Praise for
The Vineyards of Champagne

"A beautifully captivating story of wartime tenacity and tenderness that celebrates the sweetest bonds of human relationships and the courage to love again after loss. So exquisitely rich in detail you'll feel bubbles on your tongue."

—Susan Meissner,
bestselling author of *The Last Year of the War*

"Blackwell moves effortlessly between present-day France and the battlefields of WWI. . . . The allure of the decades-old mystery of missing letters juxtaposed against the history of the caves of Champagne makes for a satisfying page-turner." —*Publishers Weekly*

"Blackwell's exquisite talent at interweaving the past with the present is on full display in her latest . . . telling the universal story of grief, loss, and human resilience." —*Booklist*

Praise for
The Lost Carousel of Provence

"Blackwell uses an outsider's passion to shine a light into the dark past of a broken family and how a sweet wooden rabbit can bring them together again." —The Associated Press

"Plan your trip to Provence now. In this meticulously researched novel, Juliet Blackwell deftly navigates three time periods, taking us from contemporary California to both the Belle Époque and Nazi-occupied France as she spins a story as charming as an antique carousel." —Sally Koslow, author of *Another Side of Paradise*

"An untrusting American orphan meets a dysfunctional French family—and each turns out to possess wisdom that helps the other to heal from old, old wounds. With crystalline imagery, vivid characters, and lively prose, Juliet Blackwell redefines what family means, in a way that will touch readers long after they've read the last page. As Cady points her camera at one antique carousel after another, this novel should come with a warning: Will cause enormous desire to travel to France." —Stephen P. Kiernan, author of *The Baker's Secret*

"Narrating from several perspectives, Blackwell weaves together a tale of love lost, repressed passion, and finding a sense of belonging that should utterly charm and delight readers new to her and current fans alike." —*Booklist*

Praise for
Letters from Paris

"Blackwell seamlessly incorporates details about art, cast making, and the City of Light . . . [and] especially stuns in the aftermath of the main story by unleashing a twist that is both a complete surprise and a point that expertly ties everything together." —*Publishers Weekly*

"Bestselling author Blackwell brings us another captivating tale from the City of Light. . . . This romantic and picturesque novel shows us that even the most broken people can find what makes them whole again." —*Booklist*

"Blackwell paints a picture of Paris that is both artistically romantic and realistically harsh . . . a compelling story of Paris, art, and love throughout history."   —*Kirkus Reviews*

"Blackwell has woven a great tale of mystery, artistry, history, and a little romance. With plenty of backstory and tidbits about Parisian life in the nineteenth century, there's something for everyone in this recommended read."   —*Library Journal*

Praise for
The Paris Key

"A charming protagonist and a deep well of family secrets, all gorgeously set in the City of Light."

—Michelle Gable, international
bestselling author of *I'll See You in Paris*

"[A] witty, warm, winsome novel . . . [Blackwell's] generation-spanning tale combines intrigue and passion with a flawless ear for language and a gift for sensory detail."

—Sophie Littlefield,
bestselling author of *The Guilty One*

ALSO BY JULIET BLACKWELL

The Vineyards of Champagne
The Lost Carousel of Provence
Letters from Paris
The Paris Key

OFF *the* WILD COAST *of* BRITTANY

Juliet Blackwell

BERKLEY

NEW YORK

BERKLEY
An imprint of Penguin Random House LLC
penguinrandomhouse.com

Copyright © 2021 by Julie Goodson-Lawes
Readers Guide copyright © 2021 by Penguin Random House LLC
Excerpt from *The Lost Carousel of Provence* copyright © 2018 by Julie Goodson-Lawes
Penguin Random House supports copyright. Copyright fuels creativity, encourages diverse
voices, promotes free speech, and creates a vibrant culture. Thank you for buying an authorized
edition of this book and for complying with copyright laws by not reproducing, scanning, or
distributing any part of it in any form without permission. You are supporting writers and
allowing Penguin Random House to continue to publish books for every reader.

BERKLEY and the BERKLEY & B colophon are
registered trademarks of Penguin Random House LLC.

Library of Congress Cataloging-in-Publication Data

Names: Blackwell, Juliet, author.
Title: Off the wild coast of Brittany / Juliet Blackwell.
Description: First edition. | New York : Berkley, 2021.
Identifiers: LCCN 2020040106 (print) | LCCN 2020040107 (ebook) |
ISBN 9780593097854 (trade paperback) | ISBN 9780593097861 (ebook)
Subjects: LCSH: World War, 1939-1945--France--Fiction. |
GSAFD: Historical fiction. | LCGFT: Novels.
Classification: LCC PS3602.L32578 O37 2021 (print) |
LCC PS3602.L32578 (ebook) | DDC 813/.6--dc23
LC record available at https://lccn.loc.gov/2020040106
LC ebook record available at https://lccn.loc.gov/2020040107

First Edition: March 2021

Printed in the United States of America
1   3   5   7   9   10   8   6   4   2

Cover photo of woman by Rekha Garton / Arcangel Images; coast by Mathieu Rivrin /
Getty Images; planes by Amer Ghazzal / Getty Images
Cover design by Eileen Carey
Book design by Elke Sigal

To the Stauff boys.
To Cole, for going with us;
and to Luc, for staying with us.

And the day came when the risk to remain tight in a bud was more painful than the risk it took to blossom.

—ANAÏS NIN

CHAPTER ONE

Natalie

And we're off, to continue our adventure on the Île de Feme,
renovating a historic guesthouse and opening a gourmet restaurant!
Because when you grab life with both hands and hold on tight,
you never know where it might lead:
perhaps even to a rocky island off the Wild Coast of Brittany.
Stay tuned. . . . This tale is not over.

> —last line of the international bestseller *Pourquoi Pas?*
> *A Memoir of Life, Love, and Food* by Natalie Morgen

Things are not going according to plan.

Natalie Morgen sat at a little metal café table on the stone terrace
outside her guesthouse, watching the latest herd of tourists surge off
the ferry.

An aroma of anise rose from her glass, melding with the smoke
from her cigarette and the scent of the sea: a mélange of dead things
and salt, of the abundant seaweed and muck that marred the shallows
during low tide. Island sounds wafted over on the ocean breezes: the

histrionic seagulls squabbling over a bucket of scraps Loïc had tossed out the back door of Pouce Café, the rhythmic lapping of the waves in the snug harbor, the murmurs of visitors enjoying lunch at outdoor tables, the occasional clacking of a *pétanque* ball hitting its mark.

Natalie imagined the newly arrived tourists mistook her for a native sipping her glass of pastis—though most of the actual natives preferred beer or hard cider—and enjoying a sunny day on the beautiful island.

And sitting here like this, Natalie could almost convince *herself* that life was good. That everything was going according to her carefully thought-out plan. Lounging on the terrace of her ancient guesthouse, its rusted iron gates still secured with a heavy steel chain because the Bag-Noz was not yet open to guests even though accommodations were well-nigh impossible to come by on the Île de Feme during tourist season.

Bobox strutted by, clucking in contentment. The fluffy white hen had come with the house and had made herself a little nest in the shed. Ridiculously long snowy white feathers on the top of her head quivered and swayed with every confident step, reminding Natalie of stylish Parisian ladies in photographs of yore, parading along the Champs-Élysées in their feathered chapeaux.

Paris. What had Audrey Hepburn said? "Paris is always a good idea"? *Maybe for Audrey—she was rich and beautiful.* Absentmindedly scratching at a mosquito bite, Natalie realized she was clenching her jaw, willed herself to relax, took another sip of pastis, and turned her attention back to the ferry passengers.

Trying to get their bearings, the newcomers weren't talking much as they staggered along the walkway that hugged the thick stone seawall. Some carried inflatables and beach toys; others clutched scraps of paper with instructions directing them to their rented guesthouses or to the Ar-Men, the only hotel on the island. It must have been a rough crossing: Most of the children and more than a few of the adults were decidedly green around the gills. A storm had thrashed the region yesterday, and though to the unpracticed eye the sea today appeared calm, Natalie had lived on the island long enough to have learned a few things from the locals, such as how to read the water.

Or, at the very least, when to ask a local to read the water for her.

Even after a storm appeared to have passed, waves lingered and surged. The swells rippled out and down, the awesome energy of the sea needing time to settle, to balance, to find its footing once again, lulling sailors and landlubbers alike into a false sense of security only to slam them with choppy water if they dared venture too soon onto open sea.

Sounds like a metaphor for life. Natalie made a mental note to post this, or some poetic version of it, on her social media accounts. She should post some photos as well. It had been a while. Too long. She had a lot of followers to keep happy.

Her readers loved the snapshots of Natalie's life on an island off Brittany's Côte Sauvage, or "Wild Coast," where she was renovating an ancient guesthouse with the proceeds from her bestselling memoir. In fact, some of the new arrivals lurching off the ferry might well be women of a certain age who had read Natalie's inspirational tome about finding love and self-fulfillment through the art of French cooking, and had decided to come to the Île de Feme in search of love and self-fulfillment themselves.

But as Natalie had learned, in a most painful way, the Île de Feme was still an *île*—an island—which meant that if you didn't bring it with you, you weren't likely to find it here.

How could she explain that her Prince Charming—*le prince charmant*—the man she had fallen head over heels for, the reason she had come to Brittany in the first place, had turned out to be a lying, cheating, spendthrift schmuck who left her high and dry in the middle of their guesthouse renovation?

Even his name was annoying. *François-Xavier.* Being French, he insisted she say his entire name, every time: *Fran-swah Ex-ah-vee-ay.* A full six syllables. *Six.* She once made the mistake of addressing him simply as François and he accused her of calling him by another man's name. *A classic case of psychological transference,* she thought with grim humor, knowing what she now knew.

François-Xavier claimed it was an American thing to give people nicknames. He was forever blaming her quirks on Natalie's being American, but in this case it might have been true. In college Natalie's roommate had introduced herself as Anastasia—a mere four syllables—and everyone on their hall immediately shortened it to Ana. Natalie had fought her entire childhood against being called Nat because it sounded like the bug, which her sister Alex insisted she was: Nat-the-Gnat, small and annoying, bouncing around ineffectually, her head in the clouds, endlessly searching for some unspecified thing. Natalie had tried to retaliate by calling Alex "Al," but in that irksome way of smug elder sisters, Alex had embraced the name, stomping around the family compound, singing at the top of her lungs, loudly and proudly, the old Paul Simon song "You Can Call Me Al."

Which wasn't fair. Nobody wrote songs about gnats.

Natalie never managed to outmaneuver her four older sisters, and Alex, the closest to her in age, had been by far the most difficult.

Anyway. François-Xavier. She supposed two names suited a man with two faces. Still . . . that gorgeous face flashed in her mind: the sloping, intensely blue eyes; the sensual, full lips; the hint of dark golden whiskers glistening along his strong jaw. The way he looked at her as if she were not merely desirable but that he had waited a lifetime to meet her, that he was ready to share his life with her, wanted to create a family with her right here on his native island, where they would play *pétanque* in the sunshine, drink *apéro* curled up in front of the hearth, and cook together, transforming classic ingredients into sumptuous dinners through the dedicated application of traditional French techniques. And then they would linger for hours over elaborate meals with friends and extended family and guesthouse visitors.

That was the plan.

At the moment her cupboard contained half a box of crackers, an open bag of dry-roasted peanuts, and a single fragrant cantaloupe well on its way to rotten. Natalie had forgotten to put an order in with the mainland store that shipped to the island, so today's ferry brought no bundle of supplies with her name on it. She supposed she could buy something from the island's small but well-stocked "general store" that primarily served the tourists, but if she did, then the shop's owner, Severine Menou, would know Natalie's business, which meant soon *everyone* on the island would know Natalie's business.

Better to do what she usually did these days: eat the ample *menu du jour* at Milo's café, blaming it on her torn-up kitchen, and stick to peanuts and stale crackers—and plenty of pastis—the rest of the time.

François-Xavier would be appalled.

What was she going to *do*?

Keep your head down and the pretense up. At least until she figured out her next steps. She had told everyone that François-Xavier was on a business trip to Paris, scouting for kitchen help for the gourmet restaurant they were supposed to be opening in the large dining room of the Bag-Noz Guesthouse. No one was surprised; he traveled to Paris frequently, after all.

This time, though, François-Xavier had no intention of coming back. How long would it be until people started asking questions? Also, the construction workers hadn't shown up this week and Natalie was afraid to ask why. It might be because today was *le quinze août*, a national holiday. Or just because it was August, and a lot of French people took the entire month off for vacation.

Or maybe the workers hadn't shown up because Natalie hadn't paid her latest round of bills. When he left, François-Xavier siphoned off the majority of their shared bank account, leaving her to get by on a few hundred euros and maxed-out credit cards until she received a check from her publisher for the book under contract, a follow-up to *Pourquoi Pas?*

Her jaw tightened again. Her current work in progress was meant to be all about her perfect life with her perfect French chef fiancé, and to be accompanied by a liberal smattering of recipes and mouthwatering photos of the meals she and François-Xavier prepared—what her agent referred to as "French food porn."

Natalie took a deep quaff of her pastis, let out a long sigh, and watched as Bobox scratched the ground in her incessant search for something appetizing in the sandy soil of the weed-strewn courtyard.

François-Xavier was supposed to run the kitchen, and Natalie was supposed to run the guesthouse, and it was all supposed to be beautiful.

But things had not gone according to plan.

CHAPTER TWO

Alex

*W*hy *in the world did Nat move to such a godforsaken island?*

The Île de Feme revealed itself coquettishly, first appearing through the ocean mist like a vague mirage, the kind that shimmered along the highways on the hottest days in the remote Northern California mountains where they had grown up.

Alex squinted as she tried to make out the strip of low gray land. On the map the distance between the island and the mainland didn't look that great, but she and her fellow passengers had left the dock at Audierne more than an hour ago. The bobbing ferry had headed north at first, turning to the west only as they passed the Pointe du Raz, no doubt fighting the channel's famous currents and avoiding the perilous reefs that lurked just below the surface, a vast underwater maze protecting the island. According to the travel guide—Alex always did her homework before beginning something new—the jagged rocks had brought catastrophe to legions of sailors and ships over the years. There had been 127 documented shipwrecks in this strait, and that was only since they'd started keeping track, back in the seventeenth century.

The danger of shipwreck explained the multitude of lighthouses on the islands and along the coastline of the channel. Perched on rocky outcroppings, the towers appeared lonely and stoic. And hauntingly beautiful.

Alex had also read in the travel guide that the French had two words for lighthouses: A *phare* was a true lighthouse, usually home to a keeper in the days before the lights were automated, while a *feu*—which meant "fire"—was a smaller tower with a smaller light. The mile-and-a-half-long Île de Feme was equipped with one true lighthouse on its western tip, a large *feu* on the easternmost point, and two smaller *feux* dotting the southern coast.

Clearly, this region was well acquainted with maritime disasters. Alex found that oddly comforting. She was a bit of a shipwreck herself, these days.

Alex climbed the steep set of steps, clinging to the cold metal handrails as the boat pitched sharply. She would be windblown on the open upper deck, but breathing fresh air was preferable to being stuck in the crowded, too-warm cabin below.

Upon boarding the ferry, Alex had needed to harness every bit of self-control not to climb onto one of the seats and order everyone to don one of the bright orange life vests stacked in a cupboard. *Don't be weird,* she reminded herself for the thousandth time. *Act like the others.* Besides, her very limited French didn't include the vocabulary for "Safety first, folks!" She had contented herself with grabbing a dozen seasickness bags from a little stand next to the first aid cabinet and making a mental note of the location of an inflatable life raft.

Just in case.

As soon as they left the shelter of the harbor, the sea had become choppy and the boat was tossed about like a child's toy, heaving this way and that, leaving its human inhabitants retching and grasping onto their molded plastic seats for dear life.

Alex dug through her backpack for a package of wet wipes and handed them, along with a couple of the seasickness bags, to a young father whose little girl had lost her lunch all over the front of his sweater vest and jacket.

She wasn't feeling all that chipper herself, but keeping busy helped. It always had.

Father and child taken care of for the moment, Alex made her way to a seat and kept her eyes on the horizon, gazing at a fixed point to quell the nausea.

But seriously. Setting aside the "why" for the moment, how had Nat even *found* this place?

Her little sister was forever bragging on social media, posting photos of herself dancing in the clubs of Budapest or shopping the open-air markets of Marrakech as she traipsed around the world "looking for herself." On her blog she posted rambling descriptions of how she spent her days learning classic French cooking, and her nights hobnobbing with chic Parisians in cinematic wine cellars and cabarets. And if all that weren't galling enough, irresponsible, carefree Nat had hit the jackpot when her memoir of finding herself and food—and *love*—became an international sensation, lingering at the top of the bestseller list week after exasperating week.

Even the title annoyed Alex. *Pourquoi Pas?* Seriously? There were always plenty of reasons why *not*.

But readers hadn't agreed. Which just went to show you that people today were pathetic, casting about for direction in their sad little lives.

Was *she* now doing the very same thing? Alex's stomach heaved at that thought more than the seasickness. An island off the coast of Brittany had sounded so fantastical somehow when the thought first occurred to her back in dusty Albuquerque. It had seemed as if destiny had intervened. Anyway, she didn't need forever. Just a little while, time to regroup, to make a plan. A respite from the convoluted joke that her life had become.

Alex was out of options; she would swallow her pride. She had swallowed worse in her time.

The island slowly came into focus. A small lighthouse had "Ar-Men" painted on it in tall black letters. The harbor was full of boats, varying in size from small dinghies to good-size sailboats to large commercial fishing vessels. A sweeping curve of three-story houses with crenellated rooflines fronted the harbor, gazing to the east as though longing for the mainland. Built of native stone, the houses were covered in stucco in cheerful shades of chalky blue, pale apricot, and butter yellow, their steeply pitched slate roofs studded with red-brick chimneys.

A charming fishing village, read the caption under Nat's bio at the end of *Pourquoi Pas?* Alex had stared at that bio for a very long time before making her decision to come.

The rocking of the ferry subsided as the engines slowed and they navigated the entrance to the harbor. As they chugged toward the dock, a large silver tail broke the surface of the water. *The Little Mermaid!* Alex thought, then chided herself. It was probably some kind of huge fish, the likes of which she would no doubt soon be dining on.

Alex hadn't let Nat know she was coming. Her sister might not be thrilled to see her, but Nat wouldn't turn her away.

If there was one thing they had learned from their survivalist childhood, it was the imperative of helping one another when the chips were down. As their father, who insisted on being addressed as The Commander, liked to say as he stomped around their remote mountain compound, barking orders and checking the contents of their bug-out bags, "Nothing brings a family together like Armageddon."

It won't be forever, Alex thought, blowing out a long breath. Just until she figured out her next steps. If there *were* any next steps.

Or until her own personal Armageddon arrived.

CHAPTER THREE

Violette

AUGUST 1939

There were two portents of the coming war: the wreck of the *Santa Clarita* and my grandmother's discovery that her spells had been broken.

To live on our island was to understand that shipwrecks were a fact of life. The rocky reefs that lurked just below the surface of the water had claimed half a dozen unsuspecting ships in my lifetime, and no doubt hundreds more before I was born. The first that I remember was the steamship *Hélène*, which sank in 1929, when I was nine years old. There is a photograph of my sister, Rachelle, and me standing on the shoals and gazing out at it. To this day the ship's motor rests on the gravel path just past the hotel, a useless memorial to those lost to the merciless ferocity of the sea.

The weather was calm and peaceful the night the *Santa Clarita* met her doom. But as any islander knows, storms are not necessary to ruin even the finest ships in our reef-strewn waters. When the keeper of the lighthouse, Henri Thomas, spied the ship's flag of distress, he summoned *L'Iroise*, which headed out from the *sauvetage* to rescue any surviving crew and passengers, and to retrieve what they could of the ship's cargo.

Whenever the church bells ring out their warning, the entire town rushes to shore and huddles there to assist the survivors by offering warm drinks and dry blankets, and pitching in to salvage lumber and luggage and whatever else is in the ship's hold. A shipwreck is horrifying, but also electrifying.

Not much usually happens on our little island.

On that night the news spread quickly: The *Santa Clarita* had left Algiers and was headed to Brest with its keep full of wine. This news motivated some of the islanders more than usual.

I was on my way to the cove to help haul crates out of the shallows and onto the sand when I found my grandmother, my *mamm-gozh*, kneeling in the mud by a hole in the ground, sobbing.

"What is it, *Mamm-gozh*?" I asked, crouching beside her.

"The spells . . . the spells have been broken," she wailed.

My grandmother kept the old ways: She understood the movements of the moon and the sea, the never-ending cosmic ballet of the earth and the stars and the heavens. She taught me that just as the sea rose to be closer to the moon, the moon drew itself closer to the sea. *Mamm-gozh* was a healer who mixed soothing salves and teas and tinctures. But she also cast spells, gathering items, wrapping them in bits of muslin or paper, and tying them with cords knotted many times, each knot representing an incantation. She would bury the packets at high tide during a full moon for spells of focus and perseverance, or during the low tide on the new moon for spells of financial success and protection.

Now she knelt over a muddy hole, crying.

"Surely it's the dogs," I said. "The dogs dug it up."

"No, *ma petite fille*," *Mamm-gozh* said, shaking her gray head. "It is a sign. All the spells have been broken. This happened once before, you know. Before *la Grande Guerre*, the War of Nineteen Fourteen."

"I'm sure it must be the dogs, *Mamm-gozh*," I repeated, uncertain but unwilling to consider what else this might mean. "Let me take you home."

I grasped her arm to help her up, all ninety pounds of her, leaning over to brush the mud from the black skirts of her traditional garb, the *robe noire* that hung loose on her shrinking frame. When I was young my grandmother had been hale and hearty; we islanders are not a diminutive people. *Mamm-gozh* still had the wiry muscles from a lifetime spent collecting seaweed on the shore and coaxing vegetables from the island's sandy soil, but lately she seemed to be collapsing into herself, disappearing before my eyes a tiny bit at a time, as inexorably as the tide.

After leaving *Mamm-gozh* in the care of my mother, I returned to the beach and spent the night assisting my fellow villagers in salvaging the wrecked ship's cargo of wine. Together we dragged crate after heavy crate up the beach and down the path to the church, where we deposited them in Père Cecil's storage room behind the sacristy because the Good Father said he needed the wine for communion. No islander would contradict a priest, even though everyone knew how rapidly Père Cecil was apt to deplete the stores of "communion" wine.

By the time I returned home, the sky over the mainland was just beginning to brighten with the soft bluish tint of the new day.

I found *Mamm-gozh* in her bedroom at the back of the kitchen, sorting through her death drawer. Though bone weary from hauling the heavy wooden crates all night, I watched, mesmerized. My grandmother had always kept this bureau drawer locked.

"These are my grave clothes, Violette," she told me, running her thin, blue-veined hand over her black silk wedding gown, stockings, slippers, and undergarments carefully wrapped in oiled paper. *Mamm-gozh* had written out her funeral arrangements in detail: the text for the sermon, the three hymns she wanted us to sing to mourn her, the inscription for her headstone. She even specified how many chickens to roast for the memorial feast. "You will remember this, yes?"

I nodded.

"And do not forget to bury my plate, cup, and saucer, and my knife, fork, and spoon with me," she said. "I don't want anyone else to use them."

"I will remember, *Mamm-gozh*," I said. "But why?"

"Because they might ingest my dreams and start living my life instead of their own."

"Don't leave me, *Mamm-gozh*," I begged.

"That is not for us to say, child. The spells have been broken. I won't live through another war," my grandmother replied, shaking her head. "War is for the young, *ma petite fille*. I lost a son in the last one. I have no wish to endure it all again."

One week later—just before Germany invaded Poland, prompting France and Britain to declare war—my *mamm-gozh*, the one person on the Île de Feme who understood me, passed away in her sleep.

CHAPTER FOUR

Natalie

That woman looks exactly like Alex.

The slim, fortyish tourist was dressed in her sister's customary outfit of jean shorts cut off just above the knees, sporty shoes, and a long-sleeved T-shirt topped by a vest with multiple zippered pockets. Alex never wore anything without pockets, in which she carried not only a Swiss Army knife and matches but water-purification tablets and nutrition sufficient to last several days.

Some people dressed to impress. Alex dressed to survive.

This new arrival also carried a large backpack, ample enough for *all* the basics for survival. The Commander would have approved.

Natalie peered more closely. Same straight dark hair as Alex, same deeply tanned skin. Of the five Morgen girls, only Natalie and Alex shared their mother's olive complexion. But Natalie had gray eyes and had begun lightening her hair with subtle highlights at a Parisian salon so that she was now nearly blond.

Natalie ran her fingers through her hair and studied the length of one lock: It bristled with split ends. She needed a trim. As she noted every morning when she looked in the bathroom mirror, it was evident she was no longer in Paris. The island's part-time hairdresser did the best she could, but the results wouldn't win any awards. Natalie hadn't had a proper manicure in months, either. If she stayed on the island much longer, she would risk going feral.

It had been so much easier, and felt so much more compelling, to maintain good grooming when she lived in Paris, where there were world-class salons on every other corner.

The locals were fond of insisting that Brittany wasn't really France at all. Natalie wasn't sure about that, but the Île de Feme was definitely *not* Paris.

In addition to her unkempt hair and ragged fingernails, Natalie wore typical island summer attire: cutoffs and a tank top, flip-flops on her sandy (and unpedicured) feet, a light sweatshirt at hand in case the winds picked up. Never, not in a million years, would she have dressed this way in Paris. It was simply not done.

A nasty thought skittered into her consciousness: *Maybe if I wasn't such a mess, François-Xavier wouldn't have—*

She shook her head. *Stop it, Natalie. This isn't about you. It's about* him *being a scumbag.*

Living Well was Natalie's brand. Happiness was all about gratitude and self-acceptance, becoming the best version of *you*, not living to please a man or anyone else. That was the message she preached to her many followers on social media, and it was the resonant theme of her bestselling memoir. And she believed it. She did. But at the moment she was having a hard time . . . *living* it.

Natalie took another sip of her pastis, enjoying the way the liqueur filled her mouth, slid down her throat, and made the harsh lines of her present situation ever so slightly fuzzy.

That woman really does look like Alex.

But that was absurd. Natalie had grown up with only her parents and her four older sisters for company, and ever since breaking free of the compound—she liked to say she escaped, like in that movie about World War II prisoners of war—she often imagined them in the faces of strangers: a bank teller or the cashier at the grocery store or, most disconcertingly, someone in line at one of her book signings waiting to speak with her. But inevitably they would turn out to be regular, normal people.

This woman paused, checked the paper in her hand, scanned the street, and headed straight for the Bag-Noz, stopping at the small iron gates set into the stone garden walls. Respecting the boundary.

"Hey, Nat," the woman said, in the deep, slightly husky voice Natalie would recognize anywhere, that voice she would always associate with her childhood.

Alex.

It really *was* her.

Alex now wore glasses, and her face had thinned and settled into worry lines, making her look a lot like their overworked and overburdened mother, Carla. Otherwise, though, Alex seemed exactly the same as the last time they had been together, almost ten years ago, when the family had gathered to scatter their mother's ashes in the Klamath River, whose rushing waters Carla had loved so much.

What is Alex, of all people, doing here?

After a stunned pause, Natalie answered: "Hey, Alex. Is something wrong with Dad?"

"Not that I know of," said Alex.

They stared at each other for a long moment before Natalie gathered her wits enough to say, "Sorry. Come in. The chain's not locked."

The hinges squeaked as Alex unwound the heavy metal links and pushed through the gate. Natalie quailed as her sister's keen gaze swept across the disheveled yard: a dusty jumble of lath and plaster, an old wooden window frame defeated by years of exposure to salt and wind, a stack of slate shingles to repair the roof—and one ridiculously fluffy hen strutting about.

And Natalie herself, drinking in the middle of the afternoon, as though there was no work to be done. Shame washed over her. Just like that, Natalie was a kid again, caught reading instead of packing her bug-out bag.

The front step creaked loudly as Alex stepped up to the terrace, shrugged her heavy backpack off her shoulders, and leaned it against the stone wall of the house.

Natalie stood, and the sisters shared an awkward hug. Natalie's nostrils flared. Her sister smelled of hard travel with a hint of something worse.

"Rough crossing?" Natalie guessed.

Alex nodded. "You've got to hand it to kids: They throw up really easily. Probably an evolutionary advantage in there, somewhere."

"And you stepped in to help clean up."

"Somebody had to."

As they took seats at the outdoor table, Alex's gaze landed on the conch-shell ashtray with Natalie's hastily stubbed-out cigarette.

"Since when did you take up smoking?" Alex asked.

"Since I started making my own decisions," Natalie said. In fact, she had taken up smoking in a last-ditch attempt to keep the weight off, French-style. Not that it was working. "What are you doing here, Alex? How did you even find me?"

"It was easy enough to *find* you. You're not exactly off the grid."

A long moment of awkward silence followed.

Alex fidgeted with the scattered collection of sea glass and shells on the table, running thin, callused fingers along the edges of the glass pieces, their once-sharp edges smoothed and mellowed by decades of being tossed by waves and ground against the sand.

Along with the eyeglasses, the hesitation was new. Alex always knew what she was doing. *Always.* Natalie had been the dreamy one, the one with her head in the clouds, rarely answering a question directly because her mind was always somewhere else.

"I was wondering . . ." Alex paused and cleared her throat. "That is, I was hoping . . . Could I stay here for a while?" Her voice was strained, and her dark eyes remained fixed on the tabletop display of gifts from the sea.

Natalie blinked. "Excuse me?"

Alex repeated, more slowly this time, "Could. I. Stay. Here."

"Here? On the island? With me?"

"Here. On the island. With you."

"For how long?"

"I'm not sure." Alex lifted her gaze and Natalie noted the dark circles under her sister's eyes, read the tension in her gaze. "For a bit."

"Um . . . of course," Natalie replied. "Are you okay?"

Alex nodded.

Natalie considered pressing Alex about what was going on, why her ever-so-capable and oh-so-self-confident older sister, the sister who never needed anything from anyone, especially from Nat-the-Gnat, had come all the way here to ask for a place to stay. But there would be no point. When they were kids, Alex had excelled at their father's many "training exercises," including the one he called Withstanding Interrogation.

"The place could use a little fixing up," Alex said, her gaze sweeping over the yard. "You have tools?"

Natalie nodded. "In the shed."

"Then I should get to work."

"You just arrived. Let me show you your room so you can put your stuff away, at least," Natalie said, then downed the last of her pastis and led the way through the guesthouse's chalky green front door.

Accustomed to living amid the chaos of renovation, Natalie had learned to turn a blind eye to the mess. But now she cringed inwardly as they picked their way through the sawdust and wood curls and chunks of plaster that littered the plank floors, with piles of lumber and random tools and equipment seemingly left where workmen had dropped them.

To the right of the large tiled foyer was a roomy parlor lined with built-in cabinets and bookcases and, at one end, a huge stone fireplace. The window seat of a small nook held a stack of mildewy cardboard boxes.

To the left a huge dining room ran the length of the house, but currently the space was being used to store construction tools and supplies. The only decoration on the stained plaster walls was a framed article from the local newsletter declaring the island's own *fils natif* (native son) François-Xavier Olivier and *célèbre auteur Américain* (famous American author) Natalie Morgen had arrived to rescue the Bag-Noz guesthouse from its many years of neglect. There was a photograph of the two of them standing arm in arm on the front terrace, squinting into the sunshine, their smiles full of hope and excitement.

I should burn that damned picture, Natalie thought.

"Nice place," said Alex, craning her neck to look around.

Natalie glanced at her sister, wondering whether she was being sarcastic.

"Is your man here?" Alex asked. "What's his name again?"

"François-Xavier. He's in Paris at the moment. So, this house was built for a large extended family, and later it functioned as a guesthouse. Primarily for sailors seeking refuge from storms, but also for a few unfortunate shipwreck victims." Natalie gestured down the hall. "In the back is the kitchen and a small office where I write. My—*our*—bedroom's there, too."

She and François-Xavier had planned to move into a large master bedroom with its own bath on the second floor, but until the construction work was done—and while she was alone—she preferred the simple but cozy room beyond the kitchen.

The treads creaked underfoot as they climbed the stairs. Electricians and plumbers had opened up parts of walls to fish for wires and to inspect the pipes, leaving gaping holes in the old plaster, as though an inebriated visitor had repeatedly punched his hand through the walls in a rage. Plaster dust coated the floors and the banister in a liberal sprinkling of white chalk, Pompeii-like.

Alex remained mute as they reached the second-floor landing, but Natalie heard reproach in her very silence. She tried to shake it off.

"There are four bedrooms on this level, but the bathrooms aren't functional yet, so I'll put you up on the third story."

"That's fine," said Alex.

On the third floor were three small chambers tucked under the eaves, with a bathroom and a WC at the end of the hall. François-Xavier and Natalie had discussed trying to reconfigure the space for en suite baths, since modern tourists were often put off at the thought of sharing with strangers, but any improvements remained on their far-too-long to-do list.

"What's with the door?" Alex asked, gesturing toward a paneled door leaning uselessly against the wall.

"It's for the attic stairs. We couldn't find the key, so we took it off its hinges."

"Was there anything fun up in the attic?"

"Not really. We brought a few boxes of books down to the parlor, but that was about it."

"Too bad," said Alex. "I always imagine finding some sort of treasure in old buildings like this one."

"I think over the years family members must have taken anything of value. So," Natalie said as she turned into the first bedroom on the right, "things are a little dusty, but at least it's all functional."

A new mattress leaned against the wall, still encased in plastic. In one corner of the room were the pieces of an old iron bed frame that had come with the building. Natalie hadn't managed to get to the mainland to order lighting fixtures, so electrical wires dangling bare bulbs hung down from the ceiling and walls. But at least they worked. The walls had been patched and primed, resulting in large white polka-dots against the beige paint. Still, the quirky angles of the steep ceiling were charming, and two deep-set casement windows looked out to the little quay, the island's harbor, and the ocean beyond.

"Nice view," said Alex.

Natalie barely noticed it anymore, busy as she was fretting about fraying electrical wires and rusting pipes. But now she thought back to the first time she had walked into this room, pushed open those windows, and leaned onto the deep sill. She had taken a big breath of the fresh, brine-laden sea air and fallen in love with the whole place— even the old stained lace curtains. She remembered how François-Xavier had wrapped his arms around her, and she leaned back against him with a contented sigh, feeling wanted and useful and sexy. Her childhood of deprivation was a million miles away, and she had at last found where she was meant to be. Swept away by the romance of the moment, Natalie had decided that her life was, indeed, fabulous.

Just like it appeared on social media.

And then—plot twist!—François-Xavier left, the guesthouse renovations ground to a halt, and now her sister had intruded upon her fantasy world, resurrecting memories of Natalie's incompetent, useless former self. Like an unwelcome spirit crossing the veil that divides this world from the next, Alex had braved an ocean to invade Natalie's life on this isolated island.

Natalie studied her sister's profile as Alex gazed out the window: the subtle lines at the corners of her eyes, the stubborn set of her chin. Alex had always been an enigma to her. Theirs were two very different personalities linked only by the circumstances of birth.

"Why don't you unwrap the mattress while I run downstairs for sheets and pillows?" suggested Natalie. "Then, between the two of us, I'm sure we can manage to put the frame together."

By the time Natalie returned from the linen closet, Alex had already assembled the iron bed frame and topped it with the mattress.

"Oh, great, you figured it out," Natalie said. *Duh,* she thought. Alex could fix the nuclear grid, given a couple of days and a socket wrench. "I'll help you make the bed."

"I can do it."

"I know you can. But it's easier with two."

Alex let out a little snort, but acquiesced. As Natalie billowed the bottom sheet onto the mattress, she noted with satisfaction that she had gotten one thing right, at least: The linens smelled like fresh air and lavender. She had hung them out to dry on the heavy-duty clothesline that extended across the entire yard and was accessed through one of the second-story bedrooms, the roomy "master" suite that was supposed to be readied, one day, for François-Xavier and Natalie.

But it was one thing to air-dry sheets for herself, and now for her sister. *How am I supposed to run a guesthouse without a clothes dryer?*

This was the sort of question that sent Natalie not into a flurry of action but into paralysis, as she contemplated everything that needed to be done before she could open the doors for paying guests. When she and François-Xavier had confessed to the family that the renovations wouldn't be finished in time for the summer tourist season, they had agreed to delay the opening for the Festival of the Gallizenae in October. Just six weeks from now.

But now that François-Xavier was gone . . . maybe none of it mattered anymore.

"The sheets smell like lavender," Alex said with a small smile. "That seems so very French, somehow."

François-Xavier had teased Natalie when she proclaimed that since she was in France, by God, she would pack her ample linen closet full of lavender sachets even if she had to import them from Provence. Which she did. That reminded her: She should order some more. Could she justify the cost?

Just about everything on the island had to be brought in by boat: the mail, groceries, socks. Light fixtures and building supplies, even garden materials, had to be ordered from stores in Audierne or Quimper. Like most islanders, Natalie and François-Xavier kept a car parked at the ferry dock on the mainland to run errands. Natalie wondered if François-Xavier had taken it when he left; she hadn't yet brought herself to check.

The sisters worked together quickly and efficiently, making the bed with tight hospital corners the way their mother had trained them to do. As they held the pillows under their chins to pull on the cases, Natalie thought of the million unacknowledged traditions that were passed down from one woman to the next, generation to generation. Natalie once told François-Xavier that his method of folding socks was unnatural; he claimed her way stretched them out. They had laughed in mock outrage, and wound up making love on a pile of freshly laundered clothes.

What am I going to do?

"Every time I make a bed, I think of Mom," said Alex as she tossed the pillow onto the bed.

"I was just thinking that myself," said Natalie.

"I miss her."

"Me, too. She was such a sweet soul."

"And so depressed."

Natalie stilled. "You think so?"

"I do," said Alex with a nod. "I mean, I didn't think it at the time, but now, looking back . . ."

"I suppose life wasn't much fun for her."

Natalie tried to swallow, tamping down the grief and regret that rose, unbidden, whenever she thought of their mother. Her strongest memory of Carla was how she would take inventory in their basement storeroom, laboriously ticking off items on her clipboard, a permanent crease of worry between her eyebrows. Forever preparing, yet always feeling unprepared. It had taken the sisters too long, far too long, to realize she was sick; Carla never complained, and she always sounded so down that her faraway, quailing voice on the other end of the telephone line hadn't been alarming.

"She sure loved us kids," said Alex.

"That, she did." Natalie cleared her throat and changed the subject. "Hey, I'm sorry it's so dusty up here. Like I said, I'm living in something of a construction zone. I'll sweep up."

"I'll do it," said Alex. "It's not a problem. Nat, I really appreciate you letting me stay."

"Of course. And sorry you have to climb all the way up here, but at least there's a functioning bathroom," Natalie said, leading the way down the hall. "The toilet is separate from the room with the bath."

"Nice," said Alex, poking her head in. The toilet room was large enough just for the commode; the bathroom was more spacious, with a window that looked over the backyard, to the west.

Natalie saw the rooms through her sister's eyes: the old claw-foot tub so heavy that Natalie wondered how the former owners had managed to get it to the island, much less wrangle it up two flights of stairs. The graceful white porcelain pedestal sink, the antique brass fixtures, the lace curtains. François-Xavier and she had picked out new tiles and waited eagerly for the ferry to arrive with their supplies. Natalie had posted to her social media a photograph of them at the pier: François-Xavier holding up a sample of the tile and grinning, one arm looped around her shoulders. Her hair was blowing in her face, and they both looked so happy. It was perfect.

Their *photos* were perfect.

The bathroom was the first—and last—project they completed before François-Xavier lost interest and suggested they contract out the rest of the renovations.

"So, I'll just stow my things, and then I can get to work," said Alex.

"Why don't you relax?" Natalie suggested. "It's late afternoon; while I would appreciate anything you can do, there's no rush."

Alex gave her a look that reminded Natalie of their father: a look that said *of course* everything must be done right now, right this instant. *Waste your time, waste your life.*

Natalie felt her jaw tighten and reminded herself: *Alex* was the one asking for a favor. *Alex* was the one who needed a place to stay, not the other way around. "Suit yourself," she said with a shrug.

Still, as she made her way back down the stairs, Natalie felt five years old again.

A disappointment.

Again.

Natalie was never a good fit for a survivalist family. She was scared of bugs and squealed when bathing in the icy creek behind the cabin. Natalie fantasized about taking hot showers and attending regular schools with libraries full of books and buying food in the grocery store—ready-made, what a concept! She wondered about things their home-school curriculum couldn't answer, asked questions her parents didn't *want* to answer.

The five Morgen girls took turns providing and preparing dinner, and when it was Natalie's turn, the family went hungry. The shame instilled by her family's growling stomachs and plaintive gazes was supposed to motivate her to get better at hunting and trapping, or at the very least to learn to read the signs that would help her forage for edible mushrooms and roots, nuts and fruits, wild bird eggs.

But instead the only thing Natalie read was books. With each failure at mastering the survivalist lifestyle, she retreated further into her stories.

Once a month or so the Morgen children were permitted to visit the library in town, a humble portable unit parked alongside the Presbyterian church. Romance novels were forbidden, as was anything else even hinting at sex, which meant most mainstream novels were also off-limits. Natalie had once talked her mother into allowing her to check out Mary Shelley's *Frankenstein* on the grounds that it was a classic, but when The Commander caught sight of it, he had tossed the book into the pit toilet, proclaiming that that was where filth belonged.

On one visit, fed up with the lack of acceptable choices and worried about getting her mother in trouble, Natalie checked out Julia Child's *Mastering the Art of French Cooking*.

When they returned to the compound, her father just grunted and said, "At least cooking's useful."

Which just went to show that even committed survivalists like her parents lacked imagination. Natalie could never even dream of preparing any of the dishes—for some reason, Julia Child did not include recipes for dandelion greens or squirrel—but the cookbook opened a window to a different world: one of long, languid meals, of sensual delights, of variety and plenty. A world where a chef could single-handedly create magical transformations.

After that, Natalie checked out one cookbook after another. Her favorite was by the famous French chef Jacques Pépin. According to the book's foreword, a French cookbook was not really about the cooking, or even about the food, but about a way of life: mornings spent chatting over delicate café tables, evenings lingering over candle-lit dinners, savoring flavors the young Natalie could only dream of, conversing about subjects she had never even imagined.

Natalie had finally found her niche. She began working alongside her mother to dry the wild mushrooms and herbs they gathered in the forest for food and for medicine, to can jar after never-ending jar of vegetables from their garden. She learned to boil venison, skimming off the fat and setting it aside to make candles. They mixed wild berries and bits of dried meat, bound by tallow, to make a prepper's staple, a high-protein meat patty known as pemmican. It was a bit gruesome, but it kept a body going.

In one session of home school, Carla had taught her daughters about the cones in the human eye, how the color-blind were not sensitive to certain vibrations, and how some animals' eyes had more cones and could therefore see more colors. Natalie had seized on the idea and spent hours when she was supposed to be tracking animals instead sitting on a rock on the banks of the rushing Klamath River, trying to imagine what it would be like to experience a color she had never seen, could not even conceive of.

Reading cookbooks was like that. The intricate exotic recipes were a window to a world she had never known existed, a life with choices Natalie had never realized were out there, somewhere, in the world. When her eyes grew weary of reading by candlelight, Natalie would cradle her current cookbook to her chest like a security blanket, drifting off to sleep while watching Alex do her endless push-ups and sit-ups.

Alex was preparing for the end of the world. All Natalie wanted to prepare was a proper French dinner.

CHAPTER FIVE

Violette

According to family lore, as a girl *Mamm-gozh* was pulled out of the ocean one day when a fisherman, trawling for haddock, spotted her clinging to a piece of driftwood. She was too young to say what had happened, whether she had somehow fallen overboard or was the sole survivor of a ship lost at sea. The mayor wrote to everyone he could think of, and passing sailors spread the word of her discovery to ports far and wide, but no relatives stepped forward to claim her. So she was taken in by the family of the fisherman who had saved her, and embraced as an honorary Fémane.

In our *livret de famille*, the book in which every member is listed, *Mamm-gozh* was included as the daughter of my great-grandparents, though her name carried an asterisk: *place and date of birth unknown*.

I thought perhaps it was because of *Mamm-gozh*'s unusual history that, unlike most of the islanders, she understood that the Île de Feme was not the only world that existed, that there were other islands, other seas, other peoples. Entire continents populated by strangers with strange, and possibly enchanting, ways.

Certainly *Mamm-gozh* seemed to be the only one who understood my restlessness, who encouraged me to go explore the world, if that was what I wanted. She was also the only one who noticed how I looked at Salvator Guilcher.

Even as a child I was enthralled by him. I shared a desk at school with his sister, Noëlle, who was my best friend. When Noëlle and I dug in the mudflats for clams during low tide, I would watch Salvator scrape the barnacles off a hull or shellac woodwork, laughing and swapping stories with his fellow fishermen. Noëlle used to tease me, saying I wanted to be a fisherwoman instead of a proper girl. I didn't mind; it kept her off the scent of my true interest.

I loved to see Salvator standing at the helm of their father's boat, piloting it skillfully to the dock. Occasionally at night, when I was supposed to be in bed, I would slip out and silently trail after him as he left the café, tipsy on cider, singing and weaving his way through the village's narrow walkways, eventually turning in through the stone archway of his family home at 22 rue Saint-Guénolé.

Salvator was sloe-eyed and strong, and when he came near my heart sped up and my mouth went dry. He was eight years my senior, and had been in my sister's class at school. When I grew a little older, I used to watch Salvator's hands as he repaired his nets, the long, callused fingers surprisingly gentle and agile. I began to imagine those hands stroking my hair, my face. . . . Sometimes I looked up to find his eyes upon me.

But then Salvator left the island to seek his fortune, which only piqued my interest more. Soon his younger brother, Marc, began to drop by my house, asking to escort me to the market or to help me in the garden. I gave him no encouragement, but my parents approved of the match, as did my aunts and uncles, who pointed out that there weren't many eligible young men in our small island village. My mother lectured me that it was my responsibility to marry and to have children, to continue the family, to hand down our traditions. Marc came from a respected fishing family and was only two years older than me. We were a perfect match, my mother insisted.

My family knew of my restlessness, my wandering thoughts. The old women *tsk*ed and shook their heads at my refusal to wear the traditional garb, the *robe noire* and the black winged headdress called the *jibilinnen*, instead sewing modern clothing based on photographs in the fashion magazines from Paris.

My family feared I would be called away by the siren song of the mainland, to which the island had lost so many of its native sons and daughters.

They thought if I married an island boy, I would come back to them.

In the spring of 1940, word reached us that the Germans had invaded France from the north. We were stunned. The French army was said to be one of the best in the world. How had it been so easily defeated?

There were Bretons who welcomed the Germans, and some who went so far as to collaborate with the invaders. They had long resented the imposition of the French national government, for they considered themselves Breton, not French at all.

But that was on the mainland. Here on the Île de Feme, we simply wanted to be left alone. We were not especially loyal to the French government, but we certainly did not want the Germans—or anyone else—setting foot on our island, issuing proclamations, appropriating our space and our property, destroying our traditions.

In a matter of weeks, the Nazis established a puppet French government in Vichy, imposed control over the press, and forbade the use of radios by all but an authorized few. Our town hall, the *mairie*, received a telegram instructing the authorities to confiscate all radios and printing equipment.

We refused.

Over the centuries we Fémans have survived hunger and cold, cholera epidemics and storms, and loved ones lost at sea. Mother Nature has not defeated us, and neither will an invading army. If the Bretons are known as the toughest of the French, we Fémans are among the toughest of the Bretons. We are descendants of stubborn Druids, the castaway survivors of shipwrecks, and, as I believe, of the Gallizenae: nine magical women who once lived on our shores.

So the lighthouse keeper, Henri Thomas, defied the Vichy order, regularly listening to news reports broadcast from Britain, which had so far withstood the German onslaught. Monsieur Thomas was an old man with a shock of white hair, thin lips that gave him a hardened look to match his character, and rheumy eyes, one of which drooped so badly it was almost permanently closed. This did not seem to impair him in the least when it came to spotting the ships and fishing boats that passed through our waters. It was he who happened upon the tail end of a radio address on the BBC that called upon all brave French citizens to rise up against the enemy occupation.

Monsieur Thomas claimed his ears had tingled in excitement as he made out *Général* Charles de Gaulle's words through the static, declaring that France was occupied but she was not defeated.

So, in a way, the lighthouse keeper was responsible for starting it all. Monsieur Thomas was a *débutant*—that is, he was not a native islander—but had lived on the Île de Feme long enough to understand that the Fémans could not resist a call to take up arms, to resist.

Word of *Général* de Gaulle's address spread like wildfire, and

Monsieur Thomas invited the villagers to gather in the front parlor of his home at the base of the lighthouse to listen to the program's rebroadcast, on the evening of June 22, 1940.

It was a warm summer night, and the room was far too stuffy, crammed as it was with islanders of every age, anxious to hear the French general. Most of us lingered outside, sitting along the rock walls that defined the lighthouse yard, sipping *cidre bouché* and sharing the biscuits passed around by Madame Kestel, the baker's wife.

Monsieur Thomas placed his radio on the windowsill so the address would reach all ears.

We had never heard of *Général* Charles de Gaulle, but we thrilled at the sound of his voice as he recounted how he had escaped to London with his family ahead of the Nazi forces, and declared that he and France were far from defeated.

"This is a World War. No one knows whether the neutral countries of today will be at war tomorrow, or whether Germany's allies will continue as her allies. If the powers of freedom ultimately triumph over those of subjugation, what will be the fate of a France which has lain down for the enemy?

". . . I call on all French wishing to remain free to listen to my voice and follow me. Long live free France!"

Général de Gaulle was urging his fellow French citizens to join the Free French Forces in England, and exhorted us to rise up against the Germans and take our country back. To defy Adolf Hitler's Nazi regime and dash their plans to make our beloved country a German playground.

Excited chatter rippled through the crowd. "We must leave for England," the men said. "We must join the French Free Forces! We must save *la Belle France!*"

In that very moment, it seemed, every man of fighting age on the Île de Feme made up his mind to fight.

I was hardly listening. War seemed so abstract while my world was falling apart, right in front of me. My old friend Noëlle no longer liked me very much, her disdain having grown in proportion to my desire to leave the island. That night Noëlle showed me, with undisguised satisfaction, a letter her mother had received from Salvator announcing his intention to marry a young woman from Brest.

Salvator. *Married.* I felt stunned. Sick. I was still mourning the loss of my dear *mamm-gozh*, and now this? While the others talked of war and resistance, I could only wonder how my broken heart could continue to beat, how I would manage to breathe.

I don't remember returning home that night, lost as I was in my emotions at this news. *What did you expect?* I chided myself. Salvator was a handsome, healthy young man. He had already waited much longer to take a bride than most island men. Of course he would marry, and of course it would not be to me. Salvator had never seen me as anything other than his little sister's playmate, and even if he had, he had no desire to be anchored to the Île de Feme.

Late that night, as I was preparing for bed, I heard my name being called from outside, echoing off the walls of the stone houses: *"Violette! Violette!"*

I leaned out the window and spied Marc on the quay below, red-faced with excitement and emboldened by cider.

"I'm going to England, Violette!" he called out excitedly.

I know that, I wanted to say. *Aren't all the men going?* But I held my tongue, giving Marc half my attention. My mind was filled with concerns much closer to my heart than declarations of war.

"Violette . . . Violette, I love you," Marc shouted so that all the neighbors could hear. "I've *always* loved you. Will you marry me?"

I listened to his words, feeling numb. Salvator was marrying someone else—perhaps he already had. We were at war, and France was occupied by the enemy. How could I possibly leave the island now? There was no future for me in Audierne, or in Quimper, much less in Paris. The war had changed everything. My parents wanted me to be wed, and they liked Marc. He was a kind young man. He had serenaded me with a proposal. It was the only time I had been serenaded.

So I said yes.

CHAPTER SIX

Alex

One by one, Alex removed the items from her backpack and placed them in the chest of drawers, neatly lined up from left to right. Her traveling kit consisted of a pair of jeans, three pairs of underwear and socks, an extra bra, two long-sleeved T-shirts and two tank tops, a sweatshirt, a waterproof shell, and a fleece vest. She was wearing her favorite vest, shorts, and hiking shoes.

That was about it, as far as clothes went.

She picked up the fat red volume she referred to as her "training manual." Just the sight of it made her stomach quail, but Alex knew she needed to study. To prepare. For the moment, though, she slipped the book in the drawer under her T-shirts and brought out her small toiletry kit, just a toothbrush and a small container of baking soda instead of toothpaste, floss, a comb, her Swiss Army knife, a flashlight, some energy bars and vitamins. A French–English dictionary. A small night-light, which she plugged into the room's sole outlet. The heaviest item in her pack was a bottle of water, and she would never be caught without it.

Back in the States Alex had carried a cell phone, but when she discovered the cost of an international phone plan, she left the device in Albuquerque, stored in an old wooden chest in one corner of a friend's barn.

There wasn't much else in that chest: a few snapshots from childhood that had miraculously survived the years and numerous moves, school portraits of her nieces and nephews, assorted thank-you notes and cards from guests at the dude ranch. A well-thumbed address book that had belonged to their mother, Carla. The information was long since outdated, but Alex liked seeing their mother's handwriting and occasionally ran her fingers along the loops of the old-fashioned cursive script. A couple of pairs of worn but still wearable jeans and T-shirts, her favorite riding boots, a heavy parka. Souvenirs of a few road trips: matchboxes and postcards from Route 66, a weekend camping in Tahoe with friends, backpacking in Joshua Tree. The red leather collar from her dog, a Labrador retriever mix named Buddy who had been hit by a car while chasing a fox across the highway. He breathed his last while cradled in her lap. It had broken her heart.

Meager keepsakes for forty-one years of life, Alex remembered thinking as she closed the lid of the chest, locking it all away. Shouldn't there be more? How had the years gone by so quickly?

A line from an old song, or maybe it was a poem, came to her: "They say life is short—then why are the nights so long?"

Alex hated the nights. She hated the darkness.

Also in that chest was a handwritten list she had composed as a child, itemizing the skills she would need to face The Change. She had ticked them off as she mastered them, her father signing off on each one with his barely legible initials:

Identify and locate edible and medicinal plants

Make a fire (with and without matches)

Open a can of food with and without a can opener

Know when food is too spoiled to eat

Use of knife and slingshot

Setting traps and snares

How to fish and hunt

How to clean fish and wild game

Find water and identify if it's safe to drink

Basic first aid

Find or build a shelter in the wilderness

How, why, and when to stay hidden

How to climb a tree to get away from predators, get directional bearings, and hunt

How to read a map and use a compass

How to read the sky for directions, time, and bad weather

Be hardworking, self-starter, and a family helper—not a complainer!

Spiritual survival

The only item not checked off was the last: *Spiritual survival.* Unlike a lot of prepper families, the Morgens weren't particularly religious.

The Bible was one of the few nonlibrary books in the house, and their mother read passages aloud some evenings, but by and large their church was the wilderness; their religion was preparing. And Alex had been a true believer: If she completed her training, if she thought through all the worst-case scenarios and prepared for them, she would reach nirvana. She would *survive*.

Alex bashed her little toe on the heavy bed frame, swore a blue streak, and collapsed on the bed. The sting of tears at the backs of her eyes enraged her. *I could use a little help with the spiritual survival right about now.* Taking a deep breath, she blew it out slowly, counting to fifteen, and gazed out the window at the muted, barely-there line where the ocean met the sky.

What had she been *doing* with her time, all those years? Why hadn't she done more?

Speaking of wasting time . . . why was Nat sitting around in the middle of a sunny afternoon when there was so much to be done? But then, Nat never had been a fan of real work. As a girl she had cared only about her books and, when The Commander confiscated those, she had retreated into her thoughts.

And then she escaped altogether.

In none of The Commander's numerous doomsday scenarios had he imagined that his young "recruits," his five daughters, would eventually age out of his world and slip out of his control. Faith, the eldest, ran off with a young man she met at a gas station, returned to their mother's roots in a fundamentalist church, and was now raising a passel of children in a suburb outside of Salt Lake City. The second born, Hope, had a daughter at the age of seventeen, who followed in her mother's footsteps to give birth to her first child before graduating high school, making Hope a grandmother at age thirty-five. Hope worked as a cashier in a grocery store and lived with her daughter and grandchild in a trailer park near Mount Shasta, not far from where they had grown up. The third Morgen daughter, Charity, had moved to Denver and sent an occasional postcard with no return address, confirming that she was alive but refusing to share any particulars of her life.

And then there was Natalie.

Alex still remembered every detail of the day Nat left. Alex had driven back to the compound from her job at the lumberyard in town, her sense of dread building with each of the sixteen miles of road that twisted along the river at the base of the mountains. She found their father in his workshop, took a deep breath, and unceremoniously informed him that Nat had run away, hitching a ride with a logger heading down to the San Francisco Bay Area.

Alex had expected The Commander to rage and to yell, perhaps declare Natalie dead to him. But instead, he set his tools down on the rough wooden bench, leaned on his palms, and hung his head.

"'Frisco? That den of iniquity?" His voice was hollow, its sound much worse than rage. "Give it a few weeks. She'll be back, tail between her legs."

"I don't think she's coming back, Dad," Alex said.

"Then she'll be dead within the month."

Alex couldn't sleep that night or the next. Nat *dead*? But he was probably right. Her silly, flighty little sister. Without Alex to look out for her, how would Nat survive?

But her sister hadn't died. Quite the opposite: Freed of the compound and her family, Nat had flourished to a downright insulting degree. Somehow she found a job in a coffee shop, earned a GED, managed to land a scholarship for college, and then attached herself as an au pair to a family that roamed the world. Nat eventually settled in Paris, where she studied French cuisine, fell in love with a handsome Parisian chef, and went on to write a bestselling memoir.

When *Pourquoi Pas?* was published, Alex had been first in line at the bookstore to buy a copy, then devoured it over a weekend. Nearly four hundred pages of endlessly detailed descriptions of their childhood of deprivation, of Nat's quest to rise above it all and discover the finer things in life: literature and art and wine and food. *Especially* food. An entire chapter was devoted to Nat's efforts to master the five French "mother" sauces, which brought her to Paris, and which ultimately led her to fall in love with the perfect Frenchman.

But as Alex read, what struck her was Nat's version of their childhood. The Morgens weren't portrayed as self-sufficient and family oriented but as crazy and punitive, five girls and a wife suffering under the thumb of a madman.

Their names had been changed—Alex was called "Diana" in the book, for some reason—but since Nat had published the book under her own name, it didn't take a rocket scientist to make the connection. Their mother, Carla, had died before the book came out, and The Commander had never in his life set foot inside a bookstore. Still. When Alex discussed the book with Faith and Hope, she learned she wasn't the only one upset by it. *Pourquoi Pas?* made the sisters feel exposed and bloody, like the animals Nat used to butcher, their guts spilling out onto the clay tile of their mother's otherwise spotless kitchen floor.

And now Alex had come to beg her baby sister for a place to stay.

"Beggars can't be choosers," their mother used to say, and Alex was a beggar with a paucity of choices.

She stood and crossed over to the window, leaning forward on the deep sill, forcing herself to focus on the sights: the blue-green of the water, the stark white triangles of sails far out at sea, the seabirds riding the breezes overhead, the children playing on the beach in the little cove.

Memorize this, Alex, she told herself. *This is your chance. Remember every detail.*

CHAPTER SEVEN

Natalie

*N*atalie made her way downstairs, steeling herself against the sight of the wallpaper peeling away from the walls and hanging in random strips, the bare spots of aged plaster webbed with cracks and marred with water stains.

"Sufficient unto the day is the evil thereof," her mother used to say. Once upon a time Natalie had puzzled over what that meant. Now she knew.

She put the kettle on for tea and took refuge in her little office off the kitchen. There, her computer and notes sat waiting for her on a large 1940s-era wooden desk in front of a bay window.

In one smooth move, Natalie took a seat and opened her laptop, as if she couldn't wait to start writing. As if muscle memory would somehow compel her to put words on paper—or, more accurately, on computer screen. As if she had something, *anything*, to say that someone, *anyone*, would want to read and that hadn't been said a thousand times before.

Nothing. She had nothing.

When she was a girl, books had been Natalie's refuge. So when her memoir was first accepted for publication, she had been overwhelmed with glee at the thought of her book sitting on a bookstore or library shelf alongside the tomes that had once kept her alive, stoking her imagination, allowing her escape.

It had spurred her to write more, but now . . . ?

Natalie sat back and gazed out the ample window onto the walled garden, a wild tangle of green to the rear of the house. When she first arrived on the island, Natalie had thrown herself into weeding and digging and cleaning up the charming yard. But François-Xavier insisted their time was better spent on the interiors, and then those projects fell by the wayside as well, and somewhere along the line Natalie seemed to have lost the will to do much of anything.

Still, the foursquare design of the original walkways and old stone walls around the raised planting beds gave the garden a natural structure, and the perennials endured, blooming in bright pinks, blues, and yellows despite the neglect. Natalie enjoyed watching the birds flit about as the ocean breezes buffeted overgrown hydrangeas and rosebushes and lilies of the Nile.

She smiled as Bobox bobbed by, the ridiculous white plume atop her head quivering with every strut.

The teakettle whistled and Natalie hopped up to make herself a cup of Darjeeling. Maybe caffeine would help.

She brought her steaming mug back to the desk and stared at her computer screen for another moment, deleting the last sentence she had written—two days ago—and adding another. Then she deleted that one.

Her hands poised above the keyboard, she startled at the shriek of rusty nails being ripped out of ancient wood, followed by a hammer striking repeatedly.

Natalie's jaw tightened with every *whap*. It was their childhood all over again: Alex was hard at work; Natalie was not.

She looked out the window once more.

Natalie had glued small round mirrors onto fishing line and strung them about the garden like wind chimes, but instead of chiming notes the mirrors cast random circles of light onto the ground and the stone walls, like a string of disco lights. That was back when she thought of doing consciously romantic things, when François-Xavier would coo over her skills and compliment her on her strange way of looking at the world. Natalie suspected her offbeat sensibility came from being socialized into mainstream society far too late. She was "different" without ever intending to be, and François-Xavier never realized how hard she tried to mimic others, to fit in, to be normal.

Now Natalie watched little circles of light careen wildly along the paths and plants, as incessant ocean breezes tossed the mirrored strings about.

Sitting up straighter, she forced her attention back to her work in progress, willing herself to focus. She had to finish the book under contract. *Had to.* She needed the money. And even more than the funds, Natalie needed to retreat into her fantasy world, to pretend that she was still an author living the dream on a fairy-tale island.

In point of fact, the Île de Feme was not particularly romantic, at least not to someone who lived here full-time. The old houses were charming, the absence of motor vehicles relaxing, and the little stone pathways darling. But the island was essentially a low reef poking out of the water, one that might well be submerged as the sea levels rose, slipping, Atlantis-like, beneath the surface, the ocean waters drowning anyone stubborn enough to stay behind until the island was nothing more than a potential danger to passing boats.

From outside came the sound of sawing, and then more hammering. Natalie brought a sachet of lavender to her nose and breathed in the scent, hoping for calm and inspiration.

If it hadn't been for the sound of Alex at work outside, Natalie would have given up, maybe taken a walk to her favorite point on the rocks by the water, past the monument to the men who left the island during World War II. Not many people ventured out on the jagged rocks at the edge of the water, and this spot felt almost like her private haven in which to sit and watch the waves and the lighthouse.

Natalie could not explain why she enjoyed the sight of the lighthouse so much. It wasn't as though it *did* anything, just stood there, stoic and permanent seeming.

But since she couldn't escape her study, Natalie spent the next few hours writing, and *re*writing, a thousand words describing the labyrinthine pathways that formed a web around and through the residential part of the island. About three feet wide, just wide enough for a *charette*—the little wagon islanders used to transport things—to pass through, the walkways were formed by the stone walls of the houses and gardens, and had been built to shelter the islanders from the relentless wind and frequent rains blowing in from the ocean. But it was also said that a drunken sailor could always find his way back from the café by careening down those pathways, trailing one hand on the wall until he arrived at his quarters.

One thousand words, or about four pages. And it was the most she had written in a week. Natalie glanced at the journal where she jotted down ideas and kept her daily word count. Back when she was writing *Pourquoi Pas?* she had composed a minimum of two thousand words every day, sometimes as many as five thousand. The ideas had flowed out of her almost too fast for her fingers to keep up. She dove into that book with passion: It had been part memoir, part diary, part escape.

But as it turned out, the ending was pure fantasy.

This current work in progress was known only by the title on the contract: "Untitled Memoir Follow-Up." If she didn't get some words on paper at some point, her publisher had the right to cancel the contract and there would be no follow-up, untitled or otherwise. Natalie still had time to pull it together, but the clock was ticking.

She organized her pens, straightened a pile of unpaid bills. What Natalie really wanted to do was to get up and pour herself a drink, maybe munch on some stale crackers or even brave a trip to the general store for a package of cookies. She could go for something sweet right about now.

Maybe . . . Could she slip through the garden and out the back gate? No, Alex would notice. Alex noticed everything.

Natalie hadn't realized until this moment how much she had been appreciating her pity party of one. She wasn't close enough to anyone on the island for them to drop by uninvited, and after a period of awkwardness—*"Qu'est-ce qu'elle fait?"* "What's she doing?"—the neighbors had come to respect her "writing time." Members of François-Xavier's extended family did come by occasionally, but she made a point to get a jump on them by visiting them at their homes so they didn't have an excuse to snoop around the disaster that was the Bag-Noz.

Natalie had retreated to a tiny rock off the Côte Sauvage of Brittany, a mere speck in the Atlantic, and Alex had still managed to find her. Just how far away did Natalie have to go to rid herself of the family legacy?

She blew out a long breath. One thousand words would have to do for today; she couldn't write any more. She checked out Twitter, and watched a short video about a woman who ran sheep on the islands in the archipelago of Helsinki. Imagine living out there, all alone except for a sheepdog and some sheep. Natalie was strangely intrigued by the idea. So far away from judging eyes . . .

Then she turned her attention to her other social media sites: Pinterest, Instagram, Facebook. And her own website and blog, of course. She hadn't taken many photos lately, so she posted a couple of old ones she hadn't used yet: the sun setting behind the lighthouse; the sea glass on the beach; an artsy angle of the peeling wallpaper in the dining room that somehow managed to look funky and interesting, a sort of glamorous decrepitude instead of just dusty and decayed. Her followers were always thirsting for more; theirs was an incessant demand for Natalie to foster their dreams of travel and romance and self-fulfillment.

Natalie's platform was a big part of the reason her publisher had given her a substantial contract for a second book. She had to keep her followers happy. There was always a shiny new site to lure them away if she didn't stoke those flames.

She responded to a few fans who had written heartfelt e-mails about how *Pourquoi Pas?* had spoken to them and changed their lives. Natalie gushed to them about how a love for food, for art, for *life* could change everything.

She wanted to believe it. She *used* to believe it.

Dear Cathleen/Deirdre/Serena/Jennifer,
Thank you so very much for writing me! I truly believe that dreams can come true. If you keep your heart and mind focused on your aspirations, there is nothing too great for the Universe to grant you. . . .

Natalie felt vaguely nauseated as she typed the perky words, as if her lies were backing up on her.

Or maybe she was just hungry. She checked her watch: It was nearly time for dinner. Her sister had just arrived from abroad, and Natalie Morgen, who had made a name for herself writing a book about French food, had nothing to offer. To be fair, Alex hadn't given notice that she was coming, but still, this was *France*. Here it was against the laws of nature not to sit down for a meal with visiting family or friends. A proper French household would always have *something* to offer guests: a hunk of crusty bread, a slice of creamy pâté, a cup of savory soup, or the silky remnants of a hearty beef stew.

Natalie went out to the terrace to find Alex crouched down and inspecting the fit of the newly replaced front step.

"Hi," said Natalie.

"Hey." Alex lifted her chin.

Alex's figure was spare and athletic, and Natalie felt a surge of resentment. They had all been thin as kids, when there hadn't been much to eat and what little there had been wasn't worth eating. Natalie had put on weight upon leaving home, first with easy access to junk food and candy while she was in college, and then when she arrived in France and indulged in pastries and cheeses, potatoes and creamy sauces.

François-Xavier used to say he loved her luscious curves. He said it less as time passed, though, and the curves became more abundant. *Maybe that was why . . .*

"Thanks for this, Alex. It looks great."

"The step had dry rot. You really should keep up with this sort of thing or it will compromise the building."

"Yup. It was on the list." Natalie felt herself clench her jaw. She already felt off-kilter; the last thing she needed was her older sister preaching at her like she was a child. "Guess I can scratch that one off, huh?"

"Hey, look what I found when I was digging out some of the dirt underneath," Alex said, holding up a small mud-caked bundle.

"What is it?" Natalie asked.

"A set of keys."

The old-fashioned keys had been wrapped up in fabric and twine.

The fabric had rotted and now hung in strips, but the cord was still knotted tightly around the keys.

"Looks like these were dropped a *long* time ago," said Natalie.

"I think they were buried," said Alex. "They were pretty far down."

"Why would someone bury a set of keys?"

"Good question. You mentioned there were some doors you couldn't unlock. You might try them. Anyway, like I was saying, you got to keep an eye out for dry rot because otherwise . . . Nat? Are you okay?"

Natalie had sunk down to sit on the top step. The muddy bundle of old keys felt like the perfect metaphor for her life.

Natalie remembered a time, not so very long ago, when this kind of discovery would have thrilled her, when she would have dreamed of racing inside to open locked doors, to find something new and exciting. She used to cradle old things between her palms, willing herself to think of the other hands that had held them through the years. Back when her life was still beautiful, Natalie would have imagined trying the keys in every lock, asking family members if they had any stories relating to them, and then putting them on display in a shadow box for guests to enjoy.

What had happened to her vision, to her imagination?

Natalie coached her readers to follow their dreams and yet her own future, which had seemed so bright not so long ago, now lay before her like a gloomy gray vista, a cold ocean of doubt shrouded in salt haze.

"Nat? Are you okay?"

Alex's voice had a gentle, careful edge that grated on Natalie's nerves. Still . . . Natalie had kept her secrets for so long, a burden weighing upon her. Alex wasn't on social media, and besides, though the sisters might not understand each other, Natalie knew Alex could be trusted.

Natalie opened her mouth to tell Alex the truth about François-

Xavier and the stalled guesthouse repairs and the fact that she could no longer write and was worried about money, but then hesitated. Alex was probably leaving in a few days, and Natalie would rather Alex leave with an impression of her as a successful author, not her screwup little sister.

"I'm fine," she lied. "Just dizzy for a second."

Bobox strutted by, clucking softly.

Alex gestured with her head. "What's with the chicken?"

"She sort of came with the house."

"Does she give eggs?"

"Every once in a while, but she's pretty old, I think."

"Well, you know what Dad would say," Alex said with a barely-there smile. "She could serve as backup dinner, in a pinch."

Over my dead body, Natalie thought. "Speaking of dinner, are you hungry?"

"Getting there."

"The kitchen's pretty torn up, so I'd rather not cook."

"That's fine. I've got energy bars in my bag," said Alex.

"I was thinking of something more typical of the region. Let me take you to dinner."

Alex gaped at Natalie as if she had suggested they get drunk with a bunch of sailors and go skinny-dipping in the harbor.

"Dinner," Alex said after a beat.

Natalie nodded.

"In a restaurant."

Natalie couldn't help but smile. Alex's response was so typical of her family, and so atypical of anyone she had met in France.

"Yes." She stepped on the newly repaired step, appreciating its solidity. "It's early yet for dinner in France; people here sometimes don't eat until nine, or even later. But it's high season, and I want to be sure we get a table."

After a beat, Alex said, "Sure, okay. I'm losing the light anyway."

"Oh, really? Good." Back in the day, Alex would have insisted on working until full dark. "Why don't we wash up and meet in the parlor, and then I'll take you to the best dinner the Île de Feme has to offer? Just . . . don't get your hopes up. This area isn't known for its cuisine. We're not in Paris anymore."

"I skipped Paris," said Alex. "Came straight here."

"That's too bad," said Natalie, feeling unbearably sad but unable to articulate, even to herself, why. "A lot of people like it."

CHAPTER EIGHT

Alex

*A*lex mounted the two flights of stairs and washed up in the bath at the end of the hall.

She was already formulating a to-do list in her mind, addressing only the most obvious cosmetic issues in this ramshackle guesthouse. A thorough inspection, from cellar to attic, might reveal deep-seated problems.

Years ago, at the suggestion of a Realtor friend in Albuquerque, Alex had decided to supplement her pay at the dude ranch by becoming licensed as a home inspector. She was a natural: Alex relished crawling under houses, poking her head into the recesses of buildings, seeing what others too often did not, rooting out termite damage and cracked foundations and bowing beams.

And while her practiced eye told her this house was well-built, it was also ancient. Could this be one huge seaside disaster waiting to unfold? What had Nat gotten herself into? And more important, why had she gotten herself into it? A big old place like this should belong to someone with the skill and the willingness to work on it constantly, to fight the unrelenting ravages of time and storms and the salty sea air.

Someone like Alex. Or like the person Alex used to be.

Maybe Nat's boyfriend was the handy one. But it didn't look as if he had done anything recently. The front window project, for example, appeared to have been abandoned halfway through, the new frame cut but not yet applied, which made no sense at all.

More likely, Nat and her Frenchy Prince Charming were dreamers seduced by a romantic notion of a darling guesthouse with mellow stone walls and multipaned bay windows, ocean views, and a quaint garden, but without the vaguest idea how much the renovation would cost or how long it would take. As a home inspector, Alex had met many such buyers who fell in love with a house and refused to be dissuaded despite the laundry list of expensive repairs her rigorous inspection had revealed.

She always warned them. They rarely listened.

After taking a quick shower, Alex wiped the fog from the bathroom mirror and squinted at her reflection. She had whapped her head on a cabinet door a few days before leaving Albuquerque, and the bruise on her temple had turned an ugly jaundice green. Her hair lay flat and was an unmemorable shade of brown; her face was deeply tanned, narrow, and pinched. Her dark brown eyes appeared dull and tired. *Is that really what I look like?*

If Alex was surprised by her reflection, it was because she noticed it so seldom.

As she slipped a clean cotton T-shirt over her head, Alex thought about how, on top of everything else that had to be done to renovate the Bag-Noz, Nat and the Frenchy planned to open a restaurant. Wasn't the failure rate of restaurants something like eighty percent? Had they researched the market, spoken with potential suppliers, run a cost-benefit analysis?

But then again, this was France, where people apparently went out to eat without giving a thought to the cost or the fact that they could eat perfectly well at home.

Alex stood at the window for a few moments, watching the colors of the ocean shift and evolve along the horizon as the day grew late: slate gray, blue, green, violet. Was that subtle spectrum of colors really there, or was she imagining it? Alex had been a teenager the first time she had seen the ocean, when their mother took the girls for a rare trip without their father. They drove along endless twisty mountain roads, across the Trinity Alps, all the way to the crashing waves of the Pacific. Alex still had a visceral reaction to it, so vast, so inscrutable, so terrifying and magnificent.

But dusk was hard. Alex had looked it up and was slightly mollified to discover that her reaction wasn't uncommon: The light ceding to darkness signaled a shift that was felt by plants and animals, even fungi, and was essential to their circadian rhythms. Dementia patients were often particularly sensitive to the late-afternoon change in light, resulting in an intensified disorientation known as "sundowning."

Alex pushed the thought away. She grabbed her sweater and descended the stairs, noting how the banister wobbled beneath her hand. *Put that item on the to-do list, stat.*

When she reached the downstairs hall, she heard the sound of a shower running.

Cleaning up after a hard day's toil, Alex thought, then chided herself. Writing was work, too.

And who had had the last laugh, after all? Nat had probably made more from that one book than Alex had earned in all her years of physical labor. Their father used to say that honest labor wasn't respected the way it used to be, the way it should be, the way it would be after The Change.

But things didn't change. Not in the ways you prophesied, Dad, Alex thought as she meandered into the parlor.

The large space appeared to be the most finished room in the house, with a couch and comfortable-looking wing chairs surrounding a coffee table in front of the fireplace, two small café tables with chairs, a broad desk under a window, an ancient-looking upright piano, and a small nook with a window seat full of cardboard boxes. On the walls were various sepia-toned photographs of the island, and over the mantel hung a large oil painting of a lighthouse upon a lone rock being buffeted by violent waves. An octagonal box on a side table was splayed open, revealing a charming heart and flowers made up of what looked like hundreds of tiny shells, and the country name spelled out in a shell arc: *Barbados.*

Alex trailed her fingers along the piano's ivory keys, sending out discordant notes. *Does Nat play?* When they were kids Nat had delighted them all with the tunes she played on her little wooden recorder, and their mother had had a beautiful voice. They had spent the evenings huddled together around the fire, playing and singing, sewing and whittling, temporarily released from the incessant search for food.

Nat hadn't mentioned *that* in her memoir. The happy times. When the Morgens relaxed together, played together. There *were* such moments, weren't there?

Unlike Nat, Alex hadn't experienced their childhood deprivation as particularly traumatic. Alex had basked in their father's attention, learning woodworking skills and basic mechanics, how to hunt and fish. Preparing, always, for the frightening, unknowable future. Alex had found great satisfaction in knowing she could take care of herself, that she wasn't dependent on anyone.

Until now.

Alex wandered over to a built-in bookshelf. About half of the books were in French, a few were in German and Spanish, and the rest were in English. Most seemed to keep to the theme of the house, referencing the sea, or lighthouses, or sailor lore. Tilting her head this way and that, she read the spines, noting that while the English titles ran from the top of the spine to the bottom, the French titles were reversed.

As a child, Alex had suffered through her mother's attempt at homeschooling. Subjects like poetry and literature, even history and mathematics, seemed inconsequential, given the future they were facing. The future she *thought* they were facing. She would fidget at the rough pine table in their big kitchen, her mind ticking off so many more important things she could be doing: The traps needed checking, and she wanted to perfect her skills with the bow, shooting over and over until the arc and trajectory of the arrow became second nature so she wouldn't miss when presented with actual prey—or a human threat.

It wasn't until after she moved to the ranch in New Mexico that Alex learned to enjoy reading. There was no real work to do when she was off the clock, which left her evenings disconcertingly empty. At first she tried joining the rest of the crew watching television in the bunkhouse lounge, but she didn't understand most of the pop culture references, so she didn't find funny the things the others roared at. A drama about the plucky survivors of a zombie apocalypse initially intrigued her, but their consistently inane choices drove home just how bad most people would be at surviving a real disaster—with or without zombies—and she left the room in disgust.

One day, while cleaning a guest room, Alex had found a battered volume of Hans Christian Andersen tales. She had seen Disney's *The Little Mermaid* at one of the ranch's family movie nights, but as she perused Andersen's original story, she realized it had little in common with the Hollywood version. Alex's imagination was captured by the image of the mermaid giving up her voice, being spurned by her human lover, and ultimately becoming sea-foam upon the waves.

There were no volumes of fairy tales on Nat's bookshelf, so Alex chose *To the Lighthouse* by Virginia Woolf. Maybe it would tell her more about the island.

Alex peered toward the hallway. Still no Nat.

How long does it take a person to get ready for dinner?

Curious, she opened the flaps of one of the cardboard boxes stacked in the nook, hoping to find bathroom or lighting fixtures ready to be installed. Instead, she found more musty-smelling books, along with a few knickknacks: a small tarnished silver tray, a set of tiny forks—for appetizers, maybe?—and, underneath everything else, a dark brown leather-bound photo album.

Alex sank onto the window seat and opened the album, carefully turning the big matte black pages, the paper so old it crumbled at the edges. Some of the photographs had slipped out of their black corner tabs, so Alex stacked them neatly on the bench beside her. There were sepia-toned images of the sea, a grinning dog with a dark-spotted face, a few cats silhouetted in the windows. One photograph portrayed two girls in old-fashioned frilly white dresses standing on a rock with a wrecked ship sticking halfway out of the water behind them. Underneath was written: *Rachelle, 17 ans; Violette, 9 ans, naufrage du navire Hélène, 1929 . . .*

Alex flipped through more pages, fascinated by snapshots from the World War II era, including one of two men wearing the puffy jodhpurs and belted coats of the German army. They were walking along the quay, with a trio of women in black outfits behind them, their heads bent together, as though gossiping.

Finally, her eye came to rest on a photograph of two women clad similarly in black, from their winged headdresses to their boots, posing in the front courtyard of the guesthouse, where Alex had found Natalie this afternoon. The house and yard looked well tended, with jumbles of flowers spilling out of pots, lace curtains in the windows, and a big painted sign: BAG-NOZ. Alex made a mental note to ask Nat what the name meant—"Bag-Noz" didn't sound French.

One of the women was slim and stood with a calico cat in her arms, one hand resting affectionately on the shoulder of a larger woman who sat on the steps. Their faces were blurry, but they both wore huge natural smiles, as if they had been caught laughing.

Below the photograph, written in vivid white ink against the black page, was *Notre maison*. Our house.

"Hey," said Nat as she entered the parlor.

Alex let out a little yelp of surprise.

Nat slowed her step. "Sorry. Did I startle you?"

Alex never used to startle at things; to cover her embarrassment she said: "You look nice."

Nat had changed into a gauzy summer dress and applied a little makeup.

"Am I dressed okay?" Alex asked. "I didn't bring anything fancy."

"You look fine. It's casual here on the island." Nat frowned, coming closer to look at the album in Alex's hands. "Where did you find that?"

"Right here, at the bottom of the box."

"Seriously? I thought there were only books in there," said Natalie, taking the album from her. "I haven't gotten around to going through them yet."

"Are those the people who used to live here?" Alex asked, looking over her shoulder.

"I think they must be," Nat said with a nod. "Two sisters were the last people to run the guesthouse. I've been trying to dig up some stories about them, and photographs to decorate the place with, but haven't had much luck." Carefully, she flipped through a few pages, then looked up at Alex. "And then you arrive and, *voilà*, just like that, you find a photo album."

"Just lucky, I guess. Or maybe nosy."

"This is great. I'll have to show it to the relatives, see if they can help me identify the people in the photos. Thanks, Alex."

"No problem. Nat . . . I could help you unpack these boxes and clean up. I'm sure taking on a project like this seems overwhelming, but it wouldn't take that much—"

"Thanks," her sister cut her off. "For now let's go eat."

CHAPTER NINE

Violette

I knew I could control Marc. It sounds awful to say it so plainly, so baldly, but it is the truth. Unlike the dark, knowing eyes of his brother, Marc's eyes were as blue as a June sky, and just as uncomplicated. Looking at him reminded me of looking into a mirror: The simplicity of my countenance reflected back to me. But just as when I looked in a mirror, it was a surface image, not the real me.

When Marc gazed at me with adoration, I knew I could make him do what I wanted him to do.

My mother concurred.

"It's best that way," *Maman* said as she stirred the fish stew and checked the *farz*, while I perched on a stool, peeling potatoes with a knife. "It's best that a man love a woman more upon marriage. Over time, a woman's love grows."

"And a man's?" I asked her.

"Men love what they love," she said with a shrug. "But their devotion doesn't grow with familiarity the way it does with women. Men are attracted to the unknown, to the depths. That's why they're drawn to sea, while we remain on the island."

At the age of fifty-three, my father was one of the older men planning on leaving for England. Papa was a gruff man of few words who gave his time and attention to my brother and rarely acknowledged my sister or me. Papa was gone so much that he hardly seemed to be a part of our family, leaving before dawn to pilot his trawler out to sea in the never-ending search for fish. Upon returning to port he might come home to wash up a bit and eat dinner, but afterward he always left again, to play *pétanque* or drink with his friends at the café.

Like most island wives, *Maman* spent her time in the company of women: They came together to gather the seaweed called *goémon*, tended the gardens and the animals, cared for the children and the sick, went to church, and gossiped over endless cups of tea, their hands perpetually occupied by knitting or sewing or cooking.

Papa and *Maman*'s relationship was typical; here on the island men and women live in separate spheres, reuniting only over meals, or to sleep.

Is that why I've never fit in? I asked myself. Because I, too, was drawn to the unknown. Not to the sea, though. I had a native islander's respect for *la mer*, had seen the wreckage of too many ships, had seen too many bodies—and parts of bodies—wash up on our rocky shores. I understood its awful power.

I was drawn to the unknown of the mainland: of fantastical-sounding cities like Brest, Nantes, or even Paris. I had been to Audierne, of course, hopping a ride on the mail ferry or whatever shuttle was headed to the mainland to fetch supplies. Though not a big city, Audierne was bewildering: It had *two* butchers, and a patisserie that sent heavenly sugary scents wafting down the cobblestone alleys.

And my own personal heaven: the bookstore, which smelled of leather and must and ink, and a very old man who shuffled this way and that, shelving books and *Tut-tut*ting when children with sticky fingers came into his shop. Monsieur Saint-Just was gruff at first, but eventually my love of reading won him over. His furrowed brow relaxed, and he began to suggest titles he thought would interest me: Alain-Fournier's *Le Grand Meaulnes*, Antoine de Saint-Exupéry's *Courrier sud*, or a thick tome of Greek mythology that included my favorite tale: that of Circe, from *L'Odyssée*. She always reminded me of our very own Gallizenae.

I could rarely afford to buy anything, but I saved up to purchase Colette's *Claudine à l'école* for myself on my eighteenth birthday. But when I took my bag of carefully hoarded coins into the shop, Monsieur Saint-Just refused to accept them and gave the book to me as a gift.

Books seemed to me to be magical portals, as bewitching as *Mamm-gozh*'s collection of feathers and stone, birds' nests and bone.

The more I read, the more I yearned to venture farther than my island's rocky shores: to Paris to visit Victor Hugo's gargoyles atop Notre-Dame, to see the lacy steel of the *tour Eiffel* with my own eyes. I longed to visit the Louvre and view its treasures, but also dreamed of simpler things: to walk along unfamiliar streets and see unfamiliar faces, to mingle with strangers who hid within their hearts and minds stories of the strange, the foreign, the new.

I knew everyone on the Île de Feme and they all knew me. We had heard one another's stories countless times, told one another the same jokes and legends, passed down through generations.

A traveling mariner once brought me a "sailor's valentine." He had meant it for his sweetheart in Biarritz, but she married another while he was at sea, so the heartbroken fellow gave it to me, instead. It is an octagon-shaped hinged box with a design inside: a heart and flowers, and *Barbados* written in an arc made entirely of shells. He told me it came from the New Curiosity Shop in Bridgetown, a port in Barbados. I set it on a shelf in the parlor, where it called to me, whispering the names of faraway lands: the Bahamas and Bali, Madagascar and Mexico.

As a child I used to sit absolutely still in the parlor at the sailors' refuge as the winter nights wore on, scarcely breathing so as not to be noticed and sent home, listening intently to the sailors swapping tales of adventure. Now that I'm older I attract attention in an entirely different way and, like all females between the ages of thirteen and fifty, am banned from the refuge, the Abri du Marin. But after my parents produced only three children, rooms in the large family home my mother had inherited began to be rented out to those who needed to stay longer on our island, or who wanted nicer accommodations than the dormitories. And occasionally I linger after serving tea and *gâteau Breton* in the parlor of our guesthouse, watching salt-roughened hands holding delicate china cups perched awkwardly on their saucers, and listening to the tales of our visitors: how they sailed down the Côte Sauvage to Spain, beyond to Morocco, to outlandish cultures of strange dress and stranger customs. They told tales of lands where it never grew cold and striped and spotted animals roamed forests crowded with trees soaring into the sky as high as the eye could see, or jungles thick with leaves as big as a grown man's head.

I made no secret of my displeasure with the island, my impatience with the islanders. I refused to wear the *robe noire* and *jibilinnen*, and ventured to Audierne to buy floral cotton to make a summer dress, a soft green wool for a winter frock. While working, of course, I wore the linen apron like everyone else, but at the end of the day I could take off my apron and feel, even just a little, like a woman of the world, not a girl of the island.

Which is why it surprised everyone, not least myself, when I said *oui* to Marc's spontaneous proposal of marriage.

Marc and Salvator's mother, Gladie, was beside herself at the thought of losing both her boys at once, for word had come that Salvator feared he might be pressed into service at a work camp under the Vichy government, the *Service du travail obligatoire*, and was hoping to escape to England soon himself.

I was a balm to her, my new mother-in-law said sadly, as I joined her in her kitchen to prepare for the small, hurried marriage ceremony. Like most island women, Gladie was thrifty, accustomed to using up anything and everything. On the stove she kept a huge kettle into which she tossed bones and potatoes and carrots and anything edible, simmering it to create a rich, filling broth that seemed never to end, that was constantly added to. Fish hung from the ceiling beams to dry; Gladie was fastidious and refused to dry her fish on racks outside, where the flies would soon find them.

"At least knowing my younger son will be happy . . . at least I have that," Gladie told me through tears as she shuffled between counter and stove, mixing batter for the marriage cake.

The simple ritual was performed by Père Cecil. Caught up in the nationalist fervor, the priest even donated a few bottles of his hoarded communion wine for the wedding feast.

Marc and I had three nights together. Our marriage bed was in my small room under the eaves on the third floor of the guesthouse, looking as it did out over the ocean.

And then my new husband left, along with every other island man of fighting age.

It is no small thing to be abandoned.

We women cheered our men as they boarded their boats bound for England. Of course we did. The Germans had invaded our beloved France, and not for the first time. Many islanders remembered the Great War that began in 1914, and the rest of us had been raised on the stories, the entire island ever keen to the poignant absence of fathers and brothers and uncles and sons and lovers lost to German shells and bullets, poison gas and land mines. So what else could we do now but support our men as they responded to *Général* de Gaulle's plea to join the French Free Forces in London?

Besides, we island women are accustomed to our men leaving. It is not rare for them to go to sea and never return. There is a reason the women of the Île de Feme always dress in mourning.

Still, many of us were stunned and unsure at this turn of events. Proud of our men for going, certainly, but worried about what would happen next. How would we feed ourselves, and the children, and the old people?

I stood on the dock alongside the others to wish my new husband farewell, feeling a jumble of mixed emotions. I hadn't known what to expect on my marriage night; this wasn't the sort of thing the Fémans spoke of in public. Most mothers informed their daughters what to expect, but mine was not one to chat. So when my new husband fumbled between my legs, I had been appalled, and only a slight fuzziness from having drunk several glasses of the unfamiliar wine made it bearable. I had seen bulls mount cows but had not made the connection, had not realized that Marc would possess the same sort of thing between his legs. It seemed bestial, ugly, frightening. Marc's pawing, sweaty attentions in our marriage bed embarrassed me, and his tentative, birdlike kisses left me cold. They were nothing like the intense daydreams I had of Salvator's mouth upon mine, the ones that left me with a frustrated, unfamiliar yearning deep in my belly.

The day our men left, every villager on the island gathered at the pier. The scene was chaotic, with wives, sisters, mothers, grandparents, and children crying and hugging the men as they boarded their fishing vessels. We remained acutely aware that not only were the men leaving, but they were taking the boats with them. Life on an island without a boat was unimaginable. How would we fish? How would we live?

But we didn't ask; as was typical for the Breton character, there was much brave action and very little talk.

The youngest to volunteer was a boy of fourteen; his mother keened and begged him not to go, but he accompanied his father and two older brothers, standing proudly at the helm as the boat pushed off and receded from view. The eldest was a grandfather of fifty-six, a veteran of the Great War, who vowed his knowledge of the sea would make up for any deficiencies caused by a lack of youthful vigor.

A small musical band made up of veterans of the Great War, now old men, played a jaunty tune, and we showered our brothers, lovers, fathers, and sons with petals plucked from the island's wildflowers.

As I watched the vessels slip farther and farther away, becoming small gray figures on the horizon, I knew I was participating in a ritual as timeless as sailing itself. For as long as men have gone off to sea, their women have watched them go, hoping for the best, wondering if the mariners would be swallowed by sea monsters or seduced by sirens, taken to their watery deaths by vicious mermaids, never to be heard from again.

What I tasted in my mouth as I watched my young husband sail away, waving to him as he stood on deck, waving at me with all his might . . . was regret.

When the boats finally disappeared beyond the horizon, the band dispersed and the celebration faded. And then it was only the women slipping through the labyrinthine pathways of our little stone village, going back to a now emptier and quieter house.

Then came the next day, and the one after that.

No daily haul of fresh fish to eat and sell, no experienced carpenters hammering out constant vital repairs. No loud, gruff voices in our halls, no sounds of big boots overhead, no husbands to shoo out of the kitchen and down to the café to get them out from underfoot, no fathers to remind us of right and wrong, or brothers to tease us mercilessly. No strong arms to cradle us at night—although to tell the truth, I was just as happy not to have to deal with that last.

We had plenty to keep us busy: We tended our kitchen gardens, looked after our cows, pigs, and chickens. At low tide the children were sent to dig for snails and clams and razor shells in the mud; even toddlers were taught how to find clumps of mussels on the rough rocks. Every day we went down in teams to the rocks near the great lighthouse to collect the ribbony seaweed, our fingers wrinkling from the cold water and stinging with salt as we dragged the sea plant from the shallows, shaping it into tightly wound cakes that we set out on the rocks to dry in the sun. A factory on the mainland bought the cakes to extract the iodine; it sent a boat over once every week or so, bringing with it mail and news: The Germans were now established in Paris, and the Free French Forces were amassing in London.

So we ate our meager meals, ignoring as best we could the empty chairs at the tables, the subdued looks upon the girls' faces, the whining of the younger boys who wanted to follow their older brothers into battle, the soft weeping of the old people who remembered all too well the toll of the War of 1914.

But we weren't alone for long.

This time German forces not only invaded France but came to occupy our own little island.

CHAPTER TEN

Natalie

When Natalie walked into the parlor and saw Alex looking through cardboard boxes, a wave of panic swept over her.

Alex saw everything. She noticed *everything*. How was Natalie going to keep things under wraps with her big sister snooping around?

Of course she knew that it was only a matter of time, with or without Alex here. Pretty soon people were going to figure out that François-Xavier had no intention of returning from Paris, and then what? It would take only a single post going viral on social media for her brand to blow up in her face. What would her readers say, or her publisher? What would the islanders think? Would François-Xavier's extended family allow her to stay at the guesthouse?

"This is called the *quai des Paimpolais*," Natalie said as they walked along the seawall, the cove on one side, cafés on the other. "It's the main drag."

"It's cute," said Alex.

Small groups sat on the stone parapet, sharing beers and chatting.

Gulls whirled and hovered overhead, occasionally dipping into the shallows in search of mussels. Dogs roamed the walkway, sniffing for scraps and chasing lizards, and a Siamese cat basked in the late-afternoon sun. The air was filled with the scent of brine and seaweed, overlaid by the aroma of fish frying and stewing.

"So, Nat, why isn't anyone working on your house?" Alex asked.

I knew it. Leave it to Alex to zero in on what Natalie didn't want to talk about.

"It's August . . . ," Natalie began. "A lot of things shut down in France in August."

"Huh. Well, I'll tell you one thing: Even you, Nat, couldn't get lost on an island like this. You've got the water on one side and the houses on the other."

"True," said Natalie. "And no cars to worry about."

"I read about that. There are no vehicles at all?"

"There are a couple of very small trucks and tractors used for big jobs, but you've probably noticed that there aren't any real roads— this seawall walkway is the widest lane, and the ones running between the houses are even narrower. They don't fit anything bigger than a handcart."

Just then a young father passed by, pushing a wagon filled with a few boxes and bags with baguettes sticking out. A pigtailed girl of about three reclined on the bags, her chubby legs swinging off the side.

"Some say the pathways were built like that so drunken sailors would never lose their way," said Natalie, lapsing into tour guide mode as she recited the words she had written earlier in the day. *Maybe that's why I am having such difficulty with the manuscript,* she thought suddenly. *It isn't a memoir so much as a travelogue.* The problem was, she couldn't write the truth of her current life. Her readers looked to her for self-fulfillment and romance, not existential terror.

"But I think the real reason," Natalie continued, "is that the small pathways shelter the islanders from the winds that beset the island, and provide a little shelter from the storms. Anyway, this place was founded long before cars were even dreamed of. There are two Neolithic menhirs by the main church."

"What's a menhir?"

"A rock that's been carved or changed and set on end . . . like Stonehenge. Ever hear of that?"

"Yes, Nat. I may not have gone to college, but even *I've* heard of Stonehenge. Is this the place you had in mind?" Alex asked as they passed by the nearest eatery. "Looks a little busy."

The Pouce Café was hopping, its big yellow umbrellas sheltering a throng of tourists as young servers weaved nimbly between the tightly packed tables, carrying aloft large trays of fish and clams, lobster and *crevettes*.

Natalie shook her head and waved at Loïc, the café's bearded, rotund owner who was simultaneously yelling at a waiter and ringing up a customer. "That's a tourist place."

"That one has some empty tables," Alex said, nodding at a small café named Chez Brigitte.

"I don't feel like fish and chips," said Natalie.

"The chalkboard lists other things, like kebabs," said Alex, gesturing to the café's menu written in careful script on a little A-frame chalkboard.

"She always puts out that chalkboard, but Brigitte only serves fish and chips." *I should write something about this on my blog,* Natalie thought. She could make it sound quirky and charming, rather than merely annoying.

The café's owner, the eponymous Brigitte, emerged from the restaurant, set two glasses and a bottle of wine in front of a young couple, and ignored another couple that was trying to get her attention. A plump woman in her forties with a mop of curly brown hair, Brigitte always seemed overwhelmed and frazzled, whether she was serving one customer or twenty. Her fisherman brother-in-law kept her café well stocked with fresh cod or haddock, which made Natalie wonder whether Brigitte simply didn't feel like cooking anything else, or whether she, like Natalie, could not be bothered to get her grocery order to the ferry on time.

"Go ahead," Natalie said to Alex. "Ask her if they have kebabs today."

"Pardonnez-moi, est-ce qu'il y a keb—," Alex began in careful French.

Before Alex could finish, Brigitte folded her arms, shook her head, and replied brusquely: *"On a que fish et chips aujourd'hui."*

Natalie smiled at Brigitte and wished her *bonsoir* as they continued on their way.

"'Fish et chips'?" Alex repeated to Natalie. "They say it in English?"

"Yeah, not sure why. Speaking of which, since when have you spoken French?" Alex's accent was atrocious, but Natalie was surprised her sister knew even a single word. Foreign languages hadn't been a priority to The Commander, who apparently assumed all the survivors of the Apocalypse would speak English.

"I don't, not really," said Alex. "We had a surprising number of French visitors at the ranch, so I learned a little. Mostly weirdly specific words, like "stirrup"—*étrier*. And I made sure to learn a few travel phrases before I left, just in case. Everyone says the French speak English, but I assumed that was mostly in the urban areas."

"Most Parisians speak at least some," said Natalie with a nod. "But you're right. In the countryside it's not as common. And even those who do speak English appreciate it when foreigners make an effort to speak their language."

"In my case, I think I merely irritated your friend Brigitte."

"She's always irritated," said Natalie with a shrug. *"Toujours de mauvaise humeur.* But Brigitte gets a pass, because she's a true islander. Born here, into a family that has lived on the island for generations. Her husband, Auguste, is the cook. He's from a small town outside of Nantes, and even though he and Brigitte married right out of college and moved to the Île de Feme twenty-five years ago, he's still considered a newbie islander. I'm one, too, obviously. An outsider."

"We were always outsiders, though," said Alex. "It's a good fit for us."

"I suppose so." The thought depressed her. "I'm taking you to Milo's, which is the best restaurant on the island. It's at the very end of the curve of buildings, just a little farther."

"What's with all the animals running around?" Alex asked, trailing her hand along the seawall as they walked.

"Most islanders let their dogs and cats roam free, since there are no cars to endanger them, and they can't get lost because there's nowhere to go. We're all hemmed in by the waters of the Raz."

An orange tabby cat lounged in the walkway, gazing at them.

"Don't expect too much," Natalie said as Alex crouched down and held out one hand. "The animals on the island aren't overly focused on humans, since they have plenty to occupy themselves."

But the cat got up, stretched, and sauntered over to Alex, winding around her ankles.

It is part of the enigma of Al, Natalie thought to herself as Remy the terrier mix trotted up to her sister, demanding his share of affection. Her sister had always had a way with animals.

Alex was like a deadly Doctor Doolittle, who would eat one of those pets as soon as she'd blink if her survival required it. Meanwhile, Natalie would be left sniveling in a corner, crying for the animal even while hoping her sister would share her bounty.

"Do you know their names?" Alex asked, startling Natalie out of her reverie.

"Um, yeah," said Natalie. "The terrier pup is Remy, and the cat is Tula. The unfriendly dog glowering over there is Korrigan. It's the Breton name for a water sprite."

Korrigan was about the size of a German shepherd but her caramel coloring, floppy ears, and wolflike countenance hinted at a mixed heritage. Her lack of one eye and one leg revealed a history of trauma.

When Alex reached a hand toward her, a low warning rumble emanated from Korrigan's barrel chest.

"Guess she doesn't like me," Alex said.

"She doesn't like anybody, though she *will* accept food."

"I don't have anything to offer, Korrigan. Sorry," Alex said to the dog, then turned back to Natalie. "What happened to her?"

"They think she might have fallen off a fishing boat. She was found half-drowned in the cove by the hotel, with one foot caught in the rocks. It couldn't be saved, and she obviously lost an eye at one point as well."

"I like her," said Alex. "She's a survivor. Speaking of which, how is your health?"

"I'm, um, fine, thanks," Natalie stammered, startled by the question.

"Hope and Faith and I are all wearing glasses now," said Alex. "But you're good?"

"Yep. I had LASIK," Natalie said as two toddlers careened into them, followed closely by an apologetic dad.

"So," said Alex, "it was made very clear to me when I went through customs that I'm on a limited visa, and when it expires, I have to leave. How is it you're allowed to live in France so long? Did you marry your French boyfriend?"

Natalie clenched her teeth. No, she wasn't married.

"I have a special visa from the local prefecture because we're redoing the house. It's considered a project for the general good," she explained. "Since it's so close to the ferry landing, the guesthouse is pretty prominent, and the islanders don't like to see it in such disrepair. Doesn't look good for the tourists."

"Makes sense," said Alex. "And how does that work? Did you buy the place?"

"What is this, Alex? Twenty questions?"

Alex let out a startled, breathy laugh. "It's been a while, that's all. Trying to catch up. Clumsily, apparently."

In their family, interrogations were more common than small talk, so it was often hard for Natalie to distinguish between the two. Secrecy was her default mode—and used to be Alex's as well.

"To answer your question, no, I didn't exactly *buy* it. I signed an agreement with the family that owns it to invest some money to renovate it and run it as a guesthouse, and then we'll share in the profits."

"Invest some money" was an understatement, Natalie thought with a spurt of anger tinged with fear. She had *poured* money into the project. François-Xavier's remaining island family, his elderly aunties and his *oncle* Michou, were stout, practical people who had been beyond thrilled that their golden boy had come home to the island for good, to settle down with his American girlfriend. They had been so hopeful, so excited, so welcoming. Natalie dreaded letting them down, seeing the disappointment in their eyes, just as her family had looked at her when it was her turn to bring home food and they all went hungry.

How was Natalie going to tell them that François-Xavier wasn't on a business trip after all? That he had dumped her, her money was running out, and there was no way the guesthouse would be open in time for the Festival of the Gallizenae?

Her jaw tightened. If she kept this up, she was bound to crack a tooth, which would add yet another item to her to-do list.

They walked along the arc of shops and restaurants that lined the quay. On the sand below, children were still playing, now wrapped in towels and sweatshirts as the warmth of the sun ceded to the chilly evening. Beyond the swimming area was a small harbor lined with boats, including several on the mud, beached until the next tide came in.

"That ribbony-looking seaweed you see everywhere?" Natalie said. "It's called *algues* here and, specifically, *goémon*. In the old days the islanders collected it; they say it kept them alive during the war. It's supposed to be good for one's health."

"Have you tried it?"

Natalie shook her head. "I'm not in The Commander's encampment anymore; I can eat what I want. Algae is definitely not on the menu."

Milo's Café was the last in the row of old stone houses facing the water. Though it was considered the best restaurant on the island, tourists rarely made it this far in their search for food, so it served mostly locals.

Natalie paused for a moment to assess the situation. Half a dozen tables spilled out onto a stone terrace, taking advantage of the view, but they were all occupied. Inside, a few regulars lingered at the bar along with one obvious tourist, a nattily dressed man with light brown hair and a rarefied air about him. Natalie was most pleased to spy Christine Tanguy sitting at the end of the bar.

Christine was one of the few islanders under the age of seventy whom Natalie could actually call "friend." She had short-cropped hair and large, capable hands, and wore a tank top that showed off her broad shoulders and lean muscles. Her usual jeans and boots were none too clean, which surprised no one because Christine was fresh off her fishing boat.

On bad nights, when Natalie gave up on sleep and took a cup of tea out to the terrace, she sometimes saw Christine motoring off into the frigid stillness of the ocean. She recognized Christine's boat because it had a little cluster of lights at the top of one mast, reminding Natalie of a Christmas tree. Natalie wondered what it would be like to wake up in the hushed predawn hours, pull on work boots, and climb aboard one's boat, alone, to head out into the freezing nothingness of the dark sea, relying upon one's maritime skills to bring in a catch and then to find one's way back to this tiny sliver of an island.

"*Salut! Ça va, toi?*" Natalie greeted Christine with kisses on both cheeks and introduced her to Alex.

"Another *Américaine!*" Christine exclaimed in heavily accented English, and kissed Alex on both cheeks. "Mostly we have the Brits here. Welcome. You are come to visit your sister?"

Alex nodded. "It's been too long."

"Would you like to join us for dinner?" Natalie asked, suddenly realizing how much Christine reminded her of Alex.

"Thank you, but as soon as I finish my drink, I must go clean up," said Christine, making a show of sniffing her shirt. "Whew! I am very aromatic. I need a shower, you see? Nice to meet you, Alex. Perhaps we will have dinner together soon, yes?"

Natalie was sorry Christine declined to join them; not only did she enjoy her stories, but the fisherwoman's presence would have made dinner with Alex less awkward. Natalie wondered what she and her sister were going to talk about, just the two of them, staring at each other across the café table.

Natalie's heart sped up slightly at the appearance of Milo Le Gall, the café owner, who'd returned from serving tables to tend the bar. In the way of so many Bretons, Milo was broad, strong, and gruff, and looked capable of single-handedly harpooning a whale. He was the kind of man who made Natalie wonder what he had been like as a little boy; it was hard to imagine him without a reddish brown five-o'clock shadow on his square jaw and thick neck. As usual, tonight

Milo wore a button-up vest over a crisp white shirt with the sleeves rolled up to show his thick forearms.

Like François-Xavier's family, Milo's people had lived on the island for as long as anyone could remember, inhabiting this forbidding rock long before things like electricity and fresh water were brought over from the mainland. But although they had grown up together, François-Xavier and Milo shared a deep-seated antipathy for each other, the result, Natalie assumed, of childhood rivalries.

Lately she found this made Milo more attractive in her eyes.

"Bonjour," she said.

"Bonjour." Milo gave Natalie a barely-there chin raise.

"Là-bas?" Natalie gestured to a nearby table.

"Où vous voulez," he said, indicating they should sit wherever they wanted.

"What would you like to drink?" Natalie asked Alex as they took seats at a small table by the window. "This region isn't known for its wine like the rest of France. . . . The islanders tend to prefer beer and hard cider. I've developed a fondness for pastis, which is a kind of anise liqueur."

"Cider sounds great."

Natalie caught Milo's eye as he stood behind the bar and asked for a cider and a pastis, ignoring the roll of his eyes at her order. It was a ritual with them. Natalie always ordered it, and Milo always responded that only foreigners—by which he meant people from the South of France—drank such strong-smelling stuff.

Natalie felt herself relaxing. Here at the restaurant she felt more confident and in charge, ordering drinks in French, greeting familiar faces with breezy *bonjour*s. It made her feel more like Natalie Morgen, urbane world traveler and international bestselling author.

"If you're starving, we could order an appetizer," Natalie said, "but I've gotten into the *apéro* tradition of taking a drink before dinner."

"When in Rome, as they say," said Alex, looking at the chalk-board menu, which included several local specialties. "Do you speak the Breton language? It looks complicated, all those apostrophes and 'k's and 'x's. . . ."

"It's called *Brezhoneg*, and you're right. It's difficult to pronounce."

"I wondered about the name of the guesthouse. Is 'Bag-Noz' a Breton word?"

"It is, yes. It actually refers to a ghost ship."

"A ghost ship? Like in *Pirates of the Caribbean*? Why?"

"I'm not sure, to tell you the truth. I had been hoping to collect stories from the elder islanders, but they're remarkably reticent to speak about the past."

"Maybe they would tell you more if you spoke their language."

"Hardly anyone speaks it anymore. Those who came of age after World War Two refer to themselves as 'the lost generation' because they never learned to speak it properly. It's used in place-names and recipes, that sort of thing, but it's more a reflection of Breton cultural pride than a working language. I can say 'Cheers,' but that's about all."

"Let's hear it."

"*Yec'hed mat.*"

"It doesn't exactly roll off the tongue, does it?"

Natalie chuckled. "It's a Celtic language, related to Cornish and Welsh, brought to France in the early Middle Ages by migrating Britons. In fact, this whole area is considered one of the five Celtic nations. It's an ancient place that was settled long before modern France existed. According to the islanders, nine virgins once lived on the island, the Gallizenae. Their festival is coming up in October. It sort of marks the end of the tourist season."

Her heart fluttered. Only six weeks to finish the renovations. To be ready. But Natalie wasn't anywhere near ready. Story of her life.

"Why have a festival for nine virgins?" Alex asked.

"Supposedly they had special powers; they could command the wind, cure disease, and foretell the future. Occasionally they transformed into mermaids to save lucky sailors, whom they would take for lovers until they threw them back into the sea."

"Wait—how did they remain virgins if they took lovers?"

"Apparently the word 'virgin' was also used for women who chose not to marry and have children."

"Like us, then."

"I hadn't thought of that, but I suppose so, yes."

"And if they didn't take a shine to the men, they threw them back into the sea? Seems a bit harsh."

"Or maybe they turned them into swine, like Circe," Natalie said with a smile. She pronounced it *seer-see*, and then doubted herself. "Or is it pronounced *kir-kee*?"

"I have no idea who you're talking about, much less how to pronounce it."

"Circe is a goddess from Greek mythology. In *The Odyssey*, she turned Odysseus's sailors into swine." Natalie's words sounded pompous to her own ears; she doubted her sister knew the first thing about Greek mythology. She glanced over at the bar, wishing Milo would hurry up with the drinks already.

After a beat, Alex gestured to the view of the harbor with the ocean beyond. "This is nice. Pretty."

Natalie tilted her head. "Are you joking or being serious?"

"Why would you think I was joking?"

"This isn't the sort of thing you used to enjoy."

"It's been a while since we've spent any time together."

"True."

"You seem to have made a good life for yourself, Nat."

Natalie smiled but her monkey brain was racing. Natalie *had* made a good life for herself, hadn't she? She had cultivated a following and was under contract to write another book about how she had made a good life for herself. But . . . would she be able to get by until the next check from her publisher came through? Would the French government even *allow* her to stay if she was no longer attached to a native? And speaking of natives . . . Milo's wrists and forearms were so thick, his hands so large and capable-looking. She knew he lived over the restaurant, and now she wondered: Was there anyone special in his life?

Realizing her sister was waiting for a reply, Natalie said simply, "Yeah, it's nice here. Thanks again for fixing the porch step."

Alex shrugged. "Easy fix. So, tell me about this guy you're with."

"He's . . . in Paris, interviewing sous-chefs," said Natalie, feeling awkward as Milo approached their table with their drinks.

"But you're nowhere near ready to open the restaurant, are you?"

"We will be. He'll be back from Paris soon," Natalie said, doubling down on the lie, feeling every bit the fraud.

Milo set their drinks down, placed a small dish of peanuts on the table, and caught Natalie's eye. She knew her island neighbors wondered what the story was with François-Xavier. Milo wasn't known as a gossip, but any exciting tidbits were sure to spread soon enough. How long could she keep up the charade?

Usually Milo took care of business and returned to his station behind the bar, but now he lingered at their table. Natalie's heart beat a little faster.

"Speaking of Paris," Milo said to Natalie in French, gesturing with his head to the tourist at the bar, "that fellow over there, Jean-Luc Quenneville, missed the last ferry. Don't suppose you could put him up at your place?"

"I don't think—"

"Says he'll pay a small fortune for a room."

"We're not really ready for guests."

His gaze shifted to Alex.

"She showed up unexpectedly. Also, she's my sister." Natalie switched to English. "By the way, I should introduce you: Milo, this is Alex. Alex, Milo."

"*Enchantée,*" said Alex.

His only response was a curt nod.

"The man, he speaks English," Milo said, again addressing Natalie in French. "He's from Paris."

"Yeah, I guessed that part," Natalie replied. Jean-Luc Quenneville was Parisian from the tips of his tasseled leather shoes to the silky tie and tailored suit, everything tucked in and just so. He stuck out like a sore thumb on this island, where flip-flops and T-shirts were the norm. Still, he was smiling and chatting easily with the locals at the bar, which, in Natalie's experience, was *not* the way of most Parisians.

"He's my sister's ex-brother-in-law, sort of. Divorced from her husband's sister. They can't put him up because their new baby is sick—also because her *belle-soeur* wouldn't be happy about it. I've called everyone I can think of for a place."

"I . . ." Natalie hesitated. Her sister's arrival had already thrown her for a loop. But the Fémans—the people of the island—rarely asked for help, which meant that when they did ask, it was important. Not to mention this was Milo asking for a favor. Gruff, interesting Milo.

"He will pay two hundred euros a night," Milo added. "Cash."

"For a simple room?"

Milo shrugged. "The man wants what he wants."

Two hundred euros a night, cash. That was a lot of money. A few days ago her agent, Sandy Ramirez, had confirmed there was no way the publisher's accounting department could cut her a check ahead of schedule. Just paying for this dinner would blow her budget for the week.

Over at the bar Christine made a loud snort, downed the last of her cider, pounded the Parisian on the back, and said, "I tell you what, monsieur. *I'd* put you up for that price, if I didn't live with my mother."

Jean-Luc Quenneville smiled and raised his glass of cider to her. "Very kind of you. Let me buy your drink."

"Ah, thank you! I don't care what they say about Parisians. I like you already," said Christine with a smile as she left the restaurant, bowing to one and all. *"Merci, Milo, et bonne soirée, mesdames and messieurs."*

Natalie explained the French exchange to Alex.

"Since when do the Morgens turn down money?" Alex asked. "The room across the hall from mine looked all right. I already swept it out, and you've got a new mattress in there as well. We just need to put the bed frame together and make the bed. Easy enough."

"You wouldn't mind sharing the bathroom?" Natalie asked.

Alex looked incredulous. "Am I the only one who remembers we grew up without indoor plumbing? Remember the 'honey pot'?"

The sisters shared a grimace.

"What I really remember is we never had toilet paper," said Natalie. "We had to make do with leaves or the pages of a phone book."

Another grimace.

Milo frowned as his keen eyes shifted from one sister to the other. "I do not understand."

"Long story," said Natalie. "But if your friend or in-law or whatever he is has money to burn, why doesn't he hire someone with a boat to take him back to Audierne?"

"I suppose he wants to stay," Milo said, appearing done with the conversation. He lifted his chin in greeting to a couple coming through the door of the café before turning back to Natalie. "So, what shall I tell him?"

"Tell him yes," Natalie said. "If he's willing to deal with less-than-ideal accommodations, he's welcome to stay at the Bag-Noz."

"Bon," Milo said, and left.

Alex raised her glass of cider. "To your first paying guest. How do you say 'Cheers' again? *Yeck*-something?"

"Yec'hed mat." Natalie raised her glass of pastis, and the sisters toasted the outsider from Paris willing to pay two hundred euros a night.

CHAPTER ELEVEN

Violette

The Germans landed on a cold, foggy morning in July.

A few scouts had arrived earlier and scoped out the island, informing the residents that our lives were about to change, and setting up a table down at the quay to issue every islander an official *carte d'identité*, which included a photograph and personal information. And then on July 11, the largest ferries we had ever seen pulled up to our docks. Nearly three hundred enemy soldiers surged off and marched in formation along our *quai des Paimpolais*.

The older islanders hid in their houses, closing their shutters against the Germans the way they would guard against a storm blowing in from the sea. Others, mostly young women and boys defying our mothers, lined the seawall, curious about the new arrivals.

That's when I spied my childhood friend and sister-in-law, Noëlle, standing to one side with a bucket of fish guts in one hand, a look of sheer hatred on her face.

I sidled up to her, placing my hand over hers.

"*Arrête*, Noëlle!" I whispered fiercely, urging her to stop. "You think those rifles are just for show?"

Noëlle had confided to me that her mother lost her first love to a trench mortar in the Battle of the Marne during the War of 1914, and sometimes still cried at night, calling out to her fallen lover as well as to her beloved father, who succumbed to dysentery while serving near the Belgian border. Noëlle's uncle still suffered from the shrapnel lodged in his body. And now both her brothers had gone to fight.

Noëlle had no love for Germans.

Noëlle and I weren't as close as we were as girls, when we used to scramble over the rocks, playing pirates and discovering "fairy pools" left by the tides. Lately, since talk had turned to war, Noëlle had hardened, something deep within her calcifying, making her turn away from old friends. She would disappear for days at a time.

The fingers wrapped around the bucket's handle were stained with ink from her grandfather's old printing press, hidden in the basement of her family home. I imagined that was where she now spent the majority of her time.

"Nazi swine," Noëlle nearly spat through gritted teeth.

"Will it help your mother and sisters if you are arrested?" I whispered. "Your brothers have already gone to fight the Germans. Will you endanger those who are left on the island?"

She glared at me, tried to throw off my hands.

"Are you a *Vichyste*, Violette?" Noëlle demanded.

"Of course not. My husband is in England, too, remember? As are my brother and father."

I wasn't a German sympathizer; I just wasn't sure what they were capable of, these well-fed men in their smart belted uniforms and shiny leather boots. We had all heard the rumors and knew what had happened in the last war. The Germans were a formidable enemy, not to be underestimated.

And now that our own men were gone, what was to keep these soldiers from exacting revenge upon the women on the island? The kind of terrible, whispered revenge that men so often take out upon women and children.

Noëlle and I, and all the others, were stuck here on this island of women, of *veuves*, of fatherless children. while German soldiers took the place of our men, sleeping in their beds, sitting at their tables, their shadows dwarfing our Lilliputian walkways.

"*Arrête*, Noëlle," I repeated. "If we defy them, it can't be like this. We have to be smart about it."

She gazed at me with eyes that looked much older than they had a mere few weeks ago, before our men left, before our home was invaded.

After a long moment, she put down the bucket and we stepped back and watched as the soldiers made their show of force, marching down the quay like Teutonic phantoms, invading our lives and awkwardly inhabiting the spaces our men had left behind.

My great-grandparents had added on to their proud stone home to house their large family of eleven children, plus assorted other relatives. Later, my parents had begun taking in guests to fill the empty rooms, offering a refuge to weary sailors and stunned shipwreck survivors, and the rare visitor to the island who had no family with whom to stay the night.

And now we were to house Germans. Nearly every Féman family became an unwilling host, as the men took over marital beds and children's nurseries, couches and cots. The soldiers slept four to a room at the hotel and filled the dormitories of the Abri du Marin, but there were still hundreds in need of shelter.

It wasn't long before the rooms in our guesthouse were claimed by the officers.

I had always loved my little bedroom on the third floor. I had a view of the ocean, and the windows opened out from a deep sill. Sometimes I grabbed a book and a pillow and crawled up onto the sill to read in the soft afternoon light. But I gave up my chamber willingly, as I had no inclination to sleep near any of the German officers. I moved downstairs to share a bed with my mother in a small room off the kitchen that had once belonged to a housekeeper, and more recently to *Mamm-gozh*.

The soldiers carried with them an unfamiliar scent that took over our home as surely as they had our country: These men did not smell of fish and brine, as ours always did, but of sweat and musk and the wool of their fine uniforms. Heavy boots thundered overhead, as if warning of an approaching storm. My mother and I did our best to ignore the guttural, harsh male voices booming through our halls.

And they issued proclamations: No gatherings of more than three islanders at a time would be permitted, except for the harvesting of *goémon*. A strict curfew would apply after dark. And anyone wishing to leave the island had to file a request with the occupying authorities. Permission was seldom granted.

When our men were home, they were accustomed to telling us women what to do. Now the German soldiers were giving us orders, but unlike our fathers and husbands, these occupiers offered nothing in return.

The first order of business was surviving, persevering long enough for our men to return to the island. So we kept our heads down and avoided making eye contact with the soldiers, whether on the village pathways or in our own homes, trying not to engage even at the most basic level.

We called it "feigning blindness."

One morning I surged up from the bed and retched into the chamber pot.

"It's because of the hunger," my mother said.

I nodded, though I knew it wasn't true. It was something else, something secret within. Something I wanted to hold on to, just a little bit longer. A barely-there fluttering I was at first sure I must have imagined. But my flow had not come this month, and usually it was as regular as clockwork.

The regret I tasted as I stood on the pier and waved good-bye to Marc was now displaced by nausea. We had been together only a few nights, but it was enough. I was with child.

I felt confused, unsure. In my experience, the arrival of children meant relinquishing all else, especially dreams of something more, of a different kind of life. A child would tie me even more tightly to Marc, a man I did not love. On the other hand, there was a strange, enticing intimacy in the idea that I would now be related by blood to Salvator. And the prospect of a new life seemed like a buffer, mellowing the harshness of war and occupation.

I was not prepared, much less eager, to be a mother to anyone, but I was pleased I could bring so much happiness to our families.

That afternoon my *belle-mère*, Gladie, wept with joy when I told her I carried her first grandchild in my belly. We sat in her warm, crowded kitchen, where, despite our lack of meat and vegetables, the huge pot of broth bubbled merrily on the stove.

"Noëlle!" shouted Gladie down the basement stairs. "Noëlle, come and say hello to dear Violette! She has news!"

Noëlle came up from the basement but did not smile, even at my news, instead appearing to view me with suspicion. Was it because I had stopped her from attacking the Germans that first day? Or was she, perhaps, the only one besides my *mamm-gozh* who understood what I felt for Salvator?

Salvator.

Not long after the soldiers arrived, when we were still allowed to receive mail from England, across "enemy" lines, the busy postal clerk handed me a letter. It was from my brother-in-law, and it was addressed to me, not to his mother or sister.

I slipped it into my sleeve, hoping no one noticed and that the overworked postal clerk would not mention it and fuel the fierce island gossip network. Climbing out onto the rocks, where I liked to come to read when the weather was fine, I opened the note with shaking hands.

Salvator wrote that he had watched me for many years, waiting for me to grow up, but that in the end he knew he was too old for me. He wrote that he wished me nothing but the best, that his brother was a good man, a true man. That Marc was not tempted, as Salvator was, to go down to the café in the evenings, to drink too much and dance with barmaids, to wander the world in search of the next best thing. That his brother would make a much better husband than Salvator ever would. Finally, he confessed that even though he had told his mother he was engaged to be married, he had no intention of tying the knot. He had told his mother that to ease her mind, because she worried that he was so far from family and had for so long avoided the marriage state.

I leaned back against the rocks, looking up at the lighthouse, taking it all in.

The man I loved wasn't married. But I was. And I was carrying his brother's child.

CHAPTER TWELVE

Alex

his must be my lucky day," Jean-Luc said as he approached their table, smiling broadly.

Jean-Luc Quenneville appeared to be in his early fifties, and was attractive in a beige sort of way, the kind of man one might nod to pleasantly on the street and forget a moment later. By far the most interesting thing about him was his voice: Deep and velvety, it reminded Alex of the narrator of the wildlife show she used to watch late at night when she couldn't sleep.

"I do have to warn you," said Natalie, "we're really not set up for guests, and parts of the house are still under construction."

"Milo explained that to me," said the man. "A roof and a bed would be jolly good."

"It's settled, then," said Natalie. "We're about to have dinner; why don't we walk back together afterward?"

"Perfect. *Bon appétit!* I'll just wait over by the bar."

Jean-Luc Quenneville returned to his stool and made a stab at engaging the other men in conversation. They cast him suspicious glances.

"Poor fellow. They don't seem thrilled with him," said Alex in a low voice.

"Bretons can be a little . . . gruff. They sometimes take a while to open up."

"Like Milo?"

"What about him?"

"Gotta say, our genial host is a bit of an ass." At Nat's look of surprise, Alex added, "Sorry. Maybe that's just the way of Bretons, as you said."

"Milo's not an ass. He's . . . complicated. He reminds me of that café owner on *Gilmore Girls*. Did you ever watch that show?"

Alex shook her head. "Doesn't sound familiar."

"He was a curmudgeon, but hot. And a really good guy, under the rough exterior."

"Ah, I get it." Alex leaned back, a small, knowing smile on her face. "You've always had questionable taste in men."

"What are you talking about?" Nat replied, bristling.

"You like him."

"No, I don't. I mean, it's just that Milo's—" Nat's eyes shifted to a spot over Alex's shoulder. "Oh, *damn*."

"What?" Alex twisted around to see two middle-aged women stumble into the café, books tucked under their arms.

"Pilgrims."

"Pilgrims? Like Thanksgiving?"

"That's what I call them," Nat said, scooching down in her chair and looking out the window to avoid their gaze. "People—women, mostly—who read my book and come here looking for me."

"What, *here*? To Milo's?" asked Alex.

"Here, to the Île de Feme. There are only so many restaurants on the island, and the locals know I tend to come here, so . . ."

The newcomers approached Milo behind the bar, who pretended for a moment that he didn't speak English before relenting and nodding toward Nat and Alex. The women made their way across the now-crowded restaurant and, flustered and giggling, stepped up to the table.

"Oh, please, we don't mean to interrupt," said a neat blonde with a soft British accent wearing an expensive-looking pantsuit. The other, a petite brunette, hovered behind her. "But are you Natalie Morgen? *The* Natalie Morgen?"

Nat sat up and gave them a brilliant smile that conveyed warmth and welcome. Alex watched, fascinated, as her little sister assumed the persona of an international bestselling author: dignified, gracious, and charming in the face of the women's effusive comments. She signed their books, added a personal note to each, and asked about their own dreams of moving to a new country, of learning the art of French cooking and the sensuality that it conveyed.

"I swear, you must be the luckiest woman in the world!" The brunette sighed. "François-Xavier is just *gorgeous!*"

Nat smiled. "Every day I remind myself to be grateful. I think that's the most important thing, don't you?"

"I *do!*" the blonde gushed, and the brunette nodded. After what seemed like an interminable interlude, the women thanked Nat, nodded to Alex, apologized again for interrupting, and departed. Through the window, Alex watched them walking along the seawall and chatting animatedly, comparing the inscriptions Nat had written.

"Can't you do something about that?" Milo asked as he approached their table, frowning. "I don't like the rock star thing in my café. Anyway, you know what you want to eat?"

"I'll go with chef's choice," said Alex.

"The *menu*?" Milo asked.

"Here, the *menu du jour* is a set meal," Nat explained.

"Works for me," said Alex. "I'm not picky."

"Two *menus*," Nat said to Milo, who grunted and left the table.

"Yeah," said Alex as she watched him saunter back to the bar, ignoring several patrons who were trying to get his attention, "I'm gonna go with 'a bit of an ass.'"

Nat laughed despite herself.

The first course soon arrived and Alex gave Nat a side-eyed look. "I came all the way to France to eat a bowlful of bugs?"

"They're not *bugs*. The small ones are *bigorneaux*, or periwinkles, a kind of sea snail. They're delicious. *Bulots* are whelks, and *praires* are prairie clams. They dig them out from the sand when the tide's out. They say they're good for you, high in magnesium and potassium."

"Looks like something Dad would make us eat."

"You said you aren't picky, remember?"

"You got me there. Um, how do you eat these things?"

"Use one of these to extract the meat from the *bigorneaux*, like this." Nat picked up a tiny fork and demonstrated how to pluck out the morsel from its twisty shell, before dipping it in the garlicky *aïoli*.

"I saw a set of these little forks in that cardboard box in the parlor," said Alex. "Didn't know what they were for."

"I haven't made it through all the boxes, obviously," said Nat.

"Why not?" Alex asked.

"There's been a lot to do," said Nat. "You don't see it all—most of the work so far has been inside the walls, down in the basement, that sort of thing. Ah, here's the fish."

The main course was halibut in a mushroom sauce, served with a bottle of Muscadet from outside of Nantes. And after, for dessert, Milo brought two small plates with a square of pastry on each.

"This is a traditional Breton dessert called *kouign-amann*," Nat explained. "The butter and sugar are folded into the pastry to make layers, and the sugar caramelizes during the baking process. Doesn't sound very interesting, but it's luscious, especially when accompanied by Calvados, which is a kind of apple brandy."

Alex took a sip of the strong Calvados, then pushed the small glass across the table to Natalie. She couldn't help but notice that after all these years, they didn't have much to talk about other than the food. Alex remembered her baby sister as dreamy, excitable, irresponsible, but this was different: Nat was drinking freely and acting in a show-offy, oddly performative manner, as though they were on film or under observation. There was a definite edge to her, but Alex couldn't parse whether it was excitement or fear.

When the bill came, Nat whipped out a credit card and tossed it on the little tray without looking at the total. Natalie tried to catch Milo's eye as they left, but he was engrossed in conversation with a pair of attractive young women.

"I guess he's busy," said Nat, as if it didn't matter.

Their new boarder, Jean-Luc Quenneville, joined them at the door, trailing a small rolling suitcase.

"I honestly can't thank you enough," he said as they walked out into the warm evening air, gentle breezes blowing in off the water. "This is jolly good."

Alex smiled. "I don't think I've ever heard the phrase 'jolly good' used outside of old movies. Where did you learn English?"

"My stepfather. He was impossibly old, and impossibly British. And where did you learn French?"

"I didn't," said Alex, holding up her hands as if in surrender. "I know about two sentences. Nat's the expert."

"Hardly that," Nat said, and lit up a slim cigarette, avoiding her sister's disapproving look. She offered one to Jean-Luc, but he declined. "But I lived for a time in Paris, in the Marais."

"One of my favorite neighborhoods!" said Jean-Luc. "All those crumbly ancient buildings. Just lovely."

"Well, if you like crumbly ancient buildings, you're in for a treat at the Bag-Noz," said Nat.

They walked by a little plaza where bright overhead lights illuminated two informal teams playing a game. A dozen men and women were seated along the seawall, making teasing remarks and commenting upon the skill of the players. Children squatted and watched the progress of the ball. Three old women sat on a bench outside a house, leaning against its ocher wall.

"I understand there's a *pétanque* competition this weekend," said Jean-Luc.

"What's *pétanque*?" asked Alex.

"It's sort of like bocce ball," explained Nat. "It's played on a dirt court, or in pretty much any available square in France."

"Do you play?"

Nat shook her head. "You were the sporty one, not I."

They watched as a barefooted man with long white hair pitched a ball toward two others on the ground.

"So how's it played?" asked Alex.

"First, you throw that white little ball," said Jean-Luc, "called the *cochonnet*, which means 'pig.'"

"Why is it called a pig?"

Jean-Luc looked dumbfounded, then smiled. "I have no idea. I've never wondered about it before! Anyway, players take turns trying to throw their balls near the *cochonnet*. When all the balls have been thrown, whoever is closest wins."

"Sounds simple enough," Alex said.

"Yes, the rules are very simple," said Jean-Luc. "But there's a lot of finesse in how to throw the ball, spinning it so it stops where it lands, that sort of thing."

Right then the thrower struck his opponent's ball with his own, resulting in a loud *clack* and sending the other ball rolling far from the *cochonnet*. A raucous cheer went up from some spectators, groans from others.

Jean-Luc explained: "And occasionally a player will try to knock the opponent's ball out of the way, to remove it as a threat. Would you like to play? I could ask them if they'd allow you—"

"No, thanks. Not enough light." Alex turned and, as if on cue, stumbled over a rock that formed part of a garden border.

Jean-Luc reached out to steady her.

"Thanks," Alex said tersely, and yanked her arm away from him.

"Pardonnez-moi," he said, tucking his offending hand in his pocket. "Reflex."

The tourist cafés were still packed with customers, the tchotchke shop was open despite the late hour, and more people were strolling along the seawall, enjoying the summer evening.

As they walked past Café Brigitte, Nat raised her hand in greeting to Brigitte, who responded by shaking her head and insisting: *"On a que fish et chips."*

Only fish and chips. Ever and always.

"I feel I should warn you again, Jean-Luc," said Nat, "we're nowhere near ready for guests. The bed's not even set up, much less made. I'll take care of that right away, of course, but it's not too late to back out."

"You are doing me a great kindness by offering me a room of any sort. Silly me, thinking I could come to an island during tourist season and expect to find a vacancy."

"How long were you thinking of staying?" asked Alex.

"Indefinitely," he said, adding, "Though I don't intend to impose upon you lovely ladies forever, of course. But I . . . I find myself at a bit of a crossroads in my life and need time to consider my options without distractions. I am thinking of possibly relocating to the island."

"Well, if you're looking for a place with few distractions, this island fits the bill," Nat said.

"Will you be looking for a job here?" asked Alex.

"I have taken early retirement. It is—what is the expression?— a long story. I am—I *was*—a *fonctionnaire* for many years," said Jean-Luc.

Nat explained: "A *fonctionnaire* works for the state, like a civil servant."

"Yes, precisely." Jean-Luc nodded. "That's the term in English: a civil servant. I spent nearly thirty years working in an office that issued contracts for the procurement of items needed in government-sponsored projects. It was . . . well, I don't mind saying it was rather tedious. I spent days, weeks, months auditing line items and cost estimates, reviewing legal contracts, fielding calls from irate officials, contractors, and suppliers wondering why the approval process was taking so long."

"That sounds tough," said Alex, searching for something polite to say.

"Oh, it was," Jean-Luc said. "You see, to them, I was an obstruction, the annoying bureaucrat who stood between them and whatever it was they wanted: a new bridge, a public park, a housing development. They did not understand that I was a part of the process, what you call in English a 'cog.' This is correct? I heard it in a documentary about World War Two. I was but a cog in a wheel of a vast government that counted on its many cogs to keep itself rolling along."

Silence followed this declaration as they passed Pouce Café, jammed with tourists. Children were still playing on the beaches, their parents watching as they built sandcastles in the dark, under a canopy of stars.

Jean-Luc let out a long, loud sigh. "I take by your silence that I am boring you. Indeed, the more I try to explain this, to my wife, to my children, the more boring I seem to become. A self-fulfilling prophecy, no?"

Nat and Alex shared a look. He was their guest, after all.

"Not at all," Nat said. "You say you have children?"

Jean-Luc nodded. "A girl and a boy, though they're adults now, out of college and living their own lives. They are beautiful, and smart. I do not hear from them often, which I believe must mean they're happy."

"Will your wife be joining you on the island?" Alex asked.

He shook his head. "We divorced many years ago."

"Oh. I'm sorry."

"It is water under the bridge, as they say. Do the Americans say that, or is that a British bit as well?"

"We do say it, yes," said Alex.

"Some of us say it a lot," Nat concurred.

"Our divorce was a happy enough occasion, as far as divorces go. The lawyer said he'd rarely seen a divorcing couple agree on so many things, so I suppose that was good. And now, years later, what is the phrase? I 'bear her no ill will'? Only occasionally do I get annoyed, as when I remember a certain cigar box I unearthed in my stepfather's garage after his passing. . . . I spent days sanding and refinishing it to a soft mahogany sheen. . . ."

"What happened to it?" Nat asked.

"Odile—my ex-wife—kept it. She stores her tea in it."

"That doesn't seem very fair," said Alex.

"No, no, I suppose it doesn't. But as I say, it was a long time ago. And I was able to get a cat when I moved out. Odile doesn't care for animals—doesn't like hair on the furniture."

"Where's the cat now?" Nat asked.

"She died. Just last week." His voice caught and he cleared his throat. "That was one reason I felt the need to get away, to search for something new. I am quite intrigued by the history of World War Two; I have been to all the Normandy beaches and that sort of thing, and I found the story of the men from the Île de Feme fascinating. Then I remembered Odile's sister married a man from the Île de Feme, and the next thing you know, I filed for early retirement and came here without so much as a hotel reservation."

"That was brave of you," said Natalie as she paused at the iron gates in front of the Bag-Noz.

"I daresay no one expected it of me," said Jean-Luc, a note of wonderment in his voice. "My supervisor thought I was making a joke when I told him. I had never even contemplated such a thing before."

A short silence passed.

"Well, no time like the present to jump in with both feet, right?" said Nat. "Speaking of which, here we are: home sweet home."

Jean-Luc gazed up at the stone building's faded façade, which gleamed silver in the moonlight. "Oh, this is charming."

The iron gates screeched as they pushed them open to enter the courtyard.

"I'll fix that tomorrow," Alex murmured.

Nat led the way into the house and gave Jean-Luc a quick tour of the main floor. "The dining room is unfortunately out of service at the moment."

"Is this where the restaurant will be, then?" Jean-Luc asked as he poked his head in. He stopped in front of the framed newsletter article, peering at the photograph.

"Yes," said Nat. "Just a small capacity. Eight tables. François-Xavier is in Paris scouting for—"

"*Attends.* Do you mean *the* François-Xavier Olivier? The chef?" interrupted Jean-Luc. "Now I know why the name sounded familiar!

But he is opening a new restaurant in the *dixième arrondissement*, is he not?"

"He's . . . what?" Alex glanced at Nat. "Isn't that a neighborhood in Paris?"

Her little sister appeared ashen, even in the golden light of the hallway sconces. Nat stood absolutely still, like a deer in the woods sensing the presence of a hunter. "When faced with danger, there are three possible responses," The Commander had lectured them as small children. "Fight. Flight. Or freeze. I strongly suggest the first two." Alex and Charity had fought, and Hope and Faith had flown, but Nat had always frozen.

"Perhaps I am mistaken," Jean-Luc said, apparently realizing he had said the wrong thing. "I believe I must be mistaken."

"Nat, why don't I show our guest up to his room since I'm up there as well?" Alex said. "You go on to bed, if you like."

Nat nodded, wished them a quiet *bonne nuit*, and walked stiffly down the hall toward the kitchen.

Jean-Luc trailed Alex silently as they mounted the stairs to the third floor.

"This is just lovely," Jean-Luc said as Alex showed him the bathroom and his bedroom.

Together they assembled the bed frame and settled the mattress on it. Then Alex left Jean-Luc to unpack while she searched the second floor for the bedsheets. Unlike the rest of the house, the linen closet was tidy, filled with stacks of neatly folded sheets and scented with lavender.

Alex chose a pair, along with towels and a washcloth, and brought them up to the third floor.

"I would like to apologize if I said the wrong thing earlier," said Jean-Luc as they made up the bed. "This is not unusual for me, I am sorry to say."

Alex shook her head. "It's not you, Jean-Luc. I have a feeling the situation with my sister and François-Xavier is . . . complicated. So, tell me what you know."

"Only that he and the celebrated restaurateur Celeste Peyroux announced a new endeavor in Paris. My ex-wife, Odile, is very fond of the restaurant scene, and the site for the new restaurant is not far from where she lives. She mentioned it when I told her I was coming to the Île de Feme, since he is from here." Jean-Luc's voice was low and earnest as he added: "I certainly won't mention it to anyone. But, Alex, if this has been announced in Paris . . ."

Alex nodded. They might be on an island, but they weren't isolated from the world.

It was only a matter of time before the islanders heard the news.

After wishing Jean-Luc a good night, Alex went downstairs and knocked softly on Nat's bedroom door. No response.

She hesitated. Should she push it? Or give Nat her space? She tried once more. "Nat? Talk to me."

After a long moment of silence, Alex went back upstairs. She and Nat had never been especially close, but childhood habits died hard and Alex felt her protective instincts kicking in. Once, during one of their childhood rock climbing drills, Alex had scaled a large rock with ease and was waiting at the top while The Commander barked orders from the ground. Nat made it halfway up, then froze, her knuckles turning white as she clung to a fissure in the rock, unable to move. "C'mon, Nat. Give it a try," Alex called to her. "Nowhere to go but up, Nat. You can do it. Listen to the sound of my voice, don't look down, and climb." But Nat couldn't, or at least she didn't, and so Alex climbed back down and guided her up, one tense step at a time. The Commander swore at them both from below: at Alex, for being a softy, and at Nat, for being useless.

Alex washed up in the bathroom, then went into her bedroom, locking the door more out of habit than concern for the guest across the hall. She left the lamp on, unwilling to lose the light, shrugged off her clothes, and crawled into bed with a grateful sigh. The mattress was supremely comfortable, the sheets lusciously soft. *Must have cost a fortune,* Alex thought.

There was a reading lamp by the bed, but Alex turned on her heavy Maglite with the high beam. It reminded her of how Nat used to read under the covers while pretending to be asleep.

When they were children, Alex thought Nat was lazy, preferring an imaginary world to the hard work of real life. But when the grown-up Alex began to read for pleasure, and not just how-to manuals, she came to realize that books had been Nat's lifeline. Reading must have offered her access to other worlds, alternative lives, ways of being that did not include the nonstop search for food or the perpetual threat of the end of the world. Alex remembered Nat showing her recipes from the cookbooks she checked out of the library. Neither of them was familiar with most of the ingredients, so the exercise seemed pointless to Alex, but it was precisely the unknown elements that made Nat's eyes light up.

Alex opened Virginia Woolf's *To the Lighthouse,* flipped through the pages, and skimmed a few passages. One in particular struck her:

Life, from being made up of little separate incidents which one lived one by one, became curled and whole like a wave which bore one up with it and threw one down with it, there, with a dash on the beach.

Alex got out of bed and gazed out the window into the darkness. The sea was a black void, but a full moon silvered a shimmering slice of the water. From down on the quay below she could hear the clacking of *pétanque* balls, spectators cheering and booing. The sweet coos of a night bird—or was it an owl? The squeak of a *charette*, its wheels rumbling as it rolled along a stone pathway.

Woolf's words came to her: Was Nat caught in the curled wave of life, and on the verge of being dashed upon the beach? Just as Alex was?

CHAPTER THIRTEEN

Natalie

The next morning Natalie was awakened by the whine of a circular saw, and in the strange twilight of being half-awake, she thought the work crew had taken pity on her and returned to finish the job.

She lay there for a moment, embracing the idleness, not ready to release her vivid dreams and the priceless escape they offered. Natalie listened for the other sounds typical of island life: children laughing, the *slap-slap-slap* of thongs on bare feet, the incessant call of the gulls.

Her jaw ached from clenching it at night, from grinding her teeth. She opened wide to stretch her jaw, rubbing the sore joint.

Above the sound of the saw she heard a woman speaking and a deferential, upbeat man's voice in reply.

Alex. And the new boarder . . . what was his name? Jean-something. Luc, right? Jean-Luc Quenneville.

And then she remembered.

After Jean-Luc's revelation last night, Natalie had poured herself a generous portion of pastis and gone online, looking for more information.

It wasn't hard to find. A newspaper article about François-Xavier Olivier, photographed strolling along the Seine with a beautiful woman, both smartly dressed and reeking of Parisian sophistication. Below the image was a gossipy story about how these two "culinary legends" would be opening a "first-class" restaurant in the *dixième*. With a flick of her fingers Natalie had enlarged the photograph so that all she saw was her apparently ex-boyfriend's face. Those beautiful eyes. The larger-than-life charisma that filled a room and commanded attention. That glorious smile that had once shone so brilliantly on Natalie. That sensual mouth that spouted lies: that he loved her, that the two of them would create a life together, on this island, in this community, in this house.

Her jaw tightened; her gut fluttered. She tasted something acrid in her mouth and could not tell if it was fear or rage. Tears surged and she collapsed onto her bed, allowing the sobs to rack her body.

She had sunk so much into this place, not just money but her *self*—and it hadn't been enough, not nearly enough. *She* wasn't enough and never had been, not for her family, not for François-Xavier, not for *his* family, not for her publisher, not for her readers. *Porquoi Pas?* had obviously been a fluke. She was a fraud, a one-trick pony, a one-hit wonder. *Face it, Natalie,* she thought bitterly. *You're pathetic.*

Her carefully curated world was coming apart. The bedrock turned to sand.

And now what was she supposed to do, with not one but two guests sharing her not-ready-for-guests guesthouse?

All Natalie was sure of at the moment was that she was in serious need of caffeine. Normally she would slouch out to the kitchen in the T-shirt she had slept in to make herself a mug of crappy instant coffee because anything else was too much bother. But . . . was that fresh brew she smelled?

Natalie pulled on a robe and went down the hall to find a brand-new coffeemaker and a carafe of freshly brewed coffee. And that wasn't all. The large kitchen had been tidied up, the flatware stowed in the drawers, the cups and dishes stacked neatly on the shelves.

Natalie stared at the coffeemaker. She and François-Xavier had bought it on one of their last "fun runs" into Quimper. They had lingered in the massive Carrefour, searching each aisle even though they really needed to finish the renovation before even thinking about furnishing and decorating the place. It had been hard to resist the allure of what the Bag-Noz might look like, feel like, once the building was fully functional and filled with guests. Once their dream had come true.

Her dream. Not his, as it turned out.

The coffeemaker had sat in the pantry in its original packaging for weeks now, alongside several other appliances and a dozen boxes of filters they had bought with optimism, imagining serving their guests in the morning. After François-Xavier left, Natalie couldn't find the energy to set up the coffeemaker and deal with actual coffee beans. She had briefly considered returning the appliances to get her money back, but wavered at the thought of lugging all those big boxes down to the ferry under the watchful eyes of the islanders. The money wouldn't be enough to fix things, anyway.

But somehow, while she was sleeping, someone had put the coffeemaker to good use. She didn't even have coffee beans in the pantry, did she?

The back door squeaked as Jean-Luc came in from the yard.

"Oh! *Bonjour,* Natalie!" He kissed her on both cheeks. "I am an early riser, as is your sister, and must confess that I have a caffeine habit. Too many years trying to stay awake in the terrible office, I suppose. I hope you do not mind."

Natalie blinked.

"May I fix you a cup? Happily, the general store was open, and they had some very nice dark roast coffee beans. Your sister assured me I should open the coffeemaker. Otherwise I would never have presumed . . ."

"I . . ." She cleared her throat. "Thanks, yes, but I can serve myself."

He smiled. "That's what your sister said."

"Two peas in a pod, I guess," she said. *Not.* "What is Alex up to?"

"Your sister, she is working on a windowsill at the front of the house. She was thinking to check out the roof tiles, though, and wondering whether to make that a priority. The proprietor of the general store says her arthritis is acting up, which means there's a storm coming in."

On an island, there's always a storm coming in.

"She is rather fantastic, is she not? Your sister?" said Jean-Luc, taking newly washed pots and pans from the drainer by the sink and placing them on the open shelf above the counter, turning each so its handle faced out and to one side, at precisely the same angle. "She tells me she worked on a ranch, like a cowboy! I do not believe I have ever met such an able woman."

"She's able, all right," said Natalie, pouring herself some of the fragrant java. She hugged the mug and breathed in the aroma. After weeks of instant coffee, she savored the moment and almost forgot Jean-Luc was there.

When she looked up, he was leaning against the counter, holding his own cup of coffee, and looking at her expectantly. Natalie considered trying to make up an excuse for her reaction to his words last night, but couldn't bring herself to address it. And he seemed, kindly, to be allowing her to ignore it.

"Thank you for the coffee," she said.

"I hope you don't mind."

"Mind what?"

"About opening the coffeemaker."

"Not a bit. Thank you."

"And tidying up in here. I have probably put all the dishes where they are not supposed to go, and you will spend the next several weeks looking for what you need and cursing my name," Jean-Luc said with a broad smile. "Also, I found a very old cantaloupe that was past saving, I'm sorry to say. Your sister assured me it would be all right to organize the kitchen. I was worried I would wake you, but Alex said you always used to sleep through anything."

She managed a nod.

Still feeling fuzzy and not quite awake, Natalie studied her guest. He was so eager, rather like a bouncy puppy. She wasn't accustomed to this from the French, especially not from Parisians. According to François-Xavier and his chic friends, it was the Americans who were enthusiastic and puppylike. She tried to imagine Jean-Luc at his desk alongside the other *fonctionnaires*, churning out government-mandated paperwork, fulfilling his dreary daily responsibilities to a massive bureaucracy, year after year. She couldn't picture it.

This morning he was wearing a button-down shirt and nice slacks, but at least he wasn't wearing an entire suit. She wondered if he owned a pair of shorts or jeans.

Jean-Luc noticed her gaze and said, "Your sister tells me I must find some work clothes if I am to stay on. And I would very much like to stay on."

"Alex has a way of putting people to work, but you don't have to do her bidding, Jean-Luc," said Natalie, pasting on a small smile. "You're paying me good money to stay in this hovel, *and* you brought me coffee."

He smiled and ducked his head. "It probably sounds silly, but I am fifty-three years old, and I've never worked with my hands. I believe I would enjoy it, to remain a few days and learn from your sister. Unless you object, of course."

"If it's okay with Alex, it's okay with me."

Jean-Luc beamed at her. "Then it is settled! I shall today purchase some appropriate work clothes."

"How long were you planning on staying?"

"I am a free agent." He smiled and sipped his coffee, sighing in appreciation. "But of course I will seek more permanent arrangements. As a matter of fact, I have to leave now for an appointment with the mayor's assistant; he has promised to see whether he could help me figure things out."

"Oh good. Monsieur Le Guen knows everyone on the island."

"I also bought some bread and butter and jam for breakfast," Jean-Luc said. "Would you like me to make you something?"

"No, thank you," she said, finally waking up, grateful to feel the caffeine kicking in. "I'm not much of a breakfast person."

He nodded. "Your sister mentioned that."

"You and she had quite the talk this morning, it seems." Natalie glanced at the clock on the wall: It was ten forty-five. Alex and Jean-Luc must have been up for hours. *Have they been speculating about me and François-Xavier? Pitying me?*

"I noticed a small shop with some clothes that we passed by last night," Jean-Luc said. "Just down the way."

"Le Caradec? That's a souvenir shop, for the tourists. The islanders buy their clothes on the mainland."

"But that is perfect! I suppose, since I am a tourist, it will be just what I need."

Natalie imagined Jean-Luc would return clad in a bright yellow rain slicker and a long-sleeved Breton T-shirt. The shirt used to be part of the uniform for navy seamen in Northern France, and the original design featured twenty-one navy blue stripes—representing each of Napoleon Bonaparte's victories—against a white background. According to lore, the distinctive stripes made it easier to spot sailors who had fallen overboard. Mariners still fell into the sea from time to time, but no one wore the striped shirts anymore.

No one but the tourists.

"Well, I suppose I should let you get ready for your day," said Jean-Luc, "and I should make my way to the mayor's office. But thank you, again, for giving me a place to stay. However temporary."

"My pleasure."

"Why don't I pay for a week in advance, and we can adjust as necessary?"

"That will be fine," Natalie said. *A week means fourteen hundred euros,* she thought. *I can get by with that until the publisher's check comes through.*

"Do you still prefer cash?"

"I, um . . . cash would be great."

"Is there a machine on the island?"

"No, but the bank window is open this afternoon. There's only one, and it's only open on Tuesdays and Thursdays, from three to six. It's not far from the mayor's office; Monsieur Le Guen can show you where it is."

"*Bon!* I will be sure to go by, then. *Je vous souhait une bonne journée,* Natalie."

"You, too, Jean-Luc. And thanks for straightening up."

Natalie downed the rest of her coffee, returned to her room, pulled on a clean pair of shorts and a tank top, and went outside, where she found her sister in the lean-to by the shed.

"Morning, Nat," said Alex, looking up from a piece of wood trim she was measuring.

"Good morning. Looks like you're hard at work. Again."

"Yeah. That window project in the front was halfway done. Figured I could finish it up quick enough. Just a rotten sill." Alex had strapped a tool belt to her slim hips, and she was moving efficiently around the shed as though she had worked there for years. Laid out in precise order atop the workbench were the tools left by the workmen, as well as the shiny new ones Natalie and François-Xavier had bought.

"What time is it?" Alex glanced at her watch, a masculine-looking manacle with a large face.

"Almost eleven. I was up until three," Natalie added, feeling defensive. "Writing."

Alex nodded. "I remember how you used to stay up late, reading with a flashlight under the covers."

"And here I thought I was so sneaky."

"It infuriated The Commander." Alex gave that low, raspy chuckle that still startled Natalie. She didn't think of her sister as someone who laughed.

Their eyes met and held for a long moment.

"Sorry about last night," said Natalie.

"Are you okay?"

Natalie shook her head, feeling tears sting the backs of her eyes.

"Nat, tell me what's going on."

Natalie hesitated.

"You can trust me, you know," Alex said softly.

"I know." Natalie sighed and sat down, hard, in a wooden chair. She gazed out at the garden. "I . . . He . . ." She shrugged. "He's not coming back."

"Is that what he said?"

"He didn't *say* anything. I mean, everything was good—at least I thought it was. But he got bored here, and lost interest in the renovations, and then started taking quick trips to Paris. Then the trips got longer and more frequent . . . and finally he texted me, saying he wasn't coming back."

"He *texted* you?"

Natalie nodded, her humiliation complete. "I checked the Internet last night for news of what he's doing in Paris. None of the articles mention me. *Yet.* They haven't put it together, but they will. Soon enough, they will. And then, as The Commander used to say, the you-know-what will hit the fan."

"What do you care what people think?"

"It's probably hard for you to understand, but I have a social media presence to protect. It's like a brand. 'Living Well.'"

"And can't you live well without a man?"

"Of course." *She* could, *couldn't she?* "It's not *that.*"

"Then what is it?"

"You wouldn't understand," Natalie snapped. What did Alex know about love, anyway? Had she ever even been in love, ever known what it was like to be with someone who wanted you, needed you, loved you? Because Natalie sure had. Hadn't she?

Alex's only response was to raise her eyebrows and turn her attention back to the window frame.

"Look, Alex," Natalie said, feeling churlish. "I don't want to talk about François-Xavier. And I really appreciate everything you're doing around here to help. But you've only just arrived; don't you want to walk around and see things? The islanders are particularly proud of their history during World War Two."

Natalie fully expected her sister to say no, that she had no time for frivolous things like sightseeing, but Alex straightened, laid her leather work gloves to one side, and nodded.

"Sure, thanks. I'd love to see the island."

. . .

You saw this yesterday," said Natalie as they walked along the seawall, following the crescent of buildings. "It's pretty much the main drag of the village."

"There was a photograph of German soldiers walking right here," said Alex. "In that old photo album in the parlor. It's hard to imagine Nazis walking these paths."

"That's how I feel about most of France," said Natalie. "Have you seen that famous photo of German soldiers goose-stepping down the Champs-Élysées in Paris? Still gives me the shivers."

Though not nearly as busy as last night, the cafés were open, with tourists sitting outside in the morning sunshine, enjoying espressos and croissants. Couples strolled along the quay, and children chased dusky sparrows, trying to catch the little birds as they searched for crumbs. In the harbor half a dozen boats were moored on the mud, waiting for the tide to come in.

"It's low tide. Want to walk out to the point?" Natalie asked.

"You're the tour guide."

Natalie led the way out to a narrow peninsula featuring jagged rocks, scrubby wildflowers, and a whole lot of seaweed.

They passed a large sign that read: ACCÈS INTERDIT À MARÉE HAUTE.

"I thought '*accès interdit*' meant you weren't allowed," Alex said.

"That's only during *marée haute*, which means 'high tide.' This thumb of land gets cut off from the rest of the island when the tide's in. Occasionally a tourist doesn't heed the warnings and gets stuck out here."

"What happens then?"

"If someone on the quay notices, they'll bring a boat over to rescue them. If not, then whoever's out here has to bide their time and wait for the next low tide. But I suppose they could swim over if it came down to it."

They walked along to the very end of the spit of land, which was the easternmost point of the island. Surrounded by water on three sides, they were buffeted by winds off the ocean.

"The mainland doesn't look that far away from here, does it?" Alex squinted at the landmass rising out of the ocean to the east. "But it took more than an hour to get here on the ferry."

"It's not far, as the crow flies. But this stretch of water is called the Raz, and it's famous for its reefs. The water's full of them, lurking just below the surface."

Alex nodded. "I read about that."

"They have a saying here: *'Qui voit Feme voit sa fin.'*"

"Meaning?"

"'Whoever sees Feme sees their end.' According to the locals, the first inhabitants of the Île de Feme were castaways, sailors who survived shipwrecks and were stranded here. There are no real trees on the island, so there was no way to build a boat to escape." Alex seemed interested, so Natalie kept talking. "I always find the word 'castaway' interesting. I mean, who is casting whom away, and from where? The French word makes more sense to me: A shipwreck is a *naufrage*, and the victims of it are *naufragés*, literally those to whom the shipwreck happened."

Alex gave her a strange look and Natalie felt like a freak for researching abstract factoids no one else cared about.

Chill, Natalie. You're not Alex's inept little sister anymore.

Alex turned her back to the water to view the village from a new angle. "It's really pretty, isn't it?"

"It looks great in photographs, that's for sure. We should probably head back, though. If I got caught out here during high tide, I'd never live it down."

They retraced their steps, but rather than turning onto the quay, they kept walking west, skirting the populous area of the island.

"The island's shaped sort of like a big S, with the bottom part inhabited and the rest not as much," said Natalie.

"I recognize that guy," said Alex as they passed a bowlegged man with long white hair, bright orange cargo shorts, and bare feet petting a dog outside a business that rented kayaks and standing boards to the tourists. "He was one of the *pétanque* players last night."

"That's Tarik," Natalie said with a nod. "There are only a few hundred full-timers on the island, so you get to know people quickly here. Speaking of which, here comes François-Xavier's uncle—we call him *Tonton* Michou."

Michou was not particularly tall but had a big belly that protruded aggressively. His face was well rounded and tanned, and he sported little tufts of hair on his otherwise bald head. Michou had a tendency to slur his words and speak "into his *barbe*" even before he started drinking, but once he'd downed a few, he also got weepy, talking about his hundred-year-old mother, who had passed away just a few years ago. He didn't speak a word of English, but didn't let that hinder him and spoke to Alex at length in French, which Natalie tried her best to translate.

"He's saying he's happy to meet my sister, and he's saying nice things about me," said Natalie with a smile. "The people here tend to be very family oriented; they worry about me being so far from home."

She told Michou that she had found a photo album and wondered if she could bring it by soon for him to help her identify some of the people in the photos.

"*Bien sûr!*" he responded. Of course.

Then they bade farewell to Michou and continued on their tour, passing the last of the buildings. Spread out before them were small fields and a patchwork of gardens ringed by low stone walls.

"This is where the islanders grow vegetables. In the old days they kept cows and pigs, but now there are only chickens."

"Any game animals?" Alex asked.

"There are wild rabbits, which are considered a nuisance, though during the war they were a precious source of protein. These islanders . . . I mean, obviously things have gotten a bit easier in recent years, but they're tough, used to pulling together to endure hard times. They expect things like storms that knock out the power for days, disrupt the fresh water supply, and interrupt contact with the mainland. The *sauvetage* boats go out no matter how harsh the weather, and if a boat crew sees another boat needing help, they offer it without question, regardless of how they might feel about one another."

"Survival requires cooperation." Alex nodded. "We learned that at an early age."

"It's like The Commander used to say: Nothing brings a family together . . ."

". . . like Armageddon," they said in unison, sharing a smile.

"So, I was snooping around the Bag-Noz," said Alex. "It looks like a lot of the plumbing has been replaced, and there was some good work done on the foundation."

Natalie nodded. "We've done a lot of work already. It just doesn't look like it."

"That's the way of most renovations. The fun cosmetic stuff comes at the end. But you know, I used to be a home inspector. I could do a thorough inspection and come up with a list. It probably seems overwhelming, but if we break it down—"

"I didn't know you were a home inspector."

"You don't know much of anything about me."

That stung. But she was right. In her own defense, Natalie responded: "You don't know much about me, either."

"Of course I do," said Alex. "I read your book, and you're all over the Internet."

"Oh. That's true." It was just that Natalie Morgen, Internet sensation, wasn't the real Natalie Morgen.

"In fact, you know what most surprises me about your life here? That it's so stinky."

"It's a fishing island. And there's a lot of seaweed."

"I get that, but from reading your blog, I envisioned an island that smelled of lavender and—I don't know—crepes and whipped cream, or something. Maybe with a drizzle of chocolate."

"Sounds more like an American hot fudge sundae than a French crepe," Natalie said with a smile. "But I get what you mean. It's just that, well, my readers have a certain image of France, and what it's like to live on an island. No one wants to imagine the stink of rotten fish, so yes, I suppose I gloss over a few of the less savory details."

"And François-Xavier was part of that?"

Natalie let out a long breath. "You could say that."

"Sounds to me like the guy's a jerk. Why would you want him back?"

"Alex, the whole premise of my second book is the romantic life I'm creating right here on the island. What happens when my publisher learns it's all a farce? When my fans learn my handsome French chef dumped me? What am I supposed to tell them? *Que será, será?*"

"I'm sorry, Nat," Alex said. "Was he . . . I mean, did you truly love him?"

"Of *course* I loved him. I thought you said you read the book."

"I did," Alex said. "And you described your life really well. And François-Xavier was obviously a big part of that, and it was all very romantic."

"But?" Natalie said. "There's a 'but' in there."

"Maybe I'm just not good at human emotions, but I couldn't tell from the book if you were actually in love with him, or . . . in love with the *idea* of being in love with him."

When Natalie spoke, her voice was hollow. "What's the difference?"

They walked in silence for a few moments.

"So, here's something interesting," Natalie said, eager to change the subject. "The shipwreck cemetery. The islanders weren't sure of their religions, so they didn't want to bury them in the Christian grave-yard."

The fenced-off area had a small marker at each mound but no crosses. Some of the markers were engraved with names, while others had only a date of death.

"Seems sad, doesn't it?" Alex said. "Someone heads out to sea and winds up buried on a tiny island. . . . Do you suppose the families ever learned what happened to them?"

"I have the sense that seafarers often did not return home."

They walked past the Hotel Ar-Men, a large three-story building backing onto a pebbly cove.

"It reminds me of pictures of New England," said Alex. "With the lobster pots, the coves, the lighthouse."

"I've heard it's similar to Cornwall. Maybe that's why the Celts felt so at home here."

On a clothesline to the left, with the view of the ocean behind it, hung two dozen white lobster bibs, whipping this way and that in the wind, the bright orange lobster images flapping madly, like little crustacean flags of surrender. Natalie remembered thinking it was all so picturesque the first time she had walked by here. Now she wondered how anyone could run a lobster restaurant—and deal with all those soiled lobster bibs—without a clothes dryer.

"I love lobster," said Alex.

"Really? I don't think of you as loving food."

"Of course I love food. Everybody loves food."

"You never seemed to care."

"No way to care much about pemmican, right? And anyway, Nat, things change. Whether we want them to or not, they change."

CHAPTER FOURTEEN

Violette

Without the fishing boats, the threat of hunger hovered over us with the persistence of a malevolent spirit. A few of the stronger young women did their best with the dinghies left behind, but small boats cannot safely go out far enough in the open water to bring in much fish. So we made do with what we could collect in the shallows, gathering little feeder fish, digging up clams, and harvesting mussels and other shellfish off the rocks.

Every household kept meager stockpiles of flour, sugar, dried fish, and lard, which we doled out carefully, and there were a few cows and goats to provide milk. We no longer made butter or cheese; the milk was reserved for the children, now deprived of their fish pies and hearty stews. Our chickens gave us eggs, occasionally we managed to trap a wild rabbit, and our kitchen gardens yielded potatoes and carrots, cabbage, herbs, green beans, and tomatoes, depending on the season and the rainfall.

Since the Vichy government had officially declared our men to be deserters, we received no military pay, but even for those with francs in hand there was little to buy. Our movements were controlled by the German military, so we could no longer hop on a boat or ferry to visit Audierne at our own discretion, and the shelves of our sole island store, La Melisse, were nearly bare.

As the days and weeks ticked by, our hunger grew. Our fear even more so.

And the German soldiers *ate*. Supposedly they were supplied by the army on the mainland, yet still they helped themselves to what little we had, making a show of "paying" us for what they took—at a fraction of what the supplies were worth.

Eventually the Vichy *mairie* began issuing ration tickets, and the owner of La Melisse was permitted to receive shipments from the mainland, so our panic eased somewhat. Still, butter was impossible to come by, and cheese was but a memory. We queued up for hours for a ration of bread and lard, flour and sugar.

Daily life became a constant overwhelming obsession with the search for food on an island with limited resources.

Hunger, we learned, does not bring out the best in people. Hearing one's children cry in the night from empty stomachs was especially trying. We islanders had a tradition of helping one another, but as the months passed and the German invaders remained in our pathways, on our beaches, and in our beds, fissures developed within our community.

Some whispered that we had to get along with the Germans, to make the best of a bad situation, while others denounced those who dared make such suggestions as "appeasers" and "traitors." My old friend Noëlle had a very decided opinion about those of us who tried to remain neutral.

I hated the Germans for invading our country; of course I did.

But absent any other realistic alternative, I thought it best to try to get along as well as we could.

One evening I was drawn to the sound of someone pounding on my grandmother's piano in the parlor. He was pounding well, but was pounding, nonetheless.

I peeked around the doorframe.

I had seen the man for the first time several days before, when German officers took up residence in our home, claiming our guest rooms. He was of average height and well-built, blond, with prominent cheekbones and a strong jaw: Hitler's ideal Aryan. The other soldiers seemed to take a step back when he appeared, as though recognizing his innate authority.

I had the sense that the others would follow his lead, which meant that if he was cruel or unkind, we would be in for trouble.

Now I watched him at the piano. He was not playing the music of that very famous German Beethoven like my mother always asked me to do, or the lilting compositions of Chopin, which were the favorite of my *mamm-gozh*. Instead the officer played a jaunty tune, the kind one might hear in a talking picture, like one I had seen in Audierne a few years ago.

The upbeat music stopped when he spied me hovering in the doorway. The piano stool scraped on the wood-plank floor as he pushed it back and stood, bowing his head ever so slightly.

"*Mademoiselle, bonjour.*" His French was nearly perfect, with only a slight German accent discernible in the harshness of his consonants. "*Pardonnez-moi.* I hope I was not disturbing you."

I shook my head and turned to leave.

"Please allow me to introduce myself," he continued. "I am Rainer Heisinger."

I paused, one foot still on the threshold. I had sworn to myself that I would not speak a word to the enemy, but my mother's training ran deep and I found it difficult to be rude. Worse, blatant discourtesy might be dangerous. We were sharing our home, our land, with these Germans.

"My first name, it means *pluie* in English," he continued, his fingers trailing along the piano keys, making them tinkle pleasantly. "And your name, mademoiselle?"

"Violette. Violette Fouquet . . . Guilcher." I often forgot that I was married. "And it's madame, not mademoiselle."

"Violette?" He grinned, softening his strong features and showing his very white teeth. "So you are a flower, and I am the rain."

"You are very forward, monsieur."

The smile dropped from his face. "I apologize. Sincerely, madame. I am . . . I am not accustomed to this situation."

"What situation?"

"Occupation. War."

That made me pause. "How does *anyone* become accustomed to war, monsieur?"

He gave a sad, small smile. "By living in it long enough, I suppose. In any case, do you mind if I play this beautiful instrument? I should have asked before, but I gave in to temptation."

"I doubt it's even in tune," I replied. "No one plays anymore, now that my grandmother has passed."

"It sounds lovely to me. Far preferable to the snores of my compatriots."

I felt awkward, and a bit nauseated, and turned to leave once again.

"Madame?" he called me back. "If I promise not to be too rough with your grandmother's piano, may I play?"

He stood there, filling out his uniform in all his blond Aryan glory. Rainer was a German. An invader. Why was he asking me for permission to do anything? What kind of game was he playing?

I shrugged. *"Comme vous voulez, monsieur."* As you wish.

It seemed ironic that the man was named for rain.

On the Île de Feme, rain is life. Rain is everything. On the Île de Feme, no one complains about storms, as they are our sole source of fresh water. Also, the tempests bring the shipwrecks, and though we risk our lives to save the victims of such catastrophes, there is no denying the bounty they bring to the island: new blood in the form of those who decide to remain with us, as well as the salvaged cargo—barrels of liquor or beer, boxes of exotic spices. Occasionally, bullion or other treasure. Even the wood from the ships, hulls is a boon, for ours is an island lacking not only fresh water but also trees. We islanders seize upon the lumber with an avarice forest dwellers might reserve for salt or wine.

Rainer. He said in English, it meant *pluie*, rain.

How did he know the English language? Or French, for that matter? I knew that some Germans who lived near the border could speak passable French, but most of the soldiers who had crossed my path did not know a single word. They expected us to understand their language, and soon we learned a few phrases: *Entschuldigen Sie bitte* or *Ja, ich habe meine Papiere* ("Excuse me, please" or "Yes, I have my papers"). It was the bare minimum to get by, to survive what we all hoped—and insisted to ourselves—was a temporary situation.

So, a man named for rain came to our tiny island all the way from Germany, and was now speaking French, playing our piano, living in our home.

In the house that *used* to be our home.

CHAPTER FIFTEEN

Alex

*N*at was in full-on tour guide mode, pointing out plants like thrift, *criste marine*, and *pavot cornu*, a stubborn type of poppy that grew despite the salty earth.

"Water's a constant concern, since there's no natural source," Nat explained, pointing to one of the tanks that dotted the island. "These days, water is brought in from the mainland. But the islanders still collect rain in large cisterns like this one."

"Speaking of rain," Alex said, "Jean-Luc said he heard there's a storm coming, and I noticed the stack of slate shingles in the shed. Do you have someone coming to repair the roof soon?"

"I . . . Yes, I do, or I did. They seem to have flaked out."

"Because it's August?"

"Maybe."

Alex tried to study her sister's expression, but Nat didn't give much away.

"Couldn't you hire someone else?"

"It's not that simple. It's not like the islanders don't already have a lot to do," Nat said.

"Maybe, but I'd be surprised if there weren't at least a few who'd be willing to take it on for the right price. What about that crew, there?" Alex asked, gesturing toward three men who were repairing a stone wall. "We could ask them."

Nat shook her head. "No . . . I don't think so. Maybe you and I could do it."

Alex snorted.

"Jean-Luc said he was willing to help."

"Which is very nice of him, but from what I've seen, his handyman skills aren't much better than yours. Besides, roof repairs aren't anything to screw around with. Seriously, Nat, I think you ought to hire someone."

It was one thing to put off repairing interior plaster or applying a coat of fresh paint, things that made a home more comfortable and more attractive. But to allow the roof of an ocean-side guesthouse to deteriorate was foolish in the extreme. Repairing the roof should have been Nat's first priority, not installing pretty new bathroom tiles.

"So, when did you become a home inspector?" Nat asked. "I thought you worked on a dude ranch."

"I did, but I got licensed as a home inspector as well. But I don't need to be an inspector to know the roof needs attention—you can tell from the ground you're missing some shingles."

"Yeah, it's on the list. Thanks."

"Why not just hire someone else? I thought you were rolling in money."

"Yeah, right," Nat said.

"Did François-Xavier contribute to the renovations?"

Natalie gave a quick shake of her head and said, "*I'm* the one with the money in this relationship. Or I was, anyway."

"Does that mean you've paid for everything?"

"Pretty much."

Alex studied her for a moment. "Did you think I would judge you for being short of cash? Given the way we were raised, money problems are our birthright."

Nat gave a breathy laugh. "So at least I come by it honestly. Anyway, it's only temporary. As soon as I can send in a decent draft of this book, I'll get a progress payment, and there should be a royalty check in the offing for *Pourquoi Pas?* as well."

They continued along the narrow stretch of the pathway, the ocean on one side and bracken-covered fields on the other.

Alex tried to memorize it all. The chalky blue of the weather-beaten shutters, the little fish-shaped doorknob adorning the front entrance of a small stone cottage that looked like an overblown dollhouse. The lighthouse tower, standing tall and sure, the rocky shelves blazing gold with lichen, the strangely shaped boulders looking like figures hunkering down along the shoreline.

There wasn't much human presence beyond the hotel. Besides that one small house, there was nothing but scrub and sand and rocks and algae, the ocean to either side, as they continued down a path that led to the lighthouse.

"A very old woman lives in that little cottage, there," said Natalie. "It's called the House of Meneï. I think she may have put a curse on me."

"Why would she do that?"

"When I first got here, I was snapping pictures of everybody—especially the old women. I guess I didn't consider that not everyone wants their picture taken, much less shared on the Internet."

"Ah."

"Her name's Ambroisine."

"Great name."

Natalie nodded. "And she's got a great face to match. Very full of character. I'm sorry I blundered so badly with her; apparently she's the oldest person on the island and a font of information."

"Have you tried apologizing?"

Natalie let out a shiver. "She's scary."

Natalie veered off to the right to show Alex another small fenced area full of graves.

"This is the cemetery that was set aside for the victims of the eighteen eighty-five cholera epidemic. They didn't understand at the time how contagion worked, so they buried the victims farther away from the town, just in case. During the epidemic so many people died that no family was left untouched. That was when *les Fémanes*, the women of the island, began to wear *la jibilinnen*."

"Sorry—the what?"

"Back in the day, the women of Brittany wore white *coiffes*, or headdresses. You've probably seen them in pictures; they're pretty distinctive. They're depicted in a lot of van Gogh paintings, and local women still wear them for regional festivals. Anyway, when the cholera epidemic took so many of the islanders, the women began to wear a black mourning headdress called a *jibilinnen*."

"I think I saw photographs of women wearing them in the album at the house. But those photos were taken in the forties and fifties."

"They continued to wear them for decades, long after the epidemic passed. They say on an island there's always something, or someone, to mourn—a lot of men never return from sea. When the Germans occupied the island during World War Two, they asked the women why they wore black, 'like witches,' and the response was, *'Nous sommes en deuil pour la France.'*"

"Meaning?"

"They were in mourning for France."

"I'll bet the occupying forces loved that."

"Not many Fémans are willing to talk about what happened during the war—most of them were very young, or not yet born, of course. Still, I hoped to get some stories for my book, but they're pretty guarded. Except for this."

Natalie gestured to a large granite sculpture of the Cross of Lorraine just beyond the *cimetière des cholériques.*

"After hearing General de Gaulle's speech calling on the French to join the Allies, every man of fighting age on the Île de Feme sailed to England in their fishing boats to volunteer." Natalie read aloud the inscription carved into the stone: " *'Kentoc'h mervel'* is Breton for 'We would rather die.'"

"Wow. And they left the women and children behind?"

Natalie nodded.

"Where's *their* monument?" asked Alex.

"Their what?"

"Where's the monument to the women who had to survive on the island, find a way to keep the children and the elderly alive—not to mention deal with an invading army?"

"That rarely merits a statue."

They heard a low rumble and turned to see Korrigan, the half-feral dog, staring at them, her head low and threatening.

"She doesn't look happy," said Alex.

"She never looks happy. But she's never hurt anyone, as far as I know."

"Poor thing. I should carry some treats with me for the next time I see her."

After a moment of staring, Korrigan limped off, disappearing in the direction of the little stone cottage.

"This is my favorite spot on the island," said Natalie, leading the way out onto the shoals by the water and taking a seat on a rock.

Many of the twisting, strangely carved rock formations were decorated with lichen the chalky greenish blue color so common to French shutters and doors; others sported bright yellow and orange growth. Small tidepools held barnacles, mussels, and anemones. Gulls cawed overhead, the waves lapped rhythmically upon the rocks, and the ever-present scent of sea surrounded them: dead fish and brine. Up ahead, the island's lighthouse stood, proud and silent and reassuring.

On such a sunny, calm day, it was hard to imagine being at sea during a storm, waves breaking over the bow. . . . What would it be like to see that warm flash of light from the beacon and know, perhaps, that someone knew you were out there? Struggling. Drowning. In need of rescue.

"So, I e-mail with Hope every once in a while, and Faith occasionally," said Nat. "No word from Charity, though."

Alex shook her head. "I get a very occasional postcard from her, so I can tell you she's still alive. But she's keeping her distance."

The last time Alex had spoken with Faith and Hope, it was to inform them of her situation. Now Alex considered telling Nat as well, even starting to formulate the phrases in her head. But the impulse died before she uttered a word.

Nat hid things. She always had. Her candy bars, her thoughts.

And with Nat so invested in creating an image of her perfect life on the Île de Feme, where would Alex fit in? Would she be yet another thing for Natalie to be embarrassed about, to ignore? It was better to leave it alone. Alex would spend a little vacation "time-out" here on the island, and then perhaps she would be more ready to face her new reality.

"I feel as if everything changed after the book came out," said Nat.

"Well, we were raised never to talk to strangers. And you pretty much told the world everything."

"I know. I struggled with that. I often wonder what Mom would have thought of the book."

They fell silent, thinking of Carla. Lighthouses reminded Alex of their mother. The rhythmic turning, a bright flash of emotion, then a long interval of flat nothingness.

"She gave me her blessing, you know," said Nat. "When I told her I was going, that I had to leave."

"She did?" This was a shock. Then Alex thought back on that day, returning from town with the news, walking into the kitchen that smelled of steam from the boiling canning jars. Carla had turned toward her with the saddest eyes in the world, as if she knew what Alex was about to say before she said it.

"She gave me two hundred dollars," said Nat.

"She—what? Mom never had any money. None of us ever had any money. Where did she get two hundred dollars?"

"I have no idea." Nat shook her head, sighed, looking at the lighthouse. "I almost didn't take it. But she insisted."

"I'm glad you did. I would have given you money if I knew you were leaving."

"I couldn't tell you, Alex. You would have tried to stop me, or told Dad."

"I wouldn't have."

Nat stared at her for a long moment, seemingly unconvinced, before looking back to the lighthouse.

"I still feel like it was Dad's fault that Mom died," Nat continued. "Maybe if she had seen a doctor . . ."

"She wasn't powerless, Nat. If Mom really wanted to see a doctor, she could have. I offered to take her—actually, I begged her to let me take her."

"Then why didn't she?"

After a pause, Alex said: "I don't think Mom really *wanted* to live. I think she was weary. Dead tired of waiting for the apocalypse, of never having it come."

CHAPTER SIXTEEN

Natalie

The Morgen family didn't take the usual family vacations. No trips to Disneyland, certainly no Hawaiian getaways, and camping trips to the great outdoors would have been pointless since that was their everyday reality. But every year, The Commander ordered Carla and the kids to load up the car to attend the annual gathering of "preppers" in a dusty town about an hour away.

The year Natalie turned fifteen, the rally was held in a sad-looking outdoor mall where half of the storefronts were vacant, their dirty shopwindows still emblazoned with names like Angie's Blooms for All Occasions and Margene's Wedding Gowns.

There were booths selling just about everything imaginable: from Civil War memorabilia to essential oils and naturopathic remedies. Stands for guns and ammo vied for attention with those offering food dehydrators, tents, and prepacked bug-out bags. Long-whiskered vendors sold camo-decorated ponchos and boots and vests and even gas masks. The Commander was in heaven, and spent hours chatting with those who specialized in backyard bomb shelters and massive storage tanks meant to be buried and filled with water and gasoline.

By this time, the older girls—Hope, Faith, and Charity—had already left the family, and Carla was busy selling her herbal tea blends at a small card table, so Alex and Natalie meandered through the aisles of exhibits and sales booths. Natalie was wondering at the possibility of slipping away to see if the town had a library when a young man behind a booth advertising underground bunkers held up a small yellow pepper and asked:

"Are you here for the doomsday peppers?"

"The what?" Natalie asked.

Alex rolled her eyes and kept on walking.

"You know how they call us doomsday preppers? Well, these are doomsday *peppers*. Get it? They're superhot. Wanna try one?"

Natalie looked at him skeptically.

"I'm Ivan."

"Natalie."

"Well, want to come over and give this pepper a try?"

Ivan was tall and thin, and his nearly whiskerless cheeks were pockmarked with acne scars. But it was the first time anyone—especially a boy—had looked at Natalie as though she was someone other than the youngest Morgen daughter, the family screwup who never got anything right.

"Can you believe all the nutjobs in this place?" Ivan asked, and Natalie started to relax a bit. "Don't get me wrong. I know a lot of them. I mean, my father's in construction, and started specializing in installing bunkers after he built one for our family. It's kind of dope, really. I like to spend time down there, you know, just to get away from it all."

"What do you do in the bunker?"

"Read, mostly. How old are you?"

"Fifteen."

"I'm sixteen. I've got my license, and my dad gave me his old pickup truck, so I've even got my own ride."

"Lucky you," Natalie said. "Where do you live?"

"On the Klamath River, near Red Gulch. Ever heard of it?"

Natalie nodded. That was only about half an hour from their compound.

"So, you want to try the doomsday pepper?" Ivan asked.

Natalie hesitated, then took the pepper and crunched into it. "Not bad," she said, chewing. "Just tastes like a sweet pepper."

Ivan laughed. "It is. I just tell people it's superhot to see how they react. Scares most of 'em off." He added, in an admiring tone, "But not you."

One positive aspect of The Commander's "free-range" parenting was that Natalie was accustomed to hitchhiking to the library in town, where she now began meeting Ivan. They would look at the books together and then he would buy her sodas and snacks at the gas station. Sometimes they would take a walk down by the river, and other times go out to a small pond with a stolen bottle of rum.

Ivan was her first kiss, and he might have been more except The Commander stumbled across them in what Natalie initially believed was an example of her father's omniscience. Later she realized it had been a simple coincidence—Ivan had parked his old truck too close to the main highway that day. Her father saw it as he drove by, assumed it had been abandoned, and came to see what he might salvage from it.

The Commander's reaction to finding Natalie with Ivan wasn't as bad as it might have been. Ivan was familiar with the prepper world, knew how to hunt and to shoot, and stood up well to The Commander's interrogation. Not wanting to lose yet another daughter to the lure of "big-city boys," he invited Ivan to join them for dinner. The meal had gone well until The Commander asked Ivan his plans for the future.

"Not sure, really," Ivan said. "Ma'am, this biscuit is delicious."

"Why, thank you, Ivan," Carla murmured.

"Man's gotta have a plan, son," The Commander said. "Gotta have a plan for when the world's gonna end."

"See, I'm really not sure about that," Ivan said.

"Not sure about what?" The Commander demanded, dropping his fork and staring at Ivan. Natalie tried to catch Ivan's eye, but he was oblivious.

"I think we'll muddle along," said Ivan. "Hard to believe the world's coming to an end in our lifetime."

"That's a ding-dong thing to say!" The Commander banged the table with his fist, rattling the dishes. "Read the signs, boy! I'll tell you what. You'll be dead soon enough with that attitude."

Carla jumped up to get a just-baked peach cobbler, trying to smooth things over. When all else failed, their mother brought out the sugar.

For the rest of the meal, The Commander lectured Ivan on the many reasons he was wrong. Ivan listened politely enough, but said nothing.

Ivan's refusal to back down in the face of The Commander's ire made him even more appealing to Natalie, and they continued to meet in secret.

One day a fierce storm unleashed a downpour in the mountains, and the swollen river overflowed its banks and washed out the bridge. The Morgens huddled in their crude storage cellar, The Commander striding back and forth, announcing that *this* was how it would start, that *this* might be *It*. The end they had been waiting for, had been preparing for, had at long last begun. Natalie was petrified. She kept imagining zombies coming toward them when they emerged from the cellar, then—her science education seriously lacking—she wondered how bridges washing out and the electrical grid going down and the government spinning out of control would end up creating zombies. Wouldn't it just mean the lights didn't work?

After two days the deluge ceased and they poked their heads out of the basement to find the world exactly as it had been, just a lot wetter. It was a great relief, yet a strange sort of letdown.

When Natalie shared this story with Ivan, he said, "You know, sometimes I think they *want* the world to come to an end."

"What are you talking about?" Natalie had never heard such blasphemy.

"Think about it, Natalie. Does what our parents say really make sense to you? I mean, my parents talk about how they started stockpiling when they were young, first in response to the 1988 foreseen rapture. Then there was Y2K, then 9/11. And yet nothing has happened. Every time somebody says doomsday is on the horizon, it's like they get, like, *excited*. Like they can finally say 'I told you so' to everyone who called them crazy. They'll be the only ones prepared. Everyone else will be crowded at the entrance to the bunker, banging on the door, begging to be admitted. And then, when the world *doesn't* actually come to an end, they're disappointed."

"We must look so stupid," Natalie whispered, stunned at her own words. Her thoughts had skittered around the idea, but she had never before dared to give it voice: Her parents might be profoundly, shockingly wrong. About everything.

"Exactly!" said Ivan, and Natalie felt a thrill at his look of approval. No one ever agreed with her. "They're the ones who are the fools. But you know, I think it's even more than that."

"Like what?" Having for the first time expressed her dissent from the world she had grown up in, Natalie felt emboldened.

"Like maybe they do what they do because it's the only way they know how to go on with their lives. Some people distract themselves with stupid movies and liquor and pizza. Or drugs. Preppers do the same thing. It's just not as much fun."

As she let Ivan's words wash over her, Natalie thought of her family's supply "closet" in their basement, a hole in the ground lined with concrete blocks that was bigger than their living room. It held fifty-pound sacks of wheat, rice, oats, beans; dozens of gallon jugs full of water; toilet paper; and assorted canned goods. Once a week her mother took inventory, clipboard in hand, assessing and documenting the supply, rotating items according to expiration dates, fretting over the numbers, her brow lined with worry.

Since there was no future, they didn't worry about pensions, or retirement, or health care, but when Armageddon arrived, they would be prepared.

"Yep, that's the crux of the problem," said Ivan. He passed his hand over the disappointingly sparse stubble on his chin, a sixteen-year-old sage. "The world just keeps on a-goin'."

Do you remember Ivan?" Natalie asked Alex, watching the sea breeze playing with her sister's hair, whipping the dark tresses into snarls. Alex didn't seem to notice, apparently engrossed in the view of the cove, the lighthouse, the ocean.

"Wasn't he your first boyfriend?" asked Alex, after a moment. "That geeky prepper boy?"

Natalie nodded. "I remember one time he said something about how, after every predicted doomsday failed to arrive, the preppers didn't so much feel foolish as they didn't know what to do with themselves. They couldn't lose themselves in the kinds of distractions that the rest of the world did, so they got depressed when the world didn't end."

"I suppose that makes sense, in a weird way."

"James Baldwin said that we waste our lives, turning away from beauty, because we try to deny the presence of death. He said we ought to *rejoice* in the knowledge that death is inevitable, that we should 'earn' our death by meeting life with passion. Or something like that."

"Is he another boyfriend of yours?" Alex asked.

"No," Natalie said, surprised her sister didn't know one of her favorite writers. But then, Natalie was the only one in her family to pursue a formal education. "James Baldwin was an author and a poet. He's pretty famous."

"Oh."

Natalie pulled out her phone and took more photographs: of her sister's profile as she gazed toward the lighthouse, the tall spire painted in black and white with FEME written in black block letters on the side. She snapped photos of the almost otherworldly rock formations, the orange and green lichen, the tiny barnacles and minuscule mussels clinging to the sides of the tidepools.

"Can we go up the lighthouse?" Alex asked.

"Sure."

Along the path to the lighthouse, the flat, treeless island narrowed, the ocean near on both sides.

There were a number of tourists milling around, so Alex and Natalie stood in line to pay their fee, then waited for their turn to ascend. They passed the time in a small exhibit set up in the rooms of the former keeper's home.

There were photographs of the last lightkeeper, Henri Thomas, as well as several of the tower when it was under construction. This stretch of Brittany's coast, the Côte Sauvage, was peppered with smaller lighthouses, which were incredible feats of engineering and determination, built around the tides and the weather.

"Listen to this: 'The Fresnel lens casts light that can be seen for twenty-seven nautical miles, all the way to the coast to the north, not far from Brest,'" Natalie read aloud. "The original was built in eighteen thirty-nine, but the Germans dynamited the lighthouse when they left the island at the end of World War Two. It was rebuilt in nineteen fifty-one."

"Why would they blow up the lighthouse?" Alex asked.

"They didn't want the Allies to have any help navigating the waters. It was war. Things got ugly."

The ticket taker announced it was their turn to mount the 249 steps of the narrow, winding metal staircase, their feet clanging on each one, the muscles of their thighs burning by the time they reached the top.

Natalie hadn't been in the lighthouse since she first arrived on the island. She remembered François-Xavier had tried to beg off, but she had insisted. That was back when she was able to cajole him into doing things she wanted to do. He had teased her, acting as though he was looking up her skirt as she preceded him up the steps. Climbing the stairs of a lighthouse with her *prince charmant* . . . she had felt so carefree, so sexy, so optimistic for their future.

The moment Natalie and Alex emerged onto the catwalk, they were slammed with wind from all directions. Natalie was surprised to see Alex holding on to the railing so tightly that her knuckles turned white. Alex always used to climb rocks and scamper up trees, seemingly unafraid of heights.

The tower was so tall they could see the S of the island laid out before them, with the village huddled on the far shore, its buildings nestled together, shimmering through a saltwater haze. Innumerable rocks and shoals peeked up from the open ocean in all directions. Several of the larger rock outcroppings—not quite large enough to be called islands—sported *feux*, or small lights.

"Which is that one?" Alex asked, pointing to a lighthouse on a larger but forbidding-looking rock in the strait about halfway between the Île de Feme and the mainland. "I saw it from the ferry on my way over."

"The Phare de la Vieille. Can you believe there used to be a keeper living out there? They say it was such a hardship post that the keepers had to be rotated out every six weeks."

"I don't think I'd mind being a lighthouse keeper."

"It sounds romantic, doesn't it? But the reality was pretty harsh. Keeping a light here was one thing—there's an actual island attached; you could walk around and even grow things—but the Phare de la Vieille is nothing but a rock. One false step out the door, and you're in the ocean."

"Still."

"A lot of sailors mourn the loss of the keepers. They say it's not the same when you're out at sea at night, that knowing there was a person tending to a lighthouse made all the difference. Now that they're all automated, it's just an empty tower."

Was that what *she* was? An empty tower? The light was on, but nobody was home. *Ugh.* Couldn't write *that* on social media.

"What's that?" Alex gestured to a small stone building not far from the lighthouse, the rocks covered in lichen. "It looks old."

"A chapel was originally built there in the twelfth century. It's been rebuilt a few times since. We can take a look, if you'd like." Chilled by the wind, Natalie pulled her sweatshirt tighter around her. "Ready to head down?"

Alex nodded, and they proceeded carefully down the narrow stairwell, stepping into the small niches by the windows to allow those coming up to pass.

"It's called the Chapel of Saint Corentin," Natalie said as they walked toward the chapel. "It's also where people come to pay their respects to the Gallizenae. There's another, larger church in the center of the village that is dedicated to Saint Guénolé. He and Corentin are the saints most associated with Brittany. Saint Guénolé is considered a phallic saint."

"I hope that's not what it sounds like."

Natalie chuckled. "They say the women of the island used to stick pins into the feet of his statue, hoping for romance and fertility. But I can't help but feel like there's something special here, something ancient. Like I said, the Druids arrived on the island long before the Catholic priests. In fact, the Île de Feme was mentioned by Pomponius Mela, the earliest Roman geographer, who wrote in the very first century AD."

Natalie snapped a few more photographs. *This is good.* She could post these to her social media accounts and feel that she was getting back on track. She made a mental note to write a post about Pomponius Mela. Her followers would like that.

"How do you know all this?" Alex asked.

"Research. I'm writing a book, remember?"

"Oh, right. What's the title?"

"Still working on it. Titles are hard."

"Anyway, it's impressive," said Alex. "But then, you always were impressive."

"You never used to think I was impressive. You were always Dad's little pet, doing everything right all the time. You used to call me Nat-the-Gnat."

"I said you were annoying. I never said you weren't smart."

Natalie had always known she was intelligent and had an excellent memory, able to recite long passages from an author's explorations of life and death. But that very ability also made her doubt herself: Her mind was crowded with other people's thoughts and ideas, the ponderings of dead philosophers and poets, words and sentences and whole paragraphs from books she had read in her search for truth. Sometimes it felt like all those ideas left little room for her own thoughts.

No wonder I can't figure out how to write my damned book. Books had to be brutally honest, to come from one's heart. But *other* people's ideas were the only ones she appreciated and held close.

Another wave of panic washed over her. *What am I going to do?*

They headed back toward town, down the other side of the island, and finally turned into the narrow stone passages that wound between the houses and walled gardens.

"And yet another cemetery," said Alex.

"This is the main one," said Natalie.

"Are we allowed to go in?"

"If the gates are unlocked," Natalie said, but Alex was already pushing in the tall iron gates, the rusting hinges squeaking a protest.

Marble slabs lay atop the graves, many sporting little ovals with photographs of the deceased. Most were decorated with flower arrangements or some form of greenery.

"Many graves are still tended by family members," said Natalie. "A lot of the islanders trace their families back for generations. Properties are handed down through the family, so it's firmly rooted in history."

"There's something sort of comforting about that, isn't there?" said Alex. "A sense of permanency and roots. Or do you think it gets claustrophobic after a while?"

"I think there are probably as many answers to that as there are personalities on the island."

"I guess I've always felt sort of rootless," said Alex. "At least, since the compound fell apart and we all split up."

Natalie had never thought about it that way. She had been overjoyed to see the mountains recede in the rearview mirror of that logging truck, so very many years ago. She missed her mother, and had some fond memories of her sisters and parents together, sitting and talking around a warm fire, back when she was young enough not to realize everything she was missing. But after the horrors of The Commander's training sessions, and as she grew older and read more, her sense of not fitting in increased until Natalie realized she had to leave, to experience for herself what the world had to offer. And she had never looked back.

The cemetery gates creaked loudly, and François-Xavier's aunt Agnès appeared, a basket of flowers looped over one arm.

"*Bonjour, Tante Agnès,*" said Natalie, hurrying to her side and kissing her on both cheeks.

Agnès was in her eighties, with the sturdy frame typical of the Bretons. She wore her white hair in a short, practical bob, her hand-knitted sweater closed at the neck with a cameo brooch. François-Xavier's extended family consisted of several aunts and his uncle Michou, and though many of the younger cousins had left for better opportunities on the mainland, there were enough still on the island to make Natalie feel part of a network—or perpetually under surveillance, depending on her mood. Several of his relatives had read the French translation of her memoir and felt sorry for Natalie, especially because of her lack of family, in the way of old people who had always lived in a small, tight-knit community.

"*Bonjour*, Natalie! What a lovely surprise!" *Tante* Agnès said in French. "What are you doing here?"

"I'm showing my sister around the island. I'm so glad to see you. I'd like to introduce you to her. This is Alex." Natalie spoke in French to Agnès, then switched to English when she spoke to Alex. "Alex, this is *Tante* Agnès. She's one of François-Xavier's extended family, and Michou's cousin."

"*Enchantée,*" said Alex, who looked unsure when Agnès responded in French. "*Pardon*, that's all I know."

Natalie translated for *Tante* Agnès, who laughed and waved off Alex's concern, continuing to speak in French as she explained that she had just come to lay flowers on her father's grave.

"He went to England in answer to the call of *Général* de Gaulle, during the last World War," said *Tante* Agnès.

"I'd love to hear more about that," Alex said. "If *Tante* Agnès doesn't mind, of course."

Natalie translated Alex's request, and Agnès smiled warmly. Natalie marveled at the immediate connection her sister seemed to have made with the older woman. Not that Agnès wasn't friendly with Natalie; Agnès considered herself *une personne très sociable*, or a very social person. Unlike most of the native Fémans, she enjoyed chatting with new people, even the tourists.

But Natalie always felt as if *Tante* Agnès was holding back, holding Natalie at arm's length. Maybe it was as simple as the fact that Natalie was connected to François-Xavier. The extended family was ecstatic to have him back on the Île de Feme, but seemed to worry about how realistic his plans—*their* plans—were. It had taken numerous assurances from Natalie that she had the money and determination to restore the Bag-Noz into the guesthouse it had once been. Only after François-Xavier left did Natalie wonder if his family might have reason to question his reliability. After all, they had known him all his life.

Wish someone had warned me, Natalie thought, though if someone had tried, she suspected she wouldn't have listened. Not when her dreams seemed to be coming true.

As they stood by the grave, Agnès reached for Alex's hand, and to Natalie's surprise, Alex did not protest. Natalie translated as Agnès recounted the story of her father being killed at war.

"I was just a child at the time, of course. A toddler. So I don't really remember when he left, though I do recall my mother's reaction." Agnès nodded, a faraway look in her eye. "She was pregnant with my younger brother, and was angry that my father was leaving her and their children here, alone, to face the German soldiers. The Vichy government declared the island men traitors—or worse, *Anglais*, or Englishmen—so our families received no military pay, no support at all. It was a struggle to survive."

"How did you get by?" Alex asked.

"We had some animals, a few cows for milk. And we children helped to keep the gardens, raising carrots and potatoes, peas and beans—if we could save them from the rabbits. The Germans brought their own rations but stole whatever they liked from us. I remember going to the beach to scavenge for snails and clams in the mud, looking for mussels in the shallows, anything at all. It was a never-ending search for food. We ate a lot of *goémon*." Agnès chuckled and shook her head. "It doesn't taste like much, but it keeps you alive. I still eat it occasionally, mostly for the nostalgia. It's supposed to be good for you."

"I've heard that," Alex replied. "Did the women fish?"

"Some tried. But the men took the best boats to England."

"Could you relocate to the mainland?"

Agnès shook her head. "Even if we had boats to sail, the Germans controlled our movements. You had to be granted special permission to leave the island. The entire community was under suspicion because the men had left. Did you see the monument to the French Naval Forces? It was inaugurated by *Général* de Gaulle himself in honor of our men's enthusiastic response to his call."

Natalie nodded. "We did, yes. I was sure to show her."

"And then my father died," Agnès said, laying her flowers on a simple grave of pale pink granite. "He was inducted into the British navy with the rest of our boys because of their knowledge of the sea, and was killed off the coast of Normandy."

Tante Agnès showed them to another plot, for the large Fouquet family.

"These are the women from the Bag-Noz?" asked Alex.

"Yes, my aunts." Agnès placed a single flower in each of the sconces next to the names Violette and Doura. Both had died in the 1990s.

Natalie was distracted by the names of several babies also listed on the family plinth: Josée, Nicole, Esprit, Jean-Yves. All deceased at less than a year old during the war, from 1940 to 1944.

"Babies die," said Agnès with a shrug, the look on her face belying the casualness of the words. She pushed her chin out. *"C'est ainsi . . . C'est comme ça."*

"That's just how it is," Natalie translated for Alex, then said to Agnès: "I keep hearing references to the two sisters who ran the guesthouse after the war. But no one has any details."

"Violette and Doura . . . well, there was some gossip after the war, but . . . I don't put any stock in that. I'm sure they were loyal and brave, like all the women on the island."

"I saw a photograph of them," said Alex. "Wearing the black outfits."

"Yes, they both wore the *jibilinnen* until the day they died, long after the other women on the island had given it up." Agnès nodded, a faraway look in her eye. "As a child, I remember running to the Bag-Noz to beg for cookies. They grew herbs in their garden, made tinctures, and mixed teas. They became quite well-known for it. And when they died, they said they wanted to be buried in seaweed and shells, the treasures of the sea."

"Do you have any other stories from the war years?" Natalie tried again.

"Some stories are best left in the past," said Agnès. "If they wanted it remembered, they would have written it down. Everyone who remembers the war is dead or dying now, anyway."

Natalie clamped down on her frustration. This was a typical response when she asked the island elders about World War II.

"By the way," Natalie said, "Alex found an old photo album. If I bring it by, would you help me identify the people in the photographs?"

"I could try," *Tante* Agnès said.

Natalie and Alex walked *Tante* Agnès home, passing through a narrow walkway to a cottage made of stone, with lace curtains in the windows, a cat on the windowsill, and a lush walled garden full of flowering plants.

"I am very proud of my gardens . . . but I stay with a daughter on the mainland in the winter. Too cold and stormy on the island for my old bones. And speaking of storms, there is one blowing in, Natalie. Have you and François-Xavier fixed the roof yet?"

Natalie didn't translate this question.

"We're working on it," Natalie said. "I hope to have it done soon."

"There's a storm coming," Agnès repeated as she waved good-bye.

There's always a storm coming.

As the sisters headed back home, Alex asked Natalie: "Why did the Germans occupy this island, anyway? There isn't much here."

"Whoever controls the island controls the shipping lanes, and the Raz. Also, the island was part of the 'Atlantic Wall' the Germans were trying to establish to prevent an invasion of the mainland from the Allies based in England."

Natalie snapped a few more photos as some old women passed by.

"I would have thought you'd have your fill of photos by now," said Alex.

"They're not for me. They're for my readers."

"You're going to publish a book of photographs?"

"No, I'll post them on my social media. You know. Online."

"Oh, right."

"It's part of my job. People love photos of the island." They approached a small grass-covered plaza studded by two large rocks standing on end in front of a small church. "These are the menhirs I was telling you about. They look like they're gossiping, don't you think? Want to go check out the museum?"

"I think I've had my fill of history and sightseeing for the day," said Alex.

"It's almost time for lunch. Hungry?"

"Maybe later. I'm thinking I should get back to work. If you can't hire a crew to work on the roof, maybe we could hire a helper? You could ask Milo, from last night. He stuck you with his Parisian, after all."

"I don't know . . ."

"What about Christine?"

"What about her?"

Alex shrugged. "She looked like she might know how to swing a hammer."

"Alex, I can't ask her to do that. She doesn't have time to come fix my roof. She's busy fishing or taking care of her catch. Anyway, it's lunchtime, and people here don't skip meals. So should we go back to Milo's, or . . . ?"

"Can't we just make a sandwich?"

"We could, if I had anything to eat at home, which I don't. I put in a grocery order before we left this morning, but it won't arrive until tomorrow."

"How about buying something here?" suggested Alex as they walked by the general store, La Melisse.

"It's expensive," said Natalie, her tone doubtful. "And I don't have a bag."

"What bag?"

"A shopping bag. You have to bring your own."

"I have two good arms, Nat, as do you. Between us, I bet we can manage a few groceries."

CHAPTER SEVENTEEN

Violette

"They aren't *all* Nazis," said Marie-Paule as we gathered *goémon* in the shadow of the lighthouse. Half a dozen children—the eldest was eight while the youngest, my niece Agnès, was barely out of diapers—dug in the sand nearby, searching for clams and razor shells.

"What do you mean?" I asked, grimacing at the unpleasant slime of the seaweed, the sea brine stinging a small cut on my hand. "What's the difference between a German soldier and a Nazi?"

We had so little access to news and information that the gossip mill was running on high. The elders who had lived through the Great War were full of stories about that conflict, but to my mind, at least, the situations were hard to compare. In the Great War, the enemy had remained in the north of France, but this time the Germans had occupied our country and invaded our island. And their charismatic leader, Adolf Hitler, spewed rhetoric about world domination. . . . It was difficult to understand.

Earlier in the week a newspaper had been passed from one island house to the next, showing a photograph of German soldiers goose-stepping down the Champs-Élysées. So we knew things would be different this time.

Nazis, in *Paris*.

"A lot of the regular soldiers were drafted into the military," Marie-Paule explained. "They didn't have a choice."

Noëlle snorted. "They had a choice. We all have a choice. If every decent German man stood up and refused to fight for the Führer, there would be no war."

We women discussed the Germans often, trying to figure out who they were, what they wanted, what made them tick. When we passed them in our passageways or on the quay, they seemed gruff and pushy, their guttural language falling harsh upon our ears. But some of them—a lot—were young, boys really, with open, clear-eyed gazes that reminded me of Marc.

"Marie-Paule's right," said Irmine. "I read about it in the paper, before they got here. The Nazis follow a certain set of beliefs, but most of these men are just following orders. They do not understand the war any more than we do."

"What difference does that make?" Noëlle demanded, casting a quick glance at the young soldier who stood guard over us. He leaned back against a strange rock formation we called the Sphinx, smoking and looking out to sea. He didn't understand French, and as long as we kept our voices low, he didn't care that we talked. In a fierce whisper, she declared: "They have occupied us; they are all culpable. I would happily kill each and every one of them, slit their throats if I could. And so should every one of you."

"I don't want to slit anyone's throat," Marie-Paule said, looking troubled. "That is not what a Christian woman should do."

"Then embrace your pious principles and welcome the invaders into your bed, Marie-Paule," Noëlle said, sneering. "You appeasers make me sick."

"Noëlle, that's unfair," I said. "Marie-Paule suggested no such thing. We're all just doing our best to get by."

That brought the discussion to a halt, and we worked in silence for a while. Three of us wrenched and hauled the slimy weed from the sea, which did not gladly relinquish its greenery; two others wrung out the water; and two more wound the cakes and set them on the rocks to dry in the sun. Our arms ached from the effort, the skin on our hands and wrists wrinkling and turning white from the salt water. My stomach growled; breakfast that morning had been a cup of tea and a small potato in a little broth. I supposed I was lucky that I felt nauseated much of the time because it made me care less about not having enough to eat.

"At least we have no Jews here on the island," said Lazarette.

"That's something else I don't understand," I said. "Why don't the Nazis like the Jews?"

We used to receive our post, and newspapers, twice a week. But now the boat came once a week, if that. The newspapers were censored, so we had access only to Nazi propaganda, and those of us with men in England received no mail at all because even the Red Cross letters were intercepted.

"They despise them," said Marie-Paule with a shrug.

"How do they even *know* who is Jewish?" I asked. "I met a Jewish man last year, a sailor who took shelter with us during a storm. He had dark features, but he looked just the same as anyone else. I can't understand why, or even *how*, someone like him would be separated out from the rest of us."

"They're making them wear the six-pointed star in Poland," said Irmine. "I saw a photograph in the newspaper."

"But if they didn't wear the star, how would anyone know?" I persisted.

"Maybe they round them up at religious services. Jews go to church on Saturdays," said Corinne, who prided herself on knowing more about the world than the average islander.

"Some of them dress differently," suggested Angelique. "Like the jeweler in Quimper."

Corinne cast Angelique a quelling look. Angelique's aunt had married a man from Quimper, and Angelique visited them once or twice a year, earning a reputation for worldliness that Corinne envied. We islanders might rely on one another in times of need but we had our share of petty jealousies, made all the worse by the special disdain fostered by familiarity.

"We separate shipwreck victims when we bury them," Denise pointed out. "People of different religions are . . . different. Maybe we're no better than the Nazis."

"I thought that was out of respect for their wishes, in case they did not want a Christian burial," I said.

"Maybe. I never thought of it as segregation, either," said Marie-Paule. "But who knows? A lot of people are afraid of outsiders; living on the Île de Feme in the modern day, we are exposed to sailors from far and wide. Not everyone is as tolerant of difference."

"I'm just glad we have no Jewish neighbors on the island to be sent to work camps," said Irmine. "Can you imagine seeing your neighbors hauled off in trucks? I heard they are rounding up other people, too, and forcing them into the camps."

"What do they do in these work camps?" I asked.

Irmine shrugged. "I suppose they work in war factories for the Third Reich. Making weapons, perhaps?"

"And the Germans take their land and all their possessions?"

"That's the first thing anyone does when they invade," said Noëlle. "They take what they want. They're like badly behaved children, with no mother to scold them. *Murderous*, thieving little children."

Her voice grew louder, and the soldier guarding us roused and barked, *"Sei ruhig!"*

"That means 'Be quiet,'" Marie-Paule said, and we fell silent.

Late that afternoon our small group walked toward town, weary but satisfied. We had made a record number of *goémon* cakes, which were drying on the rocks in the sun. *Goémon* was proving to be our salvation. We incorporated it into our meals more than ever, grateful for the vitamins and nutrition. It was in demand in the war clinics and hospitals as a source of iodine, so we were able to make a deal with the soldiers: They allowed the boat from the mainland to pick up the cakes in return for most of the money we earned. A little money was better than none.

A very little.

Noëlle, of course, disapproved of the arrangement, stating that we were supporting the enemy by providing iodine for their sick and injured. But what choice did we have? The money was essential to buy food. Starving would not help win France's freedom. Even Noëlle conceded that much.

And besides . . . now that the Germans were here, living with us, playing *pétanque* on the quay, and drinking in the cafés, we saw a different side to these invaders. Some were cruel, but occasionally a soldier stopped to assist an old woman, or fed the cats and dogs that ran loose on the island. I saw their pink cheeks, the dewy youth of so many of the young infantrymen, some not yet old enough to grow a full beard.

They were the enemy, and thus to be despised. But it was hard to imagine denying these boys medicine if they lay stricken on a hospital cot.

As we reached the patchwork of stone-walled gardens and fields, we noticed a commotion ahead.

In a field, standing in front of her two cows, old Madame Canté was arguing with four soldiers. Madame was eighty years old, and tiny. She used to be fierce, reminding me of one of those diminutive dogs that attacked things ten times their size, not realizing how vulnerable they were. But after her grandsons left for England, she seemed to lose her capacity to fight.

"What's going on, Madame Canté?" asked Marie-Paule.

"They want to slaughter my cows!" wailed Madame Canté.

The German soldiers were strapping young men. They had their army rations but hungered for fresh meat.

"*Non,*" said Noëlle.

"*C'est le ravitaillement,*" insisted one of the men, referring to the policy of requisitioning our property.

"But we need the milk for the children," said Lazarette, stepping forward, ever the peacemaker. "Please, sirs, have mercy. Without our men here—"

"It is hardly *our* fault that your men are cowards who left you to starve while they amuse themselves with English whores," one of the men replied in heavily accented French. I recognized him as one of the soldiers in our guesthouse. He was handsome, but his pale gray eyes were flat and empty, and he spoke in a snide, disdainful tone. I had determined to give him a wide berth.

But now I stepped forward beside Lazarette, hoping to intercept Noëlle, who was practically vibrating with fury at my side. I feared things might escalate.

"Monsieur," I said. "*Bitte,* the milk from these cows might be the only thing keeping our children alive. Couldn't we work something out? Perhaps my mother could cook for you. She is very talented and could make something delicious out of your rations."

Madame Canté began to mewl. Her begging put my teeth on edge. Something told me these soldiers would not respond well to weakness.

I stood taller, holding my breath while the man's cold gaze raked over me.

"You are the daughter of the guesthouse," he said.

"Yes, monsieur, and my mother is a very fine cook. Please, let us go there now and we will create a tasty menu for you."

"Your father and brother are *Anglais* now as well, are they not? They have run away to England?"

I felt the color rise in my cheeks.

"Les Anglais," he said, and spat on the ground. "May they all rot in hell, felled by our German bullets."

Noëlle rushed toward him, her fingers splayed like claws, and spat on his uniform.

Livid, he backhanded her, sending her sprawling to the ground. Noëlle cried out, blood streaming from her mouth.

I started to lunge toward him but was held back by a pair of strong hands: our other lodger Rainer.

"Hans!" Rainer yelled. *"Halt!"*

Shoving me aside none too gently, he stepped up to face his colleague and they began arguing in rapid-fire German. I could make out only an occasional word, not enough to understand what they were saying. A muscle worked in the other man's jaw; Rainer's voice was low and intent, not cajoling but insistent. His expression remained implacable in the face of the other man's fury.

Rainer took out a handkerchief and handed it to Hans, to wipe his uniform.

"You have goats as well, do you not?" Rainer asked me.

I nodded.

"We will slaughter one goat," Rainer said, "and leave you the cows."

"But—"

"Or we will slaughter one cow," he insisted. "It is your choice."

I looked to the other women. Reluctantly, we agreed. The goats gave milk, but there were more of them. We had only half a dozen cows, and we needed their milk and cream.

"You will please bring a goat to the butcher to be prepared," Rainer told me. Then he turned to Hans. "And we will leave these cows to their grazing."

Hans glared and said something in German. Then he snapped his heels, held up one arm, and declared: *"Heil Hitler!"*

After a brief moment, Rainer raised his arm and, in a soft voice, repeated those ugly words: *"Heil Hitler."*

That evening, I happened upon Rainer in our parlor, sitting in a comfortable chair with one of our books in his lap. But he was not reading. He seemed lost in thought, looking at nothing at all.

I started to leave when he saw me. He placed his finger in the book as though to keep his page. He seemed to favor one leg as he stood.

"Madame," Rainer said, inclining his head slightly. *"Bonsoir."*

"Bonsoir, monsieur. I am glad to see you. I . . . I owe you thanks."

His eyebrows rose.

"For the . . . for saving our cows. The children need the milk. They are hungry."

"I am afraid it will not last, sorry to say."

"The hunger?"

He gave a sad chuckle and shook his head. "No, that will most definitely last, and probably intensify. I mean the cows. I'm a customs officer; I'm not in charge of the soldiers stationed here. I will do what I can, speak to their commanding officer, but I imagine the soldiers will get to the cows eventually. They are hungry as well."

My heart fell. I forced myself to tamp down the incipient panic, wondering what we would do without the animals. "In any case, I appreciate what you've done so far. Even a few more days with milk will make a difference."

"How is the girl? The one who was struck?"

"Her tooth is loose and she will have an angry bruise."

"I'm sorry to hear that."

"Old Madame Thérèse will make her a plaster."

My eyes fell on the book in his hands. Green leather cover, gilt letters. *Claudine à l'école* by Sidonie-Gabrielle Colette. It was a book by a woman, for an audience of women. It seemed strange to imagine the story filtered through a man's eyes and emotions.

"That is one of my favorites," I commented.

"I know," he said.

I frowned. "How would you know something like that?"

He flipped open the book and held it up. "'To my loyal customer,'" he read. "'Mademoiselle Violette Fouquet, on her eighteenth birthday. Your favorite book.'"

"Monsieur Saint-Just owns the bookstore in Audierne," I explained, relaxing a bit. "I rarely had money to buy books, so he allowed me to read in his store. He gave me that one as a present."

"Sounds like a kind man."

"Actually he's very grumpy, but we share a love of books. He has been kind to me."

"I imagine you won him over with your charm." Rainer smiled. "I hope you don't mind that I helped myself to your library."

"Not at all. Books are meant to be shared."

"I agree. It's a charming novel. Tell me, why is it your favorite?"

I felt a little thrill at the question. No one ever asked me such things. The villagers had more practical matters to attend to and had neither the time nor the interest to discuss things that weren't real.

"Have you ever . . . ?" I tried to formulate my thoughts. "Have you ever read a book and tripped over a phrase or an idea, and thought, *That's exactly how I feel!* but had not been able to put into words?"

Rainer nodded slowly. "Yes, I know that feeling very well indeed."

I quoted from the book: *"Je sais très bien, depuis longtemps, que j'ai un coeur déraisonnable, mais, de le savoir, ça ne m'arrête pas du tout.'"*

He repeated the phrase: "'I have known for a long time that I have an unreasonable heart, but even knowing that, it does not stop me in the least.' Do you feel you have an unreasonable heart, madame?"

I gave a wry laugh. "Quite unreasonable, yes."

"The unreasonable heart is a gift." He waggled a finger at me in mock admonition. "Don't let anyone try to tame it."

I smiled, then sobered upon realizing I was chatting in the parlor with the enemy. Our conversation had seemed so natural that I had forgotten with whom I was speaking.

"I saw you that first day, when we came off the boat," said Rainer. "I noticed you in the crowd."

"When you arrived on the island?"

He nodded. "You were with the young woman, the one who was fighting with Hans about the cows. What is her name?"

"Why do you ask?"

"Please, I wish your friend no harm."

Rainer's actions this afternoon suggested I could believe his words, but still I hesitated. Then I realized he could find out who she was easily enough. "Noëlle. Noëlle Guilcher. She is my *belle-soeur*."

"Please tell your sister-in-law that she must learn to control her anger. I would hate something worse to happen to her."

"Is that a threat?" I blurted. It was too easy to think of Rainer as a charming man, to chat with him about books and unruly hearts as though he were a friend.

"Not at all. I am trying to be helpful. I hope you will believe that I wish you and your friends no harm."

I stared at him. He returned my gaze but did not speak.

"What did you say today, to that officer, Hans?" I asked. "What did you tell him to make him stop?"

"I reminded him of his sister. I have known his family most of my life. We are both from Berlin."

"Is his sister the type to lose her temper?"

He chuckled and nodded. "She's a . . . How do you say it? A harpy."

"That's not a nice thing to say."

"No. But it is nevertheless true."

"How is it that you speak French so well?"

"My father's mother was French. I grew up in Berlin, but spent the summers with my grandmother and cousins in the Champagne region."

"It must be awkward to be here now, given the circumstances."

He nodded.

"You play the piano very well," I said.

"Thank you," Rainer said with a grin, then set the book down, went to the piano, and played a quick interlude. "Believe it or not, I was raised in the cabaret my father opened after the Great War. We barely got by, moneywise, but as long as there was song and dance . . ."

"*Violette?*"

I jumped at the sound of my mother's voice calling from the kitchen. In my mind's eye I saw the disapproving look on her face, the strained pursing of her mouth.

"*J'arrive, Maman,*" I said, then bade Rainer a good night and hurried down the hallway to the kitchen.

As I expected, *Maman*'s expression suggested she was disappointed in me. It was a familiar look. I disappointed her each day that I rose and refused to don the *jibilinnen*. Still, I was a hard worker, I had married an island boy rather than escape to the mainland, and I was pregnant with the next generation of islander. I felt I was doing my part.

"Why are you talking with that man?" *Maman* hissed. "He is the enemy."

"You think I don't understand that?" I asked. "I was thanking him. He defied an officer today, stepped in to save Madame Canté's cows from slaughter."

"That's not how I heard it. I heard it was Noëlle who asked for the milk for the children. That it was she who gained their respect, and their cooperation."

The gossip network on the island was impressive in its speed, if not its accuracy. It infuriated me how the popular version of events tended to paint the islanders as ever noble, strangers as unworthy. No matter what the truth might be.

"That's not what happened," I said. "We need to be careful, *Maman*. Some of the Germans are reasonable, and it would be wise to keep them on our side so that they might be willing to intervene on our behalf."

"We don't need their help. We islanders have endured—"

"I know, *Maman*, I know. We have endured cholera epidemics and the inundation of nineteen twenty-seven." I had been raised on the stories of survival and persistence, of enduring whatever was thrown at us. "And we made it through the War of Nineteen Fourteen, or at least most of us did. But this is different, can't you see? This time the Germans are here, living with us. There are rumors—Monsieur Thomas said he heard on the radio that the Nazis are rounding up Jews in Poland and forcing them into work camps."

"Why do you care about Jews?"

"Why should they be persecuted for what they believe?"

"They're not Christian."

Neither were the Gallizenae, I thought to myself. My stomach clenched when I saw my mother like this, small-minded and fiercely dedicated to her insular way of life, the way things had always been. It was at times like this that I reminded myself that the blood of the Gallizenae ran through my veins.

"I care because they're human beings," I said. "And my point is that the Nazis are extreme and they are dangerous, so if we find some reasonable soldiers, we should do our best to remain in their good graces."

I watched as my mother kneaded her dough, pounding the small ball in a dull sort of indignant resignation. My mother had always been a woman of few words, living her life by a strict set of rules and beliefs, apparently cut off from her feelings. If only my *mamm-gozh* were with us. I could still hear her in my mind, taking my side as she so often did in my conflicts with my parents: "The child's clever, my daughter. You should listen to her."

"Besides," I continued, "our men are gone and we're starving, *Maman.*"

"You don't have to tell me that."

"So if that means being pleasant to a German officer so the children will have milk, then I will do so."

Maman was already writing something down in her cookbook. It was very old, with numerous recipes scrawled on the backs of envelopes, scraps of paper, and even linen, and tucked inside. "We use everything here on the island," she taught me growing up. "Everything is useful." It grated on my nerves that she remained so intent on preserving the ways of the past, seemingly marooned on an island that hadn't existed in decades. I was enough of a Fémane to respect our people's history, to value tradition. But I wanted something . . . more.

"When our men return, things will be different," said my mother. "When your father and brother return. When your *husband* returns."

I went to wash my hands, her words echoing in my head.

My *husband*.

I glanced down at the ring he had given me, using my thumb to make it spin on my finger. It was his grandmother's silver claddagh ring: two hands clasping a heart, topped by a crown. The design reminded me of friends reaching out to each other, and I thought to myself that it was fitting. Marc Jean Guilcher felt more like a friend than a husband.

On top of the bureau where my *mamm-gozh* had kept her death drawer were framed photos of my brother and my father. My mother had placed candles and flowers before the photographs as if it were an altar. A small white porcelain statuette of Mother Mary stood over it all, her palms held out in supplication.

I wondered if my mother had a death drawer prepared. Was I expected to do the same, now that I was married? Should I wrap my wedding dress in waxed paper and tuck it away to serve as my eventual shroud? I had married in such haste that I had worn my simple flowered cotton dress, adding a small veil to mark the occasion. It hardly seemed special enough for death.

I had a vision of myself in that moment, lying in a wooden coffin and dressed in a shroud decorated with shells and feathers and seaweed, a Gallizena gone to her final resting place.

CHAPTER EIGHTEEN

Alex

$\mathcal{T}$he owner of La Melisse grocery store was a severe-looking woman in her fifties, thin to the point of gaunt, named Severine. Her long dark hair was sprinkled with gray and pulled back into a tight ponytail.

Nat greeted her as they walked in, introducing Alex. Severine responded in English: "I heard you had arrived. This is so nice to know Natalie has family here."

"News travels fast," said Alex.

"It is a small island." Severine shrugged.

As the only source of groceries on the Île de Feme, Severine took her responsibilities seriously. The resident Fémans ordered most of their groceries from the mainland, but inevitably an item or two would be forgotten, and the visitors and guests at vacation rentals always needed supplies. Tourists often failed to heed the warning that there were limited dining options, which meant long lines at the restaurants and cafés at the height of the season. So in addition to the usual corner store offerings of chips and crackers and sweets, Severine sold bread—it was shipped from a mainland boulangerie each morning, and when it sold out there was no more until the next ferry—as well as fresh fruit, a variety of cheeses, and a small selection of quality pâtés and meats. An old sign hanging on the rear wall advertised locally butchered meat, CHARCUTÉ ICI MÊME, A L'ÎLE DE FEME.

"The sign's outdated," Nat explained. "The island's butcher retired a few years ago and moved to be with his kids in Bordeaux."

"Maybe you should volunteer," said Alex.

By the time Nat was ten years old, she could skin a rabbit while keeping the fur intact. She would hang it to recover the blood, which her mother used to make sausage; locate the spots in the joints where it was easiest to cut; and swiftly break it down. Alex remembered her little sister yammering on about trying to figure out how all the parts fit together, how a creature that was once warm and sentient was now sitting on the counter, being readied for dinner.

"I don't do that anymore."

"Why not?"

"It's . . . it's not something normal people do," said Nat.

"Chefs do it all the time, don't they?" Alex asked.

"I'm a writer, not a chef."

"You wrote a lot about cooking in your book."

"I did, but I was never a *real* chef."

"You left that part to François?"

"Xavier."

"What?"

"It's François-Xavier. You have to say both names."

"I really don't."

Nat gave a reluctant chuckle. "I mean, it's a different name, if you don't say both. It'd be like calling someone Mary when their name is Mary Ann."

"Whatever. I'll just stick with 'scumbag.'"

"*Shhh,*" Nat said, glancing around to be sure no one was listening. "Anyway, grab that round of Camembert, will you? And let's get some *jambon de Paris* and a baguette. I've got the apples. We don't need much—I put in an order with Carrefour this morning, which should arrive on tomorrow's ferry."

"How does that work?" Alex asked. "Do you send a carrier pigeon or something?"

"No, I go to their website," Nat said. "You *are* familiar with the Internet, aren't you? You're welcome to use my computer if you want to check e-mail or pay bills or something."

Alex laughed. "I am part of the real world, too, Natalie. Just like you. I was asking because—I don't know—it just seems so isolated out here."

"Nothing's truly isolated anymore, unless you seek it out. Like The Commander. Have you heard from him recently?"

"He seems okay. You could write to him, you know, if you want. He's living in Idaho, near a town called Horseshoe Bend. If you arrange a time to call, there's a pay phone at the post office that he can use."

"I'll think about it," Nat said with a little shrug.

They both knew Nat had no intention of calling him. Their father didn't read much, much less darken the door of a library, but he could have heard about *Pourquoi Pas?* from one of the guys hanging out at the town bar. Alex didn't imagine Nat wanted to know what The Commander might say about her book or her current lifestyle.

As they brought their selections to the counter, Alex said: "If I live to be a hundred, I will never get over how easy it is to buy groceries in a store."

"No one understands me when I say that," Nat said. "But it does have a kind of miraculous quality about it, doesn't it?"

"No bag?" Severine asked as she rang up their purchases, and she sniffed when Nat shook her head.

Just as they were leaving, *Tonton* Michou entered the store in search of cigarettes. He greeted them like long-lost daughters, speaking rapidly and at length to the uncomprehending Alex. It was frustrating not being able to understand, but Alex forced herself to relax and allow the words to swirl over and around her, enjoying the cadence of the language, the soft vowels and gentle consonants, the repetitive *ooo* sounds.

No doubt about it, she was going to add "Learn French" to her list of skills to acquire.

As they returned to the Bag-Noz, arms full of groceries, Alex tried to take in every detail: the narrow stone walkways that wound between the village buildings, stepping aside to make way for a woman pushing a little *charette* laden with supplies, the chatty tourists, the children's grins, the pink cheeks and sunburned noses, the garishly colored beach toys. Trying to commit it all to memory.

"That will be all over the island by tomorrow, you know," said Nat.

"What will be?" asked Alex.

"That we bought food at Severine's because I forgot to place my order at the Carrefour. *And* that I forgot my bag."

"How *will* you survive the shame?"

"Also, they'll gossip about *you*. A lot of them read the French edition of the book and are curious about our family."

Alex shrugged. "Why do you care so much about what other people think, Nat?"

"That's easy for you to say. You don't have to live here."

"Do you?"

Nat said nothing. Alex studied her as they walked. Her sister kept insisting she was happy and that all was well, when it so very clearly was not. Alex thought about the stories of the perfect boyfriend, the gracious treatment of her fans even when she wanted to be left alone, the easy-breezy interaction with her absentee boyfriend's elderly relatives. All the while Nat worried about what they thought of her, what the other villagers thought of her, what complete strangers thought of her. Nat wrote in her blog as if everything were bright and sunny on an island that smelled of crepes and lavender, when in reality a storm was brewing, her roof was leaking, and the whole damn place stank of rotting fish.

"Are you happy living out here on this island, Nat?"

"What do you mean?"

"I mean just what I said: Are you happy?"

"Of course. I'm living my dream, Alex," Nat said, flashing a bright smile. "Didn't you hear what the women said last night? I'm the luckiest woman in the world."

"No, you're not," Alex said, stopping in her tracks and facing her sister. "Your so-called boyfriend abandoned you, and you're drinking in the middle of the day surrounded by an unfinished major renovation."

"I . . ." Nat trailed off with a shake of her head, but her cheeks turned a bright red and her eyes shone with tears.

"Look, how about we go home, have a bite to eat, and I'll start putting together a fix-it list? And then we can talk about where to go from there. I can help you, Nat."

Nat's eyes darted back and forth, as though looking for inspiration. Finally she seemed to relax, took a deep breath, and nodded.

"Thanks, Alex. That's a great idea. I would really appreciate it."

CHAPTER NINETEEN

Natalie

*B*ack at the house, they made sandwiches and ate quickly at the kitchen counter. Alex was itching to create the punch list of what needed to be done to ready the Bag-Noz for guests.

"What can I do?" asked Natalie, her voice flat even to her own ears.

"Why don't I go through the house and work up a list?" said Alex. "And then we can review it together. Besides, don't you have to get back to writing?"

Natalie nodded. "Okay, thanks. Shout if you get stuck behind the water heater or something."

"Will do," Alex said with a smile, as she hurried out of the kitchen.

Watching her go, Natalie thought about what Alex had asked her.

Natalie's social media followers assumed she was happy. Her agent and editor were invested in the idea of her happiness, as were the fans of her book who wished they had her life—the pilgrims who followed her path in France because she was so obviously living a dream. *Her* dream.

But . . . did Natalie really want to set down roots on this isolated rock, with nosy neighbors in a tiny village? Live in an old house that was falling down around her? An old house that came with an extended family whom she felt responsible for, but with whom she never seemed to fit in? Had she given up her life to follow François-Xavier out here, only to be abandoned when he moved on?

How had she gotten herself into this situation?

Maybe old Ambroisine really *had* cursed her. It was as good an explanation as any.

Natalie thought again of the video of the woman she had seen on the Internet with those goats. Or were they sheep? Whatever they were, the woman was on her own adventure, living alone with her dog. It seemed like a really good dog, too. Running her livestock and spinning their wool to knit things. Natalie wouldn't mind learning to spin wool, and . . . maybe even learn to knit? The point was, the woman was living *her* life, not a life someone else had decided for her.

On the other hand, such an isolated life would probably meet with their father's approval. *That* was a disturbing thought.

With Alex's arrival, a flood of childhood memories had washed over Natalie. How she had failed at almost everything, disappointed almost everyone, especially The Commander. So instead of writing about her current life on the island, Natalie wrote an essay about her childhood, hoping the act of putting her thoughts into words would help her to make sense of it all.

I have a single good memory of being with my father. It was just the two of us and now, looking back, I wonder where the others had gotten to. The older girls were probably helping our mother with the endless cooking, cleaning, and sewing, or perhaps Hope had already run off to get married. Alex was no doubt repairing something or practicing her archery; she was always busy being useful.

I heard my father call my name. My stomach clenched.

He was forever dressing me down for yet another one of my failures, calling me on the carpet to parrot his lessons or to demonstrate the proper bug-out tactic. I went to him slowly, but I went, because not obeying was not an option. But this time, this one time, it was different. I found him in his workshop, where he had arranged four pieces of wood on top of his bench in the shape of a diamond.

"What do you think this is, Natalie?" The Commander asked.

"A diamond."

"That's the shape, but what is it?"

"I . . ." My mind grasped at straws and I tried not to shrug—shrugging was strictly forbidden. "Is it a trap, maybe?"

He actually laughed. "A trap? These flimsy pieces of wood?"

"Or . . . a bug-out structure?"

He sighed, annoyed, and I feared I had gone and done it, ruined his rare good cheer by screwing up again. I froze, unsure how to respond.

He took some paper and started to wrap it around the diamond frame, instructing me to tape it at key points. Then he threaded string along the edges.

"How about now? Do you recognize it?" he asked.

"Wait—it's a kite!" I said, surprised and excited.

"That's it! Oh, I know you can buy one at the dollar store, but isn't it more fun to make it ourselves? My brothers and I used to make these on the ranch when we were kids."

"Fun" was not a word in my father's daily vocabulary. But here he was, his face shining with little-boy joy as he crafted this toy on his worktable. He was being honest, I realized. He was excited about making a kite.

My ten-year-old heart turned to the possibility of flying it, even while telling myself that there had to be a lesson in there, somewhere. I must be missing it, and would be called to account. I racked my brain. I thought of the story I had read of Benjamin Franklin and a kite trailing a key during a thunderstorm. Was The Commander experimenting with electricity, maybe? He liked to play with electricity.

He wrapped a long piece of string around a pencil and attached it to the kite.

"Follow me," he said, and led the way to the meadow, where the kite caught the breeze and began to fly, higher, higher. I jumped up and down, thrilled at the sight of the kite dancing in the air.

"See that, Nat?" The Commander said, and I nodded. "Want to try? Don't be afraid. It's not hard. Just hold it like this and keep it away from the trees."

As he handed me the string-wrapped pencil, the wind kicked up, and the kite bucked and jerked about. "Hold it tight, Nat," he said. "Don't let it near the trees."

"I won't!" I said, and for a few moments I watched the kite fly.

"Watch the trees, Nat!" my father barked. "Steer it away!"

"I don't know how!" I said, as the kite took a sudden nosedive and crashed into a tall pine tree, becoming entangled in the upper branches.

The Commander swore and shook his head, his mood now black. He yanked on the string, but the kite did not budge.

"Stay there, idiotic ding-dong thing," he yelled, and walked off in disgust.

The kite remained in the tree for months, waving in the breezes, taunting me in silent reproach, until at last a storm carried away its tattered remains.

Natalie sat back, drained but satisfied. The language needed tinkering, of course, but at least she had written *something*. Unfortunately, the story was more suited to *Pourquoi Pas?* than to the new book she was supposed to be writing. But she would figure that out later. The point was, it felt good to be writing again. And after all, it seemed her readers couldn't get enough stories of her strange upbringing.

Next, Natalie posted a few photos from today's tour of the island, and wrote a short blog post about her sister surprising her with a visit. Natalie wished she had more to say, something of greater import. But instead she wrote a few words about how great it was to see relatives.

Finally, Natalie opened her e-mail to find a note from her agent, Sandy. The subject line read: **Good news!**

She opened the message, hoping her publisher was able to give her another advance after all, or that *Pourquoi Pas?* was being translated into Lithuanian or one of the other languages that had not yet picked it up.

Instead, the note read: Your book has been optioned for a movie!

Natalie sat back, stunned. Film options rarely amounted to much, but this one came with a nice chunk of change. So she really *could* finish up the renovation properly.

Except . . . *Pourquoi Pas?* was all about finding her happiness. And she had lost it again.

Natalie brought a lavender sachet to her nose. The scent was calming. Usually.

But in this moment Natalie kept thinking about what Alex said: that in actuality the island smelled of fish, not of lavender.

CHAPTER TWENTY

Violette

*R*ainer appeared in the kitchen doorway, in his hands a large package wrapped in newspaper stained pink with blood.

"Excusez-moi, Madame Fouquet," he said to my mother, his tone respectful. "Would you be willing to cook this meat for the officers staying here? I will pay you for your time and effort, of course."

My mother's mouth gaped open, as though she were unable to find the words to respond.

"Bien sûr," I jumped in. "May we share in the meat as well?"

"There is plenty for all," he said, setting the package on the counter. "The goat belongs to the Fémans, after all."

With that, he nodded curtly, smiled, and left us.

"You would break bread with the enemy?" my mother asked me, appalled.

"Better that they eat our animals while we go hungry?" I replied in a fierce whisper. My mouth was already watering at the prospect of fresh meat, something we had not enjoyed for far too long.

"You forget yourself, Violette," said *Maman*, shaking her head.

"I forget nothing, *Maman*. You are the one who always speaks of survival. Well, now *this* is our survival. And have you forgotten that I am carrying your grandchild?"

Maman sighed and pulled her cookbook toward her on the counter, flipping through the pages in a familiar ritual, looking for the right recipe.

I began to unwrap the bloody package.

As an island girl, I was accustomed to killing, gutting, and scaling fish. Slaughtering and plucking chickens were also common, if unpleasant, chores. But the meat of cows, goats, and pigs had always left me vaguely nauseated, the sinew and the blood reminding me of the gruesome nature of our carnivorous ways.

Now, as the musky scent of the raw meat wafted up toward me, I could think of nothing but dinner.

Rainer worked with German customs control, the GAST, which was short for *Grenzaufsichtstelle*. His was an important position, which reflected his education and linguistic abilities. In addition to his native German, Rainer spoke French fluently and English and Spanish passably as well as speaking a smattering of other languages.

The GAST had decreed that ships passing the Île de Feme must pull into the harbor so that Rainer's men could inspect their cargo. Our harbor, once so full of fishing boats, now welcomed vessels from Africa and Spain, even, occasionally, from the Americas. Once daily life under occupation settled down and the bureaucracy of the Vichy government had been set in motion, the island's little store La Melisse began to receive regular supplies, most of which, from meat to coffee to soap, were distributed according to the rationing system.

Monsieur Kestel, the baker, was granted small shipments of flour and other grains, sometimes even flour made of ground turnips or tulip bulbs, and whenever he was able to bake some bread, his shop was mobbed. But no one complained about the long lines. It was a rare chance to exchange information, because other gatherings of islanders in groups of more than three were *verboten*. Waiting in line, collecting *goémon*, and being at home with family members were the only exceptions to the rule of three.

"On dit"—"they say"—became a favorite refrain, a way to discuss news and events, whether speculating on what was happening to our men in England, or wondering if a shipment of potatoes was expected anytime soon, or gossiping about the shameful Parisian women—actresses and dancers, mostly—who cavorted with German officers in cafés and cabarets, committing that greatest of sins: *la collaboration horizontale*.

On the Île de Feme, there was a clear divide between the customs officials, the GAST, and the regular soldiers. The GAST's duties were to control the ferry, inspect the ships, and wave through the boat that came to pick up the dried *goémon* cakes. The soldiers, on the other hand, were there to occupy the island as part of what Hitler called his "Atlantic Wall." Convinced the Allies would attack from the West, Hitler ordered troops to take up positions on the shores of Normandy and the Côte Sauvage, on the Channel Islands, and on the numerous rocky reefs, such as the Île de Feme, that dotted the Atlantic between France and the south of England. Above all, the Germans were intent upon controlling the port of Brest, the westernmost point of mainland France, whose deepwater docks were being used to build and repair Nazi ships and submarines.

The soldiers assigned to our island watched over our small population of women, children, and old people. They did drills and kept a lookout from the lighthouse, but otherwise their duties were few. If some were secretly relieved to be far from the fighting, others soon grew bored and restless.

The officer I knew only as Hans, the one who had struck Noëlle, worried me. He made no secret of his disdain for island life and for all who dwelled here, and appeared to be perpetually angry. I tried to give him a wide berth, which wasn't always possible since we resided under the same roof. I could feel his pale gaze on me as I served the officers dinner at our long table, and always waited until he had left the house before cleaning his room and changing his sheets.

One day, when I was returning from the bakery with a rare and precious baguette, I saw him stop my *belle-mère*, my mother-in-law, and another older woman, Madame Omérin. I ducked back into the passageway so he wouldn't notice me, and watched.

"*Ihre Papiere, bitte,*" Hans demanded in German, though he knew enough French to get by.

Had he not been so threatening, I would have rolled my eyes. The elderly women were doing nothing more sinister than carrying their empty baskets to the store, having heard a rumor that a shipment of lard had come in to La Melisse.

With shaking hands, the women produced their *cartes d'identité*, which included their fingerprints, date and place of birth, and profession: *femme de foyer*, or housewife.

Hans made a show of carefully inspecting the documents, then ran his cold eyes over their *robes noires* and *jibilinnen*.

"Why must you island women insist on wearing black?" he demanded, now in French. "It is . . . *trübselig*. How do you say that in French? Depressing."

"*Nous portons le deuil de la France,*" responded Madame Omérin with defiance. "We are wearing mourning clothes for our France."

Hans stared at them for a long moment before handing them their documents and allowing them to pass.

"*Sie sehen aus wie Hexen,*" he said in a low, menacing voice.

· · ·

What does '*hexen*' mean?" I asked Rainer that evening when we passed in the downstairs hall.

He frowned. "Why do you ask?"

"I heard your friend Hans say it today."

"I wouldn't call him my friend," said Rainer in a low voice.

"He used the term about the *jibilinnen*, I think."

"The men don't understand why the women on the island wear all black."

"Oh. What does '*hexen*' mean, then?"

"It means 'witches.'"

"He thinks we're witches?"

"It was an insult, nothing more. I apologize on his behalf."

"That isn't necessary," I said, wondering what the Gallizenae would make of these German invaders. "Some of us really are witches. But I suppose he'll never know for sure which of us is a witch. Perhaps he'll be more careful."

"Was he inappropriate? Should I speak to him?"

I shook my head, not wanting to make trouble.

"You can come to me, madame, if anything happens."

I met his eyes. They were a deep azure, nothing like the pale gray of his countryman, Hans, or the clear blue of my husband, Marc. Rainer's eyes spoke of the morning sea and the night sky, of poetry and music, and his gaze made me feel welcome, as though I had come home after a long journey. It was a strange sensation, and I would admit this to no one, but had Rainer not been my sworn enemy, I felt sure we would have been friends.

I nodded. "Thank you."

"I was about to light the fire. There's a chill in the air tonight."

We had long since run out of firewood and coal, which had to be brought in by boat from the mainland and was no longer a priority. So now we burned dried kelp for warmth. It took a huge amount to warm our stone walls, and the leaves tended to smoke more than flame. Still, it was better than nothing.

"I miss wood fires," said Rainer, wincing as he crouched down before the hearth. He rubbed his knee for a moment before filling the fireplace with a tightly wound, dried circle of *goémon* and touching a match to one leaf. "Have you read the works of Thomas Bailey Aldrich? He wrote: 'Do you hear those little chirps and twitters coming out of that piece of applewood? Those are the ghosts of the robins and bluebirds that sang upon the bough when it was in blossom last spring.'"

I said nothing, unsure how to respond.

"I suppose it sounds better in the original English," he said.

"How did you learn to speak English?"

He shook his head. "I wouldn't say I speak it, exactly."

"But you read their poets?"

"I'll read anything I can get my hands on. Aldrich also wrote one of my favorite phrases: 'What is lovely never dies, but passes into other loveliness, stardust, or sea-foam, flower or winged air.'"

"You sing and play the piano, read poetry, and make fires from kelp. Is there anything you cannot do, monsieur?"

"I can't make you happy, apparently."

"That's not true: You could make me very happy simply by leaving the island—and taking your friends with you."

"I told you, they are my countrymen, not my friends."

"Is the distinction supposed to matter to me?"

He stood, wiping his hands, and walked slowly toward me, his limp more pronounced. "I know this situation is difficult, madame. I know your father and brother are in England. I know you don't want these strangers in your house. But believe me when I say I regret the situation as well. I love your country; France is part of my own family history. I never wanted to come here as a detested invader. I am . . . It probably sounds ridiculous to say, but in many ways I am as put-upon by this war as you are. The average soldier does not profit from war, whether on the winning or losing side; it is the politicians and businessmen who benefit."

Once again, I didn't know how to respond.

"I'm doing the best I can, madame," Rainer said quietly.

It embarrassed me to feel tears sting the backs of my eyes. "I'm sorry. I believe you. I am just so tired, and hungry. Also . . . I am expecting a child."

His eyes lit up, as though I had told him he was the father.

"But, Violette! This is a blessing, no? Congratulations! That is the very best of news."

The next morning when I emerged from my bedroom, there was a sack of flour on the kitchen counter, along with a jar of honey and— wonder of wonders—a small round of butter.

"We haven't had butter since this war began," my mother said as we stood side by side in the kitchen, our mouths watering as we stared at the beautiful yellow disk. "What is this for?"

"The baby," I said, with quiet certainty.

It was astonishing, given the circumstances of war and invasion. But Rainer was unlike any man I had ever known. This German had become a friend.

CHAPTER TWENTY-ONE

Alex

*A*lex was relieved to find that the basement and crawl spaces were a little dirty but appeared watertight and, amazingly, most of the plumbing in the walls had been updated. That meant it would be easy enough to tie toilets, showers, and sinks into the existing stub-outs in the second-floor bathrooms. Of course, that meant someone would have to order new fixtures and, she supposed, have them shipped out to the island. Could those be ordered online?

Alex shone her flashlight into the holes in the walls and found some sections of old knob-and-tube wiring that should be stripped and updated. She also noted that most rooms had only a single electrical outlet. Maybe the building guidelines in France were different, but back home the code required at least one receptacle every six feet.

Unfortunately, electricity was the one area of home repair in which Alex was clueless. When they were kids, The Commander had rigged power for the cabin from solar panels and a small wind turbine, but he had routed the current through a confusing and unsafe tangle of wires. Over the years they had all been shocked by ungrounded outlets and fixtures, especially when storms blew through and charged the wires and metal surfaces with invisible energy that reached out, like the tentacles of an electrified octopus, making them wary of innocent-looking objects.

Alex inspected the building methodically, floor by floor. The third floor, which she was sharing with Jean-Luc, needed only a few ceiling lights and a paint job. The broad-plank wood floors would be fine after a good scrubbing, and a well-placed throw rug or two would make things cozier.

Alex paused at the doorway to the attic stairs and studied the stout wooden door Nat and the scumbag had taken off its hinges. The antique hardware throughout the house had been crafted with pride, and even the hinges on the attic door were beautiful. The lockset and knobs were aged brass, and the plates featured decorative scrollwork. It would be a shame to replace it.

Maybe one of the old keys she had found under the front step would fit this lock. If so, she could simply rehang the door and cross that off her to-do list. She made a mental note to check.

A dim, narrow staircase led up into one big room under the eaves. Alex kept her flashlight in hand as she flicked the switch, and light from a bare bulb flooded the space.

Two women emerged from the dark.

Alex jumped, then regained her composure.

Not *women*. Dresses. Two black dresses hanging from a beam. On a nearby shelf sat two pairs of boots, and two winged headdresses.

Alex recognized these as the *robes noires* and *jibilinnen* Nat had spoken of, the traditional outfits worn by the perpetually mourning women of the Île de Feme. One dress was extra large, but the other looked like it would fit Alex. She ran her hands along the fabric; it was softer than she would have imagined. What would it be like to wear the same costume, day in and day out, whether gathering *goémon*, visiting friends, or attending a feast day celebration? Would it be stultifying? Or would it be freeing not to have to think about what to wear, to so easily fit in with one's town and culture, like a hand slipping into a custom-made glove?

She poked around but didn't see much else of interest in the attic. Wooden and cardboard boxes filled the shelves of a bookcase built into the wall. There were two small end tables, a large ceramic lamp with no shade, a mirror, mismatched window frames, a couple of doors, and assorted small pieces of lumber. Alex made a note to bring these last down to the shed. She might be able to put the wood to use, and in any case, it was never good to leave things like this lying around as an invitation to pests.

Messes went against Alex's nature. She liked everything tidy and in its place.

More worrisome were the large tarps and pots and buckets spread around, evidence of attempts to catch water. Alex could see daylight through a few pinprick holes in the roof overhead, and water stains marred the ceiling and the broad wood floor planks.

Alex felt a spurt of anger. Water damage would destroy the building. *What is Nat thinking? Or the scumbag boyfriend?* A new roof should have been the first thing on their renovations list.

Alex brought the two *robes noires* with her as she navigated the steep attic stairs to the third-floor landing, and then down two more flights to the main floor. She hung the dresses in the parlor and went to look for Nat in her study.

"Knock, knock. Nat?"

Her sister wasn't there, but her laptop was open on the desk.

Alex sat down and looked up how to repair a slate roof. It seemed simple enough—not easy, but straightforward. She took some notes and closed the roofing websites, then noticed the tabs open to Nat's social media sites. Alex scrolled through Nat's posts, studying the photographs that made the island seem beautiful and romantic—and it *was* beautiful and romantic, at least to Alex. But it was also stark and dramatic, the way it was so low, surrounded on all sides by water.

> Guess who surprised me, coming off the ferry without letting me know she was coming: my sister! We had a scrumptious meal of locally sourced seafood at Milo's Café, one of my favorite island gems, and spent the next day strolling around the island, taking in the sights, chatting with villagers, and climbing the lighthouse steps. Who knows what adventure is next on the sister agenda?

Nat had illustrated these chatty words with photographs of Alex caught in profile, some taken when she was sitting on the rocks, others on the lighthouse catwalk, as she was gazing out across the whole of the island.

Alex wasn't happy to see so many wrinkles at the edges of her eyes, but otherwise was pleased. No two ways about it, Nat had a talent with the camera. Alex knew—she had been told often enough—that she didn't smile often, yet Nat had caught her several times with a small but sad smile playing on her lips.

Alex supposed anyone who had read *Pourqois Pas?* would not be surprised to see her looking sad.

Genuinely nosy now, Alex clicked on another open tab. This one was a Parisian news site with an article featuring a photograph of a man and a woman. Alex was so engrossed in the attempt to translate the article that she didn't hear Nat come in.

"What are you doing?"

Alex jumped. "Sorry. I was looking up some details about roof repairs . . . but then I got distracted."

Nat peered over Alex's shoulder at the photo of François-Xavier and that woman walking along the Seine. She sank into a chair by the desk, looking stricken.

"He's very attractive," Alex said softly. "I'll give him that."

Nat stared at the photo on the computer screen.

"But if you ask me," Alex continued, "he's sort of *too* good-looking. You know what I mean? Like when you see a guy with his shirt off. A six-pack is nice and all, but too many muscles are kind of off-putting. At least, that's how I see it."

Nat finally gave a reluctant smile. "What are you even *talking* about?"

"I'm just running off at the mouth. What do I know? I've never had much luck with love myself."

Alex had had sex a few times, mostly to see what all the fuss was about: a guy at the lumber mill, the bartender in town. There had been a brief and surprisingly enjoyable fling with a businessman who had come to the ranch to "find himself" before returning to his wife and kids in Modesto. But she never let anyone get close.

When Alex first read *Pourquoi Pas?* she found the chapters on their childhood galling, but much worse was Natalie's therapy-inspired discussion about what it meant to survive childhood trauma: how the typical responses were either to care too much about what others thought, or to refuse to trust and to live an emotionally stunted adulthood.

Ridiculous, Alex had scoffed, tossing the book aside. *Self-involved, navel-gazing twaddle.* Little wonder the book became a bestseller, she thought the next day as she patiently showed a young ranch guest how to tie and throw a lariat. She heard her father's voice in her head:

People like nothing better than to blame someone else, to pretend nothing is ever their fault. They're full of excuses.

But over time Alex wondered whether Nat was onto something. Her little sister had always gone through life like a butterfly, driven this way and that by the opinions of others, by the stories she read or by what a boyfriend said, in a constant search for approval.

And as for herself . . . Alex liked to think of herself as an island. She stood alone. Anything else scared the hell out of her, because in the end, the only person she could rely on was herself.

What would Nat do if people thought less of her? And what would happen to Alex, now that she herself had become unreliable?

CHAPTER TWENTY-TWO

Natalie

"So, what did you learn about the roof?" Natalie asked, wishing Alex would change the web page so she didn't have to look at François-Xavier's face.

"Oh, right. Seems slate can become spongy."

"I thought slate was a rock. How do rocks become spongy?"

"Apparently it starts to delaminate. Anyway, it's not good. I was thinking I would try to patch it with some mastic I found in the shed. It isn't ideal, but it might do in a pinch. I was just up in the attic and there are gaps in the ceiling—I can literally see the sky through a few spots. Somebody tried to minimize the damage with tarps and pots, but that's not going to be enough when the rainwater comes through."

"*If* it comes through."

"Face facts, Nat. It's going to come through."

Alex was right, of course. A light rain wasn't a problem, but the wind-driven water of a severe storm was another story altogether. The last time there was a bad storm, François-Xavier was still here. She had asked him about the roof, and he had shrugged and insisted it wasn't so bad. It could wait.

Why had she listened to him?

"We should empty the attic," continued Alex. "Get the place cleaned up. You don't want to have a lot of lumber lying around. It can attract pests. Are there termites on the island?"

"I'm not sure. That was François-Xavier's venue. I was on the hospitality and decoration end of things. Anyway, the stuff in the attic is just junk. I think I had romantic notions of what might be up there. But there was really nothing."

"Some of the wood might be useful in redoing things around the house."

"We're not back at the compound, Alex," Natalie said. "We don't have to always reuse everything."

"But why not use it, if it's an option? Keep the historic bits. Oh, there were two black outfits up there, too. I brought the dresses down and hung them in the parlor so they wouldn't get wet."

"Thanks. I thought about putting them on display for guests but couldn't figure out exactly how. Maybe I should give them to the museum."

"Hey, while I was online I also read your blog. Looks like we've had a nice visit."

"Well . . . we *have*. Haven't we?"

"Of course. It's just that . . . when you experience it in person, then read about it online like that, it seems different."

"It's part of my job, you know," said Natalie. "It's part of what I do, as an author, a *motivational* author. I create this online presence. It's based in the truth, but it's not entirely real. It's not a deposition."

Alex nodded. "I get it. Anyway, good news about the house: Most things are cosmetic fixes, but you'll need an electrician to update the wiring. But I could install the plumbing fixtures and lamps. Besides painting and cleaning, it's mostly just the roof."

"That is good news," Natalie said, relaxing for the first time in a while. "It all seemed so overwhelming. Do you think we could have the guesthouse ready in six weeks, in time for the Festival of the Gallizenae?"

"A licensed electrician probably wouldn't need more than a few days. The roof might take longer. I'm not really sure. But again, you really need a professional. Could you ask the scumbag's family for money, maybe?"

"No point; they don't have any. But I just got some other good news: My agent sold the film rights to *Pourquoi Pas?*"

"Someone's making a movie out of your book? That's amazing, Nat. Congratulations."

"Well, that remains to be seen. Someone bought the *option*, but in the long run not many movies actually get made."

"Still, that's pretty cool. You don't seem very excited about it, though."

"I would be, but I feel like . . . I feel like a fraud. I mean, no one's going to make the movie when they learn the real ending to my story, will they?"

"It's not over till it's over," Alex said. "How can anyone know the real ending, until you die?"

Natalie smiled. "Now you sound like Dad. But—"

She was cut off by the sound of the front door opening and a man's voice calling out, "Hello? Anyone home?"

Jean-Luc came into the kitchen wearing a bright yellow slicker over his suit.

"What do you think?" he asked, holding his arms out and turning around like a little boy showing off his new school clothes.

The sisters exchanged glances and smiled.

"That looks perfect," Natalie said. "You are every inch the islander."

"I am prepared for the storm," said Jean-Luc.

"You certainly are," said Alex.

"I bought a few other things," he said, holding up a bag. "A striped Breton shirt, of course, a pair of jeans, a couple of T-shirts. I haven't located a long-term rental yet, but with Monsieur Gilbert Le Guen on my side, I feel sure something will be discovered. Oh, and I brought you something," he said, reaching into his bag.

"Jean-Luc, you're already paying me a good sum to stay here. You don't have to give me a gift, too. Save it for yourself."

"I am afraid that would not be a good idea," he said, and held out a bundle wrapped in white paper. "A nice, plump chicken and some fresh vegetables. The shop owner had a shipment this morning. It would be my pleasure to cook for you."

"That's so nice of you, Jean-Luc," began Natalie, "but—"

"Scared to let someone else in the kitchen?" Alex said. At Jean-Luc's confused look, she added, "Nat's a famous chef."

"I'm really *not*," Natalie hastened to say. This was a common misconception, and one that her publisher had exploited. "François-Xavier's the real chef. I'm merely a decent cook."

"In *Pourquoi Pas?* it sure sounded like you knew what you were doing."

"Wait," said Jean-Luc, looking back and forth between the two women. "Natalie . . . you are the author of *Pourquoi Pas?* It seems there is nothing but surprises for me here at the Bag-Noz! I know this book! And you, Alex, will you turn out to be a famous actress? Or do you hold some other intriguing secret?"

He gazed at her a second too long.

"Don't be ridiculous," Alex said, with an annoyed shake of her head.

"But, of course," Jean Paul said, flustered, turning back to Natalie. "You are the famous Natalie *Morgen*! Your book was fascinating."

"It's a good read," said Alex, sounding like a proud older sister.

Natalie gave her a side-eyed glance. "You said I spilled all our family secrets."

"You did," said Alex. "But it's still a good book."

"At least I changed the names."

"But that means . . ." Jean-Luc stared at Alex. "You are the 'Diana' in the book?"

"How did you guess?" Natalie asked.

"Because of course Alex"—he blushed—"reminds me of her."

"Reminds you of who?" asked Alex.

"Isn't it . . . ?" Jean-Luc looked back and forth between the two sisters. "The name 'Diana' was a reference to the Roman goddess of hunting, was it not?"

"I'm not up to speed on my Roman goddesses," Alex said. "I thought you named me after Princess Diana."

"Why would I name you after Princess Diana?" asked Natalie.

"I had no idea. That's why I was confused."

"Jean-Luc's right," Natalie said. "I called you 'Diana' in the book because you were so good at hunting."

"I'm . . . I guess I'll take that as a compliment."

"Anyway," said Natalie, "enough talk of royal princesses and Roman goddesses. Why don't I cook us all some dinner?"

"If you would grace us with your cooking," said Jean-Luc, "I would consider myself the most fortunate man in the world."

"Nat, to your knives and saucepans," said Alex.

"All right. But I insist the two of you stay and keep me company," said Natalie. "Jean-Luc, would you pour us some wine?"

"I would be honored," Jean-Luc said, and began looking through the bottles on a small wine rack in the corner of the kitchen. "Do you have a preference?"

"You choose," Natalie said. "Something to go with this lovely chicken."

"What can I help with?" asked Alex.

"How about some chopping?" Natalie handed Alex a wooden board and a sharp knife, and tossed her an onion from the bag of groceries Jean-Luc had set on the counter. He had purchased the ingredients for a classic French *mirepoix*: carrots, onions, and celery.

Natalie noticed that Alex wielded the knife clumsily, which surprised her, given Alex's aptitude with weapons when it came to more lethal pursuits.

"So, what's on the menu?" asked Alex.

"Let's see . . . ," Natalie said. Moving around the kitchen felt good, made her feel in control. "Jean-Luc, I know Alex would be happy with anything. But do you have any particular likes or dislikes?"

"I am very amenable," said Jean-Luc.

"Why am I not surprised?" murmured Alex. "Hey, Jean-Luc, did you know Nat can butcher a rabbit in under twenty?"

"Oh!" exclaimed Jean-Luc. "I remember that part in the book! That was a very evocative scene."

"We had an unusual childhood. But now I buy meat from the store, like every other normal person."

"That's too bad," said Alex. "I've never gotten used to the sanitized version of everything in the modern grocery store."

"People don't like to be reminded of guts and nastiness," Natalie said. "At least, my readers don't."

"Some of them might," Alex said.

"Like I told you, no one wants to hear about smelly fish or rising seas," said Natalie, clenching her jaw. "People read my book to escape from their worries and concerns, like I used to do when I lost myself in the fantasy world of cookbooks when we were kids."

Jean-Luc had been trying to follow this exchange, clearly unsure how to interpret the tense undercurrent but picking up on the tone. "I do love cooking," he said to change the subject. "But I am pretty basic. What is it that you like about cooking, Natalie?"

Natalie paused to form her thoughts. "I think it's because cooking is all about culture. Want to learn about a society and its people? Take a look at what they eat and how they eat it. Making older or less tasty cuts of meat palatable by adding salt and pepper, for example. Way back when in France, there were no chili peppers or other kinds of strong spices, so the chefs in the great châteaus created intricate sauces to make bland meat more flavorful."

"I never thought of it that way," said Alex. "Cooking isn't my forte, to put it mildly. And I confess that I may have skipped some of the book's cooking sections, so I need a refresher. What are the 'five sauces' I keep hearing about?"

"The list can vary, but basically it's béchamel, velouté, espagnole, *sauce tomate*, and hollandaise," said Natalie.

"And this being France, I imagine they're all based on butter?" asked Alex.

"Surprisingly, no. Béchamel is a simple roux—flour whisked into hot milk or some other dairy to make a white sauce. Have you ever made macaroni and cheese or chicken potpie?"

"I've made mac and cheese. But it came in a box."

Jean-Luc reared back, looking vaguely appalled.

"Hey, it was cheap and it was quick," Alex said. "And it tasted good, too."

Jean-Luc shook his head.

"Sometimes I cut up a hot dog in it," Alex added, just to see the look on Jean-Luc's face. "Now, that's some fancy eatin'."

"You are teasing me now," Jean-Luc said, a skeptical look on his face. "You did not do this."

"I *am* teasing you," Alex acknowledged with a smile. "But I *did* add the hot dogs."

Natalie chuckled. "Anyway, if you *had* made either macaroni and cheese or chicken potpie from scratch, you would know that the base of both dishes is a béchamel sauce. By itself, béchamel is quite bland, which is why it is usually cooked with other ingredients and not used as a finishing sauce." *I might not know how to fix a front step or a slate roof,* Natalie thought, *but I can whip up a béchamel without breaking a sweat.*

Jean-Luc piped up: "Velouté was the first sauce I learned. I remember, I was so proud when I got it right. It took forever, as I recall."

"A proper one can take a long while," Natalie agreed. "Most French cooking requires time and patience to allow the ingredients to meld and transform."

"So what's a velouté?" Alex asked.

"It's a light roux made with a clear stock, such as chicken, turkey, or fish. The name is derived from the French word for 'velvet,' so it's supposed to be very soft and velvety to the tongue. It's usually served over fish or poultry that has been prepared in some delicate method, such as by poaching or steaming."

"May I pour us some wine?" Jean-Luc asked, having opened a bottle and allowed it to rest. "Now all we are missing is some music. On a night like this, cooking with two wonderful women, I feel we should be listening to Édith Piaf or Serge Lama."

"Sorry. We don't have a music collection, and my little computer's speakers are an offense to the ear," Natalie said.

"I believe I may have a remedy to that," Jean-Luc said. He disappeared for a moment, then returned with his phone and a small speaker system. "Does anyone have a request?"

"I vote for Édith Piaf," said Natalie.

"I see you are a woman of old-fashioned taste," said Jean-Luc. "I approve of this." The kitchen was soon filled with the strains of *"Non, je ne regrette rien."* "So, we were discussing sauces. What is next?"

"Then there's espagnole," said Natalie, "which is a basic brown sauce. It's made from beef or veal stock, tomato puree, and a browned *mirepoix*, which is the mixture of carrots, onion, and celery that you're chopping up there. All thickened with a dark brown roux. This sauce is sometimes used as the foundation for *boeuf Bourguignon* and demi-glace."

"I've heard of *boeuf Bourguignon*," said Alex. "But I've never had it."

Natalie and Jean-Luc gaped at her.

Alex chuckled. "It wasn't on the menu out at the ranch."

"That does it," said Jean-Luc. "Tomorrow night, I will bring home some beef and a good Burgundy for *boeuf Bourguignon*, assuming Natalie would be willing to make it for us."

"I'd be happy to," said Natalie.

"So what is it, exactly?" Alex asked.

"It's beef stew. Really, *really* yummy beef stew," Natalie said. Tonight she had decided upon a simple chicken fricassee, which involved slowly sautéing the chicken and the *mirepoix*, then adding wine and cream, parsley, and thyme. The aroma of sautéing onions wafted up from the stove, perfuming the kitchen and making her stomach growl.

For the first time in a very long while, Natalie felt relaxed, filled with confidence. She knew what she was doing as she moved around the kitchen, adding just the right amount of an ingredient at just the right time. When Natalie first transitioned from merely reading cookbooks to actually putting those skills to work in the kitchen, she felt as powerful as a witch mixing her magical potions. Why had she stopped?

Because François-Xavier took over. He was a classically trained chef, and she had ceded the cooking to him without a second thought. Then after he left, she had been too dispirited to cook for herself.

"What's the next one?" asked Alex. "We're only up to three sauces, and you know me: I hate unfinished lists."

"*Sauce tomate.* Unlike more modern-day tomato sauces, the classic French tomato sauce is flavored with pork and aromatic vegetables. And then hollandaise is the last one. This is the only one of the five mother sauces that is not thickened by a roux. Instead, it's an emulsion of egg yolk and melted butter."

"That sounds pretty basic," said Alex.

Jean-Luc shook his head and smiled. "It is basic, but it can be difficult because the emulsion can easily 'break.' The trick is to make a stable mixture of two things that normally don't blend together."

"And you put that on eggs Benedict, right?" asked Alex. "Even I've had that."

Natalie nodded. "Or drizzle it over asparagus, that sort of thing."

"Do you have to become an expert in all five sauces to cook French food?" asked Alex, popping a small piece of carrot in her mouth.

"Well, yes, but there are others as well, such as a *beurre blanc,* or a white butter sauce, and a brown butter sauce. . . ."

"And pretty much anything soaking in butter," Alex suggested.

"You are obsessed with butter, I am thinking," said Jean-Luc.

"Nat, whatever you're doing at the stove over there smells incredible," said Alex, inhaling deeply. "Jean-Luc, you should have seen us growing up: poor Nat trying to make our very questionable food palatable. No such thing as butter in our house in those days."

"I remember reading about that," Jean-Luc replied. "You were very young to be doing things like butchering and cooking."

"In our family everybody had to pull their weight and contribute," said Natalie. "Cooking was something I could do. Actually, it was the *only* thing I could do. And now, *voilà*, we're ready. Who volunteers to set the table?"

They ate by candlelight at the small breakfast nook in the kitchen, savoring their wine and the meal, swapping stories, comparing Jean-Luc's childhood in Paris to their upbringing in the mountains of Northern California, and discussing the relative merits of Bordeaux versus a Napa Zinfandel.

Natalie sat back, savoring her wine and feeling at home in the Bag-Noz for the first time in a very long time.

As she headed to bed, Natalie made a mental note to pay her bills, now that she had money coming in. Plus, she needed to make some calls to find an electrician and a roofing contractor willing to come out to work on the island.

But first she was going to write to François-Xavier and let him know exactly what she thought of him, and to tell him, in no uncertain terms, that she wouldn't take him back, ever. Even if it was an option. Why would she want to be with someone who made her feel bad about herself?

And then maybe she would ask old Ambroisine to curse his new restaurant.

It was past time to step up and tend to her business.

CHAPTER TWENTY-THREE

Alex

*T*he next day, Alex awoke to darkness.

There was no glow from the night-light. Fighting panic, she reached out to switch on the bedside light, but nothing happened. The blackness threatened to swallow her. Her heart pounded as she grabbed for her flashlight.

The beam came on, its reassuring light bouncing off the heavy down quilt she had pulled over her in the night. At last, she realized the wind was blowing so hard, it rattled the windowpanes.

Alex felt a surge of relief. *It isn't just me.* The forecasted storm had arrived and the whole island was dark. She took several deep breaths and willed her wildly thumping heart to slow.

She couldn't see much from the window. The sea was a deep gray, roiling under a canopy of slate-colored clouds. For the first time since she had arrived on the Île de Feme, there were no boats out on the water. She wondered what sailors had done before the days of weather forecasts, and took a moment to imagine being caught on the open ocean in a storm, no land in sight. What it felt like for poor, desperate castaways to catch a glimpse of land, to drag themselves up out of the sea and onto these pebbled shores.

Alex took a deep breath and smelled coffee. And something else. Something yeasty and baking.

She pulled on her jeans, a double layer of T-shirts, and her fleece sweatshirt for warmth, and headed down the stairs.

The flashlight highlighted the spots on the wall that still needed patching. What had Natalie been going through, feeling obligated to François-Xavier's extended family, worrying about money, anxiously awaiting her next advance? She thought of the look of terror on Nat's tearstained face at the end of their father's mandatory exercise, The Trial. Like her sisters before her, when Nat turned ten years old, she was blindfolded and marched far into the wilderness, told to count to a thousand before removing the blindfold, and left to find her way back to the compound on her own, relying upon her survivalist training.

Alex had made it back within three hours. Natalie was lost in the woods overnight.

While working at the dude ranch, Alex once helped a ten-year-old girl to mount a pony and it suddenly dawned on her just how young she and her sisters had been when forced to endure The Trial. It was only then that Alex truly understood: *We were too young. We were much too young. We could so easily have been seriously injured or even died.*

Oh, Dad, what were you thinking? And, Mom, why did you go along with him?

Maybe Nat was right, Alex thought now as she carefully picked her way down the shadowy staircase. Maybe they *had* been raised by a madman. No wonder they were all so screwed up—it was a miracle all five Morgen girls survived to adulthood.

She paused in the kitchen doorway to take in the scene: An old-fashioned gas lamp and several candles cast a mellow amber glow around the room, which was warm and redolent of something baking in the oven.

And Jean-Luc stood behind the counter, like a welcoming, benevolent lord of the manor. He was wearing his new striped long-sleeved Breton shirt and stiff jeans, and somehow the outfit looked adorable on the ex-*fonctionnaire*.

"*Bonjour*, Alex," he said, coming around the counter to kiss her on each cheek. He smelled subtly of soap and aftershave lotion.

"*Bonjour*, Jean-Luc," she replied. "You've been busy this morning."

"Gas appliances," he said with a nod. "A warm oven heats up a kitchen in no time."

"It smells like heaven in here."

"It is nothing compared to the dinner your sister cooked last night. But I made some petite pastries. I believe you call them 'morning buns'?"

He held out a wicker basket and unfolded a kitchen towel to reveal several golden buns nestled within, still warm from the oven.

"Wow, this is . . . this is *so great*."

"I found baking supplies in the pantry—flour and sugar and the like. I hope Natalie won't mind." He set a steaming cup of coffee in front of Alex. "The coffee machine does not work without electricity, but happily we have the simple solution: a drip cone."

Alex bit into a morning bun, closed her eyes, and chewed with single-minded appreciation. This was one holdover from their childhood that Alex was grateful for, one thing that set her apart from others: She did not take such things for granted, ever. Nothing like the constant threat of the change to make one appreciate the ease of modern amenities and the grace of simple pleasures.

They sat in companionable silence in the dimly lit kitchen, listening to the storm brew outside, surrounded by the aroma of coffee and freshly baked bread, the warmth of homemade food, the sensation of plenty.

"We knew the storm was coming," said Alex, licking her fingers. "But it still startled me this morning. It's so dark."

Jean-Luc nodded. "It is. Did you think to close the shutters in your room? I've done so in the public rooms of the house. It helps to keep in the warmth, and makes the house feel . . . What's the word?"

"Gloomy? Eerie? Forbidding?"

He chuckled and sipped his coffee. "I was thinking mysterious. Even romantic."

Alex snorted. "All I can think about is water damage."

"Is it really as bad as all that?"

"We'll see, I guess. It's blowing hard outside, but it doesn't look like the rain's started yet. I'll check the attic once it starts coming down in earnest. I wish I had a ladder that would reach up to the roof."

He frowned slightly. "That sounds dangerous, Alex."

"But you'd hold the bottom of the ladder for me, wouldn't you?"

"Of course I would."

She had been teasing, but the sincerity in his tone made her smile.

They heard a banging from Natalie's room.

Jean-Luc dropped his voice to a whisper. "I hope we did not wake up her."

"'Wake her up,'" Alex corrected him with a yawn.

"Pardon?"

"The phrase is 'I hope we didn't wake *her up*,' not 'wake *up her*.' Though come to think of it, you could simply say, 'I hope we didn't wake her.' It's easier."

"Thank you! I find your language so interesting, though the grammar can be challenging. It does not always make sense, if you ask me."

"I can believe it. Your language is beautiful, and also challenging, at least to me."

"Pas du tout," he said with a quick shake of his head, turning to the sink to rinse the coffee filter. "Not at all. A new language is like any new thing: At first it may seem strange, even frightening, but with time it can feel quite natural, and eventually one learns to stop translating every word and even forgets one is speaking a foreign language. There are times I cannot think of the word in French, but only the one in English!"

"I'm trying to imagine what that must be like," Alex said. "I'm not having any luck, though."

"English is a marvelously flexible language," said Jean-Luc. "You adopt words from other languages easily, make verbs out of nouns, that sort of thing. French is not so flexible. There are many rules that must be followed."

"What about *'le weekend'*?" asked Nat as she walked into the kitchen. "That was imported from English."

"Aaah, but not without resistance! Our scholars worry about such incursions into French, whereas I have the sense that you English speakers enjoy adopting other words," said Jean-Luc, crossing over to kiss Nat on each cheek. "*Bonjour*, Natalie. I hope we did not wake you . . . up."

"Pas du tout," said Nat.

"This is clearly a phrase I need to know," said Alex, repeating it to herself quietly: *"Pas du tout."*

"May I make you some coffee?" Jean-Luc offered. "The machine is not working, obviously, but I found the cone."

"Oh, thank you, Jean-Luc," said Nat. "That would be great. So, one of my favorite French words is *'râler,'* which is sort of like complaining but different."

"Ah yes. This is a way we French have of declaring our ongoing dissatisfaction with the world," Jean-Luc said with a smile as he poured boiling water into the cone of coffee grounds.

"But you always seem very upbeat," said Nat.

"You should have seen me when I was working. I was known to *râler* with frequency. But here on the Île de Feme, what is there to be dissatisfied with?"

Alex chuckled, passing him her coffee mug for a refill. "I've got to hand it to you, my friend. The power's out, the house is cold, and there's soon to be rain in the attic, but you're a happy man."

He rested his hands on the counter and gazed at her with a strange little smile on his face. He ducked his head and in a quiet voice said: "Perhaps it is the company I keep."

CHAPTER TWENTY-FOUR

Violette

*T*ime went by, the weeks fading into months.

The proclamations during wartime grew in number and severity: The only newspaper we were allowed to read was the *Pariser Zeitung*. It was full of anti-British and anti-Semitic propaganda, and harped on a collaborationist theme, extolling the beauties of Paris and the advantages of harmonious relations between Germany and France. The trading of other newspapers or other sources of news and information was strictly *verboten*. The Germans feared information, it seemed to us, and isolated as we were on the island, it was easy enough to keep us in the dark. Henri Thomas, the lighthouse keeper, still had his secret wireless radio, but was able to listen to it only occasionally since the soldiers maintained a constant presence at the lighthouse.

The stories he repeated to us, though, made me wish not to know.

When Bigou, a German shepherd who belonged to Tintin Marie, started to follow the soldiers about the island, it was cause for much speculation.

"C'est un Vichyste," said the islanders, claiming that the dog had become a follower of the Vichy, a collaborator. *"Un collabo."* They joked that it seemed fitting that a German shepherd would return to his countrymen.

Most of the islanders bore up well under the strain, but a few took advantage of the tense situation to indulge long-nursed grudges against their neighbors by passing notes to the authorities at the Vichy *mairie*, the town hall, turning in their neighbors for invented reasons.

Occasionally some of us received *colis familiaux*, or packages of supplies from relatives living in the French countryside who had more access to food. According to rumor, people on the mainland had begun bartering in what was called the *marché amical*, or even buying things on the black market, the *marché noir*.

But on the Île de Feme we had only what we had.

We were issued ration coupons in variable amounts. Children received the least; the elderly were given a little more, while working people—such as the women who gathered the *goémon*—were allotted the most. I was issued a few extra coupons due to my condition. Still, food remained paramount on everyone's mind. It was all we talked about and how we spent our days: tending our gardens, praying for rain, digging in the mud for clams, chipping mussels off rocks, coming up with new recipes for the *goémon*.

We liked to proclaim that we relied on the *système D*, for *se débrouiller*, which means to get by, to manage. We islanders had always been survivors, and we had no intention of changing now.

Very early one foggy morning, I sat on the rocks near the cove past the hotel. I liked the fog, relished the mysteriousness of it, the tantalizing promise of something different and new. I placed my hand on my belly, trying to envision what was happening within me, the astonishing life developing where there had been none. I thought of Salvator, wondered what he was doing. Perhaps sailing in the British navy? Did he wear a smart uniform and order men about? Or did he hop to the orders of his superiors? And what of my husband? Was Marc excited to be a father? I hadn't heard from him in a very long time. Early in the war we had received Red Cross letters from our men in England, but after a while the Germans cut off contact, citing security concerns. A group of women had protested at the *mairie*, but though the mayor agreed with us, he now worked for the collaborationist Vichy government and his hands were tied. So we were left to wonder about the fate of our men.

Sitting on the rock, I felt mesmerized by the flashing of the lighthouse, lulled by the mournful sound of the foghorn and the lapping of the waves.

Not for the first time, I thought about Henri Thomas, tending to the light, polishing the glass, making sure the clockworks were functioning as they must to maintain the constant rhythm of the lamp going round and round and the baritone warning of the foghorn. Ever vigilant, Henri's lopsided eyes were perpetually fixed on our seas.

As I gazed into the ocean mist, an object slowly appeared: a small boat.

I blinked, certain it was unreal, that I was imagining it. I thought of the legends of the Bag-Noz, the phantom boats that sailors spoke of, their ghostly crews forever sailing the high seas.

But as the boat came closer, I could see it was very real, with people, not ghosts, handling the rigging. What was a boat doing here in the cove?

Then two men dropped a package overboard and with wooden poles pushed it toward the shore, apparently familiar enough with the tides to know it would drift into the cove rather than out to sea. And just like that, the boat slipped away, swallowed by the fog.

I remained motionless, wondering if I should try to retrieve the floating package.

Just then Noëlle appeared on the other side of the cove. She did not see me, did not seem aware of her surroundings at all. She waded into the water with a long hook, pulled the package to her, and lugged it hurriedly down the path that led to old Madame Thérèse's cottage, and the lighthouse, before also disappearing into the mist.

Despite the scarcity of food, my belly started to rise. The growing mound fascinated me, and I liked to loll in bed for a few minutes in the morning, caressing it before getting up.

One morning, I felt a flutter. And then another.

"Maman!"

My tone must have alarmed my mother, because she rushed in from the kitchen, wiping her hands on one of the linen dish towels *Mamm-gozh* had embroidered with images of tiny mermaids, fish, and shells.

"What is it, Violette?" she demanded. "Are you all right?"

I nodded, my eyes full of tears. I sat up in bed, leaning back on one elbow and placing my hand on my belly. *"Feel."*

She set her still-damp hand on the soft lawn of my nightgown.

"It's moving," I said, letting the tears fall. "My baby is moving."

My mother smiled. "It is the quickening. It's a good sign to feel it so early. It means he is a very strong boy."

"Or a very strong girl."

"Perhaps. But why are you still in bed? Get dressed and help me in the kitchen. We have to set out breakfast for the Germans."

The presence of so many officers lodging in our house, for whom we now cooked regularly, meant my mother and I had more to eat than most of our neighbors. Packages of pork chops, horsemeat, chicken, and fish, all meant for the soldiers, arrived on the ferries

along with huge sacks of flour and potatoes. Our mouths watering at
the smells, we prepared stew and fish pie as well as Breton specialties:
kig ha farz, meat with a buckwheat stuffing cooked in a bag in broth,
and *lipig*, a sauce of butter and shallots that made me want to faint.
We ate pork with *graisse salée*, and *ragoût dans les mottes*, a kind of
lamb stew braised for hours over a smoking fire. We were cooking old
mutton rather than tender spring lamb, but none of that mattered:
We were eating.

My mother despised having to nourish our enemy, even though it
meant we ourselves were fed. So, more and more, I took over her
tasks, jotting down my own notes in the cookbook.

I could not in good conscience eat my fill while so many others
went hungry. The families of the men who went to England, and
those without homes large enough or nice enough to lodge the Germans, suffered the most. The Île de Feme had a long tradition of sharing. If a fisherman was unlucky, those who had a plentiful haul were
expected to share their catch. It was the way it had always been.

So I began to set aside small quantities of the food we were told
to cook for the German officers: a few potatoes, hard heels of bread, a
little sugar. Sometimes I would fix an extra plate of food, as though I
had forgotten how many we were serving that evening. I would slip
the food into my apron pockets, or cover the plate with my shawl, and
set out to visit the neighbors. Their faces, lined with worry, were always gruff with suspicion when they answered their doors; they were
wary and jealous of the fact that my mother and I had enough to
share. But they always accepted the food.

One night I was slipping out the back door when I heard Rainer's
voice. The officers, Rainer included, rarely ventured into the kitchen,
seemingly honoring our feminine domain.

"Madame, please. *Attendez*—Violette, wait, *s'il vous plaît*."

It was the "please" that did it. I stopped but did not turn to face him, tightening the shawl around my shoulders as though seeking warmth, while in actuality hiding the plate I was holding.

"Madame," he whispered, catching up to me. His eyes glanced at the bulge under my shawl. "You are going to get caught. As I've told you, I do what I can, but I am not in charge here."

There was no point in denying it. "What would happen if I got caught?"

He hesitated. "I don't know. Things are a bit different here on the island, but elsewhere . . . things are getting difficult, Violette. You don't know what is happening."

"How could I? You've taken our radios and newspapers, even our mail. How are we to know what's going on?"

"What you need to know right now is that I'll do what I can, but I don't know how far I can protect you."

Our eyes held for a long moment. I could feel the plate, intended for Madame Spinec and her four hungry children, growing cold.

Finally, I nodded, and spoke to him in his language:

"Ich verstehe." I understand.

CHAPTER TWENTY-FIVE

Natalie

*A*lex announced she would start the repairs on the interior walls since it was storming outside, and Jean-Luc immediately volunteered to give her a hand. Natalie decided she should get some work done as well.

She thanked Jean-Luc for the coffee and carried it into her office, closing and locking the shutters over the door and window.

Natalie thought back on the first time a storm took out the electricity and François-Xavier had hauled out the old-fashioned hurricane lamps. The lamps cast a mellow golden glow, softening the hard edges of the Bag-Noz. François-Xavier built a fire in the parlor and they basked in its warmth, drinking a bottle of wine, making plans, telling silly jokes. She had been so glad to be here on the island with him, safe from the awesome power of the storm outside, away from the big-city distractions and François-Xavier's oh-so-urbane Parisian friends, who always made her feel small, whether they meant to or not.

Natalie shoved those memories aside and took her seat at the desk. She had a couple of hours' worth of battery at least. She positioned her fingers over the keyboard.

So. Write, Natalie.

Nothing. She had nothing to say. This was getting ridiculous. Not to mention frightening. She had written that last piece, about the kite, but she wanted to write something other than more stories from her childhood. Was her odd family history the most interesting—the *only* interesting—thing about her?

She realized she was clenching her jaw.

Back when she was on tour promoting her memoir, Natalie used to declare that there was no such thing as writer's block. "The muse arrives on the wings of hard work," she had assured her audience. "You write by sitting your butt in the chair every day, putting in the work. You make your own luck."

Where was that confidence now?

Her mind wandered, and Natalie sat back and gazed at the closed shutters, imagining her windswept garden. She should probably make sure Bobox was okay, had everything she needed. Natalie pulled on her rain slicker and boots, grabbed the can of grain, and hurried out to the shed. Bobox was sitting on her roost and clucked softly at Natalie as she entered.

"Hey, sweet girl. You're already tucked in, aren't you? Pretty smart, for a chicken. Wait. . . . What's this? You made an egg!"

The pure tan oval was slightly smaller than an average chicken's egg. Natalie took it, scratched the hen's neck, patted her crazy white feathers, shook a little more grain into her trough, and made sure she had fresh water, then shut the shed door tight against the winds.

Back in her office, she set the egg on her desk and gazed at it for a moment, pondering the fact that chickens laid eggs even without a rooster present to fertilize them. Were they hoping for a miracle?

Focus on writing, Natalie.

She could hear voices from the kitchen, a low murmur of conversation barely intelligible over the building storm. Jean-Luc and Alex, one a lifelong French bureaucrat and the other a survivalist and Western ranch hand, nonetheless seemed at ease with each other, as if they had known each other for years instead of two days. What was *that* about?

Hearing them talking in the other room was annoying. But it shouldn't be. When she was writing her memoir, she had met her daily word count no matter where she was: in a crowded café or a busy Parisian park, or in their noisy atelier on the Right Bank, where François-Xavier thought nothing of entertaining friends and acquaintances late into the night. She hadn't been distracted then; she'd been inspired, whether by the muse or something else entirely, and had felt compelled to write. To be sure, she had sweated over some passages and there had been more than a few frustrating days when the words just didn't come out the way she wanted them to. But overall it was as if the ideas had been waiting impatiently, eager to be expressed, made into words on paper. And now . . . nothing.

Finally, she forced herself to write a passage about the Île de Feme. If nothing else, she could always post it on social media:

> The Bag-Noz guesthouse used to be run by two sisters, Violette and Doura. They dressed in black, from their boots to their winged *coiffes*, in the traditional island garb known as the *robes noires* and the *jibilinnen*.
>
> What must their lives have been like? Today a storm has blown out our power, and I am huddling inside, seeking shelter with my own sister, and we

have taken in our first official guest. All we need to do is pull on their *jibilinnen* to re-create the past—do you suppose we would stir up any ghosts?

Her hands hovered above the keyboard, and she wondered whether to simply spill the beans: to post on her website that her sister had arrived and that, like the sisters Violette and Doura before them, they would work together on the Bag-Noz. And to confess that François-Xavier had left.

But she chickened out and focused instead on the storm:

The islanders fear the storms; of course they do—they have an innate respect for the sea, and realize they might yet be inundated, their land and homes taken over by the ocean as they were in 1896 and 1927, when they were forced into their boats, fleeing for the safety of the mainland. But they came back, and by and large they celebrate when the dark clouds arrive. They welcome the rain with the deep passion of a people with no other natural water source. The deluge feeds the gardens, fills the cisterns with the fresh, clean water that sustains life itself. Sure, in the modern day a water tanker can bring over potable water from the mainland, but as *Tonton* Michou would say, "Nothing tastes sweeter than rainwater."

Natalie shivered. Although it was August, the cold winds and rain seemed to permeate the old stone of the house, and the air carried a frigid chill.

The kitchen had been nice and toasty. Maybe she should move her computer to the kitchen table, try writing there. Maybe the problem was that it was *too* quiet in her study, too isolated. But Alex and Jean-Luc might ask questions, wonder why she was joining them, ask to read what she had written. She didn't want to have them notice that she wasn't writing much at all. She kept thinking about that scene from *The Shining*: "All work and no play makes Jack a dull boy." She shivered again. If it was this chilly already, and the storm hadn't even hit with full force yet . . .

She should light the fire in the parlor so they would have another warm room to hang out in. That was the least she could do.

Natalie got up and went into the parlor, where she found Alex kneeling in front of the hearth.

"Hope this is okay," Alex said as she began crumpling newspaper and setting it on the fireplace grate. "I inspected the chimney yesterday; it's a little sooty but otherwise good to go."

"That's great. Thank you. I was coming in here to do that myself."

"This should take the chill off," Alex said, reaching for some kindling. "Soon as I'm done here, I'll go up and check the attic. The rain's just starting. We should make sure the tarps and the pails are well placed so as to minimize the damage."

"Where's Jean-Luc?" Natalie asked.

"In his room, I think," Alex said. "We'll get started on the walls soon."

The room was lit with candles and an oil lamp, and Natalie noticed the two black dresses hanging, specterlike, from the bookshelf.

"Can you imagine wearing a uniform like that every day of your life?" Natalie asked.

"I was thinking about that," said Alex as she placed small pieces of lumber atop the kindling in the form of a tepee. "I mean, you know I'm not partial to dresses. But I pretty much wear the same thing every day anyway."

"But that's your choice. Imagine if you had to wear just one thing."

"At what age did they start wearing the *jibilinnen*? Was it a rite of passage, or something along those lines? I saw a photograph of two girls in the album and they're not wearing them."

"I really don't know. We could ask the curator at the museum."

"And when did they stop wearing them altogether?" Alex took a wooden match from the box on the mantel, lit the newspaper, and watched the fire spring to life. She repositioned the metal fireplace screen and stood, wiping her hands on her jeans.

"Agnès told us her aunts wore them until they passed, which was a few decades ago," said Natalie. "But I think World War Two brought a lot of changes. Some of the old women continued to wear the dresses, but you only see the *coiffes* in regional festivals now."

"This one's about my size," said Alex, holding one of the dresses against herself. "What do you think?"

Natalie smiled. "I never figured you for a fan of vintage clothing."

"I'm not. But I keep thinking of the woman who wore it and what her life must have been like. *Tante* Agnès mentioned that the sisters lived here together. Were they widows?"

"I don't think so."

"Wasn't it unusual at the time for women not to marry?"

"Probably in some places, but a lot of men died in the war, and they lived on an island. There may not have been many eligible bachelors to begin with. Or maybe they were inspired by the Gallizenae and simply took the occasional sailor as a lover."

"Maybe so. Oh, hey, I looked through the rest of that box—the one that had the photo album? Check this out." Alex handed Natalie a small journal marked *Livret de famille*. "It's like a genealogical chart listing the family members."

"Yes, just about every French family has one," Natalie said as she flipped it open. "Cool. I knew it was around here somewhere. I should keep you around just to find things, Alex. You're amazing."

"All I did was unpack a box."

"Still. More than I've done in a while. But look—according to this, the Fouquet family had one boy and two girls, named Rachelle and Violette. But there's no Doura listed."

"That's weird," said Alex. "Agnès said she used to come here to beg for cookies from Violette and Doura, right?"

"Maybe . . . Could they have been together? Back then same-sex partners were sometimes referred to as sisters. Or . . . people here talk a lot about castaways being taken into families, that sort of thing. Maybe—"

They were startled by a loud banging on the door.

"I hope no one's looking for a room at the inn," murmured Natalie as she went to open the door.

On the porch stood Christine in a dripping rain slicker, holding up a plastic bag.

"I bring you fish! A beautiful fish!" She leaned to the side to look past Natalie. "Hello, Alex! In English, this is my favorite fish name: You call it John Dory."

"Oh, thank you!" said Natalie, surprised. Christine rarely dropped by and had never before brought her fish. Natalie imagined she was curious about Alex, or maybe just looking for something to keep her occupied while the storm kept her onshore.

"I think, since you got stuck hosting that Parisian and everything is closed today, you could use this."

"That's so thoughtful," said Natalie. "Come in, out of the weather."

"A little bit of rain doesn't bother me as long as I'm not out at sea in it," Christine scoffed.

"Can we get you a cup of coffee or tea?"

"Tea would be fine," Christine said, taking off her slicker while still on the porch. She shook it and hung it over a chair.

"I'll be right back," said Alex. "I was just about to check the attic."

"Leaky roof?" Christine asked.

Natalie, reverting to form, started to say, *"No,"* but Alex answered too quickly: "Yup."

"I'll go with you, to help," said Christine.

"That's really not necessary," Natalie said.

Christine looked amused. "You think you are the only one on the island with a problem roof? I will bet half the villagers are in their attics at this very moment."

Each armed with a flashlight, they began to mount the dark stairs.

"Hey, Christine," began Alex. "Do you know anything about the women who used to live here at the Bag-Noz?"

She shrugged, sticking out her chin. "Not really. Two old ladies . . . they were *very* old by the time I knew them. Died a while ago. Why?"

"Only one of them is listed as a family member in the *livret de famille*. I've asked about them," said Natalie, "but as much as the Fémans love to gossip about the living, they're pretty reticent when it comes to speaking about the dead. I get the sense that something happened during the war, something people don't want to remember."

"I'm sure a *lot* of things happen during war that no one wants to remember," said Christine.

"We found their *robes noires* and *jibilinnen* in the attic," said Alex.

Christine grinned at the way Alex pronounced the unfamiliar word. "*Jibilinnen?* Truly?"

"If they wore them all the time, why do you suppose they weren't buried in them?" asked Alex.

"A lot of the old people on the island kept death drawers."

"I'm sorry?" asked Natalie.

"Death drawers . . ." Christine trailed off as though searching for a word. "I don't know if there's an equivalent in English, or if you even do this. But here the old people used to keep some clothes, usually their wedding dress or something special like that, and they would write out the instructions for their burial so that when they died everything was ready to go."

"I can't decide whether I find that charming or disturbing," said Alex.

Christine chuckled. "A lot of the old ways are both charming *and* disturbing."

"How is it you speak English so well?" asked Alex.

"Went to university in Bordeaux."

"Really?"

"I studied art history. You are surprised a fisherwoman goes to school?"

Alex smiled. "I didn't realize it took a degree in art history. But then, I've never set foot in a classroom."

"Never?" Christine responded. "I enjoyed school, and after completing my certificate I stayed awhile, working in Bordeaux. But I missed my island and, I suppose, the old ways, as you say: both charming and disturbing."

Natalie paused when they reached the doorway to the attic stairs. She peered up, worried. "When we first got the door off, I had hoped to find some great treasure in the attic, something that might shed a little light on who the women were, or tell some great old tale from World War Two."

"But all you found was a roof in need of repair?"

"Something like that," Natalie said with a grimace, then blew out a breath and started up the stairs. "Here goes nothing."

CHAPTER TWENTY-SIX

Alex

"Looks okay so far," said Nat, sounding relieved.

"The rain only started in earnest a little while ago," said Alex, straightening one of the tarps and angling a pot directly below what looked to be a trouble spot in the ceiling. "Sometimes it takes a while to build up. You know what they say: Water will find a way."

"Yeah, great, thanks," said Nat. "You're not helping my anxiety, Al."

"Wait—do you hear that?"

"Hear what?"

Alex held up a hand and listened intently. She heard the wind and the roar of crashing waves in the harbor, but also something else. A steady tapping.

"That's a drip," Christine said.

Alex nodded and cast the flashlight beam around the attic ceiling, squinting as she peered into the corners formed by the steep angles of the roof. "Where is it coming from, can anybody tell?"

"It's not from over here," Christine said from her position near the stairs.

"I don't see anything," said Nat, flashing her own light this way and that. "I don't hear it, either."

"I do," said Alex. The beam of her flashlight came to rest on the seam where one wall met the floor, next to the built-in bookcase. She crouched down and touched her fingers to it. "Yep. Wet. It's coming from behind here. Hold on."

With one fist Alex started knocking on the wall surrounding the bookcase. Nat and Christine came over to watch.

"What are you looking for?" asked Nat.

"Yes, what are you doing, Alex?" Christine asked. "That is not the way to find a drip."

"Already found the drip," Alex said, feeling around the paneling. "But this looks like . . . Yep, here, see? This old bookcase is covering something up."

"Covering something up . . . ? Like what?" Nat asked.

"Probably just a crawl space, or a void in the eaves," said Alex, taking the boxes off the bookshelves and setting them to one side on the floor. "I'm worried the water will continue down through the walls to the third-floor bedrooms. You don't want to get dry rot. If I can just get in there . . ."

"That bookcase is built in, Alex," said Nat. "We can't pull it away from the wall."

"I know that. I just want to see . . ." Alex crouched down and shone her beam on the bottom shelf. "Aha!"

"What?"

"There's a keyhole."

"A . . . keyhole?" Christine asked.

"I love these!" Alex said.

"These *what*?" demanded Natalie.

"Hidden stuff. There was a bookcase like this at the ranch—it opened onto a little storage area. A lot of older homes have them. . . . I think there's something behind this bookcase." Alex felt like a kid discovering a secret cave. "Nat, do you have that key ring I dug up the other day?"

"In my room," she said with a nod, heading toward the stairs. "Be right back."

After Nat left, Christine turned to Alex and asked in a soft voice: "Your sister, she is okay? *Ça va?*"

Alex nodded. "Of course. Why?"

"I just wonder. She was here all alone until you come. François-Xavier is taking his time in Paris, it seems."

Alex didn't respond. Nat would tell the islanders what was going on when she was ready. Alex just hoped she'd be ready soon.

"Anyway, I have offered to help, but she turns me down," said Christine. "This is a lot, an old house like this. It is a . . . What's the word? A burden."

Alex nodded. "It is a lot, true. I think she—"

She cut herself off as she heard her sister's hurried steps on the stairs. Nat appeared, breathing hard, and held up the key ring in triumph.

"Did you run?" Alex asked, amused.

Nat nodded and smiled. "My exercise for the day. I was thinking—this island was occupied by the Germans during the Second World War. . . . Do you suppose someone might have been hidden back there?"

"What, like someone hiding from the Nazis?" Alex asked.

"Maybe?"

"I have not heard any stories of that sort of thing here during the war," Christine said. "I don't think there were any Jewish people on the island back then."

"Jewish people weren't the only ones who hid from the Nazis," said Nat.

"It's probably just a crawl space," said Alex, who was lying on her side to access the awkwardly placed mechanism, trying one old skeleton key after another.

"Then why would it be covered with a bookcase and locked?" asked Nat.

"Maybe it was a hiding place for valuables, like a safe?" Alex said. "I think . . . Wait! Got it!"

Alex turned the key and the bookcase popped open.

CHAPTER TWENTY-SEVEN

Natalie

$\mathcal{T}$he door swung out to reveal a small opening in the attic wall, about three feet high.

"*Ça, alors!*" Christine exclaimed.

"I don't know what that means, but I think I agree," Alex said, shining her flashlight beam in the opening.

"What do you see?" asked Natalie.

Alex banged her head on the top of the opening and swore under her breath.

"You okay?"

"I'm *fine*," she said, sounding annoyed. "It's probably just a crawl space."

"A locked crawl space? Really?" Natalie turned to Christine. "Is that common in French homes?"

Christine shook her head.

"I'm going in," Alex said.

No surprise there, Natalie thought as her sister disappeared into the black hole, first her head, then her shoulders, then her narrow hips and long legs. Alex always had been the first to explore the unknown, whether it was an unfamiliar trail, a cavern, or a mine shaft. Natalie used to wait behind, ready to run for help, if needed.

"I think we should call her Alex the Adventurous," said Christine with a smile.

"What do you see?" asked Natalie, anxiety warring with the excitement of discovery. Maybe there *were* skeletons in there, and she'd been living all these months with their restless spirits. Maybe *that* was why she felt so haunted.

"Not much" came the muffled voice. "Wait—found something!"

"Rats?" suggested Christine.

Alex crawled out, emerging from the access point butt first. She dragged a large wooden crate behind her, caked in grime and furry with spiderwebs.

"That's interesting . . . ," said Christine.

"Probably something boring," said Alex. "Building supplies or rusty nails or something."

Natalie nodded. "You're probably right."

"No way to know until we open it. Grab that hammer over there and do the honors?"

Natalie pried open the rusty hasp and lifted the lid.

At first it looked a like a mass of feathers and shells. But as Natalie reached in, she realized the bits and pieces were sewn onto muslin. She held one up. Pieces of sea glass were attached with wires, and a fringe was made of streams of muslin in subtle shades of pink, green, and yellow. Under the garments were headdresses and masks, equally bedazzled with shells and feathers.

"Is it a . . . costume?" asked Alex.

"Looks like it," said Natalie, pawing through the contents. "There are several in here."

"*Quel dommage.* I was hoping for a bunch of gold coins," said Christine. "Like in the *Pirates des Caraïbes*. How do you say that in English?"

"Pirates of the Caribbean," said Natalie with a nod. "Hands down the best ride at Disneyland."

"Also at Disneyland Paris. My favorite, too."

"I don't get it," said Alex, staring at the garments. "Was someone who lived here an actor or a singer, maybe?"

"Remember when we were in the cemetery Agnès mentioned that one of the women who lived here was buried in shells. Could this have been her death drawer?"

"But that doesn't make sense. If it was her death costume, she would be wearing it, right?" said Alex.

"True."

"I've never heard of anything like these clothes," said Christine. "Only the *jibilinnen*. It's true there are always rumors on such an island, but nothing that would explain this."

"They remind me of that piece of shell art in the parlor," said Alex. "You know the one I mean, Nat?"

"That's called a 'sailor's valentine,'" said Natalie. "It was here when we moved in. But these are something else entirely."

"*C'est fantastique,*" said Christine, running her hands over the beading. "They are so complex, very detailed."

Natalie picked up a feathered headdress and examined it. "This reminds me of an old-fashioned Vegas showgirl outfit, except made with locally sourced items. Hardly a traditional Breton *coiffe.*"

"Obviously it was for a special occasion," said Alex. "These don't seem like they would have given the *jibilinnen* a run for its money."

"What else is in there?" Natalie asked.

Beneath the costumes they found a stack of embroidered household linens. The fabric smelled of must from being closed up so long, but was in decent shape.

"This is quite a treasure trove," said Alex. "I mean, if you like sheets. Look, they're embroidered with little mermaids and fishes."

Natalie nodded, thinking how excited she might have been to discover these lovely old-fashioned linens just a few short weeks ago. She would have pounced on the sweet tea towels and cozies and pillowcases, imagining using them for guests visiting the Bag-Noz here on her beautiful adopted Île de Feme.

"Wait. There's something else. An old book. Now, that's more my style." Natalie picked it up and turned it over. There was no title on the cover or the spine, so she opened it.

"What is it?" asked Alex.

"It looks like a family cookbook, maybe? Some kind of a journal, with handwritten recipes, some old envelopes, a few printed recipes and pictures cut from magazines . . . and even some drawings and doodles in the margins. How cute."

"There are a few different styles of handwriting," said Alex, looking over her sister's shoulder. "Like different people contributed. It reminds me of Mom's old recipe box."

"It does, doesn't it?" Natalie passed her flashlight beam over a few more entries, lifting the fragile old pages carefully by one corner, trying to make out the different handwriting. The ink faded in and out a little, but by and large was legible. "This is great."

Outside, the storm had become ferocious, the wind doing its best to knock down the thick stone walls of the house. They heard a ripping and a banging as though a slate tile had been wrenched off the roof and flung who knew where.

Christine peered over Natalie's shoulder at the recipes and made a dismissive *tsk*ing sound. "I have no need for more fish pies in my life. The storm, she is getting worse. I should go to my boat to be sure the nets are secured against the wind. Do you need me to help you place the pots to catch drips before I go?"

"No, thank you, Christine," said Natalie. "Alex and I can manage. And thank you so much for bringing the fish! Would you like to come back and join us for dinner?"

"I thank you, but no," Christine said, heading toward the stairs. "After I check my nets I must inspect my own mother's attic for water. *À bientôt.*"

"And we've got work to do, Nat," Alex said after bidding Christine farewell. "Hear that? More drips."

As Natalie was closing the recipe book, a photo slid out from between the pages and wafted to the floor. She crouched to pick it up.

It was a group of German officers surrounded by women in ornate feathered masks and beaded costumes like the ones they had found in the crate.

"Hey, Alex, check this out," Natalie said to her sister, who was already crawling back into the access to the eaves to place a pot under the drip she had found.

"A little busy" came the muffled reply.

Natalie put the photograph back in the book, then placed the rest of the items in the crate.

Alex emerged from the eaves and dusted herself off, and together they positioned the rest of the buckets and spread out more tarps.

"Well," said Alex, casting her flashlight beam up and down to inspect the ceiling and the floor. "It's not great but it'll have to do for the moment. Hopefully this will catch the worst of it."

Natalie nodded. "Let's get that crate downstairs where it's warmer and the light's better."

Just then Jean-Luc called up from the third-floor landing.

"Alex? Natalie? *Tout va bien?* Is everything okay up in the attic?"

"We're fine," said Alex.

"We could use a hand, though," said Natalie.

He hurried up the steps.

"What is all this, then?" he asked, staring at the crate.

"Believe it or not, some vintage goodies from the folks who used to live here. Could you help us carry it down to the parlor?" Natalie said, shivering.

"I would be happy to," said Jean-Luc.

Alex grabbed one end, and Jean-Luc the other, while Natalie held the flashlights. At the top of the steps Alex stumbled slightly, then caught herself.

"You know, it is not all that heavy," Jean-Luc said. "It would probably be better for me to carry it myself. Much easier on the stairs."

"Are you sure?" asked Alex.

He nodded and smiled. "This way I can work up an appetite, since I have done so little all day."

"Okay, but don't trip."

Natalie picked up the winged headdresses and boots and followed Alex, both using their flashlights to show the way. Jean-Luc came last, lugging the crate down to the parlor. Despite his protestations that the box wasn't that heavy, he was breathing hard by the time he eased it down to the floor in front of the fire.

Natalie opened the lid to show him what they had found.

"Costumes?" Jean-Luc said when he saw the contents. "What an odd thing to find. I was hoping for a treasure."

"You're not the only one," Natalie said.

"Any idea what they were used for?"

"I'm afraid not," said Natalie, though judging by the amount of dust on the crate, it had been there for a long time. Might it have been hidden during the war and later forgotten? There had to be a reason it was in that wall. Or maybe she'd read *The Diary of Anne Frank* too many times. As a girl, she had seen parallels between Frank's life of constant hiding and fear, and her own.

"Do you think the items in the crate could have belonged to someone who was deported by the Nazis?" suggested Alex.

"According to what I read at the museum the other day," said Jean-Luc, "there weren't any Jews on the Île de Feme at the time of occupation."

"That's what Christine said, too," said Natalie. "But the Nazis went after a lot of people, not just the Jewish community."

"One of those women had pretty big feet," said Jean-Luc. "This pair of boots is enormous."

"Her dress was large as well," said Alex.

"Healthy lifestyle, maybe, what with all those vitamins in the seaweed," said Natalie as she perused the cookbook. There were numerous notes and arrows, names and dates and even weather reports, all written in an old-fashioned French script. It was going to take a while to decipher it all.

"Now, these are some nice linens," said Jean-Luc, holding up several pieces. "I can imagine the women of the family sitting around the fire, embroidering them."

"They look a bit stained," said Alex, noting a number of rusty-looking spots. "That's a shame."

"Those can often be removed with a proper washing. Old linens were meant to be handed down," said Jean-Luc. "They're quite durable. I would be happy to help launder them."

Natalie looked up from the book. "You're volunteering to do our laundry now?"

He shrugged. "My grandmother left drawers full of similar linens to my mother. I remember helping her launder them while she told me stories of growing up in France after the war. These linens will last many generations, unless . . . What do they call it? *C'est la pourriture sèche.* Is it . . . dry-rotted?"

"Fabrics get dry rot?" asked Alex. "Like wood?"

"I don't know if it is the same process, but yes. Once the rot sets in, there is no saving it."

"How can you tell if there's dry rot in cloth?"

"You take it by both sides and pull hard, like this." He demonstrated. The towel seemed sturdy enough. "If it is rotted, dust will fly and a strong person could pull it apart. This looks good."

Her eyes tired from the strain of trying to read the old, faded ink by the flickering firelight, Natalie decided to take the cookbook to her room to read when the storm passed and the electricity came back on. She removed the photograph of the uniformed soldiers and costumed women to add it to the big leather album in the parlor.

"Check out what else I found in that cookbook," said Natalie.

Alex and Jean-Luc stood on either side of her, studying the strange photograph.

"That looks like it was taken in the Abri du Marin, doesn't it?" said Jean-Luc.

"That's the building where the museum is now?" asked Alex.

He nodded. "I spent a lot of time at the museum my first day on the island. I just love local museums, don't you?"

Natalie had gone to the museum a few times when she first arrived on the island, to learn more about its people and culture. But it had been a while, and she had spent most of her time there learning about the island's ancient way of life, the women gathering *goémon*, and the traditions of lifesaving and salvaging shipwrecks.

"When do you think this was taken?" Alex asked.

"Those soldiers are wearing German uniforms from the Second World War," said Jean-Luc.

"Was there a cabaret at the Abri during the war?" Natalie asked.

"I have no idea," said Jean-Luc. "But I recognize the ceiling beams. You see how they are shaped like this? Also, look at the shape of the windows. You know the island better than I do, of course, but I cannot think of another building that has those windows."

"*Huh.* I think you're right. Before the Abri du Marin became a museum, it was the sailor's hall. Would they have entertained people there?"

"Not normally, I wouldn't think so," said Jean-Luc. "From the research I've done on the Second World War and the island, people were pretty old-fashioned, the women very modest. That was brought up during the inquests."

"What inquests?" asked Alex.

"After the war there were investigations into those who collaborated with the enemy, with some women accused of *collaboration horizontale*—sleeping with the Germans," said Jean-Luc. "In Paris it was common for women to be marched through the streets with their hair shavened as a sign of shame."

"Shaved or shaven," murmured Alex. "Not shavened."

"Thank you, Alex," said Jean-Luc.

"But that seems incredibly unfair," said Natalie. "I imagine the women were simply trying to survive or were coerced in some way."

Jean-Luc nodded. "I agree. I don't believe wartime is known for being fair."

"And you're saying they had inquests about the women here, on the Île de Feme?" asked Natalie.

He nodded. "But nothing was ever proven."

"Maybe that's why the islanders are so reticent to talk about it," Natalie said to herself as much as to them.

She looked up as the storm rattled the shutters and the wind whistled.

"Well," said Natalie, slipping the photograph into the back of the album, "now that we've discovered a treasure *and* a mystery, what do you say we get to work on these walls? I've written about enough for the day."

"You'll join us?" Alex asked. "It's bound to be very exciting: We're going to repair plaster with mesh and mud."

"Mud?"

"Very goopy plaster."

"Ah. Well, lead on, boss. Let's work for a bit, and then I'll rustle up something for dinner."

"'Rassel up'?" repeated Jean-Luc. "I do not know this word."

Alex patted him on the shoulder. "Like cowboys stealing cattle, my friend."

"Ki-yi-yippety," Jean-Luc said with a grin. "I heard that in a movie once."

CHAPTER TWENTY-EIGHT

Violette

I was sitting on my favorite rocks, weary from the morning spent gathering *goémon*, staring down into the pools of water and up at the lighthouse, alone with my thoughts, when I spotted Rainer approaching. He was negotiating the rocky shore carefully and favoring his bad knee.

"It's beautiful here," Rainer said. "Am I interrupting your solitude?"

I shook my head. "It's your island now, after all."

"We both know that's not true." He took a seat on a rock not far from me. "And never fear. We Germans will be leaving, eventually. Whether it will be soon enough to please you, I can't say."

A moment passed. I enjoyed the sensation of the fresh ocean breeze and the gentle October sunshine on my face. But there was a definite chill in the air, making me wonder what to expect in the coming winter. It almost never snows on the Île de Feme, but the violent winter storms and perpetual dampness could be bone-chilling and seem never-ending. Without fresh produce from our gardens, or enough fuel to burn in our hearths . . . it was hard to imagine how we would survive.

"*L'air, la mer, la terre,*" I said. "That's what the islanders say, that we have it all here: air, ocean, land."

"And you don't agree?"

"I love the beauty of the island," I said.

"But your heart is unreasonable."

I smiled. "I suppose so. Sometimes . . . sometimes I feel like I was born with a hollow place inside, and a wind blows through it, just as surely as the wind blows off the ocean. It is as though I can hear my own heart whistling, a hollow place where something is missing."

I stopped, suddenly feeling silly. "I am being foolish."

"Not at all," Rainer said. "I have felt something similar, all of my life."

I studied his face for a moment, to make sure he wasn't mocking me. "What do you do about it?"

"One endures the best one can," he said with a shrug. "I look at the lighthouse and wonder, did God make the lighthouse or create the storms?"

"My *mamm-gozh* used to say that the storms are here to remind us to seek out a lighthouse. She said you couldn't even see the beacon of light until it was dark, and then you couldn't help but see it."

"She sounds like a very wise woman."

"She was. I miss her."

"When did she die?"

"Just before Germany invaded Poland. I think . . . she couldn't bear another war. She lost a son in the last one. She predicted her death, knew it was coming."

"How so?"

"She used to bury things, little charms. Then one day she found them dug up—I'm sure it must have been the island dogs, but she insisted the spells had been broken. That it was an omen."

"Perhaps it was."

"You believe in such things?"

Rainer gave a low chuckle. "I like to think I'm like my father, openminded."

"My father isn't," I said. "Still, I would have gone to fight with him and my brother, if I could have."

"I believe it," he said with a soft chuckle. "Have you had any news?"

"As you know, we haven't had letters from our *Anglais* for quite some time. It is a terrible thing, not to know. It makes us suffer even more than we already do."

We sat for a while in silence. It was strange, being with Rainer. Despite his enemy uniform, despite the fact that I was a married woman, it felt comfortable being with him, as easy as sitting with my brother—easier, actually. It occurred to me that it might not do for anyone to see us together like this, alone, far from the village. But the islanders rarely came out this way unless they were going to the lighthouse or to collect *goémon*. Henri Thomas wasn't a gossip, and we women had gathered the *goémon* this morning.

"My father passed away several years ago," said Rainer. "I suppose it was just as well. He would have hated what the new regime has done to our country. He was very modern in his perspective, very tolerant."

"Like you?"

He nodded. "Like me."

"You mentioned he ran a cabaret. That must have been a fascinating way to grow up. You probably met many interesting creative people. I envy you that."

Rainer glanced around, as though to be sure no one was spying on us. "The Nazis shut down the cabaret. Said it was immoral."

"Why?"

"They have strict ideas about what is 'appropriate.'"

"I only know what little I can glean from occasional newspapers, or gossip," I ventured. "But your leader, Hitler, and his party . . . they seem rather harsh."

He let out a humorless chuckle. "Yes, one could say that."

"And is your mother alive? She must miss you terribly."

He hesitated. "She is still alive."

"Are you . . ." I trailed off, searching for words. "Are you two close?"

"Not particularly, no," he said. "She and I, we're very different people. She never cared for the cabaret, or the artistic life. She has become a devoted follower of Hitler and his ideals."

"And you're not?"

"I am regular army. We are not all members of the Nazi party."

"But I've seen you salute, *Heil Hitler*."

"I want to survive, madame. Surely you can understand that."

"That is something every islander understands," I said.

"May I ask you a personal question?" Rainer asked.

I hesitated, unsure what he might ask, but nodded.

"Why don't you wear the *jibilinnen* and the *robe noire*, like the others?"

I relaxed. "I have always seen myself as a part of the island, but also partly not. I want to go other places, see things other than what is here."

"You want to be part of the modern world?"

"Yes. Or, at least, I *used* to want that," I said, pushing the hair out of my eyes. I tied my hair back with a ribbon while working, but the ocean breeze always undid my best efforts. "Lately the modern world has lost much of its appeal."

"I've seen these rings," Rainer said, touching the ring on my left hand. "So unusual."

"It's called a claddagh. It's a traditional Celtic design."

"Is it true that they aren't always wedding rings? That the way you wear them matters?"

I nodded, switching the ring to my right hand to demonstrate. "The point of the heart facing out, like this, on the right hand, means one is open to relationships. Turned around so the tip of the heart points to the hand means one's heart is taken. On the left hand, the point up means that the wearer is engaged, and down, like this, that she's married."

"You say 'she'—don't men wear them as well?"

I shook my head. "Our men don't wear rings, only the women. It's a Celtic tradition, and we're one of the Celtic worlds."

"Interesting," he said, his eyes lingering on me.

I felt the need to say something in response to the strange sense of closeness I believed we were both experiencing.

"Rainer, I appreciate your friendship, but . . . I have to make it very clear to you that I am a married woman, and even if I weren't—"

He threw back his head and let out a loud bark of laughter. "Madame, you have nothing to fear from me in that regard. I promise you."

The next morning, I found a spot of blood on my underdrawers.

Competing emotions surged through me. This baby was hope; this baby was acceptance. It offered joy to so many, and I had been moved to tears when I felt it move within me. But this child also tied me forever to the island, to Marc, and to a way of life I wasn't sure I wanted.

But it also connected me to Salvator.

I didn't want to worry my mother, so I went to see my sister, Rachelle, who lived with her in-laws on rue du Gueveur. Rachelle was my senior by eight years, had three children, had lost one baby in infancy, and now was pregnant with her fourth. She was still bitter about her husband going to England with the rest of the island men; she thought he should have stayed to take care of their growing family.

Rachelle was a lot like our mother in her approach to life, though she looked more like our *mamm-gozh*, small and dark haired. I was the opposite, taking after my mother in looks—I was slim but sturdy, with honey-colored hair and brown eyes. But I was so much more like my grandmother in personality. Now, more than ever, I understood why *Mamm-gozh* had buried things, hoping to work her magic. I only wished I had paid more attention to her spells and incantations when she was alive, had learned from her the workings of the moon: how it calls the ocean, and bends its arc to come closer to the sea.

"It's usually not a worry," Rachelle said as she served me chamomile tea with a dollop of precious honey. "I had a little bleeding last time, when I was expecting Agnès."

I started crying, appalled at my inability to control my own emotions.

"The crying's normal, too," she said with a sigh. "But then, I'm no expert. Now that *Mamm-gozh* is gone, there is only one person on the island who might know for sure."

"But . . . Madame Thérèse charges dearly for her services."

Rachelle pressed her lips together in annoyance, handed me several coins she had squirreled away, and wished me luck.

Madame Thérèse was the village "cunning woman," the closest thing we had to a doctor. She was ancient. She knew things. I remembered when I was a little girl and announced that my *mamm-gozh* was the smartest woman on all of the island. *Mamm-gozh* smiled and said, "No, *ma petite fille*. Madame Thérèse is a *louzaourian*, a healer. She is the wisest of us all."

When I was nine years old I became very ill and my grandmother brought me to Madame Thérèse. She fed me a wretched-tasting tonic,

easing it along with a spoonful of honey. I cried when my grandmother left me there in her cottage, but Madame Thérèse tended to
me for nearly a week as I tossed and turned and sweated through
sheet after sheet. When the fever broke and I started feeling better, I
learned that Madame Thérèse dealt in the twenty-six sacred herbs,
though she wouldn't tell anyone what they were. I knew some of them
because they grew on the island: vervain, eyebright, yarrow, tansy,
chamomile, dandelion, mint. Others were mushrooms of various
kinds, and there were also ugly, twisted, dried things kept in jars on
her shelves, or hanging in drying bundles from her rafters.

"The herbs correspond to points on the body," Madame Thérèse
explained in response to my curiosity. "Vervain is the head, Saint-
John's-wort is the blood, mugwort at the waist, and so on."

I was fascinated by the herbs, even the smelliest ones, and would
have willingly become her apprentice had my mother not come to
take me home.

Much later I learned that my parents had been furious with
Mamm-gozh for taking me to Madame Thérèse, and that they had to
pay her fee to get me back, as though I were a hostage.

Now I made my way to her small cottage, the House of Meneï,
the only dwelling past the hotel on the path to the lighthouse. Most
of the island's houses are two or three stories; the small size of the Île
de Feme meant we have of necessity built toward the sky. But Madame Thérèse's cottage was but one floor, including a kitchen, a living
room, and a single bedroom. There were few windows to let in the
light, though a large one looked out to the sea. Madame Thérèse was
a woman with no family and no past, and had always been that way.
It was rumored she came to the island as a shipwreck victim, like my
own *mamm-gozh*, though some villagers suggested she was a *morgen*,
a siren, a witch.

Not even the bravest among us, however, dared to say that to her face.

I sometimes left biscuits or a pie on her doorstep to keep in her good graces. It was always business with Madame Thérèse; one didn't stop by for a mere social visit.

I hesitated now, in front of her door on which a large "H" had been painted in red paint. As I reached up to grab the fish-shaped knocker, the original brass finish having turned a chalky blue-green from the brine of the sea, the door opened.

"Violette," she said, her eyes raking over me.

"Madame Thérèse," I replied. "Why is there an 'H' on your door?"

"It stands for '*Hexe,*'" said Madame Thérèse. "They think I am a witch."

"And aren't you?"

She laughed. Madame Thérèse's thin white hair was pulled back and affixed to the top of her scalp with a wooden pin pushed through a leather strap imprinted with an exotic design—probably a gift from a grateful sailor. Her once-piercing green eyes were now foggy and she had lost several teeth. She grew shorter every year; I remembered thinking of her as huge when I was a little girl. I wasn't particularly tall myself, but now I towered over her.

Her eyes slipped down to my belly.

"*Tu es enceinte,*" she said before I had spoken a word.

I nodded.

"You want to be rid of it?"

"No," I said, though a part of me wondered if I was sure. "Of course not."

"There is a problem?"

"I . . . There was blood this morning."

"Come in and tell me about it," she said, opening the door wide.

The house was smaller than I remembered, just one room with a kitchen in the back. A single door led to her bedchamber, and there was a cot in the main room. One big window looked north, and a smaller one looked south. As I remembered, her shelves were full of shells and feathers, old jars and bottles of herbs and dried roots and mushrooms.

Hovering in the background was an adolescent girl named Ambroisine. Ambroisine's father's boat had gone down in a storm before she was born, and then her mother died in childbirth. Madame Thérèse had announced that her breech birth might be a sign that she would be a skilled healer, so when she turned twelve, her grandparents had allowed her to be apprenticed to the *louzaourian*.

"Ambroisine, bring us some of the tea I mixed yesterday," ordered Madame Thérèse.

Madame Thérèse told me to sit at the table in front of the hearth, where she peppered me with questions before handing me several bits of bone and instructing me to splay them out on the tabletop. She then proceeded to "read the bones," and we spoke of blood and periods, of the fluttering I had felt and the date of conception—the things of women.

"We women are tied to our bodies in ways that men are not," declared Madame Thérèse as she laid me down on the cot and palpated my belly, her touch sure and surprisingly gentle. "This is a gift, though it may not always seem so."

"It is the fault of the Germans she is having troubles," declared Ambroisine. Madame Thérèse silenced her with a hard look.

"The child is right, though," said Madame Thérèse. "Our occupiers are like a disease; they make us sick. *Ils nous rendent malades*."

I nodded.

"But you like one of them," said Madame Thérèse. "I have seen you walking with him and sitting on the rocks."

I should have known nothing escaped the eyes of the islanders. Not even the foggy eyes of an ancient woman with few windows.

"He is not like the others," I said.

She snorted.

"I care not what you do, nor with whom," Madame Thérèse said. "Life is pain, and war is worse. Here is my advice to you: When you leave here, you must bring a loaf of bread to the chapel and lay it at St. Corentin's feet."

"Where do I get the bread, madame?"

"That is your burden."

"I understand. But, madame, Saint Corentin's chapel was built on the heads of the Gallizenae."

"You think a little stone building will stop the Gallizenae?" Madame Thérèse scoffed as she pinched two dried leaves from a stem, placed them in her mortar and crushed them with her pestle. She mixed me a tonic, and then a salve for my skin.

"This will help?" I asked. "It is important . . . I think it is important that this child live."

"Why?"

"What do you mean?" I asked, stunned at the question.

"Why is it important that this child live, when so many others die? We sent our sons to war, did we not? As did the German families. Those boys in their uniforms, they are someone's children, too."

I placed a hand on my belly, thinking of Marc, and the happiness in his mother Gladie's eyes when I told her I was expecting. I thought of Salvator, and of the others who had left us. I thought of what they must be seeing in war: the carnage, the terror.

"I want this child," I said with renewed certainty. "It is *my* child."

Madame Thérèse smiled her gap-toothed grin and nodded. "Don't we all, *ma fille*. Don't we all."

She turned back to her counter and mixed something noxious into a base of beeswax and olive oil.

"Don't worry," she said. "Now that the Germans are here, the spirits of the Gallizenae will fill the womenfolk with power, and we will force their retreat."

I wished I could believe her.

"As for your condition, a little spotting is common," she said. "Not all babies live, you know. I have come to believe this is determined at conception: Some take, and some don't. This baby seems healthy enough and should remain so as long as you don't work too hard, and get enough to eat."

As I was about to leave, Madame Thérèse handed me a jar she had filled with the ointment she was mixing. "Bee venom."

"How do I use it?"

"It is not for you, Violette. It is for your soldier's knee. I have seen him limp. If he is a good man, as you believe, he must not let on that he is injured. These Germans, they do not believe in infirmity. They are like a pack of wolves and will fall upon those who show any sign of weakness. Now, let us discuss my fee."

CHAPTER TWENTY-NINE

Alex

*T*he ferry doesn't run during storms, so no grocery delivery today after all," Nat said as they gathered back in the kitchen after washing up.

Alex had been surprised, and pleased, at how steadily Nat worked. She was a little sloppy, but soon got the hang of it once Alex showed her how to neatly apply the mesh and the mud. Between the three of them, they had made short work of the front hall and even started on the dining room.

"Fortunately, Christine brought us a whole John Dory," Nat said, "and we have some greens from yesterday."

"And I have energy bars in my pack," Alex mentioned. "Nobody's going to starve."

Nat cleaned and filleted the fish, then sautéed it and made a quick sauce with white wine and capers. Jean-Luc fixed a salad and arranged cheese and pâté on a plate, while Alex opened a bottle of wine.

As they carried the food and wine into the parlor, Nat grabbed a box of broken matchsticks and an old deck of cards, soft with use.

Alex stoked the fire, and they took seats around a coffee table in front of the hearth, serving themselves from the food Nat laid out on a small side table while Jean-Luc dealt the cards for a game of gin.

"This remind you of anything?" Alex asked Nat.

"You mean playing cards in the storage cellar and waiting for the world to end?"

"Remember? Every damned storm," Alex said. "Mom would say, 'Let's go, girls,' and down we went to sit in the dark. I half expected the sun to turn red and the water to run like blood."

"Where do you suppose Dad got all that religious imagery from?" asked Nat. "He believed in The Change, not the biblical prophesies."

"Probably just stole it from a preacher," said Alex. "The Commander liked a rhetorical flourish as well as the next person. He's many things, but no one's ever accused him of being boring."

"Remember the time Faith didn't come home from town, and Mom thought she must have drowned trying to cross the river, sure the bridge was out?"

"What about the time The Commander started the generator and anybody who touched a metal surface got shocked because the wiring was so bad?"

Nat let out a hoot. "I was afraid to move for days. Electrical work was *not* The Commander's strong suit."

The sisters laughed, though Jean-Luc looked vaguely appalled.

"When I was a child the worst thing I could imagine was when the other children made fun of my haircut," said Jean-Luc. "Waiting for Armageddon seems . . . seems like a childhood without a future."

"Oh, we had a future," said Alex with a sigh. "It was just a grim future for which very few of us would be prepared."

"I always figured I'd wind up as zombie food anyway," said Nat with a shrug, casually throwing a card on the stack and declaring she had gin. "So I wasn't too worried about it."

She looked up to see Alex's eyes on her. "What?"

"I wouldn't have let the zombies eat you," said Alex.

"Thanks," said Nat softly. "I guess. Anyway, growing up expecting the end of the world makes it nice now, since it's a relief to know that a storm might cause a mess, but it could have been worse. It could have been Armageddon."

"I don't know, Nat," said Alex. "With some things, like water damage, one storm can make all the difference. There may be no going back."

"Let it go, Alex, will you?"

"I'm just saying, not every mess can be cleaned up."

Nat caught Jean-Luc's eyes and gestured toward her sister with her head. "Ladies and gentleman, may I present the Grump of Albuquerque."

Alex nodded her head. "I accept your accolades. Except I may have to surrender my title because I'm not sure I'll go back to Albuquerque. Maybe I'll stay on the island and become the Grump of the Île de Feme, give Milo a run for his money."

"Milo? From the café?" asked Jean-Luc, seizing on the new subject. "He *is* rather . . . What is the word in English? Taciturn? Truculent? We say *grincheux* in French."

"Spelled like the Grinch," said Nat, "though it's pronounced like *gransh*."

"Is that where Dr. Seuss got the name from?" Alex asked.

"I have no idea, but I like it," said Nat. "Maybe Dr. Seuss spoke French. There are lots of synonyms for 'grumpy' in French. *Grognon*, for example. I like that one because it rhymes with onion. Or *bougon* or *renfrogné*."

"What was the other one you taught me this morning?" Alex asked. "Re-lay?"

"*Râler,*" Jean-Luc corrected her. "The 'a' has a little hat over it. *L'accent circonflexe.*"

"You see, Alex?" said Nat. "It's easy. You'll be speaking French in no time. Anyway, Milo might be a little grumpy, but I think underneath it all . . ."

"Sometimes a grump is just a grump, Nat," said Alex. "They're not all the cute guy on . . . What was that show you mentioned?"

"*Gilmore Girls,*" Nat said, blushing.

"I love that show!" said Jean-Luc. "But tell me, do you think the French are grumpy, as a rule? Do you find me that way?"

"You're the exception that proves the rule," Alex replied. "You're the antigrump."

"I agree," Nat said. "I don't think you're a typical example of your countrymen, Jean-Luc. Must have been all those years tucked away in a government bureau, filling out forms."

Jean-Luc raised his wineglass and said: "Then let us lift our glasses to bureaucracy. As they say in Bretagne: *Yec'hed mat!*"

"*Yec'hed mat!*" Nat and Alex joined in.

CHAPTER THIRTY

Natalie

*H*ours later, the storm still raged. The card game had been abandoned, another bottle of wine had been opened and consumed, and the conversation had turned philosophical.

"It wasn't all that bad, for a divorce," Jean-Luc said. "I think people underestimate how relaxing it is to be able to live without having to justify one's actions. That was my favorite part of living by myself."

"You felt you had to justify yourself to your wife?" Alex asked.

"It is simply part of living with someone for so long. You do not want to let them down. Or let yourself down," he replied. "I bear Odile no ill will. She raised our son and daughter, and they are intelligent and kind and pursuing their own careers: Marie-Claude is in banking in Toulouse, and Gilbert plays the *violoncelle* as a symphony musician. He supplements his income by giving music lessons—do you have any idea how much just the *archet* costs for the *violoncelle*?"

"What's an *archet*?" Natalie asked.

"I don't know the English word. It is the thing one uses to play the strings. . . ."

"Oh, the bow."

"*Oui, c'est ça.* This *bow*, she is very expensive. My son asks for money rather frequently."

"And you give it to him?" Natalie asked.

"What are fathers for?" said Jean-Luc.

"*Our* father might argue that point with you," Alex said.

"I do not mind helping him. Gilbert's passion reminds me that a fervent love for something exists. I suppose that is the true work of an artist, to remind us of such things."

"Speaking of instruments," Alex said, turning to Natalie, "do you play the piano?"

Natalie shook her head. She had tried picking out a few tunes when they first arrived, but had never learned to read music. François-Xavier used to cover his ears, teasing her about her lack of musical ability.

"Too bad. When we were kids, Nat used to play the recorder," Alex explained to Jean-Luc. "She was the only one in the family with any musical talent."

"Wow, that was a long time ago," said Natalie, her head nestled on a pillow, searching the ceiling for drips. "I haven't picked up a recorder in years."

"I always loved it when you played."

"You did?"

"Of course I did. That's one of the reasons I left those candy bars for you."

"What are you talking about?"

"During The Trial, remember? Surely you found the candy bars I left for you."

Natalie blinked. "I didn't realize you were the one who left them there." Natalie could still taste that sweet chocolate on her tongue. She had been so hungry, and so frightened, and to stumble across a cache of candy bars in the forest was to experience a true miracle. Nothing, not even the ambrosia she had tasted in the finest patisseries in Paris, could compare to that one moment of sheer bliss.

"Who did you *think* left you food?" asked Alex, adding more wood to the glowing embers in the fireplace.

"I . . . I honestly didn't know. I suppose . . . I thought some hunter might have hidden the stash for later. I always felt a little guilty that I had stolen it from someone."

Alex gave a low chuckle. "Well, if you *had* stolen it, Dad would have congratulated you for it. All's fair when it comes to the End Days."

"You know what this house needs?" said Jean-Luc suddenly as he started shuffling the discarded deck of cards.

"A new roof?" suggested Alex, picking up the cards Jean-Luc was dealing.

"One-track mind," muttered Natalie.

"A cat," said Jean-Luc. "Can't you just imagine one curled up in front of the fire?"

"Dad didn't believe in pets," said Natalie. "'Animals are for eating,' he used to say."

"What about Bobox?" asked Alex. "I saw you checking on her when the storm began."

"She's not a pet. We're . . . more like acquaintances who mind our own business. We're on the same wavelength."

"I found a dog in a junkyard," said Alex. "After you left, Nat. Named him Buddy. Dad never liked him, but he tolerated him."

"I didn't know that," Natalie said. "What happened to him?"

"Hit by a car after I moved to New Mexico," she said flatly.

"I'm so sorry," said Jean-Luc, gazing at Alex. She kept her eyes on her cards. "I had a beloved cat, back in Paris."

"You mentioned that."

He nodded. "I meant to adopt a kitten, but I fell in love with a ten-year-old calico. I named her Dossier, which I suppose is a joke only a *fontionnaire* might find amusing. She had a problem, with inside her ear?" He made a twirling motion with his finger. "She would roam in circles around the apartment, keening softly to me."

"Poor little thing," Natalie said.

"It was all right. She had a good life. Most of her time was spent reclining on a little bed I made her out of a silk pillow. It was silly, I know, but I adored that cat."

"There's nothing wrong with adoring your cat," Natalie said.

"It's just that, for the first time in my life, I felt like I actually had something that was mine, you know? Free and clear. The children were always more Odile's."

"They might come back to you as they get older," said Natalie, thinking how she had grown to appreciate her mother with age. Not so The Commander . . . at least not yet. "It can happen."

Jean-Luc nodded and discarded a jack of diamonds, which Natalie immediately picked up.

"So, what happened to Dossier?" asked Alex softly.

"She lived to be seventeen, but near the end, she was sick, in pain, and I had to let her go." His voice was strained, and a sheen of tears sparkled in the light of the fire. "It was that night, after coming home from the veterinarian's office, I fixed myself a drink, and a bowl of ice cream, and turned on the television. There was a special about the Île de Feme and I was overcome by the notion of visiting. I loved the look of the place, and the lives of those living out on such a seemingly foreboding rock. And the whole story about the men leaving during World War Two, of course."

"But you didn't simply come for a visit," said Alex. "It sounds as though you're planning on staying."

"I suppose I lost my head a bit," he chuckled softly. "You should have seen my boss's face when I told him I had decided to take an early pension and left with no plan more detailed than 'going off to the Île de Feme to see what happens.' I do not know who was more shocked, him or me, or Odile, for that matter."

"That was one influential cat," said Natalie. She couldn't stop glancing over at the cookbook they had found.

Jean-Luc nodded. "She was a great cat."

"Buddy was a great dog." Alex and Jean-Luc shared a sad smile.

Natalie noticed their lingering look. *Interesting.* Maybe this island was more romantic than she thought.

"You know what?" said Natalie, setting down her cards after Jean-Luc won another round. "I think I'm going to try to write a little more tonight. I wish you both a *bonne soirée.*"

CHAPTER THIRTY-ONE

Alex

*R*ain spattered hard against the shutters, which shook and rattled.

"Don't shutters make you feel claustrophobic?" asked Alex.

"Would you prefer I open them?" Jean-Luc asked. "These old windows are not likely to withstand the wind, so it might make it a bit cold in here."

"No, you're right. We should leave them closed," said Alex.

"Would you like a little more wine?" asked Jean-Luc, holding the bottle over her glass, poised to pour but waiting for permission. "I don't suppose I will be able to sleep with this racket, anyway."

"Sure," Alex said.

Alex wasn't much of a drinker, and the wine had made her pleasantly mellow. Usually Alex preferred her own company to being with others, but Jean-Luc was surprisingly easy to be around. And that voice . . . Maybe she should ask him to read for her. She remembered their mother reading aloud to them on special occasions, when they were warm and contented. It was such a relaxing, luscious feeling to be read to.

Jean-Luc grabbed his phone and turned on a playlist.

"Do you know this song?" he asked as a warbling, old-fashioned voice started singing. "It is called 'I Have Two Loves, My Country and Paris.' It's from one of your people, the American Josephine Baker."

"An oldie but a goodie."

"This is a phrase?"

She nodded. "This is."

"I like it. A 'goodie.' Have you been to Paris, Alex?"

She shook her head. "I mean, my plane landed at the airport there, but I came straight here. Well, not straight here, exactly. I got on a bus, and then a train, and then another bus, and then a ferry. . . ."

He smiled. "You really should visit Paris one day."

Not likely, she thought. "Maybe. One day."

"It would be my pleasure to act as your tour guide."

"I thought you were moving here to the island."

"I grew up in Paris and lived my entire life there; I imagine I will visit often. It is a marvelous city," said Jean-Luc as he dealt the cards again. The candle cast a mellow glow on his features, softening their ordinariness. "In her song, Baker sings, *'Ce qui m'ensorcelle c'est Paris . . . doucement, je dis, emporte-moi.'"*

"What is she saying?"

" *'Ensorcelle'* is . . . I don't know the word in English, but when you are under the power of a sorcerer . . ."

"Bewitched?"

"Yes, this is the word. To be witched."

"It's one word, actually. 'Bewitched'"

"Ah. Goodie. She says she is bewitched by Paris, and she asks, sweetly—*doucement*—to be taken there."

"It sounds better when you don't know what the words mean."

He smiled. "I would love to hear more about your childhood."

"Obviously it was unusual, but of course we didn't realize it at the time. It was all we knew. And . . . I know it sounded awful in Nat's book, but it really wasn't all bad."

"What was a good part?"

"I liked learning new skills, and knowing I could take care of myself," said Alex, arranging the cards in her hand. "I'm still shocked at how little most people know how to do."

"I suppose most of us have never needed to hunt for our dinners."

Alex looked at her cards: She had two pairs, and discarded an unmatched king. Jean-Luc's eyes lit up as he snatched it up. Not exactly a poker face.

Note to self: Hold on to the kings.

"Hey, Jean-Luc," said Alex. "You don't have any plans for the next week or so, do you?"

He shook his head. "As I have said, the mayor's assistant is helping me to find longer-term lodging. I am also interested in an organization here that is attempting to address the sea-level rise. I have an appointment with them next week, but nothing else in particular."

"I've been coming up with a to-do list to help Nat finish up the renovations. If it's okay with Nat for you to stay here for a little while longer, would you be willing to keep helping me for a bit? I need another set of hands."

"I'm not certain my hands are very . . . What's the word? Able to fix things?"

"Handy."

"That is a word? *Handy?*" He looked delighted as he picked up another card Alex discarded. "I do love your language."

She smiled. "You know, being handy is something a person can get better at with practice, just like learning a language. And after all, you have those snazzy new jeans."

"Snazzy?"

"Fancy."

"Well, yes, I do feel rather fancy."

"Let's put them to work."

"I might disappoint you," said Jean-Luc. "My wife always said that I was nothing but a *fonctionnaire*."

"That doesn't sound very nice."

"I do not think she meant it nicely."

"Well, you *were* a *fonctionnaire*, but that's in your past, right?"

"You are right. I very much like to be handy. I have always liked to be useful. I have a funny story about this."

"I love funny stories." Alex put down her cards. "Let's hear it."

"When I was a child my mother was called in for a meeting with the teacher. We had an assignment in class to say what we would like to be. Most of the children said lions or birds or a sports star, that sort of thing. I said I wanted to be a washcloth."

"A . . . washcloth?"

"Yes, is that not the word? A flannel? The kind of towel used for washing up."

"That's the word. Why did you want to be a washcloth?"

"That is what the teacher wanted to know. It was because a washcloth is so useful, and everyone needs one."

Alex sat back and smiled. "That's really very sweet."

"Do you think so? They all thought it was odd."

"It *is* odd, but it's also sweet."

He smiled and ducked his head slightly. "And then when I grew a bit older, I decided I wanted to be a butler."

"From washcloth to butler?" she asked with a laugh. "You don't often see that kind of career trajectory."

"I did not know what a butler was, exactly. But after I realized that my dreams of becoming a washcloth were not realistic, I switched to soccer star or butler. Those were my two choices."

"Soccer star I get. But why butler?"

"I like big old houses, and I like taking care of people. And it is also possible that I read too many British novels." He put his cards down with a flourish. "Gin."

"What, already? No!"

He grinned. "I have always been gifted at this game."

Alex laid her own cards out on the table—she was missing only one card to claim gin herself. The oil lamp and candles bathed everything in a soft light. The muffled popping and spitting of the fire, Jean-Luc's hands shuffling the cards with surprising grace. Wind rattled the shutters, making it easy to imagine what it would be like to be out in a storm like this, exposed to the rain and the cold, yearning for the warmth signaled by the golden glow from within the house.

I like it here, Alex thought suddenly. She liked the Bag-Noz, the old stone walls, the briny air, even the occasionally rank fish smell. She felt . . . at home. Warmed by the fire and mellowed by the wine, Alex thought of how lucky she was, ultimately, in this very moment.

She could almost forget about that one thing lurking over her, that one thing she hadn't prepared for.

"Another round?" Jean-Luc asked, shuffling the cards.

She shook her head. "You've won all my matchsticks."

"More where those came from."

"Rain check?"

"Pardon?"

"How about we play tomorrow?"

"Of course. Let me tend to the fire, and then, may I walk you to your door?"

He arranged the remaining wood in the fireplace so that the

flames would die out, and carefully positioned the metal screen to guard against flying embers.

"That should do it," he said quietly, as much to himself as to her.

As they headed toward the stairwell, Jean-Luc carried the oil lamp and she had a flashlight, but the rest of the house was pitch-black.

Alex misjudged the height of the first stair and stumbled.

Jean-Luc reached out for her, and as before, she pulled away.

"*Pardon,*" he said. "I did not wish you to fall."

"No, no, I'm sorry. I—I think I had a little too much wine, that's all."

"Oh, I'm a clumsy sort myself. You sure you want me holding ladders for you? The two of us will make quite the pair."

"I'm willing to risk it if you are," she said with a forced laugh, focusing on negotiating the rest of the stairs without tripping.

When they reached the third-floor landing they paused in the dim hallway.

"Anyway," said Jean-Luc, "I will honored to be your extra set of handy hands."

"Thanks, Jean-Luc," said Alex. "*Bonne nuit,* is it? Or *bonne soirée?*"

"*Bonne nuit.*" He nodded. "Well done. *Très bien fait.*"

They hesitated a moment, as if there was more to say. Then Jean-Luc leaned forward and kissed her on both cheeks, French style. The slight rasp of his whiskers against her cheek, the scent of wine on his breath . . . *Remember this, Alex.*

"*Dors bien*, Alex. Sleep well."

CHAPTER THIRTY-TWO

Natalie

*A*s she had as a child, Natalie climbed into bed with her flashlight and started looking through the old cookbook.

Recipes dominated the pages, mostly for seafood: *huîtres gratinées, moules sauce moutarde, moules panées, gratin de moules aux poireaux, moules farcies.* It was hardly surprising that a cookbook by fishing villagers would focus on different types of fish and shellfish. There were also plenty of recipes for *haricots de mer*, literally "green beans of the sea," by which they meant the *goémon*. Her eyes alighted on *dessert aux algues*, a dessert made with seaweed.

Sounds scrumptious, Natalie thought. *I wonder if François-Xavier will include that on his fancy new restaurant's menu.*

Flipping through the pages, Natalie felt the link to women from another time. In the margins were charming drawings, featuring dresses and shoes. A few photos had been cut out from newspapers and magazines and pasted onto the cookbooks' pages. Names and dates followed many of the entries: *Madame Spinec, 14 Juin 1934. Madame LeRoux, 21 Décembre 1941.*

The last dated entries were from 1945. The end of World War II.

The recipes didn't stop at food. There were also instructions for concocting salves and mustard plasters, various types of teas for treating fevers and abdominal distress, and tinctures for pain and swelling. Some names had numbers listed next to them: *Lazarette, 85x64x93 entrejambe 78; Irmine 97x76x104.* "Circe" was mentioned several times as well. Were these names of islanders?

There were also several miscellaneous notes and letters, and weather forecasts predicting rain. Lots of references to rain and rainwater, as a matter of fact.

This was much more than a cookbook. Could it be some sort of almanac?

Her eyes growing weary from reading by candle and flashlight, Natalie set the cookbook aside, and turned off the light, willing sleep to overtake her.

Having Alex here with her was easier than she would have imagined—and Jean-Luc as well. It was a relief not to feel like she was facing so much all alone. And now that there was some decent money on the horizon, she didn't have to fret about her financial situation.

But she still hadn't figured out what she was going to do. Should she stay on at the Bag-Noz? How would she tell everyone what was going on with François-Xavier? What would she do about her currently nonexistent follow-up to her memoir?

Natalie remembered when she started to write *Pourquoi Pas?* after François-Xavier invited her to move into his tiny Parisian garret. She began without really intending to, merely jotting down a few memories of her stark childhood, which posed such a contrast to her new life, so full of love and adventure and food. Word by word, paragraph by paragraph, she began to dissect and to come to terms with her childhood and how it had, oddly enough, led her to where she was now: living in Paris with a beautiful man, learning the fine art of French cuisine.

But just as her literary career began to take off, François-Xavier's cooking career began to stall. Frustrated by his slow rise through the strict French restaurant hierarchy, he began to get into arguments with the chef, arguments he would inevitably lose. He started drinking too much wine at their nightly parties and calling in sick the next day because he did not feel like working. Natalie believed him when François-Xavier told her he was a true artist whose talents were not being respected or appreciated. He was on the verge of being fired when his family got in touch and begged him to come back to the Île de Feme and make something of the Bag-Noz.

She and François-Xavier had visited the island once, and she had seen it through the eyes of a tourist: the charming stone-and-stucco houses lined up in a sweeping curve along the quay, the children playing on the beach, swimmers in wet suits diving off the point, the *pétanque* games and the folks sitting at café tables and along the seawall, drinking cider. The lighthouse and the strangely twisted rock formations. The gulls and gannets and other seabirds gliding along on the air currents, buffeted by ocean breezes. The sheer romance of living on an island.

Natalie had posted to social media about that trip, shared some of the photographs she had taken of the two of them exploring the island. Her followers loved it all and clamored for more.

So when François-Xavier came home early one day and announced he had quit the restaurant and wanted to accept his family's offer, it was as if fate had intervened. They would leave Paris, move to the island and renovate the historic family guesthouse to include a restaurant where François-Xavier would finally be the chef. It could not have been a more perfect ending for *Pourquoi Pas?*

The thing was . . . it was easy to end a book on a high note. Real life rarely cooperated.

The next morning, as Natalie was pulling on her shorts and tank top, her eyes alit on the cookbook.

Overnight, an idea had begun to take shape in Natalie's mind. Instead of writing the follow-up memoir—the one that was now nothing but a litany of blatant lies about her romantic bliss on the Île de Feme—what if she used this cookbook as a guide, instead? She could fall back on what had sustained her in childhood, and what had brought her fame and fortune and love in adulthood (never mind that she had lost those last two), and she would go back to her roots: the yearning for good food, for the finer things in life. She could follow the recipes in the book, track down the descendants of the women who had contributed to it, write up family stories and vignettes of island life, and add plenty of "food porn" pics.

That sounded good, right? That would sell. Wouldn't it?

On the heels of a surge of excitement over this new idea came self-doubt, low and slinky as a feral cat.

Natalie was less and less sure of what made sense anymore, as if everything she thought she knew and understood had started to fade, melting into something she couldn't comprehend, a watercolor left in the rain. She had not felt this lost since she'd first escaped the compound, hitching a ride to the bustle of San Francisco, and was dropped off on Mission Street, adrift in a foreign land surrounded by sounds and people and a culture she didn't understand. Her knowledge of the world had been sketchy and random, having been gleaned from whatever books she could lay her hands on over the years. She had known so much more than other people about weird topics like butchery, but nothing about things like public transportation or modern conveniences.

Just as she had back then, what Natalie needed now was an entrée, a way to get the families of those who had contributed the recipes to trust her, to open up and tell her stories of their parents and grandparents, the elders who had lived through the war, or heard stories from those who had.

She needed the help of a local.

She thought about François-Xavier's aunts and uncle and cousins, but now that Natalie knew about his Parisian restaurant, she didn't want them asking any questions she couldn't answer. The same went for Christine; she was far too astute to fool with an easy cover story. What she needed was a local who wasn't a relative and who wouldn't ask a lot of uncomfortable questions.

Milo.

Alex had pronounced him a grump. But Alex had always been dismissive where men were concerned.

Milo was handsome, but in a completely different way from the sleek, urbane François-Xavier. He was so *not* what François-Xavier was: He looked like he could hunt down a moose, if need be, while François-Xavier would be lucky to outrun one. Best of all, François-Xavier had never liked Milo.

He was perfect.

CHAPTER THIRTY-THREE

Violette

I worked in the garden alongside my mother, digging in the mud for the last of the potatoes and carrots. We had a few greens as well, some kale and cabbage, but they wouldn't last long. And then we would be dependent on the supplies brought in by boat and on our ration tickets, supplemented only with dandelion greens, nettles, and more *goémon*.

My mother didn't believe in idle chat, so we worked in silence, the only sounds the *scritch* of the shovel in the dirt, the calls of the gulls overhead, and the rumble of the occasional *charette* as it passed on the other side of our garden wall. If not for the deep-seated, simmering terror at the thought of our dwindling food stocks, it would have been quite peaceful.

"There's been talk," my mother said suddenly.

"What kind of talk?"

"You are too friendly with that soldier."

"'That soldier' has a name: Rainer. And he is helping us."

"I saw you came home with a new tea. And you were seen consulting with Madame Thérèse." She fixed me with that look: disappointment but something else as well. Was it fear? "Violette, tell me the truth. Are you trying to rid yourself of the child?"

I let out a gasp, a wave of indignation and self-pity washing over me.

"Just the opposite," I said, turning back to the dirt. "I found a little blood this morning, so I went to speak with Rachelle. She suggested I talk to the *louzaourian*. Madame Thérèse assures me everything's all right, as long as I eat enough."

"That's not likely, is it?"

"We're luckier than most," I said. "Need I point out that it's because of 'that soldier' that we eat meat and bread as often as we do?"

"Watch yourself around that man, Violette. Young men and young women brought together under difficult circumstances . . . it is only natural that things occur."

I straightened to stretch my back and stared at her. My mother wasn't given to such talk.

"You are a married woman, daughter," she continued. "And he is our enemy."

"I am well aware of who I am, *Maman*. And because he is who he is, he can make our lives easier or harder with a stroke of his pen."

I have something for you," Rainer said the next day when we met in the hall. "But you must promise to keep it quiet."

"What is it?" I asked, my eyes searching his empty hands, hoping for a package of meat.

He took two letters from his coat pocket and handed them to me. One was from my husband, Marc, the other from his brother, Salvator.

"Where did these come from?" I asked. "I thought the mail from England was being intercepted."

"There's an old saying: Do not look a gift horse in the mouth."

"This is . . . this is wonderful, Rainer. Thank you. Oh, and speaking of gifts, Madame Thérèse made some ointment for your knee."

He frowned. "Who is Madame Thérèse, and what does she know about my knee?"

"She is our island cunning woman. She knows about medicines, and setting bones, and she is our only midwife. She saw you limping and made you a salve. I'll leave it in your room when I do the laundry."

We heard the sound of boots on the stairs, and I tucked the letters in my bodice.

"Danke schön," I whispered as Hans came toward us, eyebrows raised.

I hurried to the room I shared with my mother and shut the door. Greedily, hungrily, I sank onto the bed and placed both letters atop the quilt, studying them for a moment. I opened Marc's letter first. It was short and chatty, full of details of their journey across the ocean, their landing and attempts to locate and join the French Free Forces. He wrote about their tasteless bully rations, and the passion the English had for tea. He sent much affection and wished me well, stating that he hoped I was looking in on his mother and sister. He expressed, almost as an afterthought, that he was over the moon to meet his baby, and he hoped it would be soon.

I saved Salvator's letter for last. Why had he written me again? I tamped down my guilt over my disloyalty to my husband, my hands shaking as I tore it open.

Salvator's letter was descriptive and lyrical, putting me in mind of Rainer's poetry. He wrote of seeking glimpses of mermaids gliding below the surface of the sea, hoping for the glimmer of a silver tail, and what it meant to be exiled from his beloved France in order to fight for her. He described British naval traditions, how new and different it felt to serve on a vessel that did not seek to bring in a haul of fish. He could see massive schools of sea creatures just by looking down into the cool waters. Salvator had crossed paths with his baby brother once or twice, but they were not serving together. He wrote that he had shaken the hand of *Général* Charles de Gaulle himself, and that the good general had exclaimed that the fishermen from the Île de Feme seemed to make up half the Free French Forces.

As my eyes reached the last paragraph, I thought I detected Salvator hesitating, his pen hovering above the paper, unsure how to phrase his thoughts. Finally, he wrote:

> *I have heard that you are expecting a child. Most of my life people have told me I should be more like Marc: more thoughtful, more attentive, more responsible. I never minded the comparison and was always as proud of him as everyone else. But now, for the first time in my life, I find myself jealous—rabidly jealous—of my baby brother.*

I read and reread those final words, trying to decipher their meaning. Did Salvator mean he was jealous of Marc because he loved me and wanted to be with me? Or that he yearned to be a father himself? Or was there something else, some other possible meaning I had yet to tease out of those words?

It was little enough to hold on to, yet I did, hugging the letter to my heart, and thinking of the man I loved.

I showed Marc's letter to my mother but of course hid the one from Salvator. It wouldn't do for her, or *anyone* on the island, to know that Salvator was writing to me, his sister-in-law. It wouldn't do at all.

"I thought the mail was being intercepted," said my mother.

"It was. It is."

"Then how did you get this?"

When I didn't answer, she let out a long sigh and continued: "Are you going to show it to Marc's mother?"

I nodded. "I'll go now."

"Do me a favor and ask for her recipe for *yout lichon*," my mother said, handing me her cookbook. "And also her *Breton Farz-forn*. Hers is by far the best on the island. We have no milk, and precious few eggs, but perhaps I can find a substitute. And tell her she is of course welcome to any of my recipes."

I took the cookbook and hid Marc's letter in my bodice. Out on the stone walls of the quay, I noticed a large "V" painted in red. V for *Victoire*, I assumed. Who would dare paint such a thing with all these Germans swarming our island?

I had just turned into the first passageway off the quay when a soldier stopped me and demanded my papers. By now most of the occupying troops spoke a few words of French, though they still insisted on speaking primarily German. So we Fémans had learned snatches of the invaders' language—especially when they demanded something.

"*Ihre Papiere, bitte.*"

I handed him my *carte d'identité*. He was young and stern faced, and made a show of looking long and hard at the photograph and then at me. I tried to avoid his eyes, feeling uncomfortable standing so close to him in the tight passageway.

After a long moment he nodded and handed them back.

He gestured with his chin to the book in my arms, then put his hand out for it. "*Was ist das?*"

"*Un livre de cuisine,*" I responded in French, not knowing the German word for "cookbook." "*Des recettes.*"

He flipped through the pages perfunctorily, his eyes moving rapidly over the handwritten recipes. He snapped it shut with a disgusted air and gave me another stern look.

"Keine Gruppen über drei Personen," he said.

This was one of the German phrases we all knew by now: "No groups over three people."

He held up three fingers and shoved them close to my face, repeating: *"Drei."*

"Ich verstehe," I said, rearing back and tried to hide my dislike. Rainer had told me that I had no face for poker.

My heart pounded in frustration and anger when I was at last allowed to continue on my way. That I could no longer walk along the passages I had known all my life without being harassed, that I could be stopped and made to feel foolish and afraid at the whim of a soldier no more than my age enraged me. Still, I knew only too well that it could be much, much worse. Villages had been bombed, and hundreds of thousands forced to abandon their homes in *L'Exode*, the great exodus, as our compatriots fled the violence in the north of the country.

Still, it was beyond galling.

I continued on to 22 rue Saint-Guénolé. My mother-in-law, Gladie, was glad to see me, patting my stomach and fluttering around her kitchen, offering me a bowl of broth, which I accepted with relish though it wasn't yet dinnertime. Now that the morning sickness had abated, hunger gnawed at me constantly.

"Is Noëlle around?" I asked. "I have news."

"Noëlle!" Gladie called down the stairs into the basement. "Noëlle, come see who is here!"

I heard boots on the wooden stairs, and Noëlle joined us in the kitchen, wearing what was now her typical sneer. She had been angry since this war began, and I doubted it would end anytime soon. Our childhood friendship seemed as nothing in the context of what we were dealing with now.

"What are you doing here?" asked Noëlle. "What do you want, besides my mother's soup?"

"Noëlle!" Gladie scolded her daughter. "Violette, pay her no mind."

As before, I noticed ink stains on Noëlle's fingers. As a child she'd had a knack for drawing, often doodling in the margins of her school papers. Now I wondered: What was she up to, down in that basement?

"I have news," I said, presenting Marc's letter.

Gladie cooed and Noëlle's expression softened as they read his words, searching, as we all did, for meaning beyond the obvious.

"Oh, my sweet, sweet boy," Gladie said. "But he says nothing about his brother, my dear Salvator. . . ."

"I bring my mother's kitchen journal as well," I said, feeling a twinge of guilt for not sharing Salvator's letter. But I couldn't. It wouldn't do. "She was hoping you would share your recipe for *yout lichon*, and *Farz-forn*, and says you are welcome to anything of interest."

"Oh, yes, of course," Gladie said, rising to retrieve a pencil and her own recipe book.

"Where did you get this letter?" demanded Noëlle in a low voice when her mother's back was turned.

"It was . . . I don't know," I said. "It simply appeared at our house."

"Oh, I'm sure," she scoffed. "What about the others?"

"What others?" I asked.

"All the letters the other men must be writing. Why haven't *they* magically appeared?"

I shook my head, feigning ignorance.

Noëlle dropped her voice. "I have heard about you and that soldier, the GAST officer."

"What about him? He is living in our house."

"I've heard more than that."

"Then you are misinformed. It is because of him that my mother and I are able to eat," I said, my hand going to my belly. "Able to feed Marc's baby, among other things."

"But he listens to you. He has befriended you," said Noëlle.

"He has been helpful, that is all," I said, glancing at Gladie, who was hunched over my mother's cookbook on the kitchen counter, writing down her recipe.

"If he could get this letter, he can get others."

"I don't think it's that easy. By the way, what were you doing in the cove the other day? I saw you there, in the fog."

"It wasn't me," she insisted.

"You were meeting a boat that dropped something overboard. It was like a Bag-Noz, a ghost ship. It didn't go through the GAST."

"A ghost ship? *Ha!*" Noëlle's fake laugh ceded to a fierce hiss: "Just mind your own business, and get our letters from your boyfriend, Violette. You owe it to my brother, to my mother, and to your people."

Whispers began to follow me as I walked through town, weaving my way down the narrow paths.

Maybe Madame Thérèse said something about seeing me with Rainer on the rocks, or perhaps young Ambroisine had mentioned that I defended him. Or his gentleness toward the islanders had been noted. But it seemed more likely that Noëlle was the source, her anger at the Germans fueling her nastiness toward me.

Whatever the reason, people began to gossip.

I didn't care overmuch. I knew my association with Rainer was innocent. And in some ways it was a relief, the rumors throwing the gossips off the scent of my actual sin: loving my husband's brother.

As I gathered *goémon*, as I stood in line with my ration tickets, as

I fell into bed exhausted and hungry, I thought of Salvator. Would he survive the war? Would *I*? What would life be like in the future, when I gave birth to my baby, the war came to an end, and my husband returned to the island? Would we move into his mother's house, as was the local custom? And what of Salvator? Might he return to our island? My heart sped up at the prospect of our living under the same roof. It would be . . . *exciting*. And impossible.

My unruly heart.

That night, after my mother had gone to bed, I sat in the dark kitchen, reading and rereading Salvator's precious letter by the weak orange light of a single tallow candle, running my fingers over the words, accompanied only by the low, vaguely threatening rumbling of the enemy conversing in the hallways overhead.

I approached Rainer the next time I found him alone, reading in the parlor. Most of the other men had gone down to the café to drink, as they often did in the evenings.

"Thank you, again, for the . . . for what you gave me." I didn't want to say the word aloud, in case anyone was lingering and might overhear.

"Two men with the same last name writing you," he teased as he stood to address me. "I suppose there's a story there?"

"One was from my husband, the other from my husband's brother."

He nodded, still smiling.

"But, Rainer . . ." I dropped my voice to a whisper. "Does this mean you have access to the other letters?".

A cautious look came over his strong features. "What other letters?"

"Letters to the islanders from their men in England. Rainer, please, you must give them to me. It is cruel to leave people not knowing."

He shook his head. "I can't do that, Violette. I know it's not fair, but I can't take the risk. I'm sorry."

"What if . . . How would we even know if one of our men was killed or injured in the fighting? Can you imagine what it feels like, not to know?"

There was a pause, and we heard someone approaching.

"I can't," he said curtly, and turned on his heel and walked away.

The next day I cleaned the rooms and changed the beds of the officers staying on the second floor. Washing the sheets of so many, and hanging the linens on the line to dry, was no small thing. My arms ached as I carried the heavy wicker basket of wet linens upstairs.

The clothesline was suspended across the yard, and was accessed through the window of the room Rainer was inhabiting. I had seen him leave the house earlier in the day, but knocked anyway, just to be sure.

"Hello?" I said, walking in.

The room was so tidy, it was hard to believe anyone lived here. I had always been chastised by my mother for failing to make up my bed, for leaving books and hair ribbons and dirty clothes strewn about. Perhaps it was military discipline, I thought, for all the officers' rooms were tidy. But Rainer's was more so, somehow. The only thing left out was a book on his bedside: Saint-Exupéry's *Courrier sud*.

I crossed the room, threw open the casement window, and began the laborious process of hanging the sheets on the clothesline. My fingers soon grew raw and numb from wrestling the wet linens in the wind off the sea, chilly despite the day's bright sunshine.

I finished at last, picked up my basket, and remembered the jar of salve in my pocket. I left it on top of Rainer's bureau.

And then I thought about what Noëlle had said. The Germans

had no right to keep our men's letters from us. Might they be here, somewhere?

Listening carefully for the sound of footsteps in the hall or heavy boots on the squeaky stairs, I set down the basket and eased open the top drawer of Rainer's bureau. It was filled with shirts and underwear, all carefully folded. But no letters.

Again, I listened for sounds of anyone in the hall. I shouldn't be doing this, I knew; when I was growing up, my mother had often chastised me for my unbecoming curiosity and bullheadedness. What I was doing could be dangerous. But I could not resist, and eased open the next drawer.

This one contained a few assorted papers, and several pairs of folded pants. Under the pants, I spotted a slim volume of what looked like German poetry. I picked it up, studying the unfamiliar symbols and umlauts, some of the words so long, they seemed to take up an entire line. The German soldiers had been frighteningly efficient and well organized, making it easy to imagine their culture was devoid of art and poetry, though certainly that was not the case with Rainer. I tried to imagine what he must have been like as a boy, growing up in cabarets, surrounded by music and dancing and laughter and joy, the world changing around him and forcing him to go to war.

A photo fell out of the book, and I knelt to pick it up. It was a young man, and there was something intriguing about his features, which rendered him more arresting than handsome. It might have been the intense gaze. Though his hair was dark, his eyes were very light, and looked unbearably sad. I turned it over. On the back of the photo was written: *In Liebe, Sascha.*

A sound at the door startled me, and I dropped the book and the photo.

Rainer entered the room and fear surged through me. Despite his kind acts, his poetry and love of lighthouses and a good fire, this German officer was the enemy. He could have me arrested for looking through his things, or even for nothing at all.

But worse than my fear was the look of hurt in his eyes. Rainer had been amiable and respectful, and in most ways a friend. And I had betrayed that trust.

He made a *tsk* sound, and the wounded look gave way to a more neutral expression as he tossed his hat and gloves atop the chest of drawers.

"I did not expect to find you here," he said.

"I was hanging the laundry," I said, gesturing to the window.

"Is that right? And do you make it a habit to go through your visitor's things while hanging the laundry, madame?"

I shook my head.

"What are you searching for? Is it money?"

"No, of course not."

"I see," he said with a nod. "The letters aren't here, you know."

I said nothing.

"Are you working for someone?"

"What? No— Who would I be working for?"

"I don't imagine you would tell me the truth, anyway." He blew out a harsh breath, knelt, and picked up the book and photo. "Please leave, madame. I will bring the sheets to you when they are dry."

"I'm sorry," I said, excusing myself in his language. *"Entschuldigun Sie, bitte."*

"Just go, Violette."

CHAPTER THIRTY-FOUR

Natalie

The storm had passed, but Natalie wrapped the cookbook in plastic bags to protect it from any lingering showers, and pulled on her bright yellow slicker. The raincoat was one of the first things she had bought here; she had found it on sale at the souvenir store Le Caradec. Just like Jean-Luc.

At the café, Natalie peered through the window as Milo came out from the back room and walked toward the bar, looking rumpled and sexy, as if he'd just rolled out of bed. She pushed her hood back, ran a hand through her hair, pasted on a smile, and rapped on the front door.

He frowned as he came to the door.

"*Bonjour,*" she said.

"*Bonjour,*" he said curtly.

The wind blew a wet gust in Natalie's face, and she shivered as a drip of cold rainwater trickled down her neck. "There's something I would like to talk with you about," she said. "And . . . maybe beg a cup of coffee?"

"We're not open yet."

"I understand. It won't take long."

He let out a long-suffering sigh and stepped back, allowing her to come in out of the rain.

She followed him to the bar, watching the muscles of his broad back move under a blue chambray shirt. He started to heat the cappuccino machine. Natalie took off her wet slicker and hung it on the rack, where it dripped onto the tile floor.

"So, I found something in the attic last night," she began, unwrapping the journal.

Milo fiddled with the ground coffee in the little metal cup, tamping it down.

"It's an old cookbook, or a journal of sorts," she said, setting it on the bar. "From what I can tell, it's from the late nineteen thirties, up through the Second World War."

"And so?" he said, watching the coffee machine steam and hiss.

"I was wondering about trying to track down some of the people mentioned in it, maybe speak to them or, if they have already passed, speak with their descendants."

"Why?" he asked over his shoulder. The machine made spitting sounds and a dark liquid began to drip into a diminutive porcelain cup.

Natalie waited to reply, hoping for his full attention and not wanting to shout over the sounds of the machine at work.

He set the cup on a plate, added a small wrapped chocolate on the rim, and placed it on the zinc bar in front of her.

"Merci," she said.

"Je vous en pris," he replied.

She noted that he still used the formal pronoun, *"vous,"* even though they'd known each other for nearly a year. She supposed it made sense; they had never really moved beyond a restaurateur/patron relationship. *I'm assuming a lot, dropping in like this,* she thought. *Isn't that what the French always think about Americans? That we're pushy?*

This was not going the way she had imagined this conversation would unfold.

Milo set his hands on the bar and leaned on them, as though ready to take a food or drink order.

"No coffee for you?" she asked.

"Had mine already. What do you want, Natalie?"

"I was hoping to find some of the families of the people—the women—who might have contributed to this cookbook."

"I repeat: why? Who cares about the old methods of cooking fish? That book is nothing special. There's at least one in every house on the Île de Feme."

Her heart fell. Natalie had been hoping the journal would be her deliverance. It had been hidden in the attic wall. Milo was wrong; this one had to be *special.*

"It's not just recipes, though. There are letters in here, messages. . . . I think it could be really something interesting. As you know, I'm a writer, and . . ."

He shrugged, his eyes wandering back down her body, where the fabric clung to her curves. He had never looked at her that way before. Natalie felt a warmth flood her cheeks. She hadn't noticed a man looking at her like this in a very long time. It felt . . . good. Sort of. Also, disconcerting.

"Why don't you just look them up yourself?" he said, finally turning the book around and flipping through a few pages. "Why do you need my help?"

"Because sometimes I get nervous and forget my French. And you know how people are on the island. They take a while to open up. I thought, since you're a native—"

"So ask François-Xavier to help you."

"He's still in Paris," she said automatically, though she knew it wouldn't be long before everyone on the island knew the truth. *Don't think about that now.* "I'd rather not wait."

"I suppose I could talk to a few people," he said, his rough fingers resting on the letters tucked within the fragile pages of the old journal, nodding as through recognizing the names. "You'll leave this with me?"

"Actually, I wrote out the names of the people I'm particularly interested in," she said, setting a piece of paper on the bar with a list of names: the Spinec family, the Cantés, the Guilchers. "I want to keep the journal just now, read it some more, maybe try out a few of the recipes."

He looked at the list and nodded, then gazed at her for another long moment.

"Sure," he said. "I'll ask around."

By the time Natalie left the café, the last of the rain clouds had passed and warm sunshine was drying the cobblestones and the seawall. The yellow slicker slung over one arm, the cookbook tucked under another, Natalie nodded to acquaintances but let her mind wander as she meandered back to the Bag-Noz, stopping to watch the first ferry of the day pull into the harbor, accompanied by a flurry of seagulls. There was a dolphin that often met the boat, to the delight of tourists and natives alike. Why did it do that? Was it merely curious? Hoping for tourists to drop food? Or was there something else to it?

And what had just happened with Milo? Had he been *flirting* with her?

Natalie unwound the chain on the front gate and let herself into the guesthouse yard, distracted from her thoughts by the site of a frighteningly tall and spindly-looking ladder leaning up against the side of the house, Jean-Luc holding it at the base.

"What are you doing?" Natalie called out.

"Hello, Natalie! Your sister wanted to get a better look at the damage from the storm," Jean-Luc said, as upbeat as ever. "She . . . What's the word? She went right up there, like a little monkey. Skimpered?"

"Scampered."

"Yes! She scampered right up the ladder, your sister."

Natalie took a few steps back and craned her neck to see up onto the roof, hoping for a glimpse of her sister.

"Alex?" she called out. "I hate to be a drag but let me remind you that there are no medical facilities out here on the island."

"What?" came the muffled shout.

"Be careful!" Natalie shouted, then bit her tongue. In the Morgen family, the admonition to "be careful" was considered unnecessary and annoying, and therefore was rarely acknowledged.

"I am rather no help at all, I am afraid," said Jean-Luc.

"Holding the ladder's an important job," said Natalie, distracted not only by the danger posed to Alex on the roof, but by what she was no doubt discovering up there. Alex was right. Natalie should have made the roof her very first priority, no matter what François-Xavier had said.

At long last, Alex came back into view. As she reached the top of the ladder, she grasped it and paused for a long moment.

Great, Natalie thought, her jaw tightening at the thought of what Alex's hawk eyes were fixing on. *Wouldn't want to leave anything out of the inspection.*

Finally, Alex eased her way down the ladder, Jean-Luc bracing it with both hands and one foot planted on the bottom rung. When she finally got back down to earth, she sat down on the ground and wrapped her arms around her knees.

"Are you all right, Alex?" Jean-Luc asked, placing a hand on her shoulder.

"I'm fine," she said. "But I hate to say we really do need a professional. The problems are too extensive to be repaired with a little mastic, as I had hoped."

"I'll make some phone calls, see if I can get on someone's schedule before the rainy season arrives in earnest," Natalie said.

"Good idea. By the way," Alex continued, "while I was looking for the ladder, I ran into what's his name—Uncle Michou?"

"*Tonton* Michou, yes."

"He and Agnès invited us for dinner tomorrow night."

Natalie's heart fell. "What?"

"He said that he and Agnès want the two of us to come to dinner."

"But . . ." Natalie's mind cast around for a reasonable objection. François-Xavier's extended family was all well and good in the abstract, perfect for her blog and her book, but the reality meant sitting for hours over long, drawn-out meals, keeping up the pretense. Even with François-Xavier there, she had felt awkward. His family members were kind and pleasant enough; it's just that she and they had little in common, and so had nothing to talk about. François-Xavier used to complain about having to go to these family meals and quickly grew impatient with the old people. It was one reason he used to cite for needing to "get away" to Paris.

And then he escaped to Paris altogether. Didn't even tell his family good-bye.

Maybe *she* should escape to Paris, Natalie thought.

Wait. Was she becoming like François-Xavier now? Could she simply abandon the Bag-Noz, and the old people?

"But what about Jean-Luc?" Natalie said, casting around for an excuse. "We can't just leave him."

"So we'll bring him with us," said Alex. "I'm sure there will be plenty."

"This isn't California, Alex," said Natalie. "It doesn't work that way here."

"No, no, no, please—do not worry about me. I will be fine," Jean-Luc said quickly. "I have been meaning to try Brigitte's kebabs for days now."

"They have only fish and chips," Alex and Natalie said in unison.

Jean-Luc looked confused but replied, "Then I shall enjoy fish and chips. Natalie is correct, Alex. A dinner invitation is a serious thing."

"There's something else I should mention," said Alex.

Good Lord, now what? Natalie thought. "What's that?"

"They want to know if you'd be willing to do some butchering for them."

"Do some—*what*?"

"The woman at the store—what's her name? Submarine?"

"Severine."

"Anyway, she overheard the two of us talking about it and mentioned it to *Tonton* Michou. He wants you to butcher something for them. Gotta say, he sounded pretty excited."

"But . . . why are you even talking to people?" Natalie demanded. "And *how* are you talking to them? They don't speak English."

"I know a few French words, they know a few English words, and we use lots of gestures. Also, a little tourist kid helped with translation," Alex said. "Anyway, they seem nice."

"They are nice, but—"

"But what?"

"They're nosy."

"They don't seem all that nosy."

"On an island this size, *everybody's* nosy."

"Sorry, Nat," said Alex, pulling herself up to stand by the ladder. "I didn't realize it would be a problem. I can call and say we can't come if you want."

"No, no," said Natalie. "Jean-Luc's right. A dinner invitation is an important thing here. They've probably already placed their grocery order. It would be rude to back out now. Besides, we could ask them about the photos we found."

Alex's eyes shifted to the front gate. "I think someone's here to see you."

Natalie looked up to see Gabriel, a deckhand on the ferry, standing at the gate. Tall and thin, he was handsome in a gaunt sort of way and sported a number of piercings and tattoos, reminding Natalie of the young people she had known in San Francisco what seemed a million years ago.

"Bonjour, Natalie!"

"Bonjour, Gabriel. Ça va?"

"Oui, merci. Il y a des provisions pour vous."

"Ah bon?" Natalie answered. *"Merci. J'arrive tout de suite."*

"Everything okay, Nat?" asked Alex.

"Yeah, he says the ferry brought something for me."

"Groceries?"

"Maybe, but those usually come on the afternoon ferry."

"Need help?"

"No, thanks. I think I can handle this much, at least."

CHAPTER THIRTY-FIVE

Alex

After Nat left, Alex told Jean-Luc she would be right back, went inside, hurried up the two flights of stairs to her room, and closed the door. Crossing over to the window, she leaned on her hands on the deep sill, hung her head, and took several deep breaths.

Being on the roof scared the life out of me. The morning sun had long since dried the slate, so it was no longer slick, but Alex had been petrified that she would misjudge her footing and slip, maybe even tumble off the side. She had spent thousands of hours climbing trees and rocks and cliffs as a kid, negotiating uneven surfaces and dizzying heights as if by instinct. But no longer.

She wasn't *able*.

Who *was* she if she couldn't *do* things?

Alex gazed out at the water. It was a bright day, and the storm had scrubbed the air clean. It was so clear the horizon line was the vivid marine blue of the ocean against the pale robin's egg of the sky. A couple of impossibly fluffy clouds floated way up high, as though painted by an artist who mass-produced sofa-size paintings sold at big-box stores. The waves were dotted with pure white triangles of sails, kayakers hugged the shoreline, and fishing trawlers chugged slowly toward the harbor, their keeps no doubt bursting with the catch of the day.

Alex had always been *able*. Her father would pose a challenge for her—shooting, honing knives, orienteering—and she would excel at it. She thought of the list of skills she had been tasked with mastering, each set of her father's initials a sign that she was worthy, she would survive, she was prepared.

But now . . . Alex wouldn't be able to fix the damned roof, even if she knew how.

Alex came downstairs just as Nat returned, pushing a *charette* filled not with groceries but with packages and cans of paint. Close behind her trotted Gabriel with a similarly laden *charette*.

Nat stopped outside the gate, breathing hard.

"What's all this?" asked Alex as Jean-Luc hurried over to open the gate and help Nat and Gabriel.

"I ordered this stuff ages ago," said Nat, looking irritated as she pushed the *charette* through the gate and came to a stop near the porch steps. "I waited for it anxiously for weeks, then forgot all about it. Typical."

"What is it?"

Nat blushed. "I know a lot of the walls aren't even repaired and prepped yet, but François-Xavier and I worked out a color scheme for each floor of the house. The top floor—your bedroom and Jean-Luc's—were going to be in shades of the sea, blue and green and aquamarine. The second floor in floral shades, buttercup yellow and lilac. The main floor was going to be in shades of cream, but with this wallpaper in the parlor. It's a vintage design. . . ."

Gabriel lingered by the gate, apparently interested in their discussion.

"Very pretty. But what are these?" Alex asked, holding up a plastic-enclosed bundle of cloth in a garish assortment of colors.

"That was supposed to be curtains, for the kitchen." Nat grimaced.

"You chose these?" Alex asked, trying to keep a straight face.

"I swear the colors didn't look like that on the website," Nat said.

"The wallpaper's nice," said Alex, as she picked up one of the heavy rolls, which displayed an ocean theme, with mermaids frolicking among the waves. Against a pale aqua background, a brown woodcut-style of mermaids, shells, and horns o' plenty twisted so the design at first seemed abstract, until you looked more closely and saw the figures.

"It reminds me of the paper in my grandmother's house," Jean-Luc said. "I hung it for her."

Alex cocked her head. "You know how to hang wallpaper?"

"Uh-oh, you're in for it now, Jean-Luc," Nat murmured.

"I do," Jean-Luc said, looking a bit confused. "It was a long time ago, but it is not that difficult. It is mostly a matter of measuring carefully."

"I can also to help," said Gabriel, in heavily accented but clear English.

"Gabriel, is it?" asked Alex. "Thanks for the offer. How can I get in touch with you?"

He gave her his cell phone number and said, "I work on the ferry most days but not Tuesdays and Wednesdays."

Nat, Alex, and Jean-Luc carried the paints and wallpaper into the house, setting them in the dining room alongside other building supplies and random pieces of furniture.

Alex expected Nat to go hide in her office, but instead her sister picked up a broom and started sweeping the hallway.

"I can do that if you want to get back to writing," Alex offered. She might not be able to handle roofs, but she could still wield a broom.

"It's okay. I'm sort of at a crossroads in this project, anyway. Let me ask you something. . . ." Nat paused and leaned on the broom handle, apparently searching for the right words. "You like to read now, right?"

"I like to read some things," Alex said. "Why?"

"Would you be interested in reading a cookbook if it also told stories about the history of the island?"

"I guess," Alex said with a shrug. "I'm not the one you should ask, though. I've bought precisely one book in my life: yours. But why are you talking about writing a cookbook? I thought you were working on a follow-up to *Pourquoi Pas?*"

"I was, but real life isn't cooperating."

"Because Monsieur Scumbag took off to open a restaurant in Paris with another woman?"

Nat winced. "Way to sugarcoat it, Alex."

"Isn't it better to face the truth and move on?"

"Whether it's better or not doesn't really matter since I don't have a choice. The book I proposed and sold to my publisher is not going to have the ending I imagined it would."

"Life can be awfully inconvenient that way."

"But here's the thing: I can't stop thinking about the journal we found in the attic last night. I was up late last night, reading through the entries. There are letters from World War Two, notes about herbal remedies, and a whole Celtic medical system I've never heard of before. It's this really fascinating relic of an entire way of life that's now gone."

"Sounds interesting," said Alex. "So how do you get started?"

"I need to talk to as many islanders as possible."

"Hey, you should bring the journal to dinner tomorrow and ask *Tonton* Michou and *Tante* Agnès about it."

"Maybe. I actually went to talk to Milo about it this morning."

"Why Milo?"

"He's a native islander, knows everyone on the Île de Feme."

"Aren't you, like, sort of related to half the island through François-Xavier?"

"That's the problem. It's all too . . ." Nat left off with a shrug. "Too close, too incestuous, I guess. I was hoping to talk to some of the other families first. And I'm not looking forward to answering a lot of questions about François-Xavier."

"Yeah, sorry again about accepting that dinner invitation. I should have asked you first."

"No, it's fine," Nat said. "I owe them a visit anyway."

"You're going to have to tell them soon, you know."

"I know. I'd just like to get things a little farther along first, that's all."

"Hey, you know what might be fun for dinner tomorrow?" Alex said. "You could make one of the recipes from the journal, see how it turns out."

"As a matter of fact," Nat said, "that's exactly what I was thinking."

CHAPTER THIRTY-SIX

Natalie

The next day, Natalie laid the cookbook on the kitchen counter, noting again the assorted stains, dried splashes, and distinct handwriting of the various entries. It was exciting to hold in her hands such a tangible link to the past. One section was titled *recettes de Mamm-gozh Gladie.* Recipes from Grandma Gladie.

Natalie read a list of ingredients and instructions.

The classic Breton dessert *kouign-amann* seemed as good a recipe to start with as any, she thought, and gathered butter, flour, and sugar. She finally located the heavy mixer and beaters stowed away on a deep shelf beneath the window and hoisted it onto the counter.

Their mother had kept recipes in a metal box, most written on index cards, but by the time Natalie was old enough to read them, the Morgen family hadn't had access to the ingredients. The Commander kept the family on a strict budget, so things like flour and oil were bought in limited quantities. Mostly they ground their own dried corn and used the fat from the animals they hunted, so the Morgen girls grew up eating corn muffins made with rendered deer fat instead of cookies and bread. Still, Natalie loved the way cooking connected her to her mother, and to her grandmother before her, to aunts and family friends whom she had never met.

For tonight, she decided to start with a couple of classic Breton desserts, no doubt the first recipes young aspiring chefs learned at their mothers' elbows.

As was probably true for many if not most culinary traditions, and was certainly so for French food, the type of ingredients was less important than their quality and the way they were used: whipping egg whites into stiff peaks, folding the yolks carefully into the rest of the dry ingredients, the length of time the dough was allowed to rise.

"It smells luscious in here," said Jean-Luc when he and Alex came into the kitchen later that afternoon.

"It's *kouign-amann*, we had some when we ate dinner at Milo's," said Natalie. "And this is *Breton Farz-forn*, which is made with a lot of eggs and rum and raisins."

Natalie was suddenly overtaken with nerves. She had called ahead to tell *Tante* Agnès she would bring dessert, but now she wondered if that had been such a bright idea. What was she thinking, making traditional desserts for people who had no doubt grown up eating them? She should have ordered an exquisite fruit tart from the patisserie in Audierne, like a normal person.

Fueling her doubt was that the *Farz-forn* appeared lumpier than she thought it should, and the *kouign-amann looked* all right but didn't have the distinctive aroma of caramelized sugar that the dish was known for.

"It's a little tough to cook from these recipes," Natalie said. "They don't have any oven temperatures or baking times. They just say things like 'cook till done in a moderate oven.' What the heck's that supposed to mean?"

"Did you compare them to modern recipes, see if they have that information?" asked Alex.

Natalie nodded. "I did. But still . . . the desserts don't seem quite right. This book was a general reference, but probably I should be learning by watching an expert do it."

Jean-Luc looked up from the recipes he was reading. "I do not know much about this kind of cooking," he said. "But some of these recipes seem a little . . . odd. See how they specify to use rainwater? Is that not odd?"

"A lot of it's odd," said Natalie, frustrated "Maybe measurements and all that weren't standardized yet? When did cookbooks start being published? Weren't recipes mostly handed down from mother to daughter?"

"I know that Georges Auguste Escoffier was very influential in France," said Jean-Luc. "He worked with some of the finest hotels, incorporated some recipes from old châteaux kitchens, and helped to popularize haute cuisine."

"But that was at the commercial level," said Natalie. "The everyday cooking, the cuisine most of us are most familiar with, is far more basic and traditionally learned as girls helped their mothers in the kitchen."

"I helped my mother in the kitchen," said Jean-Luc.

"Somehow that doesn't surprise me," said Natalie with a smile. "And I certainly have no problem with it, but I'm talking about back in the day. When this cookbook was written, in the late nineteen thirties and into World War Two, I think everyday cooking was mostly considered women's work."

"I suspect you are right," said Jean-Luc. "In any case, the desserts, they smell good. And I imagine if the amounts are off, the family will inform you of it tonight. We French rarely hold back such opinions out of politeness."

Natalie knew it only too well.

CHAPTER THIRTY-SEVEN

Violette

 *R*ainer remained cool toward me for a long while. At first I assumed it was because I had been snooping in his room, but as the days went by and he held himself apart, I began to wonder if it was something more. He was unfailingly polite to me and my mother, but he smiled less and less. He no longer played his jaunty tunes on the piano, or lingered to chat with his fellow officers, much less with me.

One day I knocked on Rainer's bedroom door. I knew he was in, and hated to disturb him, but my mother had sent me to gather the laundry from the line because the clouds were threatening rain.

He called for me to come in, but when I did he remained sitting on the side of the bed, frowning, a letter in his hands. His usually neat bedroom was in disarray: There were a pair of trousers on the floor, a bottle of wine left uncorked, books and papers scattered over the unmade bed.

"Rainer?" I asked, setting down my basket. "Is everything all right?"

He shook his head.

"What is it? Is it your mother?"

"No, in fact I haven't heard from her in some time. But I just received a letter from a university friend. Things are happening, Violette. Terrible things. In Poland, Romania, Lithuania . . ."

I wasn't entirely sure where those countries were, not being a great student of geography. But I knew Hitler's forces had invaded those poor nations, just as they had France.

"It is worse than anyone thought," he began. "Worse than I could have imagined. The 'work camps' we've been hearing about? The prisoners there . . . they are not simply working for the war effort."

"What do you mean? What are they doing?"

He hesitated. "There is a saying in German, *arbeit macht frei*, that work will make you free. But Violette, the Nazis are putting people to death in these camps."

"I don't understand."

"They are *killing* the prisoners, Violette. Murdering them. And it's not only the men. They're sending entire families to their death."

The thought overwhelmed me. It was hard even to wrap my mind around such atrocities.

"Women, too?" I asked.

Rainer nodded. His voice was hollow when he added: "And children."

We sat for a moment in horrified silence, trying to comprehend what this meant.

"I don't understand the hatred toward people for being Jewish," I said after a long moment. "We all pray to the same God, do we not?"

"It's not only Jews. Anyone who speaks out against the new regime, or anyone the Nazis deem 'antisocial.' Invalids or the mentally inferior. Slavs. Gypsies. Homosexuals."

I shook my head. "But . . . they can't just kill people indiscriminately, without regard to any kind of human decency. That doesn't make sense."

"None of it makes sense. But I suppose that when soldiers begin to murder little children, any hope of decency is long gone."

A long moment of silence passed between us. Only the ticking of the clock, the squeak of *charette* wheels outside the house filled the room.

"Is this happening in France as well?" I asked finally.

Rainer shook his head. "I don't think so. Not yet, anyway. I suppose I could be wrong. There are so many rumors. . . ."

"But you're a soldier. An officer. How can you not know?" I asked, my words tinged with anger.

"I am told the same propaganda as everyone else, Violette. I have tried to learn more from what my friends and relatives write in their letters. But everyone is so cautious these days, afraid to speak out or oppose the Nazi party. Hitler has stirred up hatred in the hearts of many in my country. Not all of us, obviously, but enough. It makes me so very discouraged, and ashamed."

After another long pause, I asked: "What does this mean for you?"

"I honestly don't know. Out here, on the Île de Feme, it is easy enough to convince myself that I'm not part of the problem." He went to stand by the window, looking out over the back garden and beyond to the sea. "Sometimes I think about the men of this island, what it must have taken for them to board their boats and sail away, to leave behind their wives and mothers and children . . . for your husband to leave *you* behind. I wonder if I would have been so brave."

"I believe you are very brave."

Rainer turned and looked at me with the saddest eyes I had ever seen on a man. When he spoke, his voice broke: "I am a coward, Violette."

One day, outside on the quay, there was a scuffle and yelling. A crowd had gathered around, the women in their black outfits looking like an agitated murder of crows, ringing the disruption.

I ran out and down along the seawall. The pale-eyed officer I knew as Hans held two adolescent boys by their ears, pulling them out on the wharf as though intending to throw them into the water. They cried and whined, and one had a bloody nose.

"What happened?" I asked Marie-Paule. "Is that Benoit and little Ronan?"

She nodded. "They were painting V's for *Victoire* on the walls," she answered in a low voice.

"I wondered who was doing that," I whispered, looking around and hoping to see Rainer. "Those little scamps. But what is the officer planning to do to them?"

"I hope just throw them in the sea. Not . . . I hope it's nothing worse."

The tension between Hans and the islanders had been growing. Earlier in the week, Hans had discovered and smashed Henri Thomas's radio, and the only reason the lightkeeper was not arrested was the Germans needed his expertise with the light and foghorn. Hans had also discovered Père Cecil's cache of wine, and requisitioned it for himself and his fellow officers. A soldier capable of stealing communion wine from a priest, the islanders muttered, is capable of anything. But the German's larcenous ways did not bother me nearly as much as the way he looked at me, at all the young women, with a soul-crushing mixture of lust and disdain.

Hans shouted in German at the crying boys. They kneeled at his feet, not understanding what he was saying. Apparently frustrated at their lack of response, Hans drew his leg back as if to deliver a kick, and the crowd of women surged forward.

Just then Rainer came running from the quay. He planted himself in front of Hans, speaking German in a low but firm voice. The only word I recognized was *"kinder,"* which I knew meant "children."

Hans replied angrily, his tone radiating contempt. I couldn't understand him, either, but did hear the word *"Anglais."*

Rainer continued to speak in that quiet, serious tone I had heard before when he was attempting to resolve a confrontation. I wished I spoke German; all I could glean from their argument were a few words with French cognates: *"familie," "kabarett,"* and *"homosexuell."*

The men stared at each other and then Hans barked an order and a young soldier handed him the boys' paint bucket. Hans held the bucket over the boys and poured the red paint over their heads. It streamed down their tearstained faces and dripped onto their chests, like blood.

Now speaking French, Hans suggested the boys jump into the ocean to get clean. And then he stalked away.

Later that afternoon, I spied Rainer out on the shoals, in my favorite spot, staring at the lighthouse.

I clambered over the rocks to join him.

"Thank you, again," I said, "for interceding on our behalf."

He said nothing.

"What do you think Hans was planning to do to the boys?"

He shrugged. "Nothing good, you may be sure of that."

"What did you say to him?"

"I told them they were just children, and he knew very well what mischief children could get up to, especially when their fathers weren't around. His own father was severely injured in the Great War, and was unable to leave his bed."

"He seemed very angry."

"Hans has always been angry, and I fear this war has fueled that anger. But he has put in for a transfer, and I hope he will get it. This island is far too tame for him. He would like to be in Paris, or even on the front. He has always been a man of action."

"You mean a man of violence."

Rainer sighed. "That, too."

"I thought I heard him say something about a cabaret."

He grimaced. "Very good. You'll be speaking German in no time."

"Was he talking about your father's cabaret?"

"Right again. As I told you, the Nazis declared it an 'immoral attraction.' It doesn't mean anything," Rainer said with a shake of his head. "He was just trying to insult me. He knows his commanding officer respects me as a reasonable man, so Hans doesn't want to push me too far, lest I make a case against him."

"Well, that's good, then, isn't it?" I asked.

"Maybe. But if Hans doesn't get his transfer, I will have a target on my back."

We sat in silence for quite some time, both of us looking up at the lighthouse.

I kept thinking of Salvator and how impossible my situation was. Within a matter of months I had gone from being a carefree, headstrong girl desperate to leave the Île de Feme, to a pregnant, clumsy woman married to a man I liked but did not love. What kind of future did I have to look forward to? I was bone-tired of the incessant hunger, of the soldiers and their random provocations and bullying, of wondering what was happening with our men, of this wretched war—the reasons for which I still did not understand.

I teared up. I never used to cry so easily; it made me angry.

"What is it, Violette?" Rainer said softly.

"You wouldn't understand," I said.

"I might surprise you. Tell me."

"I am in love with my brother-in-law," I blurted. Saying it aloud, hearing those words I could not take back, petrified me. And yet I could feel the slightest shifting of my burden, as though the weight of the secret was lessened. Père Cecil always preached that confession was good for the soul, but why would I tell a German soldier, when I never would have admitted these feelings to my priest?

"Your . . . ? Oh my," said Rainer with a shake of his head. "That is something worth crying about."

"I married Marc, but it is his older brother I love. Whom I have always loved. Marc is a good man, but Salvator is that one I yearn for. I can't seem to stop my unruly heart."

"Is Salvator the father of your child?"

"No, oh, no, of course not." I blushed at the very idea, but couldn't keep a wry chuckle from escaping my lips. "That would be an even worse problem, wouldn't it? No, the child is my husband's. And now I am part of a family that includes the man I love, Salvator, but I am forever denied him. I just don't feel the same way about Marc as I do about Salvator, and I can't imagine how I ever will."

"That is indeed"—Rainer paused, as though searching for just the right words—"*difficult.*"

"Yes, thank you," I said tartly. "I am aware of that."

"Wait. I'm not done. Of course it is a problem. But think of it this way: Do you realize how lucky you are, to know whom you love, to be able to be near him, to be related to him in some way, even if not in the ideal manner?"

I let out a sigh, frustrated at my inability to put into words what I had been hiding in my heart.

"You can't know how it feels to love a man when you're not supposed to," I said.

"Oh, but I do."

"I don't mean the way a man loves his brother, or an officer loves his men. I mean romantically, as a woman loves a man."

There was a long pause. Rainer trailed his fingers in a tide pool, not looking at me, but said, so quietly it was as if he were speaking to himself, "I mean the same."

"You . . . What are you talking about?"

He shook his head. "Never mind."

"Rainer, I have noticed that when you speak quietly, it is something important. Please tell me what you meant."

Another long moment passed, but he remained mute.

"When you were arguing with Hans earlier," I ventured, "he used the word *'homosexuell.'* It sounds the same in both our languages."

When Rainer finally straightened and turned to face me, the stricken expression on his face both terrified me and broke my heart.

"That was because of my father's cabaret. Hans resents me and will do anything to discredit me."

"That does not surprise me. But there is more, isn't there?"

He hesitated. "Do you remember that photograph you found in my drawer?"

"From Sascha."

He nodded.

"It was signed *'in liebe',*" I continued. "*'Liebe* means 'love,' right?"

He held my eyes for a long moment, and nodded again.

"You're in love with Sascha? But he's a man."

"Yes, he is."

I had heard of such things, whispered in a crude joke or risqué tale at the café. But I wasn't entirely sure what it meant. That a man could love another man, as a man does a woman? I thought back to my wedding night, and the two nights that followed, and tried to imagine a man in my place. How would that even work?

I cursed my lack of knowledge, about people, about relationships, about sex. Monsieur Saint-Juste kept Gustave Flaubert's *Madame Bovary* and Pierre Choderlos de Laclos's *Les Liaisons dangereuses* in a locked cabinet behind the counter in his store, their forbidden nature making them all the more enticing. He would not allow me to read them, thinking to protect me, but now I wondered whether it would not have been better to have gone into my marriage bed with more information. If only I had been able to read more, to learn more, not just about sexual relations but about the world in general.

"I have shocked you," said Rainer.

"No, it's not that. I mean, yes, I guess I am a bit shocked. . . . I didn't realize."

"You didn't guess I might be in love with a man?"

"I didn't know it was even a possibility. I'm not very worldly, I suppose. Why did you tell me?"

"I'm not sure. I guess because you trusted me with your secret, I thought I could trust you with mine."

"It is a secret, then?"

"Violette," he said, a fierce tone entering his voice, "you must understand: No one can know what I told you. *No* one. People like me are being sent to the camps. If anyone were to find out . . ."

I searched his face. "Why would you be sent to the camps?"

"Being homosexual has been illegal for a long time, but it was tolerated before the war, at least in Berlin. But now . . ." He shook his head. "The Nazis say we are degenerates, not worthy of life."

"But . . . that's *appalling.*" As I said it, I realized: Rainer might wear the German uniform, but he was a victim of this war, just as we islanders were. "I think you're a lovely man."

"Thank you, Violette," he said softly, though he winced at my words.

"And I will never say a word to anyone," I assured him. "*Never.* We shall keep each other's secrets, you and I."

He nodded.

"And Sascha, is he also like you?"

Rainer chuckled. "He is, yes. I mean . . . he returns my affection. I met him at my father's cabaret, as a matter of fact. I occasionally filled in for one of the performers, dressing up as a woman for a show. Sascha plays the piano—much better than I. He's talented and funny, and so very smart. He's not the easiest person in the world, but I've been enamored of him from the start."

"Where is he now?"

"He is still in Berlin. He wasn't eligible for service because of a lung condition. He writes to me occasionally, though not so often as to arouse suspicion." He paused and looked out to sea. "It is a terrible thing, to love someone in secret. To *fear* that person, to fear the love one feels. To fear the response of one's own heart, one's own body. As though one's very nature is wrong, twisted."

"You aren't wrong or twisted, Rainer," I said. "You are simply who you are. I'm no expert, and I suppose I don't know much about the world, but in my eyes, you are a wonderful man."

"But that's just it. . . . I don't know how to explain this to you, or even to myself, but I've always felt more like . . ." He trailed off.

"Like what?"

"I know it makes no sense, but I've never felt more myself than when I dressed up as a woman, in those long-ago cabaret days. But afterward, when I put on my regular clothes, I would feel somehow . . . empty. Wrong. I can't explain it, even to myself."

I gazed at him for a long time, not truly understanding what he was saying but reading the suffering in his face, hearing the strained emotion of his words.

I squeezed his hand. "Rainer, all I know is that you are who you are. And for me, you have made this terrible time of war . . . endurable. It might sound strange, but I wish you would stay here with me on our island of women forever."

I leaned into him. He was solid and warm, and when his arm wrapped around me, I felt safe, and understood, for the first time since my grandmother had died.

"I wish you could have known my *mamm-gozh*," I said with a sigh as I laid my head on his shoulder. "She would have loved you."

As we were picking our way back along the rocky shore, we encountered Hans and two soldiers on their way to the lighthouse.

Hans smiled unpleasantly, his eyebrows raised. He said something to Rainer, and his colleagues snickered.

"So, this one, this one is not as innocent as she seems, eh?" Hans said in French so that I could understand the insult. "But she grows fat with child. Is it yours?"

Rainer fixed him with a cold stare. "You forget yourself, Hans."

"Trust me, my friend, I forget nothing. *Heil Hitler!*"

"Heil Hitler," Rainer answered, returning his salute.

Hans sneered and walked away, laughing and speaking in rapid German with the two soldiers.

"This is not good," said Rainer to me. "This will cause trouble."

"I don't see why. If Hans is trying to say you are a homosexual, this will only help your reputation."

"Yes, Violette. But it will ruin yours."

Rainer was right, of course. I did my best to ignore the whispers, much worse than before, that followed me as I walked through the village the next morning. I held my head high and headed to the shore to collect *goémon*.

Noëlle had gotten there before me, and the women did not greet me with their usual warm *bonjour*s. As I worked, I heard Noëlle utter *Vichyste* under her breath.

"Do you have something you wish to say to me, Noëlle?" I demanded, straightening.

"I have nothing to say to you," she replied.

"Then keep your unkind thoughts to yourself," I said. "Anyone else?"

The women shook their heads and returned to collecting the *goémon*.

Although I had never felt as if I fit in on the Île de Feme, the rejection I saw in the eyes of those whom I had known my entire life cut me to the quick. As the days went on, I read condemnation in the eyes of Marc's mother, and even my own *maman*. But I could not tell the truth.

Rainer felt like the only one on the island who truly understood and cared about me, yet I felt I had to give him a wide berth. He was right. We had been too free, too open with our friendship. Knowing our relationship was innocent had blinded us to the perception that we had sinned.

One afternoon, while I was working in the garden, Rainer approached me. I looked around, worried someone might see us.

"We're alone," he said, extracting a bundle of letters from a knapsack. "These are the letters from the *Anglais*. You must be very careful. If you are caught with them . . ."

I nodded. "I won't be caught."

"But if you are—"

"If I am, I'll say I found them at the cove, that one of the English boats must have dropped them."

"No one will believe you."

"No one believes me anyway. I'm becoming accustomed to it." My neighbors needed to hear from their loved ones. And I needed redemption in their eyes. "I'll carry them in the cookbook, say I'm collecting recipes. What could be less suspicious?"

The islanders assumed I had gotten the letters by sleeping with Rainer. The better sort felt torn: on the one hand, disdainful of my betrayal, but on the other hand, happy to accept the extra rations I brought them and, now, the precious letters. And no matter his uniform, Rainer had shown himself to be a reasonable man, even the staunchest Féman could see that.

November came, and then December. As weeks turned to months, we muddled along. Storms thrashed the island, flooding our walkways, the winds ripping off shingles and occasionally upending charrettes. We were always cold, even when it was not raining. The winds blew off the water, icy and relentless, and collecting *goémon* became even more miserable, our hands chapping from the salt and the cold.

As I visited neighbors, I continued to work on the cookbook, now with renewed interest. My mother approved of my collecting recipes, so it was something we could do together, at least. And it gave me an excuse to visit the neighbors, most of whom by now seemed to have made peace with the fact that, although I was sleeping with Rainer, he was helping us. We soon realized that we could pass messages back and forth through the cookbook I always carried with me.

And whenever I was stopped in the pathways I would produce my papers, but the young soldiers were uniformly dismissive of a cookbook, something so trivial, so feminine. They never looked closely at the "recipes."

One day, my ankles swollen, feeling awkward with my growing belly, moving around the kitchen, cooking for the officers while making notes in the cookbook, I wondered: Had I become my mother, just one more island woman bound forever to this rock? And was it such a bad thing?

My unruly heart.

CHAPTER THIRTY-EIGHT

Alex

*A*lex loved everything about dinner that night.

It reminded her of the rare occasions when the family visited The Commander's parents, who lived in a regular ranch house with a real indoor toilet and hot water and soft beds and frilly curtains and little ceramic figurines. Alex's very favorite part of that house was the family photos hanging on the walls, which gave her an appreciation of the past and a suggestion of the future. Living on the compound, in The Commander's world, was all about surviving the here and now. There was no time to be sentimental about the past or hopeful for the future.

After Agnès and Michou greeted them at the door with smiles and kisses on both cheeks, Agnès showed Alex around the main floor, with its crowded but neat living room and dining room.

Agnès's house was similar to the Bag-Noz: Most of the big houses on the island had been built in the eighteenth and nineteenth centuries of stone from the same quarry. But where the Bag-Noz was very much a work in progress, Agnès's home had a warm and lived-in look, with lace curtains in the windows, the rooms crowded with old furniture, tchotchkes, and framed paintings of the island.

Alex knew it was tedious for Nat to have to translate everything, especially since Agnès and Michou thought nothing of talking over each other and rarely paused to take a breath.

Luckily, joining them for dinner was another couple, both of whom spoke some English: Severine, whom Alex recognized from the grocery store, and her husband, Ismael, a portly, red-faced fellow with an easy laugh.

"We have one more guest coming," said *Tonton* Michou. "But she always runs late."

Just then Christine walked in without knocking, saying, "I heard that, old man. I had to shower off the fish guts, you know. I thought you'd appreciate that."

Tonight the fishing boat captain was wearing clean jeans and a T-shirt under a blue button-down shirt, her feet in sneakers. Had Alex seen Christine walking down the street in downtown Albuquerque, she would never have guessed she was French.

"*Voilà*, the Americans are here!" Christine proclaimed, greeting everyone with kisses on the cheek. She handed Agnès a blowsy bouquet of roses and hydrangeas, which the older woman rushed to put in a pickle jar and set on the dining table.

They sat around a small table in front of the fire for aperitif, during which Christine insisted everyone taste Uncle Michou's home-brewed mead, which the French called *hydromel*.

"I've heard of mead," Alex said. "But I've never tasted it. What is it?"

"It's fermented honey and spices," Christine said. "It'll keep you going on long, cold nights."

"I'll bet," Alex said. The mead was extremely sweet and not especially to her taste, but Alex enjoyed the tiny little glasses in which it was served, which made her feel as if she were in a dollhouse.

"I wanted to show you all a few things we found at the Bag-Noz," Natalie said, passing around the photo album and the cookbook.

Agnès and Michou were particularly interested, making little *hm-mm*s and *oooh*s as they looked through the pages.

"Do you recognize anyone in the album?" Alex asked.

"One or two, of course," said Agnès. "This is Violette and Doura in front of the Bag-Noz, but you knew that. And this might be my cousin Jacques, but it's hard to tell. . . ."

"We had a question about Doura," said Natalie. "Everyone says she and Violette were sisters, but there's no Doura listed in the *livret de famille*."

"Oh! *Que diable . . . ?*" said Agnès, pointing to the photograph of the uniformed Germans in a cabaret. "What is this one?"

"We were hoping you could tell us," said Alex.

Michou leaned over one shoulder to see, and Severine peered at it from the other side.

"Do you recognize where that photo was taken?" Nat asked.

"It looks like the Abri du Marin," said Michou.

"That's what our friend Jean-Luc thought as well," Alex said. "Was the Abri a café of some sort during the war?"

Agnès shook her head. "I've never heard of such a thing."

"Do you recognize any of the women?" Nat asked.

"Not with those masks, certainly. But they can't be Fémans, can they, dressed like that?" Agnès asked Michou. "Of course I was too young to remember anything from the war years. And Michou was not even born. So we are perhaps not the best ones to ask." She passed the photo album to Severine. "Let me see the cookbook. Oh, this looks like one from my mother right here," Agnès said, delighted.

"Look, she put in her recipe for *Strïmpous de mamm-gozh*. I should make that for you one day."

"What is it made of?" Nat asked.

"Pork, prunes, onions, tripe—specifically, three pork stomachs and the large intestines."

Nat translated the ingredients for Alex.

"Mmmm," Alex said, and Christine laughed.

"What do you think these numbers mean?" Nat asked, referring to the digits next to several women's names.

"They look like measurements to me," said Agnès. "You see? '*Entrejambe soixante-dix centimètres.'*"

"But . . . *entrejambe* would be an inseam, right?" said Natalie. "So it's not for a dress?"

Agnès shrugged and shook her head slowly.

"We also found two *robes noires et jibilinnen*," said Alex. She had looked up how to say this earlier in the day and tried her hand at the French. *"Nous avons trouvé aussi deux robes noires et jibilinnen aujourd'hui."*

Agnès hooted in delight and beamed at Alex.

"Did you ever wear the *jibilinnen*, *Tante* Agnès?" Alex asked, with Nat's translating help.

"Non." Agnès shook her head. "After the war it fell out of fashion. The young people then . . . we weren't interested. We never learned *Brezhoneg*, and we didn't wear the *jibilinnen*."

"My sainted mother did," said Michou, his eyes misting. "Until the day she died."

"Can you tell us anything about the feathered costumes in the photo taken at the Abri?" asked Nat.

Michou and Agnès both shook their heads.

"Could the women be dancers brought in to entertain the German soldiers?" suggested Ismael.

"That would make sense," said Nat, "though it doesn't explain why we found the costumes hidden in the attic."

"The only one on the island old enough to remember would be Ambroisine," said Agnès. "She's at least a hundred years old, if she's a day."

"I've heard Ambroisine is a little . . . hard to approach," Nat said. "But she's related to Milo, and he's agreed to help me try to track down some of the people who contributed to the cookbook."

Eyebrows rose slightly on every face around the table.

"Really? Milo?"

"You don't need Milo," said Christine. "*I'll* introduce you. She loves me."

"Why would she love you?" Nat asked.

Christine grinned. "There is no 'why?' Only 'why not?'"

Nat smiled. "And what do you mean by that?"

"Only that there isn't a house on the island into which I'm not welcome. Except for the Telesphore house, but they don't count."

The others nodded and sipped their mead.

"What happened at the Telesphore house?" Alex asked, intrigued. "Or should I not ask?"

"A misunderstanding involving a haddock and a . . . How do you call this? A wrench, the kind where you change the *truc-machin-chose* . . . ?" Christine turned to Nat. "How do you say *truc* in English?"

"Thingamajig."

"So this story involves a fish and a wrench and a thingamajig?" Alex asked.

"The details do not matter," said Christine with another wave of her hand. "The point is, Ambroisine is not my grandmother, but I adopted her. And I have learned a lot from her. She's a healer, you know. Learned from the old *louzaourian*, the Celtic healers."

"I've never heard of them," Nat said.

"We don't have a real doctor on the island," said Christine. "Ambroisine has stitched up more men than Dr. Frankenstein."

Tante Agnès announced that dinner was ready, and they all got up from the little table in front of the fire and moved to the slightly larger table at the other end of the room.

Dinner was simple: They began with *rillettes de maquereaux à la moutarde*, or mackerel rillettes in mustard sauce, served on small pieces of toast. This was followed by *cotriade*, a kind of fish stew, accompanied by fresh crusty baguettes.

"I've been meaning to ask," said Alex. "Why is the guesthouse named after a ghost ship?"

"There are always legends of ships that wander the seas," said *Tonton* Michou, wiping crumbs from his chin. "I remember hearing those stories when I was little."

"There are a lot of myths alive and well here on the island," Agnès added. "It is because we live so close to the ocean, and many things are not explainable."

"I heard that during the Second World War, any boat approaching the island was supposed to come into the harbor for inspection and to pass customs," said Severine. "But sometimes boats or ships would appear at night or under a cloak of fog and approach the other parts of the island. The Germans were not able to catch them."

Nat translated all of this to Alex, who raised her glass in a toast. "To the Bag-Noz who defied the Nazis."

"*Yec'hed mat!*" cheered the others.

"I like the legend of Ankou," *Tonton* Michou said. "Ankou is the coachman of death—if you hear his carriage pull up, you know you're going to die. Especially on the Île de Feme, since we have no carriages here."

"Perhaps on the island Ankou drives a large *charette*," suggested Ismael, and they laughed.

"My favorite is the story of Dahut," said Christine. "Do you know it?" Alex shook her head.

"They say her father was the ruler of a great city called Ys, which was being swallowed by the ocean."

"Rather like our Île de Feme," said Ismael.

"Sorry. The city was called *ees?*" asked Alex.

"It's spelled Y-S," said Nat.

"Ys was built on land reclaimed from the ocean," Christine continued. "But the sea takes what it wants. So the king built a system of dikes to keep the city safe during high tide, and the gates were operated by a special gold key he wore around his neck."

"Dahut was very wicked and stole the key," Severine chimed in.

Christine mock-glared at her. "Who's telling this story? Anyway, I don't see Dahut as wicked as some do. It was said that she took lovers at night and threw them into the ocean in the morning when she was done with them, but surely she was misunderstood. Just because she was picky, does that make her evil?"

Alex laughed. "I imagine her lovers had a different perspective."

"Anyway, Dahut stole the key from her father to open the gates to let someone in, but forgot to close them, or something like that, and the whole city flooded. Her father was the sole survivor, and as he was escaping on his horse, Dahut tried to ride with him, but the king pushed her into the ocean. His own daughter. Can you believe that?"

"Our father might have done the same," said Alex.

"Probably would have," Nat agreed. "Did Dahut drown?"

"That's where we come in," said Severine. "According to legend, Dahut swam here, to the Île de Feme, where she was taken in by the Gallizenae, the nine women who lived on the island and practiced magic. The Gallizenae were able to transform themselves into—how do you say, *sirènes?*"

"Mermaids," said Nat.

"'The Little Mermaid' is my favorite fairy tale," said Alex.

"They weren't that kind of storybook mermaid," Christine said. "The Gallizenae mermaids were capricious and occasionally vicious. I like them. Sometimes they're shown with wings and claws, like fierce birds."

Agnès made a dismissive sound and waved a bony, blue-veined hand. "I never believed those mermaid stories," she said. "I mean, perhaps a long time ago they existed, but not any longer."

"They say the ocean is female, psychologically speaking," said Ismael. "Because the ocean is deep, mysterious, and unknowable, which is why it casts terror in the hearts of men."

The women at the table stared at him.

"Why is it female to be deep, mysterious, and unknowable?" asked Nat.

"Because the man who came up with that particular psychological theory wasn't brave enough to just ask a few simple questions," said Alex.

Nat translated this, and everyone laughed.

"I've heard it said that the mermaids sailors reported seeing were actually seals or dolphins," said Severine. "The lonely mariners simply imagined beautiful women swimming by their boats, poor fellows."

"Speaking of dolphins," said Ismael, turning to Alex, "did the dolphin greet the ferry when you came into port?"

"The island has a dolphin ambassador?"

"It hangs out in the harbor, follows the fishing boats. But sometimes it greets the ferry."

"Wait a second—I *did* see something in the water," said Alex. "As a matter of fact, my first thought was of a mermaid."

"That was probably him! Or her," said Ismael.

"Not sure how one tells," said Christine. "So, Ismael, how goes the climate initiative?"

To Nat and Alex she explained: "Ismael is a scientist and has been working on sea-level rise for the island."

"I hear it's a real threat," said Alex.

Ismael nodded and helped himself to another scoop of stew. "We're focused on publishing a small-case study, to see if we can produce enough electricity through solar and wind to become a zero-emission island."

"We've been having a few electrical issues over at the Bag-Noz," Alex said, ignoring Nat's silent entreaties.

"Really?" He looked at Nat. "I would be happy to take a look, if you would like. In fact, have you considered letting us install solar panels on the roof? We received a special grant from the government. If your roof is the right shape, it's practically free. I don't know why I didn't think to mention it before."

"I'm afraid the roof would need to be repaired first," Nat began. "I—"

Ismael waved away her concern. "We could arrange to have the repairs done at the same time we mount the panels. Only if you agree, of course, but I'd be happy to take a look and see if it would work."

"That's a great idea," Alex said.

"Yes indeed," Nat said. "Thank you."

"Anyway, zero emission or not, we're in danger," said Ismael. "Most of the Île de Feme is only a few meters above sea level, eleven at our highest point. Climate change is a challenge to our very survival."

"We'll lose the entire island if the sea level continues to rise," said Agnès, in a small, sad voice. "We'll be swallowed up, just like Ys."

There was a long silence, everyone lost to their thoughts.

"Maybe that's why I feel so at home here," Alex whispered to Nat as they stood to help Agnès collect the dinner dishes. "It'll be the End Times for the island."

CHAPTER THIRTY-NINE

Natalie

*N*atalie watched as Alex—straightforward, non-French-speaking Alex—managed to win over every single person at dinner. Natalie had known all of them for nearly a year, and yet they seemed more at ease with Alex than they ever had with her. What was *that* about?

Not that they weren't friendly to her. They frequently invited her to join them for dinner or *apéro*, though she usually declined, she realized. Especially recently.

But perhaps there was more to it than that. Alex was a survivalist, and when it came right down to it, the Fémans were, too. They looked at the world through a different lens from the "city folk" who expected everything to be easy. They snorted at the way the tourists whined about the rain, or bemoaned the lack of food options on the island. There was no theater and not many recreational activities except for kayaking, swimming in the ocean in the summer, maybe a *pétanque* game or two. When the electricity went out, which was not infrequent, the tourists didn't know what to do with themselves.

Meanwhile, the islanders lit a candle and read a book, chatted over a slice of *kouign-amann*, or played cards.

It was a simpler life, lived within the constraints of the ocean and the storms, their only consolations the wild beauty of the island and the bounty of the sea.

Sometimes Natalie reminded herself of the tourists in Paris, walking along the Seine, their backs to the view as they posed for selfies, grinning into their phones. Fueled by a strange mélange of hope and fear, they hardly seemed to even see the City of Light as they desperately curated their exterior lives, making things look beautiful on social media to mask the inward jumble of thoughts and feelings, the icky, ugly, messy innards.

After they cleared the table of the soup plates, Michou placed on the table a huge cheese platter, including a local cheese called *tome le ty pavez*. The cheese was followed by a simple green salad. And then it was time for dessert.

Tonton Michou began to pour *cidre bouché*, a kind of flat hard cider that was served it in terra-cotta mugs and often paired with pastries.

When Natalie's desserts were brought to the table, there was much *ooh*ing and *aah*ing, and Alex embarrassed Natalie by explaining how long they took to perfect. Unfortunately, when the group tasted them, they realized something was missing. The desserts weren't bad, but they weren't great, either.

"It might be the butter. The butter has to be very cold," Agnès said, nodding in concentration. "I would be happy to show you, Natalie. Alex mentioned you know how to butcher. Perhaps we could work out an exchange. We have some chickens we would like to have killed."

"I . . . uh . . . sure," said Natalie. "At some point."

"I really like the *cidre bouché*," said Alex.

"Then you must take the bottle with you," said *Tonton* Michou.

Later, after clearing the rest of the dishes, Natalie decided it was time to go. At the door they traded effusive thank-yous and *bonsoirs*.

"One more thing, Natalie," said Agnès, handing her what look like a bundle of dirt wrapped in burlap. "This is a rose root ball, from the yellow rose you always admire. You told me it made you think of your mother. I would like you to have it."

"That's so thoughtful of you, *Tante* Agnès," Natalie said. It was so typical of the islanders to give up a rose for the memory of a near-stranger's mother. *"Merci beaucoup."*

Christine grabbed her coat and walked out with them.

As the three women left the warmth of Agnès's home, they were enveloped by the salty, damp night air. The breezes carried the sweet scent of something in bloom, and a night bird cooed softly.

"We'll go to see her now," Christine announced.

"Go see *who* now?" Natalie asked, lighting up a cigarette and ignoring her sister's disapproving look.

"Ambroisine," said Christine.

"Now?"

"She's a night owl," said Christine. "We'll bring her the *cidre bou-ché*. She'll love it."

"I have to confess something, Christine," said Natalie.

"Can't wait to hear this," Alex muttered.

"I think Ambroisine cursed me."

"Oh, I doubt that," Christine said. "The only reason she curses people is for taking her photo without permission. Also, liars, she does not like this."

Two for two, Natalie thought. *Yup, I'm cursed.*

"Just out of curiosity," Alex said. "What happens if she *did* curse Nat?"

"I think . . ." Christine looked at Natalie and burst out laughing.

"Serious? Okay, good thing we have *cidre bouché*. And you have more cigarettes? We give her those, too. I told you, she likes me. It will be fine."

There were walkway lamps within the village itself, but the only light on the path that led past the hotel was from the sliver of a moon high overhead. Luckily each woman was armed with a flashlight, and the circles of light bobbed as they strolled along. On either side of them, along this narrow stretch of the island, the ocean was a dark mass just barely shimmering in the mellow moonlight. Up ahead, a single window in the little stone cottage glowed orange.

A low growl brought the trio to a halt. Korrigan stood in the middle of the path, her head hung down in a threatening manner.

"That's why I brought some bread," said Christine, tossing a few crusts to the dog, who wolfed them down, then turned and trotted off to stand at the door of the cottage.

"Does Korrigan belong to Ambroisine?" Natalie asked. "I thought she was a stray."

"Korrigan belongs to herself, but she is often at Ambroisine's cottage. They are well suited: They are both grumpy and powerful, eh?"

There were lace curtains in the cottage windows, the vegetable garden was well tended, and Natalie had occasionally spied smoke rising from the chimney, but she had only once seen a soul come in or out. That was the time, not long after arriving on the island, that she snapped the old woman's photograph as she and François-Xavier had been returning from their visit to the lighthouse. Natalie remembered the scene vividly: The afternoon sun had cast a golden glow over the old woman, who stood beside her cottage, a black cat in her arms, looking out to sea as if waiting for a loved one to return to her. Or so Natalie had imagined.

When Ambroisine spotted her holding up her phone to take her picture, the old woman had let loose with a long, profanity-laden stream of rapid French, only part of which had Natalie understood. François-Xavier had taken Natalie's arm and hurried her past the cottage, shouting apologies over his shoulder.

Natalie's stomach fluttered as Christine lifted the little fish-shaped knocker to rap on the front door.

"Ambroisine, c'est moi, Christine!" She called out, then pushed the door in, explaining loudly that they were in possession of cider and cigarettes and that her American friend was profoundly sorry for having taken her photograph.

Korrigan slipped by them and curled up on a small rug in front of the fire.

Christine introduced Natalie and Alex to Ambroisine, who simply nodded, her sharp eyes appearing to size them up. Christine and Natalie joined the old woman at her kitchen table but Alex's lack of French made her hold back, and she lingered by the fire.

"It is so lovely to officially meet you!" Natalie felt herself overcompensating, becoming overly friendly with this woman, but could not seem to stop. "I've walked by this darling cottage *so* many times, and always wondered what it was like inside. Thank you for inviting us in."

Christine poured *cidre bouché* into earthenware cups and handed them out. Lighting up one of Natalie's cigarettes, Ambroisine sat back and gazed at Natalie.

"I hear you know how to butcher," said Ambroisine.

"Excuse me?" Natalie responded.

"I've got a rabbit. Trapped it myself. It was after my cabbage."

"I was noticing how lush your garden is," Natalie said. "But I never see you working in it."

"I garden at night, in the moonlight, as it should be done. The rabbit's in the cooler."

"I . . . I really don't do that anymore," said Natalie. "I haven't butchered an animal since I was young."

Ambroisine glanced at Alex, who shrugged and said, "She's a good butcher. At least, she used to be."

"Ha!" The old woman gave a gap-toothed smile and pointed at Alex. "You see? I like this one."

Natalie glared at her sister.

"That's the deal," continued Ambroisine. "You butcher for me, and I'll answer your questions." She tapped herself on the chest. "*I* am the one who knows things no one else knows."

"Fair's fair," Christine said.

"All right," Natalie replied, defeated by this logic. "You have a deal."

She set the cookbook on the table and showed Ambroisine the photograph of the Nazi soldiers and the women in masks and feathered costumes.

"This is from the last war, World War Two," Ambroisine said with a nod. "I was there. I was . . . twelve or thirteen, at most."

"*Vraiment?* There was actually a cabaret on the Île de Feme?" asked Christine.

"For one night, one night only," said Ambroisine said, speaking slowly. "For one night the Abri du Marin was transformed into an underwater fantasy, and the island women were transformed into beautiful winged creatures, sirens, sent to bewitch the German soldiers."

"Why have I never heard of this?" asked Christine.

"It was a great secret."

"Nothing's a secret on this island."

Ambroisine chuckled, stubbed out her cigarette, and lit another. "Oh, but there *are* secrets, *ma chérie*. Many secrets, though not so many who still know them. Your *mémé* was there that night, in costume. She was very beautiful."

Christine made a snorting sound. "My *mémé* wore the *jibilinnen* every day of her life."

"Not on that night, she didn't."

Christine appeared thunderstruck at the idea of her grandmother dressed in feathers and entertaining German soldiers. She poured more cider into Ambroisine's cup, refilled her own, and said, "Now this, I have to hear."

"It's a long story, far too long to tell you this late at night," said Ambroisine, fixing Natalie with a look. "You come back with that rabbit, properly butchered, and perhaps I'll tell you more."

"Tomorrow?"

"*Non.* Tomorrow, I am busy. You come the next day and you bring more cider. Also, bring this one with you," she said, gesturing to Alex, who was now petting Korrigan. "I like this one."

The trio walked in silence back toward the village, each with their flashlight, Alex holding the burlap-wrapped rose root ball, and Natalie carrying Ambroisine's rabbit by the hind legs.

"That was . . . unexpected," said Christine after a long silence.

Alex chuckled.

"I wished she'd told us more," said Natalie. "What's with the secrecy?"

"I'm surprised she was that forthcoming, frankly," said Christine. "Ambroisine is not one to gossip. She must feel the story is ready to be told, after all these years."

"Then why not just tell us?" Natalie said.

"A flare for the dramatic, perhaps?" Alex suggested. "Or maybe she just wants to be sure you butcher her rabbit properly."

They reached the village and started down the narrow stone pathway.

"Take a left here," Christine told Alex as they reached a T.

"It's a bit of a maze, isn't it?" said Alex.

"It is, but one learns," said Christine. "And if you're ever lost, just keep walking. You'll come out to the ocean eventually, or at worst you'll exit on the other side and see the hotel."

Just then a couple of women approached, speaking American English.

"It *is* her! I think that's her!" said one.

Christine raised her eyebrows and smiled, staring at Natalie.

"Excuse us," said the other woman as they neared. "But are you Natalie Morgen, author of *Pourquoi Pas?*"

"She is," said Alex.

The women looked a little nonplussed at the poor dead rabbit in Natalie's hand, but chatted excitedly nonetheless, asking about her life on the island and the gorgeous François-Xavier.

Natalie handed the rabbit to Alex, pasted on a smile, murmured a few pleasantries, and signed their books. Then she posed for a round of selfies.

After thanking her and walking away, one of the women said to the other: "Remember that part in the book about butchering the poor rabbit . . . ?"

CHAPTER FORTY

Violette

*R*ainer stopped me in the hall and held out an envelope.

"Another letter?" I asked.

He hesitated. "I'm so sorry, Violette. But . . . I think you should sit down. It looks like an official notice."

I froze, seemingly forgetting how to breathe. After a long moment I took a gasp of air and accepted the envelope, holding it in shaking hands.

"Can I help?" Rainer asked.

"I need . . . I need my mother."

"Of course," he said to my back as I made my way to the kitchen, where my mother was washing dishes.

I collapsed into a chair at the small breakfast table.

"Maman . . ."

"What is it, Violette?"

Rainer was right. It was an official notice. My husband, Marc Jean Guilcher, age twenty-two, had been killed in an accident off the coast of Cornwall.

. . .

I was not in love with Marc, but his loss hit me as a sick shock. He was a sweet island boy whom I had known all my life. We were supposed to be parents together. As bad as it was to read the notice, it was infinitely worse to have to inform Marc's mother and sister. As if someone had cut her puppet strings, Gladie collapsed onto the kitchen floor, sobbing inconsolably. Noëlle leaned down, hugged her, and looked up at me with empty eyes.

"Leave us. Just leave us, Violette."

I did not want to abandon Gladie but could not think what else to do, so I went out to the rocks and looked up at the lighthouse. Trying to comprehend. To understand.

How could this war—and the things Rainer told me about the Nazis—be condoned by God? Had I done something to offend Him? Had we Bretons, we French, done something to bring this cataclysm down upon our heads?

Tears stung my eyes, but I did not wish to cry any more. Earlier I had sobbed so much in my mother's arms that I had to fight to breathe. My face was so red and puffy that when I arrived at my mother-in-law's house, I had no need to show her the official notice.

She knew before I said a word. Knew her world had come apart.

I kept envisioning Marc's guileless blue eyes. I wondered if they were shadowed in pain at the time of his death, if he had suffered or was among the lucky few granted a blessedly rapid exit from this life. I couldn't stand to think of the anguish in Gladie's eyes, the way she had moaned like a mortally wounded animal. Why should a good woman such as she be condemned to experience the deaths of so many loved ones?

I tried to concentrate on the glimmer of lights prancing upon the waves. A pair of dolphins jumped out of the water in graceful arcs just offshore. Sometimes they followed the fishing boats, frolicking about, apparently without a care in the world.

And then I felt a cramp in my belly so strong and deep that it took my breath away. It went away after a moment.

It is too early. Far too early. I remained perched on the rocks, petrified, my hands cupping my belly protectively, trying to regulate my breathing, my eyes searching for the dolphins, believing if I saw them, somehow, everything would be all right.

I felt another stabbing pain, and something wet between my legs. When I stood, narrow ribbons of blood streamed down my legs, staining my ankles.

I have to get to the House of Meneï. It wasn't far. I started to climb down from the rocks but it was slow going, as I had to stop frequently to breathe through the pains.

And then, just as I wondered whether I would be able to make it, I spied Rainer on the path. He had spotted me and started walking toward me, and then began to run.

"Violette! Is something wrong?"

"I have to get to Madame Thérèse!" I cried.

He sprang onto the rocks and picked me up in his arms, cradling me like a child. Picking his way back to the path, steady despite his bad knee, he hurried toward the little stone bungalow.

I don't remember much of the rest. How Rainer brought me into Madame Thérèse's house, banging on the door, and setting me gently on the cot. How the cunning woman forced me to drink a tonic, and did the best she could. How my baby was born.

Far too soon. Far too small. Far too blue.

"A little boy," said Madame Thérèse quietly, her tone somber.

Her young helper, Ambroisine, tried to take him away, but Madame stopped her.

"*Arrête*, Ambroisine. Let her hold him. She needs to hold him."

I cradled him to my chest, murmuring to my lifeless son, until the warmth seeped from his tiny perfect body.

I named him Esprit Fouquet Guilcher. We buried him the next day in the village cemetery, alongside too many others.

I stumbled through the hours of every day in a daze, resenting the sunshine on my face. Not wanting to eat. Angry even at the need to relieve myself. It all seemed so banal, so tied to this earthly world that my young husband, and now our desperately young child, had departed.

My mother tried to observe Christmas in some small ways: She hung a few streamers of shells and greenery about the front hall, and Rainer built a cozy fire in the parlor every evening. Sometimes he would read to me as I sat in a rocking chair, wrapped in a quilt, watching the embers glow. We dropped any pretense of not being fond of each other; how could I care about consequences now?

But even the home I had always known, with its precious window seats and bookshelves, its ocean views and cheery kitchen and cozy parlor, had become a place of sadness, like everyplace else the war had touched. My mother and Rainer tried to care for me, to offer me their love and support, but I could not love myself.

Nothing mattered. Nothing.

One day I opened the bedroom closet and spied my grandmother's *robe noire*, the dark linen hanging like a specter. Her *jibilinnen* sat on a nearby shelf. Clothes I had sworn I would never wear.

The traditional black outfit had always seemed to me a symbol of the past, of a constant mourning that I wanted no part of. I had yearned for music and laughter, not the daily struggle to survive that was life on the Île de Feme.

And now, though it had been only, what—six months? Six months since our men left, yet I had aged a decade, maybe two.

I am a widow. And a . . . Why was there no word for a woman who has lost her child? No word to describe what I was now, no phrase that could possibly convey this chasm of loss and anguish. I hadn't kept my baby safe. My precious Esprit was gone without a single cry, and he had taken my spirit with him, into the ether.

Nothing mattered anymore. I had little food but didn't want to eat. I had no bed or home of my own but didn't sleep, didn't need a home.

I sat on the closet floor and stared at the *robe noire* and *jibilinnen*. Hours passed. And finally I realized: This was my place. These were my clothes.

Awkwardly, I slipped the black dress over my head, contorting myself to latch all the hooks and eyes in back. Standing back, I pulled the winged headdress over my light brown hair and gazed at my reflection in the full-length mirror.

The mourning witch within my soul stared back at me and I understood: This was the last outfit I would ever wear.

CHAPTER FORTY-ONE

Alex

*B*ack at the guesthouse, Alex noticed the light under Jean-Luc's bedroom door and wondered whether he was up late, reading. She felt an absurd impulse to knock on the door, to wish him a good night.

Why did it feel so easy to be around him? It was a novel sensation; Alex had had a few women friends in her life, but never a man. Yet sometimes . . . sometimes Jean-Luc looked at her as if he wanted to be more than friends. It made her heart speed up when she found his eyes on her, but it also stirred something else: anger. Even fear.

Alex was an island. She didn't need anyone. She didn't *want* to need anyone.

So she stifled the impulse to knock, instead entering her own room and closing the door. The night-light cast its reassuring glow. She snapped on the bedside lamp and went to the window to look out over the dark ocean, thinking about Ambroisine in her little stone cottage, and Korrigan, and the evening with *Tante* Agnès and Michou and Severine and Ismael and Christine. She liked them all, each a character in his or her own way.

Their dinner conversation came back to her: Sea-level rise put the island in peril. The Île de Feme couldn't simply build walls to keep the waters out.

Alex pictured the inundation, the salty waters flooding these rooms, turning these historic homes into ghostly underwater relics. She imagined swimming through the halls, diving down the murky steps. A part of her felt ready for the sensation of luminous waters closing over her head, leaving her to haunt the submerged stone pathways.

She thought of "The Little Mermaid," and pondered Dahut making it all the way to the Île de Feme's rocky shores to join the Gallizenae who had once inhabited and protected this island.

Alex crawled into bed, read a few more passages of *To the Lighthouse*, and drifted off.

She dreamed that she was drifting, far underwater, looking up toward the surface, searching for light, straining to see, as the darkness of the ocean depths closed in on her.

CHAPTER FORTY-TWO

Natalie

Jean-Luc was very excited to find the dead rabbit in the kitchen and volunteered to help.

"You want to butcher an animal?" Natalie asked.

"I would love to assist, if I may," said Jean-Luc.

"You are full of surprises, monsieur. You know that? Okay, let's set up a table outside. It's easier."

Out near the shed, they placed three wood planks across two saw-horses, covered the surface in newspapers, and laid the rabbit out.

It was surprisingly easy to take the animal apart, even after all these years. It was so awful, so brutal, and yet it had always seemed to Natalie the highest hypocrisy to cry over an animal being butchered but then to eat it with pleasure. What did it mean to skip the all-important step, the hard part before one was allowed to consume?

It was ugly, yes. It certainly didn't smell like lavender. And yet it put dinner on the table. The Commander used to say that if we asked an animal to give up its life for our benefit, the very least we could do was bear witness to its sacrifice, face-to-face. He had gotten that part right, at least.

"Reminds me of when we were kids," said Alex, joining them, a cup of coffee in her hand.

Natalie continued methodically dissecting the rabbit, keeping the bony parts with little meat to use to make a rich stock.

"And what do you do with . . . *les abats*? I don't know the term in English," Jean-Luc asked as he watched every turn of Natalie's wrist.

"*Les abats* are the organs, the kidney, heart, and liver," Natalie explained to Alex. "They use everything here."

"Just like we used to." Alex nodded. "I'm still surprised at how much people throw away."

Natalie looked up at the sound of a horn blast, followed by the raucous calls of gulls. She checked her watch. "There's the afternoon ferry. The groceries I ordered ought to be at the dock."

"Oh good," said Alex. "Need some help?"

"No, this time it will all fit on one *charette*, not nearly as heavy as painting supplies. But, Jean-Luc, would you mind wrapping this meat up while I wash my hands and run for the groceries? Just put it in the *frigo*."

"It would be my pleasure."

The next day Natalie and Alex took the rabbit, neatly wrapped in butcher paper, back to Ambroisine's cottage. In a woven wicker basket they also brought a bottle of good quality cider, a fresh baguette, and some cake. Alex insisted on including a few leftover tidbits from last night's dinner for Korrigan.

When they arrived, Korrigan did not growl but accepted the treats, and even allowed Alex to place a gentle hand on her head.

"I'll need carrots for a decent rabbit stew," Ambroisine grumbled as she moved around the kitchen, stashing the cake and bread and set-ting the meat out on the wooden butcher-block table. "You should bring some next time. Where is Christine?"

"Still out on her boat," said Natalie.

"Then I cannot tell you about the cabaret. Her grandmother was there; it's only fair that she hear the story."

Damn it, Natalie thought, and clamped down on her frustration. She wished she could just download the information she was after, as if the old woman were a computer.

"I have other stories you might be interested in."

"I'd love to hear anything you have to say. Is it okay if I record you?" Natalie asked, bringing out her phone.

"Certainly not," Ambroisine said with a frown. "Write notes if you want, but put that thing away. I don't trust those devices."

As she brought out a notepad and pen, Natalie translated this last for Alex, and the sisters shared a smile.

"I knew Violette from the village, of course," said Ambroisine. "I remember when she came here, to this very room, to get help from Madame Thérèse, the *louzaourian* who taught me."

"This is Violette from the Bag-Noz?" asked Natalie.

"Of course. I thought you wanted the story."

"Yes, sorry. But first: Could you tell me about being a *louzaou-rian*?" asked Natalie.

" '*Louzaourian*' means 'healer.' I understand the twenty-six sacred herbs, how they relate to the parts of the body, and their healing powers."

"What are the sacred herbs?" asked Natalie.

"Are you a *louzaourian*?" Ambroisine demanded.

"No," said Natalie.

"Then it's none of your business. If you want to come apprentice with me, I will teach you. *Si non, occupe-toi de tes oignons.*"

Natalie translated for Alex—essentially "mind your own onions"—and the sisters shared another quick smile before Natalie turned to Ambroisine. "So, you said Violette came to see Madame Thérèse? Was she sick?"

"She was pregnant."

"I didn't think Violette had any children," said Natalie.

"Do you want to hear the story or not?"

"I want to hear."

"Then stop interrupting me." Ambroisine went on to tell that Violette had come to the cottage seeking help after spotting a little blood. She wasn't entirely sure she wanted to have the baby, but by the time their interview was over, she was certain. The old woman went into great detail as to the tea and tonic Madame Thérèse had given to Violette, and even found the entries in the cookbook: "You see, right here."

"Your teacher, Madame Thérèse, shared those recipes with other islanders—people who weren't *louzaourians* themselves?"

Ambroisine smiled. "Ah, good question. In this case, yes, she did. It was not typical, but during the war Madame Thérèse feared for our people under the yoke of the Nazis. She wanted any other women who might be pregnant to remain healthy."

"I noticed a lot of remedies included in the cookbook," said Natalie. "That surprised me."

"Why?"

"Well, because . . ." Natalie hesitated, not wanting to say the wrong thing and unintentionally insult Ambroisine.

"Because we think of cooking food and treating illness as very different things," Alex interjected.

Ambroisine laughed. "Of course you do, because you are foolish. They are one and the same. The food we eat, the medicines, the herbs. And that's not all," she said, patting the journal. "During the war, this book was used to pass messages among the islanders."

"Why was that necessary?"

"The Germans did not allow more than three people to gather. The only exceptions were when harvesting the *goémon* and when standing in line for supplies. So Violette began to bring the cookbook from one home to the next, and when she was stopped she told the soldiers she was gathering recipes. The soldiers were dismissive of women's business. What harm could a cookbook do?"

"And what harm *did* it do?"

"You come back next Monday with Christine, and I'll tell you."

"Couldn't you tell me now?"

Ambroisine simply fixed her with a look, called Korrigan over, and tossed the rabbit's heart to the dog.

CHAPTER FORTY-THREE

Alex

The residents of the Bag-Noz fell into a comfortable routine.

Alex and Jean-Luc arose early, shared a simple breakfast, and got to work patching windowsills and exterior walls when it was sunny, or focused on repairing the interior walls when it was rainy. Natalie would eventually stumble out of her room in search of coffee, then go off to do the interviews that Milo had arranged, collecting cookbook stories from the women and cajoling them into posing for photos.

Christine stopped by now and then with fish or cider to share, and stories to tell. Evenings were spent preparing dinner, which they enjoyed with the wine Jean-Luc contributed, playing cards and staring into the parlor fire in companionable silence.

Nat was called on to do more butchering as word of her skill spread across the island. She returned to Agnès's house to prepare her chickens, and in exchange learned to cook *kouign-amann* at the elbow of a pastry master. Later, Nat told Alex she had substituted regular tap water for the rainwater specified in the recipe in the Bag-Noz cookbook, but Agnès had laughed and insisted the recipe did not call for water at all.

"Why would they specify rainwater in the recipe, then?" asked Alex.

"I have no idea, and neither did Agnès," said Nat.

Nat spent most mornings writing, but in the afternoons when she had no interviews scheduled, she would help Alex and Jean-Luc with wall repair and general cleanup. When the money for the film rights to *Pourquoi Pas?* was deposited in her bank account, Nat took pleasure in tending to her overdue bills. Glad to be paid, the workers returned to retrieve their tools and finish up their projects: applying weather stripping to windows and doors, making a few more porch repairs.

Nat and Alex had dug through the rest of the cardboard boxes in the parlor, hoping to unearth information on Violette and Doura, but found only more books to fill the library shelves. They tidied up the dining room and set up the eight tables that Nat and François-Xavier had acquired when dreaming of their restaurant, what seemed like forever ago. Nat removed the framed newsletter article from the wall and tossed it unceremoniously into the fire.

Alex was particularly pleased when a newly energized Nat began to work in the garden, intent on preparing a spot to plant the yellow rose in honor of their mother. Jean-Luc suggested putting in a *pétanque* court at the side of the house, linking the front courtyard to the rear garden, and Nat immediately seized on the idea and looked up the proper dimensions to see if it would fit.

As he had promised over dinner at Agnès's house, Ismael came by to inspect the roof of the Bag-Noz, assisted by young Gabriel. He pronounced it ideal for solar panels, and gave Alex the name of someone who could complete the slate repairs for a fair price. Then he and Gabriel took a look at the wiring indoors and, with Jean-Luc's assistance, began to rip out and replace the old frayed knob-and-tube wiring.

As Alex watched them work, she thought about The Commander's insistence that his girls never rely upon others, especially strangers. Ismael and Gabriel were virtually unknown to her, and she had only known Jean-Luc for a short time. But here they were, fixing problems that had worried her since she arrived, and that she was sure had been a preoccupation for Nat for a much longer period.

Jean-Luc and Alex decided to start painting the walls of the third floor, as the plaster repair there was completely dry. They carted the cans of paint, brushes, rollers, and pans up the two flights of stairs, and started in Jean-Luc's bedroom.

Alex couldn't help but notice, with an approving eye, that he kept his chamber as neat as she did hers.

"Too bad we don't have that . . . What do you call it?" said Jean-Luc as they set out tarps to protect the floor from paint spatters. "In French we say *ruban de masquage.*"

"Sorry. You lost me," Alex said. "Describe it?"

"It is used in many ways but for painting is usually blue and comes easily off the wall."

"Ah, I think you mean masking tape. Painters just call it blue tape," said Alex.

"Blue tape!" Jean-Luc repeated as if memorizing the words. "We do not have any of this blue tape."

"Nope. I don't believe in it."

"But it is . . . real."

She smiled. "I mean, I don't use it—it's expensive, and in my experience, the paint tends to leak through anyway. It's better to be careful, and then if you make a mistake you can see where you need to repair something."

He pushed out his chin and inclined his head. "If you say so, Alex, then I will be very careful. I will not believe in blue tape, either."

"That's the spirit," Alex said.

The blue-green paint Nat choseias just right, Alex thought as they painted companionably, side by side. Not too pastel but not too bold, either. Even as a kid Nat had a knack for making things pretty, doing what she could to brighten up the tired interior of their cabin.

But Alex found it funny when people spoke about "ocean colors"— the sea was so changeable, even from one minute to the next, ranging from deep turquoise to slate gray, and everything in between.

"I wonder if I should change," Jean-Luc said with a quick intake of breath. "I forgot I am wearing a dress T-shirt."

"How can a T-shirt be dressy?"

He plucked a bit of the snowy white fabric and held it out. "It is not snazzy, I admit. But it is very good quality. It is called a dress T-shirt because it is for wearing under a nice shirt. You see?"

"I do see," she said with a grin. "You're a classy guy, monsieur."

Alex leaned down to dip her paintbrush in the bucket, then straightened and turned, not realizing Jean-Luc had moved a step closer, and her loaded brush left a bright streak of paint on his T-shirt.

"Oh no!" Alex said, her free hand going up to her mouth. "I'm so sorry! And you just got through telling me that this was your special T-shirt, too!"

Jean-Luc gazed at the splotch of blue-green paint, bright against the pure white of his formerly pristine T-shirt.

"Alex?" he asked. "Did you do that by purpose?"

"First of all, the phrase is 'on purpose,' not 'by purpose,'" she said, trying not to giggle. "Second of all, I one hundred percent did *not* mean to do that!"

"I believe you," he said, then reached out with his wet paintbrush and booped her in the middle of her cotton shirt, leaving a large aqua dot.

"Hey!" Alex said in mock outrage. "You can't do that!"

"I do not know what you are talking about," Jean-Luc said. "It was an accident."

"No, it most definitely was not," she said, then reached up and put a dot of paint on his nose. "And neither was that, my friend."

Jean-Luc's eyebrows rose so far, she thought they would blend into his hair. "I am shocked, *shocked* at your actions," he said, and flicked his brush at her, sending a shower of droplets her way.

"Oh, it is *on*!" Alex yelled, and spattered him with a fully loaded paintbrush. "*En garde*, Frenchy!"

"Do not underestimate the French, my dear *Américaine*!" he replied as he bounded out of reach. "We are a cunning and an agile people! Have you never heard of *Les trois mousquetaires*?"

"Um, wild guess: *The Three Musketeers*?"

"*Précisément! En garde!*"

She and Jean-Luc danced around the tarp, wielding their brushes like miniature swords. For a moment they appeared evenly matched until Jean-Luc tripped over the paint tray, which was fortunately empty of paint, and fell down on the tarp.

"Score!" Alex yelled, and went in for the kill shot, but he reached out a hand and pulled her down next to him. She went down with a thud. "Ow!"

"Oh, I am so sorry!" he said immediately and crawled to her side. "Alex, are you all right?"

"I'm fine," she said, laughing, and reached up with her paintbrush to put another dab of color on his bewhiskered cheek.

Laughing and panting, their eyes met and held.

"What the hell is going on up here?" Nat called from the doorway. "Are you two fighting . . . ?" She trailed off at the sight of Alex and Jean-Luc entangled on the floor and covered in spattered blue-green paint, then whipped out her phone and starting snapping photos, and Alex imagined she and Jean-Luc would star in Nat's latest social media entry.

"We, uh . . . ," Alex said as they quickly got to their feet. Jean-Luc's face was bright red.

"Having a few technical difficulties with the new paintbrushes?" Nat asked, trying not to laugh. "The paint's supposed to go on the walls. You know that, right?"

"We were . . . um . . . ," Alex trailed off, clearing her throat.

"We were fooling around," said Jean-Luc.

"That's what it looked like," said Nat.

"We were just *kidding* around, is what he meant," Alex clarified.

"An unscheduled break, *patronne*," said Jean-Luc, using the French word for 'boss.' "*Pardonnez-nous*. It won't happen again."

"So, what's up?" asked Alex, her cheeks burning. "Care to help paint?"

"I was actually headed out to the garden to measure out the *pétanque* court. Could I borrow Jean-Luc for a moment?"

"Of course," said Jean-Luc.

Alex watched his back as he left. Now that Jean-Luc was working outside so much, he had lost the pallid complexion of an office drone, and she couldn't remember a time when she thought of him as ordinary. In the evenings, she and Nat sometimes played cards or watched the fire and listened to his resonant voice reading from one of Nat's anthologies of short stories.

Nat kept suggesting Alex take a few days off to enjoy what Île de Feme had to offer tourists, to check out the kayaking or the swimming beaches, and every once in a while, Alex would go down to the little beach on cool mornings before the crowds arrived to collect sea glass, searching the dark water for any sign of dolphins, and remembering her vivid underwater dream.

But most days, Alex preferred to work. The more time she spent on the Bag-Noz, the more she fell in love with the old stone walls, the nooks and crannies, the palpable sense of history she felt on every step of the staircase.

Alex tried to commit every bit—each piece of sea glass, each corner of the Bag-Noz, each narrow pathway that meandered through the village—to memory.

Remember, Alex. Remember.

CHAPTER FORTY-FOUR

Violette

*R*ainer didn't say a word when he saw me wearing the *robe noire* and *jibilinnen*.

"It belonged to my grandmother," I said.

He nodded.

"Toward the end she shrank so my mother made her a smaller one," I said.

"It suits you," he said.

"Does it?"

"I used to think of you in clad one of the bright costumes from my father's cabaret. But now . . ." He paused. "I am so very, *very* sorry, Violette."

*W*eeks passed, though I had little memory of the time. I put one foot in front of the other, cleaning the house, doing the laundry, and harvesting the *goémon* until I was so exhausted that I would fall into bed with some hope of sleep. It came rarely.

One day Noëlle sent a note asking me to come by her house. We hadn't spoken in so long that I was surprised, but also curious. As I walked through the village I saw purple petals crushed underfoot against wet stones, like fallen butterflies, and realized it was now spring. My hands were thin, almost skeletal, as I drew my black shawl around me tightly, despite the mildness of the day.

I neared the house at 22 Saint-Guénolé and hesitated, unsure if my mother-in-law would be there and, if so, what to say to her. I had encountered Gladdie many times since we lost Marc and Esprit, and the empty, endless pain in her face mirrored my own.

I was relieved to find Noëlle home alone.

"You need to get your boyfriend to do something for you," Noëlle said without preamble, or even the most meaningless of greetings.

I didn't bother to deny that Rainer was my boyfriend. There was no point. Noëlle believed what she believed.

"What is it?"

"Marceline Carmèle, a native of the Île de Feme, must be allowed to return. Your man controls the port, does he not?"

"Rainer is the head of the GAST, the customs office. He is not 'my man.'"

"Whatever. He is in the position to do you a favor. He owes that much."

"What makes you think he owes me anything?"

"This war has taken your husband, and now your child. You are owed."

I stared at her. It had been months since that terrible day, and I still could not laugh, however joylessly. "I am not owed anything, Noëlle. As Madame Thérèse says: Life is pain, and war is worse."

"Anyway, you will talk to him, convince him to allow Marceline to return to the island. It was not her fault she was caught in Nantes without papers. I have them here."

Noëlle gestured at a pile of official-looking documents, including a *carte d'identité* with the photograph of a young woman, not much older than we.

"I don't know who this Marceline Carmèle is, but she's not from here."

"Of course, she is. You don't know everyone," Noëlle continued.

"Yes, I do. I've lived here all my life. What going on, Noëlle?"

"Tomorrow or the next day, Marceline will be at the dock in Audierne, and your boyfriend must permit her to come to the island."

"Without any papers."

"She forgot them. They're right here. You are an islander, Violette. Remember?"

"I remember that in school you excelled at penmanship and drawing," I said, perusing the documents. "So, are you forging fake identities now, with your grandfather's old printing press?"

Noëlle's face registered surprise and something else much harder to define. Something like hope. "She needs our help, Violette. And we need hers."

"For what?"

"She's been injured. Madame Thérèse has agreed to take care of her. She needs someplace to be nursed back to health."

"And to hide from the Germans."

Noëlle said nothing.

"It won't work, Noëlle. Even if I could do as you ask, no islander will believe she's a native. We've never seen her before. Someone will give her away."

"Leave that to me. All you have to do is convince your boyfriend to allow her passage to the Île de Feme. Will you do it?"

I hesitated. "Let me think about it."

. . .

I had not entirely made up my mind what to do when I sought Rainer out that evening. I found him in his room alone, distraught, a crumpled letter in his hands.

"What's wrong?" I asked. "What's happened?"

"Sascha has been arrested."

"Arrested?" I breathed. "Why?"

He shook his head. "Sascha is no friend to the current regime, and those who speak up too loudly are"—his voice broke—"cut down. Our friend in Berlin wrote to tell me that the SS arrested Sascha last week, but he has heard nothing more."

"I'm *so* sorry, Rainer," I said. "Is there anything you can do? As an officer . . . ?"

"I am a customs officer, that is all. I don't have any influence with the Gestapo, and I don't know anyone who does."

I felt tears stinging my eyes. "We have both lost so much to this insanity."

"I used to tell myself that out here, I was not really involved. But now . . ."

"You should escape! Go to England. If you took a decent boat, you would be able to make it!"

"I can't simply leave."

"You can. You *should*. I would if I could."

Rainer gave a humorless chuckle, and brushed my cheek with his hand.

"Liar," he said in a voice so soft and gentle, it brought more tears to my eyes. "You wouldn't leave your people. You couldn't bring yourself to."

We stood at his window, watching the flashing of the lighthouse.

"I have to ask you a favor," I said, my heart pounding in my chest.

Its very thudding was reassuring somehow. After the shock of Marc's death, and then the loss of my child, I thought I might never feel my broken heart beat again. "I don't want to ask, but I feel that I must."

"What is it?"

"There is a native Fémane on the mainland who needs to be allowed to return to the island."

"What's the problem?"

"She doesn't have her identification papers."

He gazed at me a long moment. "Why not?"

"I have them." I pulled them from my *robe noire* and handed them to him. Marceline Carmèle. Place and date of birth: Île de Feme, Finistère, 1919. "Perhaps you could take them with you to Audierne. Marceline is expected to arrive at the ferry dock tomorrow or the next day—you could give them to her so she can come home."

Rainer studied the papers, and then searched my face. "What is going on, Violette?"

"Marceline is sick and needs to be with family."

"What's wrong with her?"

"Women's troubles, nothing contagious. What possible threat could she be?"

He let out a harsh laugh. "I do not underestimate women."

"Most of your colleagues believe we're harmless, worried about nothing but cooking and knitting and gossiping."

"Most of my colleagues are fools."

"Please, Rainer. Do it for Sascha. For every innocent person who is being arrested, sent away for no good reason."

Rainer looked out to sea for so long that I thought he wouldn't answer. At last he said: "Promise me that none of my men will be hurt. They may be fools, but they're under my protection."

"I promise. Marceline needs to come home, that's all. She'll come here to the Île de Feme, and that will be the end of it."

· · ·

But that wasn't the end of it, not by a long shot.

Marceline did appear at the Audierne pier the next day, and Rainer recognized her from the photo, though she was frailer in person. A pinched, unhealthy pallor was common to those of us living under wartime rations and worries.

But by the time the ferry docked at the island, Marceline was near fainting. Not wanting to call more attention to her arrival, Rainer told her to wait until the men had disembarked and the supplies had been unloaded before helping her off the ferry and bringing her to the guesthouse. They burst into the kitchen while the others were at dinner, Marceline clinging to him, unable to stand on her own.

My mother and I rushed her into our chamber.

"I'll fetch Madame Thérèse," I said.

"No, I'll go," insisted Rainer. "Madame Thérèse will be stopped, and if they discover she has medicine or medical supplies . . ."

"You're right," my mother told him. "You should go."

My mother placed a cold cloth on Marceline's forehead and tried to spoon some sweet tea into her mouth.

"Poor thing has a fever," my mother said. "What is this all about, Violette? Noëlle says she's an islander but I've never seen the girl."

"It is important that she be from here," I said. "That's all."

She nodded. Since I had lost my husband and my child, and donned the *robe noire* and *jibilinnen*, my mother gave my opinions more respect.

Madame Thérèse rarely left her cottage except to tend to her garden. But she came to the guesthouse that evening, young Ambroisine trailing behind her and carrying her basket. Rainer told me later that twice they passed the guards. He had explained that he was escorting them to a family dinner, held by special permission of the prefecture.

Madame Thérèse and young Ambroisine entered the kitchen, gave us a nod, and disappeared into the bedroom, shutting the door behind them. Rainer, my mother, and I waited in the kitchen in tense silence. *Maman* made tea and passed us each a steaming mug. It felt like hours passed.

Finally, the bedroom door opened.

"She has a bullet in her side. It doesn't appear to have hit any vital organs, but it's been there too long and festers," said Madame Thérèse in a hushed voice, washing her hands at the sink. "She needs surgery and treatment for the infection. I've applied an iodine and mustard plaster, and can keep the fever at bay for a while, but if the bullet is not removed, she will die."

"How long?" asked my mother.

"A few days, maybe a week. I've seen people survive worse, but she's already frail. . . ." She shrugged.

Just as we were digesting this information, Noëlle stormed into the kitchen. Upon learning of Madame Thérèse's diagnosis, she glanced at Rainer and asked to speak with me in private.

"Did she give anything to you? Was she carrying anything?" Noëlle whispered.

"Like what?" I asked.

"Microfilm."

"Microfilm of what?"

"Don't ask questions."

"I *will* ask questions," I insisted. "I have that right. My husband died for our cause."

"My *brother* died for our cause." Noëlle suspected I had not loved Marc the way a good man's wife should have loved him. But she said: "Photographs of the shipworks at Brest. It is critical that the British get that information. Otherwise Marceline's life has been sacrificed in vain."

"She's not dead," I said. "Not yet. We'll search her things and see if we can find the microfilm, Noëlle. But we have to save the poor woman's life as well. Otherwise, we are as bad as the enemy."

Later that evening, Rainer pulled me into his room.

"I'm being asked about her," he whispered.

"Who's asking?"

"Hans, of course. He heard there was an unaccompanied woman on the ferry and has already contacted the Gestapo. We have to get her off this island, and soon."

"We'll hide her somewhere." I thought of the secret crawl space in the guesthouse attic, but that was meant for valuables, not humans. A person could hide there for a few minutes, maybe a few hours, but no more.

"Where? They'll tear your homes apart looking for her. And if he finds her here, Hans might well burn this place down with you inside."

I hadn't told Rainer about the microfilm, but he was no fool and must have suspected the story I told him was a lie. Noëlle and I had gone through Marceline's things, and found the microfilm tucked into a lipstick case. How odd that something so small could cause so much trouble.

"All right. That means she has to leave the island. But how do we do that?" I asked myself as much as Rainer.

"The military transport is out; I might as well gift wrap her for the Gestapo," Rainer said.

I rose and went to stare out the window. The lighthouse beacon shone, its constant rhythm reassuring. It made me wonder. . . .

"The smugglers' boat. It comes to the island occasionally and drops things," I said.

"Smugglers? Or spies?"

I shook my head. "I don't know. Does it matter?"

"It should matter to me, but at the moment, it doesn't. How do you get in touch with them?"

"I don't. But I know someone who does. Maybe this person could arrange for the boat to come get Marceline."

"You would need a signal of some kind to coordinate the pickup."

"Like what?"

"A radio would be best. But the lightkeeper's radio was destroyed, and as customs officer, I have no access to the communications equipment."

My gaze returned to the window. "What about the lighthouse?"

"What about it?"

"Aren't there codes sailors are familiar with? What's it called, the one with dots and dashes?"

"Morse code?"

"That's the one. The lighthouse beacon is visible all the way to Brest! A boat crew could decipher the message easily."

"So could anyone else who saw it."

"But surely, only if they were looking for it. Otherwise, wouldn't they just see the lighthouse beacon?"

"I think . . . I think it's insane to even contemplate such a thing," said Rainer.

"As customs officer, you know when all the regular boats come through. So we wait for this one. I call it a ghost ship, a Bag-Noz, since it's so mysterious. When it's nearby, we'll signal it with the lighthouse beacon."

"How will you do that?"

"Henri Thomas will help us."

"But there are soldiers posted all over the island, and by now they're familiar with the beacon's pattern. How do you propose to hide the signal from them?"

"That's a good question." I slumped on the deep sill of the window. "We have to distract them somehow. How does one distract soldiers?"

"How does one distract bored young men?" Rainier gave me a sad smile. "How do you think? Wine, women, and song."

"Too bad we're not in Paris," I said.

A long moment passed.

"You may be onto something," Rainer said slowly. "The soldiers on the island are jealous of the soldiers stationed in Paris, who get to go to nightclubs and shows. What if the island women put together something to distract them? The soldiers miss the company of women dressed in something other than the *robe noire* and *jibilinnen*."

"Are you suggesting we put on a show? In costume? Like the ones you told me about, in your father's cabaret in Berlin?"

"Exactly. Gather the men around you, like Circe wielding her magic, and render them blind to what is going on, right under their noses."

"It sounds awfully farfetched. What if it doesn't work?"

"Then heaven help us all," said Rainer softly.

CHAPTER FORTY-FIVE

Natalie

$\mathcal{A}$s she read through the recipes, Natalie began to worry the idea of an annotated Île de Feme cookbook would not appeal to her readers. France's cuisine was justly renowned, but Brittany's drew more upon its Celtic roots, with a heavy emphasis upon fish stews and meat pies. It was nutritious, hearty food, and it kept sailors warm out on cold waters. But it was not exactly haute cuisine.

In Paris, lobster would be served steamed or grilled. Or as lobster thermidor, or braised in a delicate meunière sauce. Creamy lobster bisque, grilled with *beurre blanc* and served with shallots and white wine. Steamed with Champagne, orange, and fennel fronds *en papillote* . . .

Here on the Île de Feme, lobster was usually tossed into a stew. It was a delicious stew, but it was still a stew.

That evening, Natalie made *kig ha farz*.

"Well?" she asked Jean-Luc and Alex.

"It's good," said Alex. "Very filling."

Natalie's mouth twisted a bit. "'Very filling' isn't the sort of description that draws a crowd these days. What do you think, Jean-Luc?"

"It's a bit . . . What's the English word? We say *fade* in French."

"Bland, tasteless, boring, insipid, tame," Natalie translated, her tone glum.

"I've always admired your command of the English language, Nat," said Alex with a smile in Jean-Luc's direction. "But honestly, it's not as bad as all that."

"I appreciate that, Alex, but you're not exactly my target audience. You'd eat pemmican without complaint," said Natalie, pushing her plate away. Jean-Luc was right. The food was indeed *fade*.

"I'd probably pipe up these days," said Alex. "And this butter sauce is really good."

"Thank you, but butter doesn't a cookbook make," said Natalie.

"I know a few Americans who would like it. What's on the menu for tomorrow night?"

"I was thinking of trying the *ragoût dans les mottes*, which is a kind of lamb stew."

"I love lamb," said Jean-Luc.

"It's supposed to be cooked very slowly in cast iron in the fireplace, over a smoking fire."

"How do you make a smoking fire?" asked Alex.

"I'm still figuring it out. We could have some peat brought in by ferry, but that seems like overkill. I've got dessert, though." She hopped up and brought over the *kouign-amann* cooked according to Agnès's instructions, topping it with a salted caramel sauce.

"I *really* like the caramel," said Alex, and Jean-Luc nodded vigorously.

"Everyone likes the caramel," said Natalie. "It's butter and sugar and sea salt. What's not to like?"

"Oh, hey, Jean-Luc," Alex said. "I almost forgot. I bought you a present."

She handed him a bag, and he took out a T-shirt from Le Caredec, bright turquoise with a garish picture of the Île de Feme surrounded by dolphins and mermaids.

He looked at her, eyebrows raised.

She laughed. "I know it's not exactly your style, but this way you can get it as full of paint as you want, no worries."

"Thank you, Alex," he said warmly, kissing her on both cheeks.

After dinner they retired to the parlor and played a few hands of cards, but after winning three games in a row, Jean-Luc excused himself and went to bed.

"Oh, by the way, Ismael said the Bag-Noz was a good candidate for the solar panel grant," Natalie told Alex. "But we'll have to do a basic upgrade first. He left the name of a couple of people he works with, so I'll get some estimates. Thanks again for urging me to finish things up."

"No problem. I feel like I want to be a part of this place. I'm becoming bewitched by your island, after all. How did Jean-Luc put it? *Ensorcelle?*"

"It's the same word in English, 'ensorcelled.'"

"I didn't know that. Like I've always said, you're such a smarty-pants."

Natalie didn't feel particularly smart as she visited more of Milo's relatives, each time bringing the cookbook and asking about it. Milo always came along, crossing his arms and leaning against the wall, like a grumpy bodyguard. She could never tell who he thought he was protecting: her or the people she was interviewing.

Eventually, Natalie grew closer to her neighbors as she sat in their kitchens and sought out their opinions and advice, asking for their help transcribing and interpreting measurements, figuring out what was meant by a "warm oven," or "butter the size of an egg," clabbered milk, and hartshorn.

During the visits, Natalie also asked about tales from World War II. Most people recounted hearing stories of how hungry everyone was, and the anger toward the soldiers and officers billeted in their homes. Also the system of *le ravitaillement*, the Germans requisitioning what they wanted, especially tobacco and coffee and meat. Even when they paid for the goods, it was only a fraction of what they were worth.

But when Natalie showed them the cabaret photo, the gray heads would shake. *"Je n'ai aucune idée."* "I have no idea."

Natalie began to feel that she was biding her time until she was allowed back into Ambroisine's kitchen. The old woman knew the whole story; she would bet a pretty penny on it.

Natalie tried to work up some enthusiasm over Milo, but was disappointed to realize that he wasn't particularly kind or attentive to the people they visited. He paid no mind to the old people's aches and pains, and ignored their dogs and cats. He didn't ask his elderly relatives if he could help bring in firewood, or fetch something from the attic, or if they had enough groceries.

Jean-Luc would have been all over that sort of thing, Natalie thought, and her sister's words came back to her: *Sometimes a grump is just a grump.*

Still, Milo was sexy in a gruff sort of way, and it was flattering to find his eyes on her from time to time. It had been so long since she had felt wanted, desirable. Also, it would drive François-Xavier nuts to know that she was spending so much time with his old nemesis, though she didn't suppose he was still plugged into the Île de Feme's gossip network. Maybe she should post some photographs of herself with Milo on social media . . . but that would be outing herself, wouldn't it?

It was all so complicated.

Late that night, Natalie let herself into the quiet guesthouse. Jean-Luc and Alex had already gone to bed, and Natalie realized how much nicer it was to be sharing the place with them than it had been living here alone. She wouldn't have expected everything to be so easy, so homey.

She made herself a cup of tea and checked her e-mail—no surprise: François-Xavier had not returned her message, and she doubted he ever would. So Natalie wrote up the island tales she had gathered so far, matched them with recipes and observations about the island, and sent it all off to her agent.

Upon hitting "send," Natalie blew out a long sigh.

She could only hope Sandy would approve.

Would you help me rearrange the furniture in here?" Natalie asked Alex the next day.

Alex looked around the parlor. "Dad always said never to rearrange the furniture. You have to be able to navigate in the dark."

"Like I care about his opinion. Let's try moving the couch to that other wall."

The two sisters began to move the surprisingly heavy couch.

"Oof," uttered Alex.

"Did it ever occur to you that our father was afraid of a lot of things?" Natalie asked. "I mean, I never really thought about it as a kid, but as an adult it strikes me that he lived a lot of his life in fear. Why else spend all your time preparing for the worst?"

"Well, he feared the government, though come to think of it he never really explained why." Alex shook her head. "Still does, I suppose. But now he's . . . old, Nat. Harmless."

"Does he still have his guns?"

"Okay, so not totally harmless," Alex said, giving the couch one final shove. She gazed about the room. "I don't think the couch works well here—it kind of sticks out, don't you think?"

"You're right. Let's put it over there," Natalie said, and they began moving the couch back to the other side of the room.

"I think losing the ranch he grew up on affected him deeply," Alex said. "I don't know. I never heard the whole story of what happened. But maybe that was when he stopped trusting anybody but his wife and kids."

"And then we betrayed him by leaving."

"That wasn't a betrayal, Nat. That was just life."

"That's not how he saw it."

"*I* didn't leave him," Alex said. "And he repaid my loyalty by betraying me."

Natalie paused and looked at Alex. "What exactly happened? I don't think I ever heard the full story."

"He sold our land right out from under me. He didn't discuss it with me and didn't give me a dime of the money he got for it, either, even though I was the one who paid the taxes on it *and* supported him and Mom all those years. I mean, it's not as if they qualified for Social Security, since neither one ever had a real job. And then he bought some land outside of Horseshoe Bend and took off. Serves me right, I guess," Alex said with a humorless laugh. "He told us not to trust anyone. I should have listened. Let's try the couch over there."

"Actually, what he said was 'Never trust anyone but family,'" Nat said, pushing the couch into position.

"Which means he was a traitor *and* a liar," Alex said. "I like the couch this way."

"I do, too. But now the rug's not working. Grab that end, and let's turn it a hundred eighty degrees."

"I suppose trusting anyone is like building a house on sand," Alex said, bending to pick up her side of the rug. "The only person you can truly count on is yourself."

"I don't think that's true," Natalie said. "I don't think that's true at all."

"You don't? After what the scumbag did to you?"

"Clearly, when it came to François-Xavier, I made a bad choice. And it's not the first time. I don't think I have the best taste in men. . . ."

"Are we talking about Milo now?"

Natalie shot her a glare. "*No.* But I'm talking about trusting people in general. I had a lot of help you know, when I moved to San Francisco. You can imagine how naive I was, how likely to be hurt. But I met a really nice girl who let me sleep on her couch, and then the people at the coffee shop were kind to me. Genuinely so. They offered me friendship, helped me figure out how to navigate the world, and didn't expect anything in return."

"I'm glad, Nat. Really glad." Alex sank onto the couch. She could still remember that hollow, aching feeling when The Commander said Natalie would die in the big city. "Yes, this is a much better arrangement."

Natalie joined her on the couch. "I think so, too. Good teamwork."

"So, about Milo. There's some gossip going around about the two of you."

"Alex, you've been here, what, two weeks? And you don't speak French? How is it you're already part of the rumor mill?"

"That's an excellent question. If you ask me, it takes about three days, tops, to be absorbed into the island gossip network. Resistance is futile."

"So what are people saying?"

"People don't like you and Milo hanging out together, Nat. You've got to come clean with them about François-Xavier, at least. Otherwise they'll blame you for being unfaithful when it's really all his fault."

"I know. You're right."

"And you know what Christine said about Ambroisine and lying. She might just hex you again, and I'm not sure how much more you could stand at this point."

Natalie chuckled. "Hey, she said we could go back tomorrow if we bring Christine with us, and she'd tell us more. Want to come?"

"Are you kidding me? I wouldn't miss out on a chance to see Ambroisine, much less her dog."

That afternoon, Alex was out running errands. Natalie went to the kitchen in search of a snack and found Jean-Luc heating the kettle for tea.

"Natalie, may I ask you a question?" he asked.

"Sure." She leaned on the counter. "What's up?"

"I wonder . . . I certainly do not mean to overstep. But I am worried about your sister."

"What do you mean?"

"I . . ." He looked uncomfortable. "It's the stumbling . . . and sometimes she appears a bit dizzy or disoriented. And there are the bruises. . . ."

"Bruises?"

"She bumps into things. Often. I just wondered if she needed anything . . . if there was anything I could help with."

Natalie opened her mouth, but no words came.

"I should probably discuss this with her directly, but she seems a bit sensitive. I know with the paperwork here in France, this sort of thing needs to be handled carefully, but I know a good doctor in Paris. Is she eligible for national health care?"

"She said she was fine," Natalie said at long last, her mind racing. Was something wrong with Alex? *Alex?* Alex never got sick; she sloughed off sprained ankles, bruised shins. When they were kids she once lost a fingernail and merely bound the bloody finger with an old shirt until it stopped bleeding and the nail grew back.

"Perhaps she is," said Jean-Luc, blushing. "I assumed something was wrong, and that was why she quit her job and came here to be with you."

"She's just visiting," said Natalie. *Out of the blue and after ten years of no contact?*

Had Alex ever actually said *why* she had come? Had Natalie ever asked her? Alex being sick would explain why her sister had followed her all the way here, off the Wild Coast of Brittany. She certainly hadn't come intending to renovate an old guesthouse.

Their eyes held for a long moment.

"Well, good, then," said Jean-Luc. "I would not want to intrude. I just . . . I like your sister a great deal. She's unlike anyone I have ever known. She makes me laugh, and seems to find me interesting, which still surprises me! And if there is one thing my career as a *fonctionnaire* has given me, it is the ability to navigate bureaucracies. I would be more than happy—I would be *eager* to help."

"Thank you, Jean-Luc," said Natalie. "That's very kind. But you're right. My sister is a very private person. I think we should let her tell us in her own time if there's anything wrong."

He nodded. "Of course. You know her best."

Natalie's words sounded cool, but her mind was racing. Should she call Faith or Hope to see if they had any insights? With the time difference it was the middle of the night for them. She could send some e-mails, see if they'd tell her anything.

It was hard to imagine something being wrong with Alex. She

was always so strong, so able. But their mother had been, too, and they hadn't realized she was sick until it was too late.

Natalie mounted the stairs and entered Alex's room. The bed was neatly made, Woolf's *To the Lighthouse* on the bedside table—either Alex was the slowest reader in the world, or she'd given up on the rather dense novel. Not that Natalie blamed her. As an English lit major, Natalie had read plenty of Woolf, and certainly appreciated her brilliance, but for pure diversion there were a lot of other books downstairs Alex might enjoy more. Natalie made a mental note to suggest some.

Next to the book were a flashlight and a water bottle, but that was it. No dirty socks, no items tossed on the floor, nothing. Natalie, in contrast, had lived out of a suitcase for months after she moved in with François-Xavier.

She eased open the top drawer of the bureau. Alex's few things were lined up like neat little soldiers. Underwear, T-shirts, a folded pair of jeans. Under the shirts she spied the spine of a book—

"What are you *doing*?" came Alex's voice from the doorway.

Natalie jumped. "Oh, um, sorry."

"You're going through my *drawers*?"

"I'm sorry, Alex, really. I was just curious to see if you were still as neat as you were as a little kid. Anyway, Jean-Luc mentioned something to me, and I wanted to ask you—"

"Get out," said Alex.

"What?"

"Didn't you hear me?" demanded Alex. "I said, get *out*."

CHAPTER FORTY-SIX

Alex

*N*at walked stiffly through the door and Alex slammed it shut behind her, leaning back against it, trying to calm her breath and her pounding heart. To quell her anger and shame.

Why should you feel shame? Faith, their supremely sensible older sister, had asked when Alex confessed her feelings.

Alex couldn't explain why, but it felt like a weakness. Something Alex couldn't stop, couldn't overcome.

And on its heels came anger, hot and fierce.

Damn. She had overreacted, which wasn't fair to Nat. Not that anything about this was fair. But then, "Life isn't fair" was one of The Commander's favorite sayings.

Alex blew out a long breath. Her little vacation had allowed her a brief respite, on a rather magical island, to pretend everything was fine. But the island wasn't actually magical, and there were no Gallizenae around to fix her. Things were getting worse; it was time to make some decisions. Take some steps.

Where would she go? Back to Albuquerque? Faith had invited her to come live with her near Salt Lake City. Alex didn't especially care for Faith's husband, but she would enjoy spending time with her nieces and nephews while they were still young. Still . . . what would she *do* there besides hang out? *Could* she simply hang out? It wasn't in Alex's nature not to be useful.

In any case . . . she needed to come clean to Nat, let her know what was happening. Nat had always been smart, but now she was also worldly. Much more so than Alex, and probably far more adept at dealing with the brave new world than Alex was.

Maybe Alex should just get over herself and ask her baby sister for advice.

Alex made her way down the two flights of stairs, pausing for a moment to take pride in the new paint job. It made a huge difference. Another few weeks and most of the cosmetic work would be finished, and most of the electrical, with Ismael's generous help. That still left the second-floor bathroom fixtures, and of course the furniture and other supplies. . . . But if they kept on track, they would have this place ready for guests by the Festival of the Gallizenae in October. Maybe not perfect, but ready enough.

Alex was heading for Nat's office when she heard the sounds of crying coming from outside.

She peeked out the kitchen window and saw Nat kneeling in the mud, her head hanging down. Sobbing.

Had their fight bothered Nat that much? This seemed a bit of an overreaction.

The kitchen door squeaked loudly as Alex let herself out into the garden, but Nat still didn't look up. It was only as Alex neared her sister that she saw the too-still mound of white feathers, the longest, fluffiest ones wafting silently in the breeze.

Bobox.

"Ah, Nat, I'm sorry," said Alex, squatting in the dirt beside her sister and wrapping her arm around her, holding Natalie as she sobbed.

Nat's tears seemed out of proportion to the death of a chicken—after all, they had dined on a lovely *poulet au estragon* just last night.

But then Alex remembered the bitter loss of her dog, Buddy, and how for weeks, even months afterward she would suddenly break down and cry in public, feeling like an idiot, but not caring because no one had known Buddy like she had, had seen him covered in mange and fleas and assorted wounds inflicted by who knew what, his ribs protruding, desperate for food, for a safe place to sleep, for someone to love and to love him in return. She had spent an hour coaxing him out from under an old car at the junkyard where he'd sought refuge from the cruelty of humans, and he had only slowly learned to trust her, had blossomed with food and baths and consistent affection, the look in his eyes gradually changing from fear to trust and love. It might sound silly to someone who had never had a Buddy in their life, but that mutt had given her the courage to break away from not only her father but from that whole world, to leave behind once and for all the doomsday plans and bluster. Buddy had helped teach Alex to trust herself, to lift her eyes from the looming threat of The Change and make friends in the here and now, to appreciate what she had while she had it.

Buddy's love was the purest thing Alex had ever known.

But then, dogs were famous for devotion. As Alex gazed now at the white hen, her little orange beak open as though in surprise, it was hard to imagine Nat had felt something similar for Bobox—for *poultry*—but who was Alex to judge?

Alex pushed Nat's hair out of her face, wet with tears.

"Don't you dare make a crack about frying her up for dinner!" Nat said in a fierce whisper, then hiccupped.

Alex shook her head. "I won't. I wouldn't. She was a good little hen."

"She was." Nat sniffed loudly and let out a shaky breath.

"She was," Alex repeated. "And you gave her a good life."

"I tried," Nat said. "I mean, I didn't even know her that long. . . ."

"She seemed pretty happy to me," Alex said. "Hey, I have an idea. What if we buried her right there, in that corner where you were going to plant the yellow rose for Mom? It would be a pretty memorial, seeing the roses blooming over her."

A long moment passed. Nat took another deep breath and sat up, pulling away from Alex. She ran an arm over her face.

"That's a good idea," she said in a small voice. "But I—I don't think I can touch her."

"I'll do it," Alex said. "You know what? There's an old wooden box in the shed. How about I make a little bed for her out of those ugly curtains you got for the kitchen?"

"They really are ugly, aren't they?" Nat said with a reluctant smile.

"They really are. But they're soft. And aren't hens color-blind, anyway?"

"Are they?"

"Remember when Mom taught us about the cones in our eyes, how there were colors we couldn't even imagine?"

Nat nodded. "I remember. But I don't remember what she said about chickens."

"Me neither. But I'm pretty sure Bobox won't mind, no matter how many cones she has. I'll take care of her, Nat. Don't worry."

"Thank you, Alex."

CHAPTER FORTY-SEVEN

Natalie

$\mathscr{B}$y the time they were patting down the dirt over Bobox's grave, the late-afternoon light was dimming. Alex stood, turned too quickly, and bumped into Natalie.

"Oops, sorry," she murmured.

"No worries," said Natalie. She watched her sister for a moment. "Alex, why are you here?"

Alex tilted her head. "I'm helping you with Bobox."

"I mean what brought you *here*, to the Île de Feme?"

Alex paused for a moment, then said lightly, "It's not enough to want to visit my sister?"

"Not really, no. I can't help feeling there's more to it."

Alex gave a humorless laugh. "I need . . . I needed a place to land for a little bit."

"You're welcome to stay as long as you want. But . . . are you all right?"

Alex looked away.

"Alex, are you sick?" Natalie asked.

When her sister still didn't answer, fear knifed through Natalie. *Jean-Luc was right.*

"I notice you've been stumbling," continued Natalie. "You never used to trip over anything. And there have been other things. I mean, I know it's been a while since we spent a lot of time together, but . . . can't you tell me?"

Alex seemed to be fighting back tears. Alex *never* cried. Natalie was the designated crier in the Morgen family.

Finally, Alex choked out: "I'm not dying or anything. So there's that."

"That's good to hear."

"Not really. In a way it's worse than that. I mean, it's not *worse*. It's just . . ."

"Tell me. Please, Alex."

Alex hesitated, but then decided it was time. "You know how I got so upset when you were looking in my drawer?"

Natalie nodded.

"I didn't want you to find my book of Braille."

"Braille? As in the print for the blind?"

Alex nodded.

"Why . . . I mean, how is it you read Braille?"

"I don't. I'm trying to learn."

"Because . . . ?"

"Nat, I'm going blind."

CHAPTER FORTY-EIGHT

Alex

I don't . . . I don't understand," Nat stammered. "What's wrong? How bad is it?"

"I still have some vision, obviously, mostly right in the center. I started losing my night vision first. Then my peripheral vision got bad."

Nat opened her mouth, but appeared to be speechless.

"It comes on slowly," Alex continued. "It's sort of like looking through a hole in a fence—part of what I see is light and bright and the rest is blurred out and dark. I call it the 'creeping blackness,' and it's been caving in on me a tiny, terrifying bit at a time."

"That sounds awful."

Alex found Nat's blunt words somehow comforting. "It is."

"Can't it be stopped? There must be some sort of treatment."

Alex shook her head. "There's ongoing research but as yet nothing is especially effective, at least in my case."

"Have you seen a doctor?"

"Several."

"I'm talking about actual medical professionals," Nat said. "Not just old women with herbs?"

Alex let out a chuckle. Getting her eyes checked had been the first time in her life she'd been to an "actual medical professional." Until the black creeping began, Alex had been healthy to the point of absurdity, evading flus and colds and sidestepping even the most basic complaints.

"I went to real ophthalmologists with modern equipment and everything," said Alex. "The best specialists in Albuquerque, and when they couldn't help, I tried a few in Phoenix and in Salt Lake City. It's called retinitis pigmentosa. It's genetic, so it runs in families. We're lucky it's only me. I insisted Faith and Hope get their kids tested, but so far everyone's good. I take it you haven't had any problems? You would have noticed by now."

Natalie shook her head. "What about Charity?"

"I've sent messages, but no reply."

"Okay, so what are the next steps? We'll take you to see a doctor. I'll find someone in Quimper, or better yet we'll go to Paris. . . ."

"You think the French have a miracle cure they've been keeping a secret?" Alex scoffed. "Even if they did, I don't have that kind of money."

"National health care, remember?"

"I'm not French, though. Would I qualify for health care as a nonresident?"

"Probably not . . . but even if you have to pay for it, I'll bet it's cheaper here than back home. I saw a doctor in Paris once and it cost me less than half the dinner bill at Milo's Café."

A long moment passed.

"So . . . what are your plans?" Nat asked.

Alex would have assumed she had a plan, too, had it been any other problem. She thought again of Nat as a kid, climbing that stupid rock and halfway up becoming too frightened to move, how Alex had called down to her: *The only way to go is up, Nat. Keep climbing.* Alex had been so sure of herself then. So strong and healthy, always ready to act. Now, for the first time in her life, she truly understood the urge to freeze, to pretend that nothing was happening, even though she was hanging off the edge of a cliff.

"I have some time to figure things out. A little time yet. Hey, did you know Louis Braille was French?"

"He's the inventor of Braille writing?" Nat asked.

Alex nodded. "Napoleon needed a way for messages to be deciphered in the dark, so they developed a system called 'night writing' based on feeling the words instead of seeing them. Louis Braille developed the Braille alphabet based on that."

The day Alex read about Louis Braille and the Royal Institution for Blind Youth in Paris, it had made her think of Nat, and gave her the idea of visiting her sister. In search of what, exactly, Alex wasn't sure.

"I didn't know that," said Nat. "But, with technology and voice systems today, do people still use Braille?"

"Apparently, they do." Alex shrugged. "It's not easy to learn, though. I was never great at reading or studying, anyway. I must be an idiot to think I could teach myself something like Braille."

"Maybe I could help," Nat offered. "We could learn it together."

"Maybe," Alex said, turning her face up to the sky. The sun was going down, the clouds taking on a moody, pinkish golden streaky nature. Sunshine had always been important to Alex. It energized her, made her happy, and was a big reason why she had moved to the Southwest. What would it be like to lose the last of her vision, to live in perpetual darkness? Panic gripped her, and no amount of telling herself *she would find a way, she always found a way, others managed it and she would, too,* assuaged that fear.

She would be in the dark, forever. Alone.

As if sensing her thoughts, Nat put her arm around Alex's shoulders, and after a moment, Alex rested her head on her little sister's sweet-smelling hair. Had they ever stood like this, she wondered, Nat holding her rather than the other way around?

And then she heard Nat chuckling.

"What's funny?" Alex asked.

"I was just thinking about us—Jean-Luc, me, and you, the three of us hunkered down in this ramshackle old building. A useless bureaucrat, a stressed-out writer, and a blind handywoman, waiting out the storm."

They laughed.

And then they cried.

Nat and Alex had planned to go to Ambroisine's the next evening, after Christine came back from her day at sea and had a chance to "shower off the fish guts," as she liked to say.

Jean-Luc had been gone much of the day, touring the island with the climate-change group that Ismael worked with, as well as meeting with the assistant mayor.

He seemed unaccountably nervous when Alex passed him in the upstairs hall.

"Alex, I wonder if I could talk with you a moment?" Jean-Luc said.

"Of course. Everything okay?"

"Yes, yes, I am okay, or at least I think I am. Alex, I try hard to be a good man. But I am not . . . I know I am not anything special. I have worked hard to raise my children, and I was proud to support them in their studies, in their hobbies. But I do not believe they think of me very often."

"I'm sure that's not true."

"No, no, it is. I do not mind this. It is the way it should be. We raised them to be independent, and they are off on their own now, with their own lives. In the future, if they have children, perhaps we will spend more time together—I hope we will. I think I would be a good *grand-père.*"

"I think you would be, too," Alex said.

"But for this moment now, it is just fine. . . . I am on my own."

"I'm not sure I'm following you, Jean-Luc. What's on your mind?"

"My point is, I have spent most of my life doing my duty. Doing what is required. I do not regret it—to quote Edith Piaf, *"Je ne regrette rien"*—but now, for the first time, I can do what I choose to do. I am not a young man, but I am healthy and with luck I have a good part of my life in front of me, and a decent pension from the government. I want something different for myself, to explore a different aspect of myself. That is why I came here to the island." He smiled. "As I mentioned, it was unexpected."

"I'll bet it was."

"I think I was as surprised as anyone. I was open to anything when I came here, and I have found something I never knew."

"Okay . . . Jean-Luc, I'm still not sure what you're talking about."

"I have given it a lot of thought and this is what I would like to know: Alex, could you see yourself having a future with me?"

"What do you mean?"

"I just mean that if you would like to stay here in France, I will help you."

"I don't need any help," she said, her voice flat.

"But, Alex, I feel as though the normal rules of society do not apply in this situation. I mean, why *should* they apply? I care for you, and I want to be sure you have what you need. I believe I can give you that."

She shook her head. "I thought you were going to tell me you had found another place to live or something. This is . . . this is crazy."

"And is it so wrong to be a little crazy?"

"That's not the point. I mean, what are you talking about, a future together? We barely know each other. We haven't even *kissed* each other."

His voice dropped. "Did you want me to kiss you, Alex?"

As a matter of fact, she *had* thought about kissing Jean-Luc, but that was hardly the point. A moment passed, while Alex tried to think of what to say. Shame washed over her, even though she knew she shouldn't feel such an emotion in response to a medical condition over which she had no control. Still, she felt blindsided. Literally.

"I did not mean for this to be a big deal . . . ," he said, hedging.

"It feels like a big deal to me."

"Alex, it's just that I would be happy to help take care of you."

"I don't need someone to take care of me," Alex said, her shame morphing to anger. "What I *need* is my sight back."

His eyes widened. "You're losing your sight?"

"Didn't you know?"

"How would I know? I only wondered if you needed some help."

"What I *need* is for you to find another place to live, Jean-Luc. Sooner rather than later. I will take care of myself."

CHAPTER FORTY-NINE

Violette

*N*oëlle was surprisingly amenable to our plan, though Marceline's deteriorating condition did not leave us much choice. She needed to be rescued, or she would die. Noëlle explained that the boat, which we now referred to as the Bag-Noz, or ghost ship, was expected to pass off the coast of Brest three nights from now. She had a code she could use to make the message unintelligible to others, and to let the crew know it was not an ambush.

Noëlle was also invaluable in convincing a large group of the island women who no longer trusted me to go along with our plan.

"I always loved the story of Circe, who changed Odysseus's men into swine," I said as we discussed plans for the proposed evening of wine, women, and song.

"They're already swine," said Noëlle. "I like the part about them falling asleep. Too bad it's not forever."

Rainer did his part by suggesting the idea to his fellow Germans:

The women of the island needed more supplies to feed their growing children, and wanted to keep their cows to provide milk. The women had proposed an exchange, Rainer explained: For one night, the Abri du Marin would be transformed into a fantastical cabaret, and the soldiers agreed not to slaughter the cows. In addition, every soldier's entrance fee would be extra ration tickets or nonperishable items from their own canteen.

Over generous servings of cider, Rainer smiled and asked the men: Didn't they deserve a night of raucous good fun? Nothing ever happened on the island and there was nothing to do but watch the *jibilinnen*-clad women scurrying along the passageways, avoiding contact with the soldiers, speaking only with reluctance. What would it be like to enjoy their feminine company for one evening, to get a peek at the women hidden under their voluminous black skirts?

With so little time to prepare, it was not possible to speak to every woman on the island. So we used our efficient gossip network to spread the news, and Rainer sketched some simple sewing patterns in my mother's cookbook. In these "recipes," "rainwater" referred to Rainer, and "Circe" referred to the upcoming event.

The old book was passed around to every Fémane on the island, from neighbor to neighbor, one after another. Each woman indicated what she was prepared to contribute, whether it was sewing costumes or decorating the Abri du Marin or preparing refreshments. The younger women who were willing to entertain the soldiers added their measurements to the book if they did not feel confident in sewing their own costumes.

We stayed awake nearly all night for two nights in a row, setting everything up: sewing and decorating, coordinating, and preparing Marceline and her all-important lipstick for the rendezvous with the Bag-Noz.

It was a huge risk. If we were found out, the punishment would be severe, But it was a risk the women of the island seemed willing, even eager, to take.

We had gotten special permission for a number of us to gather together to sew. Our one great asset was the disdain in which most of the soldiers held women. In the soldiers' eyes, women were meant to cook and sing and dance for their amusement. We were good for nothing more.

"So assign a man to guard them if you are concerned," Rainer suggested one night at dinner, when the always-suspicious Hans objected to our proposed sewing circle. "That way you may be sure the women of this godforsaken island are not plotting to overthrow the Third Reich."

He said this last with a smile and a wink, and the other officers at the table laughed. Hans looked annoyed but said nothing further. What harm could a women's sewing circle cause?

Using my sailor's valentine as inspiration, we boiled rabbit hides to make glue, and used the sharp tines of our tiny silver *bigorneaux* forks to drill in delicate seashells holes just large enough to pass a needle and thread. My mother looted her own death drawer to contribute satin from her wedding gown, and others scavenged through their drawers and trunks for bits of silk and lace, buttons and hooks and eyes, fringe and fabric for the ornate costumes. Even the children did their part, scouring the island and the beaches for feathers and shells, pretty pebbles, and fistfuls of sea glass.

My heart swelled with fear and pride at the sight of so many black-clad figures gathered in our kitchen and dining room, bent over their sewing projects, silver needles flashing: Marie-Paule, Irmine, Lazarette, Corinne, Angelique. The older women, too, joined us: my mother, and Madame Canté, and even my *belle-mère*, Gladie, who came out of her mourning seclusion to do what she could to help the cause, weeping softly while she sewed.

While the rest of us worked on the elaborate costumes, two of the most talented seamstresses concentrated on making Rainer his very own *jibilinnen* and *robe noire*.

Near dawn of the second day, exhausted from sewing all night, we finally ushered the last of our neighbors out of the guesthouse. After they left, I helped Rainer slip his custom *robe noire* over his head, doing up the dozens of hooks and eyes that closed the gown in the back.

He ran his hands along the sleeves down to the skirt almost reverently, as though the traditional black dress were a holy artifact.

"I used to play dress-up as a child," he confessed. "There was an old trunk filled with boas and skirts, hats and scarves, and my father encouraged me to try things on. He believed in encouraging a child's imagination and creative expression. It felt so natural. It wasn't until much, much later that I realized my desire to dress as a woman made me a freak."

"You are in no way a freak, Rainer."

He gave me a sad smile. "Tell that to my mother. Most boys don't want to wear girl's clothing, as she was quick to remind me."

"Most girls don't think like me, either," I said. "You and I must each have unruly hearts."

"I used to gaze at myself in the mirror when I put on skirts, feeling the way they brushed my legs, knowing they suited me better, somehow."

"And just look at yourself now," I said, turning him toward the looking glass.

He gazed at his reflection for a long moment, his large hands passing over his chest and waist. Then he met my eyes, and when he spoke, there was a note of wonder in his voice:

"It fits me so well."

"Ah, but that's not all." I fitted his new *jibilinnen* over his short blond hair. "Now you are very fetching, indeed."

"I'm a little . . . tall and wide."

I smiled. "We islanders are a sturdy people. You look like a true, strong Fémane."

CHAPTER FIFTY

Natalie

While she waited for Alex to get changed, Natalie opened her laptop, called up a search engine, and typed in "retinitis pigmentosa."

As frightened as Alex was at the prospect of losing her sight, Natalie was willing to bet that what unsettled her sister most was the thought of losing her independence, of being forced to rely others. Alex was a stoic, an adventurer, someone who, when fate rolled a boulder in her path, found a way to go over it, around it, or through it.

But she wasn't prepared for this.

Natalie read numerous articles posted to websites devoted to eye health and eye diseases. The prognosis for patients with retinitis pigmentosa was not good, and the existing treatments were of limited value. Alex might lose all her sight, or she might be left with some ability to detect motion and sense light and dark. Either way, she was going to need help.

This time fate had thrown a boulder at Alex that was too heavy, even for her.

And that meant they would have to figure out another way. Natalie took a deep breath and squared her shoulders. Approaching a problem this big was like writing a book—you couldn't sit down and write the thing all in one go. You wrote word by word, one sentence at a time, chapter after chapter.

Not that Natalie had taken such advice with her own writing lately, she thought with a rueful sigh.

Break it down, make a list, get to work. Starting with ways to mitigate the impact of Alex's loss of vision upon her daily routine. Her sister could learn to use a cane to get around without tripping and could listen to audiobooks instead of reading. Those were easy to take care of. She would also qualify for financial assistance from Social Security, and while it wouldn't be a lot of money, every little bit would help. Natalie could help her get started with the paperwork on that right away.

Natalie scrolled down through more search results, and a website for guide dogs caught her eye. She read some more, then sat back in her chair and smiled.

That would lift Alex's spirits, she thought. *A new Buddy.*

Later, as the sisters headed to meet Christine at *chez* Ambroisine, each with a basket of goodies slung over one arm, Natalie noticed Alex waving and nodding to Loïc at the Pouce Café, to Brigitte as they passed by her *fish et chips* restaurant, to Tarik and Madame Cariou and old Monsieur Toullec. Alex had been on the Île de Feme such a short a time, and already fit in so much better than Natalie, though Natalie was the one who prided herself on being so worldly and adaptable.

Speaking of adapting . . .

"So, here's a thought: a guide dog," said Natalie as they walked through the narrow pathways of the village.

"Funny you should say that. I was wondering if Korrigan could be my guide dog," Alex said. "Assuming Ambroisine is amenable."

"Not to mention Korrigan."

Alex chuckled. "Her, too."

"The problem is that Korrigan could only lead you around this island. Real guide dogs are trained to help you cross the street in traffic, that sort of thing. They call it a 'guide dog lifestyle.' You have to go to the center and stay while you get trained."

"I thought the *dogs* were trained."

"They train you, too, I think is the point. The two of you together. The dogs are true service animals, and have little jackets to let people know not to pet them."

"Korrigan doesn't like to be petted," said Alex. "I think she'd be great."

"You're not taking this seriously."

"Oh, but I am," said Alex.

"At least think about it," said Natalie. "I could help you get signed up, and pay for your plane ticket. After all, I've got all that rent coming in from Jean-Luc, in addition to the book money."

"Oh, about that . . ."

"What?" asked Natalie as they emerged from the heart of the village and headed down the pathway toward the hotel, the ocean on one side and fields of vegetables on the other.

"On the plus side, you now have an empty, newly painted, fully rentable room upstairs."

"What happened?"

"Jean-Luc . . . He . . . We . . ."

"You like him."

Alex gave a quick shake of her head. "It's worse than that."

"You love him?"

"*No.* No. He . . . he says he wants us to have a future together."

"But that's really sweet. Isn't it?"

"It isn't a love thing. It's a *pity* thing. He says he wants to take care of me, like his dizzy old cat." Alex frowned, looked out at the darkening ocean, and switched on her heavy flashlight against the fading light. "I don't need his help. His *charity*."

She spit out the last word as if it were a curse.

"I doubt he meant it that way," said Natalie softly. "I know we haven't known Jean-Luc long, but from everything I've seen, he's a good man. I'm sure he meant only kindness. And besides, I think it might have a little something to do with love, or at least strong *like*. Have you seen the way he looks at you?"

Alex shrugged. "Whatever. It's better without him around."

Natalie wasn't so sure, but decided to let it go for now. "What time frame are we talking about, Alex? I read up on retinitis pigmentosa, but it seems like the disease is pretty variable. Where are you at on the spectrum?"

"It's strange. Some days are better than others. My night vision and peripheral vision are compromised, and my field of vision is growing smaller over time. Pretty soon it may be all gone."

Alex crouched, set her basket on the ground, and started rearranging the already neatly stowed baked goods and bottles of cider they were bringing to Ambroisine. Natalie realized, as she hadn't before, the frantic nature of her sister's busyness, how she used it as an avoidance tactic.

"We have to prepare, Alex," Natalie said.

Alex stilled and admitted in a fierce whisper: *"I don't know how."*

"I know you don't. Neither do I. But I'm here. We'll figure this out together."

Christine met the sisters at Ambroisine's door with her typical effusiveness. If she noticed their subdued mood, she didn't mention it, and launched into a story about getting her net caught in her dock neighbor's motor this morning as she pulled out of the harbor.

Inside the cottage, Korrigan glowered at them from her post by the fireplace. Ambroisine greeted them and began poking through the baskets to see what they had brought her. She nodded, apparently pleased, and told them to stash them in the kitchen. Then she invited them to sit with her at the table and, without preamble, began to speak.

"There was a young woman named Marceline Carmèle. That wasn't her real name, of course; she was with the French resistance, and had managed to take photographs of the Nazi shipbuilding facilities in Brest. She was shot at some point and came to the Île de Feme in search of medical attention. My mentor, Madame Thérèse, was called in to try to help her."

Natalie translated for Alex, while simultaneously jotting down notes.

"The young woman had already developed a high fever from the infection and needed the bullet removed. Madame Thérèse was a skillful healer but she was not a surgeon. We did the best we could, but the young woman had to be taken off the island for proper surgery."

"Wait," interrupted Christine. "How did she get here, to the island? Was she a Fémane?"

Ambroisine shook her head. "She came with false papers. Violette's German soldier granted her entry."

"Who was 'Violette's German soldier'?" asked Natalie.

"His name was Rainer," said Ambroisine. "It means *pluie* in English, does it not? I don't remember his last name. Anyway, he helped us."

"Was he in love with Violette?" Natalie asked.

"Do you want to hear the story or not?" snapped Ambroisine.

Christine poured a generous portion of cider into the old woman's cup. "Yes, please, we would like to hear more."

Ambroisine nodded, mollified. "The Germans had long since found and destroyed Henri Thomas's radio, but Noëlle Guilcher was in touch with a smugglers' boat that made regular runs between France and England, avoiding the German patrols. It sometimes came close enough to the island to deliver packages. But they had to find a way to signal the boat, and the only way they could think of to do that was to use the lighthouse."

"The lighthouse?" Alex asked. *"Phare"* was one of the words in French that she recognized.

"Yes," said Ambroisine. "The plan was to signal the smugglers' boat when it was safe for it to come to the cove and pick up Marceline. Noëlle had a code to use to communicate with them. The problem was how to distract the soldiers while all this was going on."

"That *would* be a problem," said Natalie. "Weren't there hundreds of soldiers on this tiny island?"

Ambroisine nodded and lit a cigarillo. "This was why they needed the help of the island women. The men, the German soldiers, were bored because there wasn't much to do on the island. They were young, and while many of them were glad to be far from the fighting, others wanted to see more action. And all of them were far from their homes, jealous of their colleagues who were in Paris, enjoying the cafés and revues that went on there.

"So Rainer proposed to the men that the women would create a spectacle for them, for one night only."

"A spectacle?" asked Alex when Natalie translated the phrase directly.

"They mean like a show, with dancing and singing," said Christine.

Alex smiled. "Like 'Hey, kids, let's put on a show!'?"

"Something like that," Natalie said to Alex. It *did* sound pretty far-fetched; perhaps Ambroisine was exaggerating for the sake of a good story. On the other hand, they had found those costumes tucked away in the attic, and that photograph of the cabaret. . . . Natalie looked up to see that Ambroisine's eyes were on her, as though she were waiting. "Sorry. Please continue."

"The women turned their energy to making costumes. Time was of the essence, as the boat was due in three days. The women used whatever they had: material from old wedding dresses and lace from nightgowns, candy box silk liners and old linens, whatever they found tucked away in drawers and attics. But most of the decorations were gifts from the ocean: shells and feathers, with sea glass for beads. They used all their skill to transform the Abri du Marin into an underwater fantasy, for one night only."

"Pretty gutsy," Alex muttered. Christine translated for Ambroisine, who nodded in approval.

"It was indeed. This generation of island women wore the *robe noire* and *jibilinnen* every day of their adult lives. And they were fiercely patriotic, so the idea of 'consorting' with the enemy was anathema to them. But Violette—or Noëlle—convinced them it would be a valuable contribution to the war effort."

"I still don't understand how I've never heard about any of this," said Christine. "Why were there no rumors, and only that one photograph?"

Ambroisine grinned. "Noëlle took that photograph, in case she needed to blackmail someone later. Always scheming, that one. But the reason no one talked about it was simple: Their men never would have understood."

"You mean the men who sailed away and left the women to deal with the invading army by themselves? Those men?" Alex said.

"It was a different time, child," Ambroisine said softly. "This island is very old-fashioned in some ways, and was still more so back then. The women were embarrassed even to be seen not dressed in black, much less clad in feathered costumes."

"Did you join the women in the show, Ambroisine?" Christine asked.

"Madame Thérèse forbade me from going. She said I was too young."

"But you went anyway, didn't you?" Alex asked, and Ambroisine smiled.

"Of course I did. I snuck in and hid behind the stage curtain to watch what was happening. It was beautiful, the Abri du Marin transformed, and all the women dressed as sirens, feathered and bejeweled."

"And what kind of show did they put on?" asked Natalie.

She laughed. "A short one! Madame Thérèse had brewed a sleeping draft that the women mixed into the beer and cider served that night. After a few songs and a dance or two, the men fell sleep. They awoke the next morning with a terrible headache and assumed they had drunk too much."

"That's amazing," said Christine. "So that's where the costumes came from?"

"I suppose so. They were hidden away in attics and basements. None of the women wanted their men to know what had happened. A few rumors leaked out, mostly fueled by the old men who were, of course, not invited that night. But the women kept their secrets, and even when France was liberated and the collaboration investigations began, none would say aught against the others."

"That's true courage," Alex said.

"And Violette was in love with one of the soldiers?" Natalie asked.

Ambroisine nodded, but seemed lost in thought. "That's what

people said. Whether it is true or not . . . ? All I know is that Rainer, the German officer, helped the island women that night. When his mission was accomplished, he turned his back on the Nazis and started for England in a boat too small to make the journey. Sadly, he did not get very far. They found some of the wreckage just offshore."

"Were they able to signal the passing boat? Marceline was rescued?"

"She was rescued, yes," Ambroisine said, stubbing out her cigarillo.

"Why wasn't there a formal inquiry?" asked Natalie. "Given what the Nazis were capable of, I would have imagined they would have investigated this thoroughly, maybe even torn the island apart to find the guilty parties."

"The Germans covered it up." Ambroisine chuckled. "The unit's commanding officer did not wish to advertise that a group of women had distracted his soldiers and even the guards at the lighthouse, and the soldiers themselves were afraid of being reassigned to the Eastern Front if the German High Command learned what had happened. So they kept quiet, too. It was better for everyone that way."

Natalie had been translating the story to Alex, who was petting Korrigan. They all sat for a long moment, contemplating those women so long ago duping their German occupiers to save a life and to help the cause of freedom.

"I have a question," said Alex after a moment. "They say the two women who ran the Bag-Noz, Violette and Doura, were sisters. But according to the family's *livret de famille*, Violette's sister, Rachelle, lived with her husband in his mother's house. So who was Doura?"

"I've talked enough for one night," said Ambroisine. "Alex, you must go to the Chapel of Saint Corentin to lay a loaf of bread at his feet. And you're welcome to take the dog, if she wants. Korrigan goes where she wants."

"Um . . . okay," said Alex. "Does it matter what kind of bread?"

The old woman chuckled. "Not in the least, but it must be fresh, not stale bread you would throw away. To have meaning, it must be a sacrifice."

Alex nodded. "Yes, ma'am."

Ambroisine peered at her. "Don't you want to know why I say this?"

"I assume you have your reasons," Alex said with a shrug.

Ambroisine gestured at Alex and said to Natalie: "I like this one. This is the one I like."

"Yeah." Natalie smiled. "I like her, too."

The Bag-Noz was not the same without Jean-Luc.

Natalie missed his cheery moods in the morning when she came out to the kitchen. She missed his *coffee*. But mostly she missed the way Jean-Luc used to make her sister smile, how Alex lit up when he was around, became relaxed and chatty.

Through the grapevine Natalie learned that Jean-Luc had started working with Ismael at the climate change initiative, and had found an apartment next door to Monsieur Le Guen, the mayor's assistant.

She made a mental note to go by and say hello, make sure he knew there were no hard feelings, at least on her part. Natalie had the distinct impression Alex would come around eventually. She had found Alex in Jean-Luc's room the other day, gazing out the window. Alex claimed she was making sure the room was ready for guests, but Natalie was certain there was something deeper at play.

Still, Alex had never been particularly astute at dealing with her emotions. Maybe once she had a plan for the future she would be able to make the mental space for Jean-Luc.

Speaking of mental space . . . Natalie had a phone appointment with her agent. She sat at her desk, looked out at the garden, and steeled herself.

"Sorry, Natalie," said Sandy, "but the market's been flooded with cookbooks. Unless you're a celebrity chef or some kind of Food Network personality, they're just not selling."

"But people love cookbooks."

"They do, but not from *you*. I mean, just how many fish pies do you think your average American is interested in reading about? Unless you can make it a diet cookbook. Any way you can do that?"

"The Île de Feme *diet* cookbook?" Natalie said, irked. "Are you kidding me?"

"Hey, it's fish," Sandy said. "That's good for diets, right?"

"Not when it's cooked in a pie."

"True. Now, the salted caramel topping, that's great stuff. I love that stuff. But it won't sell books all by itself."

"But what about all the island color? The stories from the elderly islanders, the legends, the photos . . . ?"

"They don't want a travelogue, either. Natalie, your readers want love, romance, adventure. *Excitement*. Frankly, this thing reads flat. I mean, I'm sure I could find a place for it, maybe get your publisher to issue it alongside the real book. But I need the one they contracted for."

One of the things Natalie used to like about Sandy was that she didn't mince words. If her agent didn't like something, she said so, which was the sort of in-your-face directness Natalie had grown up with. At the moment, though, Natalie would not have minded a little kid-glove treatment. She already felt raw and vulnerable, and Sandy's bluntness wasn't helping.

"Listen, don't take it so hard. This is what happens when your debut book is a breakout success," Sandy continued, her tone a bit gentler. "There's nowhere to go but down. I've seen it play out a hundred times. Nothing personal, but we need more . . . *inspiration*. You're an inspirational author, after all. That's your brand." There was a pause. "So, how's François-Xavier?"

"He's fine." *Did Sandy know? Should Natalie tell her?*

"Good. Keep your eye on the ball, Natalie. The cookbook's a cute side dish, but it's not the main course."

Trying to process this latest news from her agent, Natalie walked out to the cove, kicked off her shoes, and let her feet sink into the sand, then spent a good half an hour poking around and collecting shells and sea glass. She thought of the costumes in the trunk in the parlor, and of the outlandish tale Ambroisine had told them about the one-night-only spectacle at the Abri du Marin. Funny that the building now housed the island's museum. She made a mental note to speak to the museum's director about donating the two *robes noires* and *jibilin-nen*, plus the cabaret costumes. But maybe she should first get Ambroisine's permission to share the Circe story. No need to flirt with any more curses.

As she strolled along the seawall toward the Bag-Noz, Natalie noticed a clutch of half a dozen young women lingering outside the gates, taking selfies.

Damn it. It was too late to duck into the passageway and enter through the garden gate. She had already been spotted.

"Wait. You're her, right?" asked one pretty young woman who looked like she was in her early twenties. Her eyes flickered over Natalie's windblown hair, casual dress, all the way down to her sandy feet. "You're Natalie Morgen the author?"

Natalie considered trying to deny it, but figured it would only make things worse. So she straightened her shoulders, pasted on a smile, and waded into the fray.

"I am, yes!" she said. "Where are you all from?"

"We're on a study abroad in Paris, but we've read your book."

"Oh, isn't that lovely?" said Natalie. She noticed none of them carried the book with them, so she assumed they had not come in search of her autograph. So why were they there?

"So, where's François-Xavier?" one of them asked.

"He's in Paris at the moment," said Natalie.

One of the girls giggled and asked if she could get a selfie with Natalie, and Natalie agreed. Then they all joined in, and started posting from their phones, giggling more.

"The thing is, Natalie, we just took these in Paris," said one of them, showing her a selfie with François-Xavier and Celeste Peyroux. "They said they're opening a restaurant together there. Don't they look cute together?"

Natalie felt her face flame, and wondered how obvious it was in bright daylight. *I should have seen this coming*, she thought, feeling like not only a fraud but a fool. She looked longingly at the front door of the Bag-Noz.

"So we were wondering," said another young woman. "What's going on? Are you two still together?"

"I gotta say," said still another, "he doesn't sound like a man who's coming back here. He said he wouldn't live anyplace but Paris."

"Big words for a guy without a nickel in his pocket," said Alex, who was suddenly standing at the gate, no doubt attracted by the hubbub. The gate squeaked as she opened it. "I keep forgetting to fix that," she muttered, then turned to the crowd.

"The next time you see François-Xavier"—Alex practically spat his name—"be sure to ask him how he can afford to live in Paris and open a restaurant, considering he hasn't had a job since his last position as a line cook more than a year ago. Could it be he's now mooching off his rich new girlfriend?"

The young women looked surprised.

"He's super hot," one said.

"You think so?" Alex asked, her tone skeptical. "Maybe it's just me, but I don't want a man who can be bought. When it comes to love, you get what you pay for."

"What do you know about love?" one said tartly.

"Not a lot, but more than you apparently. Just think about it. In any case, don't you have your own lives to lead? Run along now, pretty ones. Go break some shallow hearts. That's it, shoo."

The young women laughed a little uncertainly and sauntered off. Alex wrapped her arm protectively around Natalie and led her inside.

"Are you okay?" Alex asked as soon as she closed the front door behind them.

"I wish you hadn't said that about the money. It makes me look like an even bigger fool than I already am. Also, give the devil his due: François-Xavier's a really good cook."

"And a rotten human being. My conscience is clear."

"Alex, you are looking at a so-called 'inspirational' author who has no manuscript, no boyfriend, no money, and is fresh out of ideas."

"I take it the call with your agent didn't go well?"

"You could say that. And you heard those people out there—it's going to be all over social media, and all over this island. What am I going to *do*?"

"This is just a shot in the dark, Nat," said Alex, "but have you thought about just telling the truth?"

Natalie made a snorting noise, and Alex handed her a tissue.

"I don't know anything about maintaining a platform or a social media presence," said Alex, "much less writing a whole book. I can barely manage to compose a grocery list. But it feels like it's time for you to embrace who you really are, however trite that might sound."

Natalie sniffed. "I was thinking maybe I could post some photos of me with Milo."

"Seriously?" Alex gave her a scathing look.

"Hey, it's better than nothing."

"You're missing the point, Nat. I mean, do you even *want* Milo or François-Xavier? Imagine there was no one following you on social media and no one on the Île de Feme even knew who you were. Would you still want to be with either of them?"

No. The answer popped into Natalie's heart before her brain could formulate a response. Slowly, she shook her head.

"Well, then?" asked Alex.

"Then what's my next step?"

"That's the real question, isn't it?"

Natalie grabbed a big floppy hat and a pair of huge sunglasses, hoping not to be recognized and waylaid again, and started walking as long and hard as a person could on the Île de Feme. It was only about a mile and a half, but she figured scrambling over the rocks counted as extra. At last she reached the lighthouse, climbed the tower steps, and stepped out onto the catwalk.

The wind immediately caught her hat, and as she grabbed for it, she knocked off her sunglasses, which fell to the rocks below. Natalie watched as the straw hat wafted on the breeze, headed out to sea.

So much for disguises.

Natalie gazed down upon the little stone chapel and thought of the Gallizenae stirring up the winds with their magical charms, transforming into mermaids as they pleased, and forbidding men from entering their sacred groves or perching on their rocky ledges.

Could the Gallizenae be sending Natalie a not-so-subtle sign?

She thought once more of what James Baldwin wrote, that true joy comes alongside the knowledge that we will die one day. In this way, if no other, The Commander had it right: Tomorrow was not promised to any of us, and if it did come, it would almost certainly not arrive in the form one desired or anticipated.

Where their father erred, though, was in insisting that if one prepared well enough, tomorrow wouldn't defeat you.

Which wasn't to say that a person in California shouldn't have an earthquake kit, or that a Féman dealing with sea-level rise shouldn't know how to navigate a boat. But perhaps it was precisely the ever-present threat of those disasters that helped people to embrace their authentic lives, to live fully in the here and now.

Because no one sees the lighthouse beacon until it's dark, and it's never more welcome than during a storm.

Natalie wasn't even sure what that meant, but the words came to her with such force that she quickly descended the winding steps of the tower and marched the length of the island back to the Bag-Noz, went straight into her study, and sat down at her computer.

She wrote: "I've been living a lie."

And then she hesitated.

Way to start, Nat, she told herself. *Don't stop now.*

She took a deep breath, and plunged in, the words flowing out of her. She would have to revise and polish, and she honestly had no idea if anyone would want to read any of it. But it was her truth and she was not about to staunch the flow. *Never deny the muse,* she always told prospective writers. Maybe it was about time she took her own advice.

> I moved to Paris and fell in love, and then my Prince
> Charming and I moved to an island off the Wild Coast
> of Brittany, and I thought I was living a dream. I was

invited into a beautiful old stone home that needed fixing up, given a promise of running a guesthouse and restaurant, and even welcomed into an extended family.

But here's the truth: I've been lying. To my friends, to my family, and—perhaps least forgivable of all—to my readers, to the people who believed in me and supported my dream all these years.

And needless to say, I've been lying to myself.

I moved to the Île de Feme with a man I loved, and who I thought loved me. And it was beautiful—for a while. And then the whole affair took on the rank odor of a fish left out too long in the sun.

I moved to the Île de Feme, and my life fell apart.

CHAPTER FIFTY-ONE

Violette

While most of the island's women were busy in our sewing circles, another team of women and children decorated the Abri du Marin. As with the costumes, the decorating team was constrained by a lack of resources, but they made do: Noëlle came up with a series of colorful posters in the style of Toulouse-Lautrec that brightened up the Abri's dark wood walls, and the children made long garlands from seaweed studded with feathers that were strewn from beam to beam. Every household on the Île de Feme, it seemed, had contributed something—tablecloths and candles, dishes and silverware—to make the setting inviting. Heirloom vases held wildflower nosegays; prized silver candlesticks glittered in the lamplight.

Meanwhile, Madame Thérèse and Ambroisine concocted a very special elixir. Madame Thérèse refused to share her recipe, leaving us no choice but to trust that she knew what she was doing.

She handed me a jar along with instructions, saying: "This must be measured out very carefully. Too little and they won't sleep. Too much and we will have hundreds of dead soldiers on our hands, and the vengeful wrath of the Nazis will descend upon the Île de Feme."

On the night of the spectacle, my hands shook as I measured the liquid precisely, adding it drop by drop to the barrels of cider that the German soldiers themselves had contributed from their supplies.

Still wearing my *robe noire* and *jibilinnen*, I lingered behind the barrels and watched as the soldiers began to arrive at the Abri, in high spirits at the prospect of the evening's entertainment. They joked with one another, nudging and winking. I could not understand their words, but was again struck by their youth. Most were mere boys, far from home. I doubted they understood why they were here, on this island off the coast of Brittany, any more than we did.

I prayed I had applied the sleeping potion properly. I prayed my actions would not harm anyone.

"*Halt!* This is a crime," a harsh voice barked.

I froze and slowly turned around.

"I thought it was you," said Hans, his pale eyes sweeping over my *robe noire* and *jibilinnen*. "I was anticipating seeing you bedecked in the gifts of the sea, a veritable Venus rising from a clamshell, guest-house girl."

Hans knew my name. He just refused to use it.

He continued: "Is Rainer the only one to see what lies beneath those black skirts?"

I forced myself to remain calm, to play along. "He wouldn't let me dress up," I said with a pout. "Rainer has promised to marry me now that my husband has perished."

"*Ha!*" Hans scoffed. "I must say, my respect for Rainer has grown. I have underestimated him. Still, it is a shame. I was looking forward to the view."

Noëlle walked up and looped her arm through his. "There is plenty to see, *mein Herr*. Allow me to show you."

I watched, speechless, as my old friend flirted with the despised enemy. Her ink-stained hands were hidden by long white gloves that reached past her elbows, a high feathered headdress adorned her dark hair, and a beaked mask hid her eyes. But the rest of her was exposed in such a manner that I felt myself blushing. Shells and feathers had been sewn onto a skillfully crafted patchwork of silk and muslin that clung to her breasts and waist, ending in a short skirt made of a fringe of shells that clacked when she moved.

The island women were typically modest, even amongst other women. I had not seen Noëlle's legs since we were children, much less the outline of her breasts. And the way she was posing now, her chest thrust out, leaning into Hans . . . she could well have been Circe herself, taming a lion or bewitching one of Odysseus's men.

When Hans spoke his voice was husky. "Now *that's* more like it, madamoiselle."

The Abri was filling quickly with men in neat but drab army uniforms. In contrast, the feathered island creatures flitted this way and that, like fantastical beings. They had transformed into Circe's sirens, whirling and swooping, feathers swaying and shells shaking.

The men's slack-jawed expressions, from officers to the youngest soldier, reflected fascination and desire. Or perhaps the elixir was already having an effect. Part of me yearned to stay and watch the island women cast their spell over these soldiers, these invaders. But we each had our role to play and mine was elsewhere.

It was now or never.

While Noëlle mesmerized Hans, I slipped out of the Abri du Marin. There was no one to stop me; even the soldiers assigned to guard the shore had been invited to the spectacle. Nothing ever happened on the island, and the officers could hardly deny the men a single evening of fun and frolic.

So no one noticed as two black-clad figures hurried along the path toward the lighthouse.

As we had planned, Rainer veered off in the direction of the Chapel of Saint Corentin and was soon swallowed by the dark night.

A lone soldier stood watch at the base of the lighthouse. He was very young, and I recognized him as one who was kind to the elderly and was often seen giving the island cats tidbits from his own meals.

"Halt! Was machst du hier?" he demanded as I approached.

"Entschuldigen Sie, bitte," I said, before reverting to French. I held up my offerings and hoped he would understand my meaning. "I come from the festivities. I bring you a slice of *gâteau Breton* and a little beer."

"Das kann ich nicht akzeptieren, fräulein," he said with a shake of his head.

"Pourquoi pas?" I asked, gazing at him through my lashes. "They left you all alone, didn't let you have fun with the others. It's just me. . . . What could happen?"

We didn't speak each other's language, but I got my point across.

I sat with him and listened while he spoke in German for what felt like a very long time, refilling his mug of beer until finally Madame Thérèse's elixir put the young soldier to sleep. Rainer joined me then and together we tied him up, and I stayed with the unconscious man as Rainer went into the lighthouse and up the stairs, his steps ringing out loudly on the metal treads, the sound reverberating in the tower. If all went to plan, Henri Thomas would be waiting for him at the top to help with the signal.

The young soldier was sleeping and bound with strong rope, so I went to stand by the chapel to see what was happening. I closed my eyes for a moment, praying. After what seemed like hours, the tower beacon started flashing, long and then short, in code.

I smiled, prayed again, and thanked the Gallizenae. I had no bread to leave them, but I pledged to them my eternal allegiance and gratitude.

And then a shot rang out.

I reached the base of the lighthouse just as Rainer appeared at the bottom of the stairs, holding his abdomen with bright red blood spilling over his hand.

CHAPTER FIFTY-TWO

Alex

*A*lex hadn't noticed the dusk descending, the light fading.

She had gone out to the rocks ahead of another predicted storm and become so lost in thought—about Jean-Luc's outrageous offer, and the fact that she missed him, and about what she was going to do next—that she hadn't realized how late it had gotten. Now everything seemed confusing, alien, the shadows and textures blurring into unintelligible shapes.

I waited too long.

Her heart raced, her breath came in rapid, harsh bursts.

Don't panic, she told herself. *You've been through worse. Remember The Trial? You were only ten years old and you survived.*

Of course, she could see perfectly when she was ten. . . . Alex caught herself. *Stop it. Focus. If you have to spend the night out here, it won't be fun but you'll survive. Rain and wind won't kill you.* She was not an infant. She was simply going blind.

Still, panic clawed at her throat, encouraging her to scream her anger and rage and fear into the gusts of wind blowing off the ocean, because why not? No one would hear her, and maybe she would feel better.

Having given herself permission to give in to her fear, Alex felt herself growing calmer. *There's a lesson in there. Okay, let's start at the beginning.* She had gotten herself here; she could get herself back home. She had limited use of her sight, but she had her other senses. She remembered Natalie describing how drunken sailors made their way back to their rooms by keeping one hand on the walls of the island's narrow passageways. Problem was, she wasn't in town; she was out on the rocks. So first things first, she had to get away from the rocks and back into the village.

Slow and steady, she told herself. *Slow and steady wins the race.*

Alex took a careful step, then another, reaching out with her hands to feel for the rocks. She stubbed her toe on something but caught herself and maintained her balance. *Good,* she thought. *That's good. One step, two steps . . .* With the next step her foot caught between two rocks, and she stumbled and went down hard, falling on one knee, and a searing pain shot through her. She paused, but the pain passed, which meant nothing was broken.

Great, Alex, become not only blind but also lame.

Her breath was ratcheting up with every gust of wind. She was panicking. *Think of The Trial.* Think of Nat's face when she realized it was you who left the candy bars for her, as if anyone else could have done so, as if there were a candy bar fairy sprinkling treats throughout the forest to lead lost little girls back home to their survivalist compounds.

Alex smiled at the thought, let it soothe her. Nat had suggested training a Seeing Eye dog, using a cane, making accommodations. Their childhood roles had been reversed, and now Nat was going to help Alex figure it all out.

She made it another step, and another, using her hands and her feet to feel her way along. *This is going to take forever,* she thought, but what did that matter? It's not as if she had to worry anymore about losing the light. . . .

After what seemed like hours, she managed to reach the edge of the village and the entrance to a pathway that would lead her to the quay. From there, she should be able to feel her way to the Bag-Noz. No sweat.

She walked along, stepping with care, and thought again of Jean-Luc. His decency, his desire to help, which, though intended kindly, had enraged her. Alex reminded herself, again: She was not an infant. She could survive what life threw at her; she always had. Including this storm. She *would* survive the storm.

And then her foot slipped, and her ankle twisted as she fell into a jagged hole in the cobblestones because she had been unable to see the bright orange traffic cone warning of its presence. Her ankle throbbed, and the hip she landed on stung. *Add it to the long list of bruises I'm already sporting,* she thought. She took a deep breath, rolled out of the hole, and sat on the wet cobblestones, her palms stinging as she picked out the gravel and the dirt.

Now the tears came, bitter and raw.

Ow ow ow ow, she crooned to herself. Resentment bubbled up into her throat like acid. Why her? What had she done to deserve this? What was she going to do with herself now? How would she survive a disaster for which she was entirely unprepared?

I didn't see it coming, Alex thought, then laughed at herself. *Get it? Didn't see the blindness coming?*

And at that moment, Alex knew that if she had the option to slip into the stone below her, to be carried out over the sea, absorbed into the mist that danced upon the waves, she would have done so. Right then and there, she would have willingly disappeared into the seascape, to become part of this stubborn village forevermore. She would become part of the foam upon the waves, like the Little Mermaid.

Wrapped up in her thoughts, her ears filled with the howls of the furious wind, she did not hear footsteps approaching and was surprised when two feet appeared before her.

Jean-Luc. He was wearing that ridiculous yellow slicker, the hood pulled up, a flashlight in one hand.

She couldn't see well enough to read the look on his face. Was he feeling angry? Afraid? Bureaucratic?

A crack of lightning brightened the sky just before the rain began to fall in earnest, stinging her cheeks. She closed her eyes, wondering if the rain masked her tears.

Long moments ticked by. Finally, Alex opened her eyes, looked up at Jean-Luc. He reached out a hand.

"Alex," he said quietly. His voice was like velvet, capable of coaxing a wild animal to his side, persuading Korrigan to trust him, convincing her to believe in him. "Take my hand, please, Alex."

That made the tears fall harder. There was no pretending it was rain now. Alex was racked with sobs, lost, and scared. Stuck, like Natalie had been during The Trial, or hanging off the side of that damned rock, with no recourse, no resources, no knowledge of what came next or how to deal with it.

"Let me help you."

She stared at his outstretched hand but did not move. "I'm not your damned disabled cat."

"I do not think that you are. But, Alex . . . sometimes the strongest thing a person can do is to accept help."

"I'm not an invalid."

"No, you're not. You're in need of a helping hand, and one happens to be right here, waiting for you. Quite eagerly, as a matter of fact."

She stared at his hand. Broad, capable, practically glowing in the lamplight. She could see it clearly. In that moment, it was the only thing she could see.

Jean-Luc stood silently, waiting for her to reply. After another moment, when she said nothing, he sat down next to her on the cobblestones, pulling down his hood so he could look at her.

"Get *up*," she said. "You're being ridiculous."

"Then we will be ridiculous together."

"I can make it alone."

"Of course you can. You are Diana the Huntress."

The rain poured down upon them, plastering their hair to their heads, running in rivulets down their faces. For a few moments they sat there, side by side, in silence.

"I'm not Diana anymore," Alex muttered. "No such thing as a blind huntress."

"None of us is the person we used to be," Jean-Luc replied. "Not I, not Natalie. The Île de Feme itself is not what it used to be. Is that not right? Even Diana got old."

"Raphael never painted her that way."

He chuckled. "No, he did not. But perhaps he lacked imagination."

Alex stared at him.

"The thing is, Alex, lives must always change, and we must make the best of it."

"Pourquoi?" she asked.

"Pourquoi pas?"

Alex let her head drop back, closed her eyes, and felt the cold rain on her face.

Pourquoi pas? It was the question Nat's book had asked, the question that had annoyed Alex for so many years. There were so very many reasons.

But in the end . . . why not?

Alex reached out and took Jean-Luc's warm hand with her cold one. Together, they got to their feet.

CHAPTER FIFTY-THREE

Natalie

*N*atalie could see it all so clearly now. She had been trying to live someone else's life, according to what other people wanted from her.

But what did she want from herself?

Now that she felt free to admit how wrong she had been about everything, the writing once again came—not easily, but steadily. She had something true to say.

The central message of *Pourquoi Pas?* hadn't been wrong, after all, she realized. Natalie still believed in pursuing a dream, in working hard for what she wanted. But real lives, unlike books, didn't just end. There was no such thing as a Happily Ever After, because the story continued, and a person had to keep working hard and adapting, because life happened, dreams died, and new ones took their place.

She wrote:

> Sometimes gratitude is just a platitude.
>
> I've been thinking about the fact that the inner life,

our quiet core, has little currency on social media. But in the end, it's all we truly have, and it is precious. It can't be found in anyone else, and no one else can see it. It's a secret. And there's nothing wrong with secrets, as long as they're true.

We all live in society, and we all have an outward persona. But each of us must also have days—or weeks, or months—when we allow our inner life to swell up inside of us until it touches everything, every nook and cranny, and we can feel it everywhere.

If we never take time out to let that happen, then we run the risk of simply accumulating facts and platitudes and other people's ideas until they begin to rattle around inside, as annoying and heavy and jangly as loose change in a coat pocket.

Such a person can make a lot of noise, but never really feel anything—nothing but a hollowness, with the wind rushing through.

Because no one sees the lighthouse beacon until it's dark, and it's never more welcome than when spotted during a storm.

"Hey, Nat?" Alex called from outside her study. "Oh, sorry. Are you writing? I don't want to bother you."

"That's okay. I was just finishing up some thoughts. By the way, I heard back from Sandy: She loved what I sent her yesterday. Seems the book industry is trending away from 'inspirational' stories to 'authentic' narratives. According to Sandy, readers *want* to hear about my having fallen on my face."

"Failure is the new success, huh?"

"I was born for this."

"That's great, Nat," Alex said with a chuckle, taking a seat by the desk. "I'm so glad for you."

"It feels good to be telling the truth. Who knew?"

Alex smiled. She had stood by her sister's side when Natalie told François-Xavier's extended family that they were no longer a couple, and that he appeared to have no intention of returning from Paris. No one seemed overly surprised at the news.

Natalie did, however, agree to keep the guesthouse renovations on track for a "soft" opening in time for the Festival of the Gallizenae, now just a week away. She devoted her mornings to writing, but spent the afternoons with Alex and Jean-Luc, aided at times by Gabriel and Christine and other neighbors who were pitching in to finish the repairs. Once the electrical wiring was redone, the roof repaired, and the plumbing fixtures installed, all that was needed was to finish up the painting and papering, refinish the wood floors, and make sure they had enough linens and dishes for guests.

Natalie had been closer to finishing than she had imagined, way back when she sat on her terrace, smoking and drinking and pretending she wasn't panicking.

Once they got through the festival days and the official end of the tourist season, Natalie promised to help the relatives find someone to take over the day-to-day operations of the Bag-Noz. As much as she loved the place, she had come to realize that she was not a good fit for full-time island living: Natalie yearned to travel, to wander the streets of foreign cities, to return to California to put to rest some old ghosts. She might even visit Horseshoe Bend and look in on The Commander. To face him as an adult.

But first things first.

"I wanted to tell you," Natalie said, "I've got that film option money deposited in my account, plus a nice royalty check. So I think we should go see that doctor in Paris that Jean-Luc knows, just in case. Also, we could go back to California so you could check out the guide dog program, or maybe even travel a little, see a bit of the world before . . ."

Natalie trailed off.

"Before I go completely blind," Alex finished her sentence. "Please, Nat, you can say it. It's not a secret anymore."

"My point is, we don't have to be stuck out here on this island."

"Hey, some of us would love to be 'stuck out here on this island.'"

"Really? I mean, it's a great place to live for a little while. But for good?"

"That's what I came to talk to you about," Alex said, seeming to choose her words carefully. "My world has never been as big as yours, Nat. I *like* small places. I probably would have stayed on that mountain my whole life if Dad hadn't sold me out. And while I've enjoyed traveling a little, I really would love to have a home. Someplace small, manageable. Especially considering my circumstances."

"Wait," Nat said. "Are you saying what I think you're saying?"

"Obviously, I'll need help," said Alex. "But Jean-Luc and I have been talking about it. . . . It was his idea, actually. I know it's probably crazy to think that I could—"

Natalie cut her off with a quick shake of her head. "It's not crazy that you could do just about anything you put your mind to, with a little help. I mean, driving is probably off the menu, but there are no cars on the island anyway."

The sisters shared a smile. In recent weeks, Jean-Luc and Alex had been spending time together. A *lot* of time. And not just working on the Bag-Noz—they took long walks, sat out by the cove near the lighthouse, even shared romantic dinners at Milo's and finally tasted Brigitte's *fish et chips*.

"Why didn't I think of that? You and Jean-Luc could stay here and run this place," Natalie said, a note of wonder in her voice, "become the proprietors of the Bag-Noz. It seems so perfect somehow."

"I'm hoping the Olivier family will be open to the idea. Jean-Luc and I have been working up a business proposal for them, with suggested profit shares and all that. Jean-Luc's good with numbers and paperwork, as you can imagine."

Natalie smiled. "The family likes you better than they ever liked me, anyway."

"That's not true," said Alex. "I have the sense you never really showed them the real you."

"Yeah. I'm working on that."

"So, if you're not running the Bag-Noz, what will you do?"

"I've got a whole list," said Natalie. "I have to finish this book, obviously. But I also need to kick my nicotine habit, and go see a dentist. And I'm dying to walk the streets of Paris, not to mention getting a proper pedicure and haircut. And then . . . who knows? Maybe I'll become a goatherd on an island in the Helsinki archipelago, like that woman I saw on the Internet."

"I thought she ran sheep, not goats," said Alex.

"Whatever."

"You might want to know the difference before you go into the business, is all I'm saying."

Natalie grinned and took a swig of her coffee. "Excellent point."

"I've got a better idea. Stay here, as our chef."

Natalie nearly spit out her coffee. "I'm sorry . . . what?"

"Hear me out: just for high tourist season. Jean-Luc and I have decided that it doesn't make financial sense to open an actual restaurant here, but we could offer our guests breakfast, *apéro* in the evenings, and perhaps the occasional special anniversary or birthday dinner."

"But I'm not a chef."

"Yes, you are, Nat. You always have been. You might not have credentials from a hoity-toity Parisian culinary school, but people love your food, and you love sharing it. You could spend the summers here, stay through the Festival of the Gallizenae, and then leave before things get too cold to traipse around the world. I understand the winters in the Helsinki archipelago are a bit chilly, so the whole goat—or sheep—thing might need to be put on the back burner."

Natalie sat back, thinking. She could spend time with her sister and Jean-Luc, enjoy the beauty of the ocean, watch *pétanque* battles, collect sea glass—in short, savor island life—but not be hemmed in by the waters of the Raz. She could *cook*. She could travel. She could "traipse around the world" and still come back to a home. A real home. Her sister's home.

She felt the sting of tears in her eyes, and knew that Alex's proposal was just right.

"So, two sisters could run this place again," Natalie said.

"There's a nice sort of symmetry, isn't it? Although we'll have to make room for Jean-Luc."

"There's plenty of room for him. The man is nothing if not accommodating."

"Also, we're getting a cat," said Alex. "This place needs a cat or two."

"What about Korrigan?" Lately the dog had been spending more time at the Bag-Noz than at the House of Meneï.

"Korrigan will deal. She's a survivor."

"Aren't we all?"

"Oh, one more thing," said Alex, reaching behind her and handing Natalie a framed photograph.

"It's the two sisters, Violette and Doura!" said Natalie. "Thank you so much for framing it."

"I thought you might want to hang it up in the parlor. But look what else I noticed when I was looking back through the photo album." Alex handed Natalie the photograph of the German officers walking along the quay. She pointed at one of them. "Look closely at this German officer's face. Now look at Doura."

Natalie studied one after the other and smiled. "I've got to say, Alex, for a woman who's losing her sight, you've got a very good eye."

"Am I crazy, or is that the same person?" Alex asked.

"Looks like we're going to have to bribe Ambroisine with more cider and cigarettes to get the whole story, but I think you may well be right."

CHAPTER FIFTY-FOUR

Violette

1947

$\mathcal{T}$he story of the Gallizenae always begins *"Il était une fois,"* or "Once upon a time," as though it were a fable. To me it is truth.

For as long as anyone can remember, my family has lived on this forbidding strip of granite off the coast of Bretagne, taking into its fold the occasional sailor or castaway, but never abandoning the Île de Feme. The blood of the Gallizenae runs through my veins.

And I believe their spirits came to help us that night.

Much later, after our panicked, painful struggle to arrive at the House of Meneï, Henri Thomas told us the whole story. He had been waiting at the top of the tower, as we planned, but a second soldier had shown up, surprising him.

The soldier demanded to know what the old man was doing. Proper keepers polished their Fresnel lenses during the day, not in the dead of night. Monsieur Thomas spoke more German than he let on, but feigned ignorance, speaking in a torrent of French about foreign ships in the water, hoping to distract the soldier long enough for Rainer to arrive and subdue him.

When Rainer's footsteps rang out on the steps, the soldier yelled, *"Halt! Wer geht dahin?"*

When he appeared at the top of the stairs, the sight of Rainer's *robe noire* and *jibilinnen* gave the soldier pause.

Rainer did not hesitate but leapt on the soldier. There was a struggle, and Rainer was able to get the soldier in a choke hold until he blacked out.

Then Henri Thomas and Rainer used the tower light to send the signal in Morse code several times, praying it would be seen by the crew of the Bag-Noz, the ghost ship working with the resistance, wherever it might be.

"We'd better go," said Monsieur Thomas. "If anyone on the island noticed that, there will be a lot of questions. Go with God, Rainer. *Vielen dank, mein freund.*"

They turned to leave, then stopped in their tracks.

The soldier had roused, and was holding his gun but seemed confused.

"Was ist los?" Demanding to know what was going on, he raised his weapon in their direction.

Rainer spoke in a high-pitched voice, saying something rapid in German, which Monsieur Thomas did not understand. The soldier, still unsteady on his feet, pointed the gun at the lighthouse keeper.

Rainer leapt on him. There was a struggle. Rainer managed to knock the man out again by banging his head on the metal stairs.

But the gun, in between them, went off, its explosive retort ringing through the lighthouse tower.

. . . .

As far as anyone in the German military knew, Rainer Heisinger deserted the army that night and attempted to sail to England. When bits and pieces of the boat were found washed ashore the next day, he was presumed drowned.

To an islander, destroying a boat is the equivalent of the ancient Romans sacrificing a bull. The women did it without hesitation to save him.

Before we left that night, I untied the soldier at the bottom of the tower so when he awoke he could only say that one of the witchy women had cast a spell on him, that she came bearing cake and the next thing he knew he had fallen asleep. He could not identify her because "all the women in black look the same." The poor soldier at the top of the tower suffered a severe blow to the head and thus could remember very little. Even after recuperating all he could recall was that a fat woman appeared, and Monsieur Thomas was waiting for her. But the old lighthouse keeper claimed that the woman was his lover who had arrived for a clandestine assignation, and in his surprise the soldier had fallen backward and banged his head by accident.

Since nothing was found to be awry with the light or the tower, and the Germans still needed Monsieur Thomas's expertise to maintain the light and the foghorn, the matter was dropped.

Noëlle told us the men at the "cabaret" fell asleep, just as we had planned, and she, Irmine, and Marie-Paule were able to carry Marceline to the little cove, where she and her lipstick met the Bag-Noz and sailed across the channel to England.

Madame Thérèse nursed Rainer back to health in the basement of the House of Meneï where he was hiding, for hers was the only home in which the Germans never set foot. Madame Thérèse claimed it was because of the powers of the Gallizenae, though we thought it also had something to do with the fact that they truly considered Madame Thérèse to be a witch, a *Hexe*.

The bullet had passed clear through Rainer's side, so Madame Thérèse and Ambroisine were able to stitch him up, and for weeks they applied plasters and concocted drafts to avoid infection and treat his fever.

Once he recovered, Rainer continued to wear his *robe noire* and *jibilinnen*. He grew his hair out, and amazingly, the German soldiers appeared not to recognize him. He rarely went out in the daytime, and if he did, all they saw was a blond woman dressed in black, tall and broad. We islanders are a sturdy people; our occupiers did not see past the traditional garb.

Noëlle made him a convincing set of documents under the name of Doura, which means "water" in the old language. Here on the Île de Feme, water is life.

But he was not asked for his identification papers, not even once.

By then the occupiers were feeling rather defeated, anyway. They never did figure out what had happened the night of the spectacle, why they weren't able to hold their liquor. Embarrassed by being taken in by a group of women, they did not report what had happened to their superiors. But they did blow up the lighthouse when they eventually left the island, leaving passing ships in danger for years afterward. Life is not fair, and war is worse.

When the Allies finally defeated the Nazis and the war came to an end, a few villagers accused me of having committed *collaboration horizontale* with Rainer. But they did not shave my head and walk me through the streets; at least I was spared that indignity, unlike many poor women in Paris and elsewhere.

Most of the island women understood, and without admitting what they had done that night of Circe, they defended my innocence.

We Fémanes never again spoke of that night. We hid the costumes in the nooks and crannies of our homes; I made room in a trunk packed with my *mamm-gozh*'s embroidered linens and hid the trunk in a locked closet behind an attic cupboard.

Madame Thérèse advised me to wrap the keys to the hidden closet in a scrap of black satin, and then to bind it with a cord, knotted many times while I chanted a prayer to the Gallizenae. I was then to bury the keys "underfoot," so I dug a hole under the step to the front terrace, vowing never to tell anyone the tale of our wartime adventure.

Rainer returned to Germany after the war to search for Sascha. He shared the agony of so many when he discovered that his *amour*, his love, his smart, talented Sascha, died of pneumonia in a concentration camp in Sachsenhausen just weeks before the Red Army liberated it.

Afterward, my heartbroken friend returned to the Île de Feme and donned the mourning costume of *robe noire* and *jibillinen*. Rainer kept the name Doura. When our men returned from England they were full of questions, but the women simply said Doura had come to us during the war. No details were given, and there were more important things to worry about, such as reclaiming our homes, returning to fishing, and rebuilding the lighthouse.

Doura and I lived together contentedly after that, running the guesthouse, which we renamed the Bag-Noz in honor of the boat that came out of the fog to help us that night as well as the many spirits that roam our seas.

Visitors sometimes ask me whether I never wanted to leave the island.

I *have* traveled. I have visited Paris many times, and I took trips to Nantes and Bordeaux, and even down through Biarritz to Donostia-San Sebastián on the coast of Spain. But I always came back; I have been part of this island since the Gallizenae, and these rocky outcroppings are as much a part of me as my *jibilinnen*.

My brother-in-law, Salvator, and I are now friends. Whatever spark we might once have felt died during the war, and was buried by the deaths of Marc and my dear Esprit. I was pleased, for Gladie's sake, that Salvator returned to the Île de Feme after the war. He brought with him a nice English girl he met in London, and she seems to be fitting in. They have opened a café on the quay that serves what they call *fish et chips*.

Madame Thérèse passed away before the war was over, and the young Ambroisine tried her best to fill her shoes, but at her tender young age she finds it hard to get people to trust her. Still, she is hard-working, and I have shared with her the recipes for tinctures and salves from my own *mamm-gozh*. I believe she will do well.

Before the war began, I used to doubt myself. I pretended. I denied my unreasonable heart.

Now that the trials of war are over, I am who I am, for better or for worse. I wear the *robe noire* and *jibilinnen*. I remain unmarried. I have become a healer and once pulled off a rather unbelievable bit of sabotage to defy the occupying army. I have traveled my fill and I have taken occasional lovers. But the island always calls to me, bringing me back.

Just as it does to my sister, Doura.

These days as we stroll along the quay or pass through the narrow pathways of the village, I sometimes hear children call us *witches* behind our backs.

I prefer "latter-day Gallizenae," but it doesn't really matter.

In the late afternoons, when the guests are out and the sheets are washed and the floors are mopped and our teas and tinctures are prepared, Doura and I relax and take *apéro* together on the porch of the Bag-Noz.

There we sit, watching the fading light of day, petting our cats and listening to the island sounds: chatting tourists and squawking seagulls and *charette* wheels rolling along stone walkways.

Together we sit in joy and mourning and sisterhood.

Epilogue

*T*he blind woman makes her way down the pathway, running one hand along the wall to one side, her cane tap-tap-tapping on the worn stones in front of her. A wolflike dog named Korrigan sticks close by her side.

"*Bonjour, Alex,*" says a man's voice. "*Et Korrigan.*"

"*Bonjour . . . c'est Monsieur Tarik?*" Alex responds.

"*Oui, ça va, très bien,*" he replies.

Alex smiles. She knows her neighbors' voices now, almost all of them.

Alex had run to the store to pick up a few more baguettes and milk for a pair of unexpected guests who arrived on the afternoon ferry. Severine carefully placed the items in her backpack, and a woman in line behind her helped Alex to slip the pack onto her back.

Her neighbors, the islanders—even the tourists—are very helpful.

As she walks, Alex thinks about Violette and Doura, and Operation Circe, the women cajoling the Nazi occupiers into an evening of laughter and song and drunken slumber. She thinks of the men of the island loading onto their fishing boats on that June morning in 1940 and leaving behind their island, their wives and mothers and sisters and children, to risk their lives fighting for *la Belle France*. She thinks of Agnès and Michou, Christine and Brigitte, Severine and Ismael and even Milo. All these tough, independent islanders who refuse to leave this forbidding rock, despite the sea level rising.

Alex's own personal Armageddon has indeed arrived; she can no longer see more than occasional shadows and bright lights.

The loss is heartbreaking. Wrenching. She misses so many things: that little line of the horizon where the ocean meets the sky, the glow of a candle, the rosy cheeks of happy children, Korrigan's fierce but loving eyes . . . and the sweet, steady expression on Jean-Luc's face, which, once upon a time, she had found boring.

There are many things she can't do now, but there are still many things that she can. Christine takes her out on her fishing boat—a life preserver strapped securely around her—so she can feel the sea spray on her face, and Alex is able to help pull in the nets full of fish. At home, she counts the stairs as she descends, and they refrain from re-arranging the furniture—which is probably covered in the hair of their two recently rescued cats. She hangs laundry on the huge line, and in the evenings, over *apéro*, she sometimes throws the *cochonnet* onto their new pétanque court, and Jean-Luc laughs and tells her she's getting better. She has not yet mastered Braille, but Jean-Luc found a pack of playing cards marked with those distinctive bumps, and she is learning as they play together in the evenings. Alex also has discovered audiobooks, and has been making her way through the writings of James Baldwin and so many others whom she has never read; Nat recently sent her a new study list from Cairo.

The tourist season won't start for another month, and Alex yearns for the time to pass quickly so that her little sister, the once annoying little Nat-the-Gnat, will come back to the island, and back to the Bag Noz. Back to them.

Alex knows the village's web of passageways by now: first left, second right brings her to La Melisse general store; continuing on to the second left and the third doorway brings her to *chez Tante* Agnès. She has learned the way to Milo's, to Le Caredec tourist supply shop, and is working on making it all the way out to the *grand phare*, the big lighthouse, all by herself.

And although Korrigan isn't really much of a guide dog, having her nearby while progressing through the narrow passages makes Alex feel stronger. She is no longer afraid. Alex has learned something her parents never understood: that following the drama and pain and tragedy of The Change, some die, and some survive.

And some are reborn altogether.

Natalie stands on the open deck of the ferry, straining to catch a glimpse of the Île de Feme as it emerges from the ocean. The low gray strip of land seems to wink at her through the salt haze, filling her heart with an unfamiliar emotion: She is coming home.

In her suitcase are carefully wrapped souvenirs from Egypt and Norway, California and Paris. In her travels, Natalie wandered through vast open-air markets and poked around tiny curiosity shops, and every time she happened upon something special—something tactile, so Alex could feel it—she knew she would bring it back home, to the Bag-Noz. To her sister.

Alex has no idea she is coming.

When they finally dock and the passengers surge off the ferry, clutching bright inflatable beach toys and picnic baskets and trailing their rolling suitcases, Natalie lingers and chats with the crew while she waits for the crowd to disperse. Then she disembarks and walks to the guesthouse, pausing outside the iron gates.

A fat orange cat perches on a windowsill, and Korrigan lazes in the sun. The yard is tidy, flowers overflow their pots, and a carved wooden sign reads: BAG-NOZ GUESTHOUSE: NO VACANCY. Good thing Natalie called ahead to tell Jean-Luc she was arriving and would need a room.

Alex is sitting at the little café table on the porch, snapping green beans.

"Hey, Alex," says Natalie.

Her sister stills, holding a bean between her hands. She tilts her head.

"Wait. Is that . . . *Nat*?"

Nat pushes through the gates, rushes up the steps to the porch, and envelops her sister in a bear hug.

"You weren't supposed to be here until next month!" Alex says, returning her sister's hug.

"Beats the hell out of me why, but I missed this place," Natalie says, hiding her face in her sister's neck, adding in a fierce, muffled whisper: "I missed *you*."

"I honestly can't believe you're here," says Alex.

"Me neither," says Natalie, taking a seat at the table. "I finished my manuscript, and my agent loves it. The working title is *Butchery: A Tale of the Messy Innards*. Too on the nose?"

Alex chuckles. "Maybe just a tad."

"Anyway, I finished up, and I couldn't think of anywhere else I wanted to be more than here. Lord, do I have some tales to tell! And I want to hear *everything* about what's going on with you, and Jean-Luc, and the island."

"Well, *Tonton* Michou found himself a girlfriend."

"No!"

"But the big news is that Brigitte is now serving kebabs."

"No!"

"Seriously! She's decided to branch out." Alex smiles, reaches for her sister's hand, and squeezes. When she speaks, her voice is rough with emotion. "Hey, you know what? Whenever I hear the afternoon ferry pull up to the dock, it means it's time for *apéro*."

"Looks like I arrived just in time."

Author's Note

The Île de Feme as portrayed in *Off the Wild Coast of Brittany* is based on the actual Île de Sein, a small fishing island in the French region of Finistère in Brittany. During World War II all the men of fighting age sailed their fishing boats to England and joined the Free French Forces, leading Charles de Gaulle to proclaim that the majority of his troops seemed to be made up of fishermen from the Île de Sein. Of the 128 island men who left for England to fight, 15 were killed; the Vichy government referred to them as *"Anglais,"* and their families were denied any military pay or benefits. In January 1946 the Sénans, or people of the island, were honored with the prestigious *Croix de la Libération*, and in September 1960 a large monument of the Cross of Lorraine was erected on the island and dedicated by none other than Général de Gaulle himself.

As in the novel, the women, children, and old people were left behind to deal with the German soldiers who occupied the island for the duration of the war. In truth, locals report that the majority of the troops were *propre*, or appropriate, in their behavior toward the islanders. However, as was the case in much of occupied France, persistent hunger haunted the island's populace; besides missing their fathers, the lack of food is the single most resonant memory of many surviving Sénans.

The parts of the story including the cabaret night, the sabotage of the German army, and the characters Violette and Doura are completely fabricated. The Bag-Noz is loosely based on a decrepit old former guesthouse that stands near the ferry landing.

If you ever find yourself in the Finistère region, I urge you to hop a ferry in Audierne and take a ride to the Île de Sein. Whether you go for one day or stay for several, you'll find a charming fishing village, historic buildings, megalithic menhirs, plenty of cider, and fervent *pétanque* battles. There are kayaks and standing boards for rent, several cafés, and an amazing museum with displays pertaining to shipwrecks and salvage operations, the experiences of the islanders during World War II, and long-ago daily life on the island. Large historic lighthouses on and near the Île de Sein include the Ar Men, La Vieille, and Tévennac.

The Île de Sein is a stark, beautiful island that is part of the regional natural park d'Armorique. If you would like to stay the night, be sure to make reservations ahead of time. As in the novel, there is only one small hotel on the island. There are also short-term rentals and guesthouses available, but during tourist season it can be hard to find a room.

Finally, beware: According to legend, nine virgins known as the Gallizenae once bewitched sailors and other visitors to the island. You might well fall under their spell, just as I did.

Acknowledgments

Sincere thanks to Monsieur Ambroise Menou, assistant mayor of the Île de Sein, for your generosity with your time, historical knowledge, and regional cooking tips! Thanks are due to the entire staff of the fantastic Île de Sein museum. And a heartfelt *merci* to all the residents of the Île de Sein—especially Madame Louise—who took time to talk with this chatty American tourist, for answering questions and sharing family stories and recollections.

My brilliant historian sister, Dr. Carolyn Lawes, is an invaluable source of academic research, emotional support, creative brainstorming, writing suggestions, plot ideas, and continual edits—especially in the final throes of my deadline sprints. I honestly don't know what I would do without her, particularly how I would write without her.

To Lena Ingram, fabulous reader/sensitivity editor for the manuscript. You are a wonderful woman and it is my honor to know you—here's to meeting face-to-face one day soon when the pandemic is a thing of the past. Special thanks to amazing author and librarian Shannon Monroe for introducing us!

The writing life can be isolating, and I am eternally grateful for my writing community and support system. As always, thanks are due to my editor, Kerry Donovan, for reading through several versions of the manuscript. To Dr. Nicole Peeler for early thoughts, and for finding my theme! To Rachael Herron for her ideas and astute feedback. To Adrienne Bell, plot doctor extraordinaire. To my entire writer circle, especially Sophie Littlefield and Faye Snowden. To Xe Sands, thank you for your consistent support and for becoming the voices in my head as I read through my own books! To my website maven, Maddee James, thank you for all the support and friendship. And finally to my literary agent extraordinaire, Jim McCarthy, for always being there for me.

I wrote a good part of *Off the Wild Coast of Brittany* while under quarantine lockdown. The overriding anxiety and worry, the feelings of isolation and generalized fear, gave me a tiny taste of what life on the Île de Sein might have felt like during wartime. As in Violette's story, true friendship is my salvation! Many thanks to dear friends Dr. Claudia Escobar, Susan Baker, Suzanne Chan, Sharon Demetrius, Bruce Nikolai, Karen Thompson, Sara Paul, Anna Cabrera, Pamela Groves, Jan Strout, Mary Grae, Bee Enos, Greg Enos, Chris Logan, Brian Casey, Kendall Moalem, Muffy Srinivasan, and the whole Heskett clan: Nan, Jackie, Toni, Sherri, and Jason Hamilton. To my fabulous neighbors the Barnettes, please know that Don is and always will be missed. And to our beloved Sea Ranch neighbors Dan and Denise Skinner, and Linda and John Harrel. *Amour à Didier, et à Sylviane La Croix.*

Mucho amor a mi familia Wanda Klor, Natasha Ybarra, and Eréndira Ibarra, and to Christine Jurisich and her family—always in my heart. Thanks also to Thiago Klor de Alva, best baby brother in the world. To the beautiful, brainy, brash Amelia and her lovely mom Sophia Munzar.

And special thanks to Hanna Toda for letting me be "Mama." To Susan and Bob Lawes: Thank you for being there, always. And to Nugget, the best dog in the world.

And, finally, to Eric Stauffenegger for putting up with living with a writer, for all the wine, and for reminding me that it's okay to stop writing and enjoy *apéro*, each and every day.

OFF *the* WILD COAST *of* BRITTANY

Juliet Blackwell

Discussion Questions

1. "It's an island; if you don't bring it with you, you won't find it here." Most of the full-time residents of the Ile de Feme were born on the island, but others are *debutants*, or newbies. What do you think draws people to wild, unpredictable, remote islands like the Île de Sein, the real island that the Île de Feme is based on?

2. What aspects of living on the Ile de Feme would you find most challenging? The isolation, the interdependence among neighbors, the climate, the tourists—or something else? Think about today, and then about during World War II. Would you have what it takes to survive and thrive?

3. Is *Off the Wild Coast of Brittany* a story that, with minor adjustments, could have taken place somewhere else? How does the landscape create and shape this story? In what ways is the isolation of the island woven into the fabric of the novel?

4. What aspects of Natalie's journey do you most relate to? What about Alex's journey?

5. What is it that each sister finds most dissatisfying about her life, and why?

6. Would you say that Alex and Natalie start the novel in different emotional spaces and end up at the same place? How would you characterize the journey of each?

7. Natalie's pursuit of education is an act of rebellion against her family and their values. How does her journey differ from her other siblings' acts of rebellion? How is it the same?

8. Throughout the book, Natalie works to challenge and sometimes dispel the "truths" that her father taught her, while Alex finds it harder to go against him. Was there ever anyone in your life whose views you accepted, only to find yourself later disagreeing with them? How do you know whether something is true?

9. How did Natalie's relationship with her father evolve? With her mother? Did your perception of her parents change as you read further? Did your perception of her relationship with them change? If Natalie and Alex had been mothers themselves, do you think their views of their upbringing would have been affected?

10. What did you think of telling the story from the alternating points of view of the two sisters? How might the story have been different if it was told from only one sister's point of view?

11. If you had to trade places with one character in the book, who would it be, and why?

12. What do you think the characters' zodiac signs are, and why?

13. What sort of influence did their father, The Commander, have over Natalie and Alex as children? As adults? Do you think The Commander is ultimately someone to be feared or someone to be pitied?

14. Natalie has one good memory of being with her father. How do you think the kite story illustrates their relationship?

15. Had you been brought up in the Morgen family, would you have reacted more like Alex or more like Natalie? Or maybe like neither?

16. Alex actually thrived under her father's harsh lessons, and excelled at being able to do things and take care of herself. How does she explain her life before she understands the harsh truth of her childhood?

17. Natalie's ex-boyfriend, François-Xavier, plays a key role in the story, yet he never makes an actual appearance on the page. If you can imagine a scene between Natalie and François-Xavier, what would Natalie say to him? What might Francois-Xavier say to Natalie? (Bonus round: What would Alex say to François-Xavier?)

18. During World War II, how did the women of the island exploit the sexism of their time and place to challenge and endure the German occupation?

19. Why did Violette decide to marry Marc? How did the loss of her baby change Violette?

20. What roles did Madame Thérèse and Ambroisine play in their societies?

21. Whose approach to defying the Germans do you think was better: Noëlle's or Violette's? What determines when it is better to challenge an enemy openly and when it is better to find a way to coexist? How do you think you might have reacted under similar circumstances?

22. Had you been a woman on the island in 1940, would you have encouraged the men to go to Britain to fight? Or to stay behind with their families? And if you were a man in those times, would you have wanted to join the war effort in England?

23. Alex asks Natalie why there is no monument to the women of the island. Why do you think this is? Have you ever wondered something similar?

24. Not all German soldiers were members of the Nazi Party—many were conscripted into the military or, like Rainer, had little choice. How far do you think you would go to defy such a regime if you were a German at the time?

25. Were you surprised by Rainer's revelation to Violette? What attitudes and social forces at the time dictated how Rainer could, and could not, live his life? How do you think he might have experienced things differently in today's world?

26. Blackwell tends to use mysteries from the past to help her present-day characters understand and grapple with their own issues. What problems from the past do you think shed light on those of the present for Natalie and Alex? For Jean-Luc? For Violette and Rainier?

27. If you could ask each of the major characters in the book one question, what would you ask, and why?

Don't miss Juliet Blackwell's

THE LOST CAROUSEL OF PROVENCE

Available now

PRESENT DAY

OAKLAND, CALIFORNIA

*C*ady had never realized how many empty platitudes people voiced when confronted with grief, how they felt compelled to say something, to say *anything*, in response to a situation that had no answer, no response. No solution.

In point of brutal fact, there was nothing to say. Maxine had died.

One moment she was there, Cady's ever-present rock in the shifting sands of life. And the next she had fallen to the floor behind the register, struck down by a sudden heart attack. Maxine had disappeared into the ether, just like that, along with her snarky comments and wise eyes and calm, slightly haughty demeanor that never failed to assuage Cady's inner demons. She was gone. No one else in this life would be lucky enough to know Maxine Caroline Clark.

All that remained of the old woman was her shop, called Maxine's Treasures, its junky (or artsy, depending on your perspective) inventory, and the back room, where Cady had set up her photography studio and darkroom. Even though Cady had no intention of taking over and managing Maxine's antiques store, she wasn't ready to give up her studio. Not to mention that she'd been living in the back room of the shop—which was not strictly legal—since she'd lost her relatively affordable apartment to a condo development several months ago.

What now? Where would she go? What would she do?

Maxine was family. She was all Cady had.

A desperate, breathless weariness reached out its icy fingers to grip Cady's bones. And it wasn't the strain of carrying her wooden carousel figure, Gus. She saw reproach in the rabbit's glass eyes as she maneuvered him into the shop; could this last shred of hope gone be her comeuppance for having tried to sell him?

Maxine had given Gus to her ten years ago, on Cady's wedding day. The marriage hadn't lasted long, and the only thing Cady took from it—besides bitter experience—was Gus-the-rabbit.

It was embarrassing to admit, but Gus had always made her feel . . . loved.

According to Maxine, Gus was a genuine piece of carousel history, hand-carved by the famous French sculptor Gustave Bayol. Which would have meant he was worth thousands—maybe *tens* of thousands. But this morning Cady's last-ditch financial dreams had been dashed by an earnest young man named Scott Ripley. Peering through a huge magnifying glass, the *Antique Forum*'s acknowledged expert in nineteenth- and twentieth-century European carvings had examined the rabbit's loosening joints, noting how the bands of basswood had pulled away from one another at the tops of the legs, and the gap where the neck section met the body. Carousel figures are hollow, built like boxes with slats of wood joined, laminated, then carved, and primed to conceal the joints. Not only were the sections falling apart—Gus's ears were now barely connected to his slightly tilted head—but the bright paint and gold gilding were flaking off, with gesso primer showing through in patches.

At long last Ripley had straightened, shrugged, and pronounced: "It's not a Bayol."

"You're wrong," Cady said. "Look again."

"Your rabbit is most probably European, and from Bayol's era, at the turn of the twentieth century. In some ways, it is very much in his style; Bayol carved farmyard animals with sweet expressions like this one, so that fits. But a hallmark of Bayol's carvings was their simplicity. His work almost never included flourishes like the lily of the valley here," he said, pointing to the offending flower. "And this rose carved in high relief, with the detailed thorns? I don't even know what to say about *that*."

"But Bayol did custom work, right?" Cady replied. "Couldn't a client have asked for the flowers?"

He shook his head. "I know Bayol's work well; I'm also very familiar with the American carvers Dentzel, Looff, and Carmel. Like all artists, carousel carvers leave their imprints on their work, like signatures. Also, Bayol nearly always attached a small plaque to the saddles of his carved animals, and yours doesn't have one. Your rabbit might have been carved by one of Bayol's apprentices, or a competitor—if you could establish its provenance, it would be worth more."

Cady's impulse was to argue with Ripley, to rail at him and cast aspersions on his professional qualifications, not to mention his parentage.

But it wasn't his fault. Maxine had been wrong. It wasn't surprising: Maxine always had insisted upon seeing possibilities in the junk other people threw away.

So Cady had concentrated on reining in her emotions, fighting an almost overwhelming, and wholly uncharacteristic, urge to burst into tears.

Get it together, Drake, she had scolded herself. *We've been in worse situations than this one. Much, much worse. We'll just have to come up with another plan.*

As a child Cady had developed the quirk of using the royal "we" when talking to herself; otherwise the only "we" in her world was wishful thinking. Later, the "we" came to mean Cady and Maxine, and finally, now, Cady and Gus-the-rabbit. It was a silly, childish habit, but Cady had more important things to worry about these days, such as where she was going to get the money to escape the wildly expensive San Francisco Bay Area, to move to a town where normal people could work a regular job and afford a decent place to live, and where she could become a foster mom, or maybe even adopt a child. The thought of change terrified her, but she was desperate to create the sort of family that she'd always wanted for herself. True, being a photographer wasn't the best career option in a small town, but she didn't care what she did for a living. She wasn't proud.

The important thing was to start over. To reinvent herself. Cady yearned for the anonymity of a second chance, a clean slate, a tabula rasa. To make a home someplace where no one knew where she came from, where no one knew she had nothing and no one.

No family connections, no Maxine, no . . . baby.

Without volition her hand went to her stomach. The only bump there now was from stress-eating her way through countless bags of potato chips and boxes of Petit Écolier cookies—scraping off the chocolate in an embarrassingly juvenile ritual—as she sat on the couch for weeks, watching endless reruns of *Hoarders*.

The nurse in the emergency room had smelled of antiseptic and was very nice in the impersonal way of a kindhearted person saddled with far too much to do. She had instructed Cady to finish the round of prophylactic antibiotics, to abstain from sex for six weeks (no problem there—Cady couldn't imagine being intimate, ever again, with anyone), to get plenty of rest, and to be prepared for sudden hormonal shifts as her body adjusted to what her medical chart referred to as an "SAB": spontaneous abortion.

The baby Cady had accidentally conceived in an exceedingly rare one-night stand, then after weeks of fear and trembling had decided to keep and come to love, had been lost in a gruesome rush of pain and cramps and blood, a gutting experience referred to simply as an SAB.

An SAB.

Cady's appalling, alien urge to cry must be due to shifting hormones. Nothing more. Surely.

First Maxine had died. Then Cady's own body had betrayed her. And now even her precious carousel rabbit had turned out not to be who she'd always thought he was.

Cady was on a merry-go-round, and no matter how fast she galloped, she kept winding up at the same place.

Her eyes stung, tears threatening. *So . . . okay.* Maybe she would allow herself a few quick minutes of weeping in the back of the shop, while cursing Mr. Scott Ripley of the *Antique Forum* and his so-called expertise.

Then she would come up with a new plan.

$\mathcal{T}$he banging on the door wouldn't stop. Cady had hung the Closed sign on the window of the shop door, alongside a note about Maxine's death. But some of Maxine's regular customers could be as persistent and annoying as a broken tooth.

"Go away!" she yelled from the back room.

The banging continued. She turned the television volume up.

"Cady?" A woman's voice. Olivia.

Cady often thought of Maxine as the only person in the world who loved her, but there was also Olivia Gray.

They had met years ago, right after Cady got divorced, in an adult education course on photography—genuine, old-fashioned photography and film development, taught by a cranky old man who didn't take to what he called "that modern digital crap."

Olivia was everything Cady wasn't but had always wanted to be: pretty, petite, quick to smile at others and to laugh at herself. It was the first time Cady had understood the concept of a girl crush; she was enamored, sneaking glances under her bangs during class, following Olivia out to the vending machines during break.

One night the machine ate Olivia's rumpled dollar. She banged on it ineffectually and yelled, *"Gol-darn it!"*

Cady had never heard anyone say something like that except on television.

"Early training," Olivia explained to Cady, with an embarrassed smile and a chagrined little shrug. "My mom's a stickler for polite language. If she gets really, really mad she might say, *'Dammit!'* But then she always follows it up with: 'Pardon my French!'"

Cady smiled, hitting the machine just so while reaching in the back, the way she had learned to do as a bad kid with no spending money. The mechanism started to hum and a PayDay bar banged down into the metal trough.

"There you go."

"Thanks! That's a neat trick. So, what's your name?"

Olivia didn't even know her name? It figured. *Stuck-up jerk.*

But nipping at the heels of anger was shame: Try as she might, Cady just didn't pick up on social cues like other people did. She wondered whether it was something integral to her—some mysterious bit of genetic code she had inherited from her unknown parents—or if it derived from her detached, frenetic childhood. Ultimately it didn't matter. She had always known she wasn't . . . *likable.*

She turned on her heel and stalked back to the classroom.

After class, as Cady was gathering her things, Olivia made a beeline across the room. "So, I'm an idiot in general. And I can never remember names."

Cady shrugged and zipped up the battered leather backpack she had scored at the flea market for five dollars.

"I'm a bit of a sleuth, though. Not to mention stubborn," Olivia said, holding out her hand. "It's nice to officially meet you, Cady Drake. I'm Olivia Gray. How do you do?"

Cady stared at her hand for a beat.

"Like I said, I know I'm clueless," Olivia continued. "But since we're the only two people in this class under the age of forty, I was wondering, do you want to go grab a drink?"

Maxine's voice whispered in her mind: *"Get over yourself, girl. Don't assume everyone's out to get you."*

So Cady nodded, and they stopped by George O's. It was a seedy dive bar, typical for this part of Oakland, but when they walked in, Olivia's eyes lit up like a child's on Christmas morning.

"This is great," she announced, taking in the dartboard, out-of-date Halloween decorations, and half a dozen men slouched over the bar. She ordered bourbon on the rocks, and Cady did the same.

"So," Olivia said as they took their drinks to a table. "'Cady' is a pretty name. I saw on the roster that you don't spell it the traditional way, K-A-T-Y."

"Yeah," said Cady. "I mean, I came with it."

Olivia smiled. "I always hated my name."

"Why?"

"The kids used to taunt me at school, calling me Olive Oyl," she said in a low voice, as though confiding a shameful secret.

"Gee," said Cady after a beat, "that must have been very traumatic for you."

Olivia looked surprised, then started laughing. "You just made a joke! And here I thought you were serious all the time." She held up her glass. "Let's have a toast. To quote Humphrey Bogart in that movie: 'I think this is the beginning of a beautiful friendship.'"

And oddly enough, it was. After the photography class ended, they enrolled in French language courses, then Thai cooking, then botany. Olivia and her boyfriend, Sebastian, had Cady and Maxine over for dinner, and when they married, Cady stood up with them at City Hall. Olivia loved to tag along at antiques flea markets, asking questions, and furnishing her falling-down West Oakland Victorian one piece at a time. Eventually she landed a job at *Sunset* magazine, and steered the occasional freelance photography job Cady's way.

Through the years they joked about who had the upper hand in the "Trauma Olympics," and whenever she invoked her childhood, Cady was the hands-down winner. But Olivia had struggles of her own.

"Cady!" Olivia called again through the door of Maxine's Treasures. "Open up. I brought coffee, made with my very own hands."

With reluctance, Cady emerged from the back room and crossed the crowded shop floor.

"I don't want any," Cady said through the glass pane of the front door.

"Too bad. Open up."

Cady undid the dead bolt and crouched down to remove the rubber stopper she always shoved under the door. It made her feel secure.

"Here," Olivia said as soon as the door was open, holding out a commuter mug and pushing past Cady into the store. "It's French roast, your favorite. You're welcome."

"I was sleeping."

"No you weren't," Olivia said, raising one eyebrow as she looked over the jumble of inventory. "And you obviously haven't been spending a lot of time cleaning."

"Not my strong suit."

"So, have you been working?"

"A little."

Olivia led the way into the back room, where they sat down at the little table by the kitchenette. Belatedly, Cady realized there was plentiful evidence of her recent dissolute lifestyle: crumpled Cheetos bags and cookie packages, old Chinese food take-out boxes, an empty vodka bottle.

"Liar," said Olivia, taking in the scene. "What have you *really* been doing?"

"Crying." Cady collapsed onto the sofa.

"But that's good, right?" Olivia said, sympathy shining in her big chocolate-colored eyes. "You never used to cry. I count that as personal growth."

Cady let out a humorless bark. "Only you could see crying as a positive."

"So, I was thinking," Olivia said, fiddling with her coffee mug, which boasted the garish orange-and-black logo of the San Francisco baseball team. "There are a lot of merry-go-rounds in Paris. Loads of them. I remember from when Sebastian and I went there on our honeymoon. A carousel in every public square, it seemed like."

"And?"

"You love photographing carousels. Have you ever thought of doing a *book* of photographs?"

"Of Parisian carousels?"

"Yes! Why have we been studying French all these years if you're not going to put the language to good use? And you never know what you might find. The food, the wine, the cobblestone streets . . ." She let out a sigh. *"C'est magique!"*

Cady managed a small smile. "You think everything is magical."

"And you think *nothing* is. But you're wrong." Olivia took another sip and let out a long, contented sigh. She had a way of savoring her coffee as though it were the elixir of life, the cure for maladies, the font of all contentment. And perhaps it was: Olivia was the sunniest person Cady had ever known. Before she met Olivia, Cady had believed sustained happiness was the stuff of fiction, found only in fairy tales.

"When did you become a San Francisco Giants fan?" Cady asked in a blatant bid to change the subject.

Olivia laughed, holding her mug out and inspecting the logo as though she'd never seen it before. "I have no idea where this came from. It just appeared, as things are wont to do around my house. But I like the way it feels in my hands."

Random items "appeared" at Olivia's place because people were forever passing through for dinners and parties, spending the night or staying for weeks at a time on the couch, leaving behind towels, a hairbrush, a coffee mug. But Olivia took the ever-shifting landscape of her home in stride, as though things appeared and disappeared by some enchanting sort of magic.

That would drive me crazy, Cady thought. She liked things organized, predictable. Even in the apparent muddle of Maxine's shop, Cady knew where each and every item was.

"Anyway, stop trying to change the subject, because I'm not falling for it," Olivia said as she set the mug down. "Maybe a change of scenery is exactly what you need. And you've photographed our local carousels enough."

"You're forgetting our road trip to see the world's largest carousel at House on the Rock."

"Not that I have anything against Wisconsin, but I was thinking Paris might be a slightly more dramatic change of scene."

Cady shrugged. "I'll think about it."

"Here's the thing, Cady: My mother always told me not to offer unsolicited advice. But I'm going to anyway, because I love my mama, but I love you, too, and you haven't had anyone besides Maxine to give you the advice you need."

"You do realize," Cady said, "that you are not required to fix my life. I'm—"

"*Excuse* me," interrupted Olivia. "When I was in the hospital, who brought me Thai noodles and Cherry Garcia Ice Cream?"

"You could have gotten as much from a delivery person."

"Is that right? And would this alleged delivery person have given me her absolute devotion and forced me to survive chemotherapy, not to mention surgery? Would said delivery person have read the entirety of *84, Charing Cross Road* to me when I was in the hospital, then popped the cork on a bottle of champagne when I finished my chemo? Would she also have watched endless rounds of basketball with Sebastian to keep him from going crazy from worry?"

"That was selfish on my part," said Cady. "You're my only friend."

With gut-wrenching clarity, Cady remembered the moment, three years ago, when Olivia divulged she had been diagnosed with breast cancer. In that instant Cady came to understand the true danger of loving someone: the absolute panic at the thought of her leaving this earth.

Olivia's only response was a gentle smile.

"And where would I even get the money to go?" Cady wondered aloud. She glared at her disappointing rabbit, propped in the corner.

Olivia perked up, sensing a potential victory. "Your landlord has been offering you cash to buy out the shop lease, right? And you can liquidate the inventory, which will add up to something. And *I'll* lend you enough for the plane ticket."

Cady snorted. "Like you and Sebastian have so much to spare?"

"We have some savings set aside for a rainy day; and in case you hadn't noticed, my friend, it's raining cats and dogs. Metaphorically speaking."

"It's *my* rainy day, not yours."

"Details." She waved off Cady's concern. "What good is money if I can't help a friend? And I believe in your art. What's that old saying? 'Anonymous was a woman'?"

"What does that have to do with anything?"

"Because you're bound to remain anonymous if you don't get your art out there for people to see. Taking student portraits might pay the bills, but you're an *artist*. And I can be your patron! Sort of. At least I can manage a plane ticket."

As photographers went, Cady did pretty well. She hauled her heavy camera bag all over the Bay Area, from Marin to Morgan Hill, from the beaches of the Pacific Ocean to the Tahoe ski slopes, and never turned down a job. She photographed weddings, bar and bat mitzvahs, first communions, anniversaries, birthdays, and family reunions. She had regular gigs taking yearbook portraits at local schools, including the Berkeley French American International School. And she did occasional shoots for *Sunset* magazine, and a few home design catalogs.

Still, paying her bills every month was one thing, but putting aside a nest egg was something else altogether.

"Thanks, Olivia, but running away to Paris for a couple of weeks isn't going to solve anything."

"Think of it as running *to* something. Anyway, I have to get back to the office. But just promise me this," Olivia said, as she gathered her things to leave. "You won't close yourself off to possibility. If something exciting falls in your lap, you'll take it."

"Exciting? Like *what*?" Cady demanded, irked. She loved Olivia, but when was the last time something great had "fallen into her lap"? That was the kind of thing that happened to charmed, suburban-grown people like Olivia, not unwanted orphans like Cady. Cady had had to work and scheme—and occasionally steal—to get anything she had.

But Olivia lifted her eyebrows and flashed a cat-that-ate-the-canary smile. "One never knows what the future might bring."

Cady laughed in spite of herself, gave her friend a hug, and watched as Olivia ambled back to her car, turning her face up to the morning sun, taking time to wave at a passing bicyclist. Olivia saw the beauty in everything: the sunrise, the city lights twinkling off the bay, a stranger on a bike.

Whereas Cady, when faced with the same scene, saw the smog, the congestion of the freeway, a traffic hazard.

Cady leaned her head against the doorjamb for a moment, ignoring the dust collecting on the shop's inventory, trying not to look at the spot behind the register where Maxine had fallen. She wasn't doing right by Maxine—or even by her landlord, for that matter. She wasn't doing right by herself, or Olivia, or anyone.

She didn't think of herself as a true artist, as Olivia had suggested. But . . . surely Cady Anne Drake had *something* to offer this world?

If only she knew what it was.

Juliet Blackwell is the pseudonym for the *New York Times* bestselling author of *The Vineyards of Champagne*, *The Lost Carousel of Provence*, *Letters from Paris*, and *The Paris Key*. In addition to writing the beloved Witchcraft Mystery series and the Haunted Home Renovation series, she also coauthored the Agatha Award–nominated Art Lover's Mystery series with her sister.

CONNECT ONLINE

JulietBlackwell.net
JulietBlackwellAuthor
JulietBlackwell

Ready to find
your next great read?

Let us help.

Visit prh.com/nextread

Penguin
Random
House